RAINBOW WALKERS

DORIS SCHWERIN

VILLARD BOOKS · NEW YORK · 1985

Library of Congress Cataloging in Publication Data
Schwerin, Doris.
    Rainbow walkers.
    I. Title.
PS3569.C5697R3   1985   813'.54   84-40483
ISBN 0-394-53950-8

Grateful acknowledgment is made to the following for permission to reprint
previously published material:

Harvard University Press: Excerpt from a poem by Emily Dickinson. Reprinted
by permission of the publishers and the Trustees of Amherst College from
The Poems of Emily Dickinson, edited by Thomas H. Johnson, Cambridge,
Massachusetts: The Belknap Press of the Harvard University Press. Copyright 1951,
© 1955, 1979, 1983 by the President and Fellows of Harvard College.

Sheila Lalwani Payne: Excerpts from three Chinese poems taken from *The White
Pony: An Anthology of Chinese Poetry* edited by Robert Payne. Copyright 1947
by Sheila Lalwani Payne, published by the John Day Company in 1960. Used with
permission of Sheila Lalwani Payne. Rights in the United Kingdom administered by
David Higham Associates Ltd.

I would like to thank the following people, who graciously extended themselves and shared the realities of their disciplines with me: Dr. Joseph Irgon, Judge Whitman Knapp, Joseph Glass, M.D., Prof. David Haber, Myron Winick, M.D., Prof. Charles H. Stern, Paul Silverstein, Esq., Dr. Sandra Baum. Let me add, they are in no way responsible for the manner in which I ingested their gifts, improvised, dreamed, and subsequently created the world in this book. I thank my husband, Jules, for patient and supportive years of listening, encouraging, aiding in the research necessary for the facts of science and law to become fiction, and perhaps too, the other way around.

. . . This is *the token of the covenant
which I make between me and you and every
living creature that* is *with you, for
perpetual generations:*

*I do set my bow in the cloud, and
it shall be for a token of a covenant
between me and the earth.*

GENESIS 9:12, 9:13

ONE

AN ENTRY IN THE JOURNAL OF DR. HIRAM WESGROVE, MARCH 1981

Yesterday was a shocker. I broke with M. after all these years, my colleague, my friend, one of the last of the old Harvard crowd. I was certain he would join me in a strong stance, but he didn't. What a surprise, no, not surprise, horror! I had expected a solid front when it came to responsibility and the guidelines for genetic intervention. He accused me of rigidity, censorship; he became an enemy in front of my eyes. I saw something unpleasant behind his eyes, and I felt he was almost capable of saying it: "You Nobel Prize winners! What makes you think you can get up on a soapbox and be a genius of morality too, just because you were singled out for honors in your own field?"

I'm more shocked with myself than with M., I suppose. He proved to me again what I have never wished to face—the scientist is no more prescient, less greedy, more obliged to humanity than the ordinary person, though God knows he should be! M. said, "You can't stop progress, old man. The genetic cookie is going to crumble where it may, and you're going to have to trust your colleagues, so you work with your cells toward your end, and we'll work with ours toward our end."

He called me "old man"? How dare he! He knew he had infuriated me beyond the possibility of further friendship when I said, "Evidently Hell's your limit!" He knew we were parting company after all these years. Sad. Very sad. Why do I keep forgetting that life is nothing but surprise?

I

Maxwell Treading knew the land so well, but the grandeur of it never ceased to startle him. No matter how often he flew over it, its beauty rose up like an unexpected wind. The gorgeous Sierras did it to him every time. Grandeur! A tourist-guide word, but hell, some words survived the indignity of overuse. With such a display as kept rising up beneath the helicopter, what American could deny emotion or think of himself as less than a lord of the world; for was not his country the most beautiful, changeable, the most surprising of all terrestrial wenches?

The hyperbolic tint to Treading's thoughts made him smile. He leaned back under the greenhouse, the plastic bubble of his helicopter, to enjoy every sensual second of the looking —the terrain flashing up and the sharp, blue air pealing like liberty bells.

The flight from Stockton to the foothills of the Sierras was about sixty miles. After that, the plane entered Emigrant Basin, a primitive area of huge, jagged peaks, some snowcapped mountain ranges, deep valleys with raging torrents, extinct craters, rock-strewn slopes, forested areas with range for sheep and deer. Some of the peaks rose to nearly 12,000 feet. Another fifty miles

or so was the California-Nevada border where they were heading; to the north, was Lake Tahoe and Reno; to the south, the
dry lakes, desertlike regions, grazing land intermingled with
medium-high mountain ranges, offshoots of the Sierras.

Blinding sunlight was drenching everything—the sheer
cliffs dangerously close on every side, the tops of massive forests,
open spaces with glacier meadows, lakes, gorges of swirling
water. It was all shimmering, multicolored wine in a mammoth
goblet.

The helicopter was dipping, rising, gliding from side to
side. Treading looked at the pilot, a taciturn young man newly
hired by his San Francisco office. Pilot and craft were executing
the swooping, zigzagging around the sharp peaks with the ease
of virtuoso ballet dancers performing a pas de deux. "You're
good!" Treading exclaimed. "No matter how many times I fly
over this stuff, I always get a funny feeling in the soles of my
feet." He laughed. "Maybe it's not in my feet, but in my soul!"

There was no response, not even a sliver of a smile. Jesse
Simmons didn't like to talk; anyway, he was hired to fly, not
talk. On his first trip with the boss, how was he to know that
one of the many pleasures of "the big man" was to pull on
people's tongues? Treading, slyly observing the pilot's face, decided the man must be in his midthirties, but the steel gray
under the western tan, the tension around the mouth, the long,
horizontal gashes of wrinkle on the forehead showed stress of
more years than that.

"You obviously know this territory like the back of your
hand," Treading commented.

"Yes, sir. Grew up in Stockton, worked charter out of there
for my father, he owned a strip . . . before I joined the Air Force
and went to 'Nam."

"You were in that mess? Good Lord. And, then?"

Simmons didn't pick up on the *And, then?* "We could have
mopped it all up over there, if we'd'a had the backing we needed
from home."

Treading wasn't going to touch that statement. He persisted with another "And then?"

"Overseas in Germany till last year."

"Married?"

"Till last year."

"German girl?"

"No, Vietnamese."

"Any children?"

"One."

"Boy or girl?"

"He's with his mother. She went back home."

"Racial mixtures make for beautiful children," Treading mused. He was busy playing a private game—creating a life scenario with snatches of information from a stranger—so he was unaware of the pilot's facial response to his questions, the look of an animal picking up danger signals, whiskers quivering, wide-open eyes . . . along with a twitch in the cheek so active it was visible to Tom Lipsky, a metallurgist in the employ of Treading for many years, who was sitting behind the two men. There was no way Lipsky could give a sign to the pilot, some look or gesture that could say, "Listen, don't take offense, that's the way the guy is, nosy, but what a boss."

Treading wasn't going to give up on trying for conversation. "What do you think of the world, Jesse?" He expected an answer, flip or otherwise, but there was none.

The pilot's jaw dropped slightly. He looked at his new boss out of the corner of an eye, then refocused on the peaks ahead. If they'd been in a bar, he would have gotten up and walked away.

Treading persisted. "Ever seen a leopard go after a wildebeest? I did, in Africa. This business of one animal having to eat another for survival—pretty mind-boggling plan, isn't it?"

The peaks were finished; they were coming to dark, undulating hills and beyond them, the flatland. A herd of deer was scattering before the sound and shadow of the helicopter.

"But the deer don't go after anyone," Treading added. "What are we to make of that? That they're God's true innocents?"

Jesse Simmons turned to look squarely at Treading for the first time since they'd refueled in Stockton. He might as well have said, "Are you crazy?" because it was all over his face.

Maxwell Treading, wizard of finance, founder of Global Materials, Ltd., uranium mining king, was unaware of the look because his attention was suddenly drawn away. He wanted a close fix on the land rising up ahead. "Take it down lower, Jesse, low as you can, right now! And we'll be just about where the new tract begins." Geological survey maps and aerial photographs fell to the floor from his lap as he leaned forward. "Here we go, right now!" he commanded in a boss's voice, not a philosopher's.

Simmons obeyed instantaneously. No problem. The guy wants a bird's-eye view? He'll get it, even close enough to lasso a gook like the Colonel in 'Nam used to. . . .

There is a sudden lurch. The helicopter drops too precipitously, not from human error; everything is going crazy and a giant hand is pulling it down. There is a nauseating crack of a sound. Simmons tries frantically to right the craft, but there is a second cracking sound as the three men stare at the uprushing ground; they brace themselves, in horror, for what looks like an inevitable crash.

Helpless as a tissue-paper kite, the shiny new helicopter plummets into a crown of trees with a deafening scream of crumbling metal into shattered tree trunks. Then, silence in the cloudless early afternoon.

Smash! It breaks up the memory bank like a half-finished jigsaw puzzle flung against a wall. Treading's brain was in a confusion of pieces, creating images *not of the present,* but of 1948, the eastern shores of Lake Maracaibo, the Bolívar coastal field.

Sticky Venezuelan crude was oozing out of him. Warm, black liquid was spouting from his hip, or was it his head? The workers made a new oil well blow, or did they make him blow? He was the one who must have blown! He was punching the owner of Carib Oil in the stomach. That indiscretion was easier for the owner to forgive than seeing the twenty-year-old Americano engineer siding with the workers yelling "Strike!"

against slave wages. For *that,* one must teach the Americano a lesson!

Someone in uniform had pulled him from his bed, dragged him outside and put a gun to his head. He was going to die in stinking Venezuela, on his first job in an oil field. What a revolting crap game!—if life could end like this and not where he'd beaten the rap for two years, fighting the Japs on a Pacific island worse than this fascist rathole!

The owner of the oil field stood between two more soldiers. "Don't kill him. The United States will look for him. Just beat him up enough to shut his mouth."

You don't just stand there, you punch the bastard. Then, the soldiers came at him.

He woke up on a boat in the Gulf of Mexico heading for a Texas port, on his way back to his mother's ranch outside Moab, Utah. Where else? Disgusted that he'd not saved a penny on his first job, elated that he knew who he was when the chips were down. He wasn't some s.o.b. who looked the other way so as not to see the pain, man's inhumanity to . . . There was a song buzzing around his head. It sounded like it was being plucked on broken bedsprings. "Just like a tree that's standing by the waa-ter, we shall not be moved." What happens when you have a mother who sang you union songs to put you to sleep when you were small? You get beaten half to death in Venezuela!

Was he on the boat? *This* was a different hurting.

Worse! His hand moved up his right thigh feeling the warm, sticky, Venezuelan crude. Take glue, his brain ordered. Glue the broken time together or it'll slip away. He was a little boy gluing a toy plane, slowly putting one delicate piece of balsa wood to another, making something whole, making a tiny window, a wing, a propeller. Now, open your eyes and see what you've made. Look! He couldn't.

Maxwell Treading was slowly regaining consciousness because of the pain. Amazement opened his eyes wide. *He wasn't on a boat heading back to Houston!* The sun was beating down through trees. He was wrapped around a tree, but it wasn't "standing by the waa-ter." It was in a desert and *he couldn't move.* Even so, the pieces were coming back together, making the picture of what had happened; he said his name to himself, to verify the miracle.

If being thrown clear of a crash, waking up and finding your juices oozing from a hole in your hip and a couple of bones sticking through the skin of your leg was lucky, then he was. He raised himself up. There it was, about seventy-five feet away, a dead metal bird lying on its side, punched and slashed out of shape, unrecognizable as a helicopter except for its bubble. What a technological joke—the weakest, most vulnerable part of the whole remained! God, where were they? He made out Jesse Simmons, his upper body on the ground, sticking out of the passenger side. It was too far away to see if he was breathing. Where was Tom Lipsky? Still in the back in that twisted mess? God! Where *was* Tom?

Treading sank back and looked up at the cloudless sky. No sun now. He picked up his hand as though it belonged to a marionette. Every move up was excruciating. The smashed face of his watch said 12:56. He tried to think about where they were, to reconstruct. They were in a hollow. The helicopter had braided itself into scrubby Douglas fir. He was under a spruce tree. It was going to get very cold if they weren't spotted by dark. Absolutely alone. A vast silence. He decided not to pray. God might not like a hypocrite.

The manager of the airport in Stockton, California, was calling the Forest Service to report a helicopter with its owner, Maxwell Treading, and two employees three hours overdue. "Their schedule for return here was 2:00 P.M., to refuel on their way back to San Francisco. No radio communication. We can't raise a signal. Something's wrong. It was perfect weather all day, wasn't it? We'd better begin a search. Alert all ranger stations in the vicinity of Emigrant Basin for flares. Their flight plan was straight across the basin to the border, give or take a couple of miles."

Treading had gotten himself into a sitting position against the tree; he looked up at the sky with all the will he could muster —to will a rescue plane any second, any minute, before nightfall. Suddenly, there was a moan. The pilot's head was turning from side to side. Simmons was alive!

The sky went from twilight to dusk and the moan became louder. Simmons was conscious, if you could call it that; he was delirious, crying, talking gibberish. It was unbearable. Treading began to wish he were alone to live or die, whichever was going to happen. He screamed, "Shut up!"; screamed it again. It quieted his own pain and fear. He began to talk to Simmons, hoping the sound of his voice could cut through the man's delirium.

"You're not alone, Jesse, I can't move, I can't get over to you, but I'm not far away. They'll spot us, fella, hang on. It's the big test. You've been through it before, so have I . . .

"You're a great flyer, Jesse. It wasn't your fault, it was the fuckin' machine, I heard it crack. I'm gonna sue them out of their minds. You'll be rich, kid, if we get out of this."

The pilot's gibberish wasn't letting up. Treading was talking to himself, but he kept on, he had to. "It's not our time to die, I know it . . . I know it . . . Even stars don't die. Nothing dies, it changes . . . it changes . . ."

There was the sound of a low-flying plane. Everything around Treading was dark green turning to black. Jesse Simmons suddenly went quiet.

Then, there *wasn't* the sound of a low-flying plane. Not an hour later or an hour after that. They hadn't been spotted. How could they be, in a hollow of spruce and fir? A voice in Treading kept on talking but he couldn't hear it anymore, he could only feel the words . . . "Oh, God . . . oh God . . ." as he felt himself fainting, sinking into the earth and long shadows.

2

If Martha Treading's spirit had been floating around the California-Nevada border that night, she would have poked her son incessantly to stay awake. He kept slipping into sleep, his body going into shock from the wounds, loss of blood, the intensifying cold. Perhaps her spirit *was* there. *Something* kept waking him, reminding him he had inherited an iron will to prevail— from his mother. She would have been eighty-five if she were alive. "Seventy-six, going on Methuselah" she described herself the last year of her life, not knowing it would be the last, when she was suddenly incapacitated by heart disease, sick for the first time in her memory.

Who else could be nudging him with such determination but Martha Ackers who'd married Jonathan Treading, the strange, sullen mining engineer? He had appeared one day in her little town of Jamaica, Vermont, swept her off her schoolteacher feet because he could quote Walt Whitman by the yard, taken her all the way to Utah to settle on a seedy ranch with five hundred acres, some worried-looking cattle, and unused soil— his inheritance. She had come to a desertlike place, blazing hot and freezing cold; it stretched endlessly with its sagebrush, cacti, trees stunted and gnarled out of shape. In the distance, there were mesas or buttes breaking the flatness. She thought they looked like giant punctuation marks in a monumental sentence that the land had composed only for the eyes of the horizon. The bigness forced her to clutch her husband's hand, adjust her heart's lenses, put from her mind that leafy, green Vermont with its weatherworn, comforting hills and meadows. Not only the land was forcing her adjustment; she had married a man she scarcely knew. Jonathan Treading's silences, so attractive and mysterious in the beginning, were becoming longer, more disquieting, and his actions, even more strange. He began to disappear, sometimes for months on end, leaving her alone. She turned herself into a sunburned desert woman, walking or riding the acres of her husband's inheritance. She wasn't afraid of hard work. It was in her Yankee blood to be good at anything she made up her mind to.

After two years of this strange life with a man who would leave, return, and ask her forgiveness, it was a wonder *she* didn't leave and go back to her parents. Perhaps she would have, if tragedy hadn't taken the Vermont farmhouse, apple orchards, and *them* in a terrible fire. There was nothing to go back to.

She began to love the bleakness and isolation, the challenge of the rabbit, mesquite country, its Indian trails deepened by buckboard wagons, still the only transportation between the frontier communities of ranchers in the 1920s. Martha built up the ranch, bought cattle, sent for books on the geology of the godforsaken place. She taught school for the sons of neighbors in return for farm and ranch work. There was nothing but time to be used well, as her husband came and went from jobs in mines as far away as Canada and South America. Jonathan Treading had made a mistake. He should never have married. He was a morose, depressed wanderer, sunk into silence, begging her forgiveness each time he returned.

In one of those *returnings,* six years after their marriage, Martha became pregnant and in 1926 her son, Max, was born. His father stayed put after that for the longest spell—four years. Jonathan seemed happy about having a son; he went to work at the Bingham Canyon mine two hundred miles away, where *his* father had worked a lifetime before him. Jonathan made the trip home to the ranch twice a month. He was there to see little Max learn to walk and ride a pony at the same time, learn to read and write by the time he was three. A wondrous child had come from Martha and himself.

When Max was almost five, Jonathan Treading left one morning and never returned. It was a man of smoke Martha had fallen in love with. She had uprooted herself, endured humiliation, privation, rejection. But, she would prevail. Sink into private agony, disenchantment? Never! If she hadn't been able to conquer the arid marriage, she was going to conquer the arid land. But, most of all, she was going to enjoy her bright, astounding little boy who'd come out of smoke. Her mission was to fill his little cup to overflowing. His existence was enough to validate everything. Not only that . . . She would read and study, have a hunch about the land that had brought her nothing but unhappiness. She would hire a geologist to come, look at the soil, and evaluate the land. And she would strike oil in its northeast corner.

Martha Ackers Treading never returned to the East, not even when her son became rich and renowned and pleaded with her to visit him in New York. He even offered to build a replica of the farmhouse of her youth—she had described it so many times and with such nostalgia—hoping to cajole her back.

Max Treading would describe his mother as "an ore-smart poet. She was the only teacher I ever had, and *was* she a damn good one!" He loved his wiry, bony mother in her dusty leather dresses, her long face with its high cheekbones, her large, green eyes filled with intelligence and an unsettling direct stare. Except for the weathered skin-white hair, she had kept the same spirit as she'd had at twenty-five . . . when her husband first set eyes on her—a tall, handsome, thoughtful young woman, assured of spinsterhood in Jamaica, Vermont, because of her fussy, superior ways. She wore somber colors, her long fingers twitched, and everything about her seemed to be nervously connected. There was a surprising femininity about her, with her dark, shiny hair forever escaping its hairpins, her pale skin and thin nose that turned up without warning; yet the local young men felt she was like the purple thistle with its quick sting and tough, spiny leaves. That was the Martha who had fallen in love with Jonathan Treading and allowed herself, in a moment of insanity, to be dragged West. All because they had sat on the sofa in her parents' parlor and talked about Emerson and Thoreau, quoted Walt Whitman to each other—the talk like a white-water river in the spring, and she thinking she would faint from its intensity.

But, she had prevailed, till the day she died.

What other *spirit* could be nudging her beloved son into wakefulness!

Lest *he* die.

It was night. The immense desert sky filled with stars. Max's body was stiff with cold. He groped about his hip, where he had imagined the Venezuelan crude spouting from a terrible pain. The blood had dried and he was feeling crust. He was freezing and on fire with fever, lying at the base of the stunted spruce tree. Suddenly, he was pulled into total consciousness by the sounds of sputtering, flame! The fuselage of the helicopter was burning!

An automatic response forced him, commanded him . . . He dragged himself like a wounded snake across the space between his tree and the wreckage. Jesse Simmons was still lying on the ground, his head near a wheel. Max grabbed him by the neck, pulled him clear, Simmons mumbling words from the tongues of the possessed, fighting being moved, resisting Max's superhuman effort to get him away from the fuel tank, inch by inch. Suddenly it blew up with a roar. Both men were seared on their backs by a fire hand that went after them and then miraculously pulled back. The pilot let out a horrible scream and struck out at Max, who let go of him about fifty feet away from the flaming wreck. The initial explosion had caught them, but the fire was pulled upward and in the opposite direction, or the two would have been burned alive.

Max got himself back to the safety of his tree. He was alert with pain, shocked into an awareness he felt would be his last. He watched Jesse Simmons crawl off into some underbrush and listened for his babbling, prayed for it this time. There was none.

The pilot was dead. Max sank into unconsciousness again. No spirit could nudge him awake.

On top of a mountain pass in the Sierras, a forest ranger suffering from insomnia stepped out onto his observation porch to have a smoke. It was 2:30 A.M. He spotted fire and rushed to phone an observation post lower down. "Can't be lightning, we haven't had a storm over here; have you?" The answer was no. "I calculate it's Emigrant Basin near Sonora Falls. Go out and check me; maybe it's the missing 'copter." He hung up and called Stockton. Stockton called San Francisco.

From late afternoon to midnight, planes had been looking for Maxwell Treading, the financier, and two other men who were missing and probably down in a crash. The search was going to begin again at the first light. Doctors and nurses were waiting in Stockton to be flown to a crash site. Max's own doctor and one of his daughters flew from New York to Stockton—to wait.

For three hours, two forest rangers on mules made their way along the mountain trails, their eyes riveted on the spot of fire in the valley. It was becoming harder to detect in the growing light, but they were coming closer; they knew it from the acrid smell of burning fuel; it kept pulling them in the right direction. There it was! In the hollow of spruce and fir. They stopped on the ridge to make the decision of which way down, then kept fanning their powerful lanterns from side to side as they came closer.

Treading woke, shaking with fever. From the base of the tree, he could see the boots of the pilot sticking out of the underbrush, now that the light had come. He turned away from the sight.

Light, but no rescue. He knew he wasn't going to make it

and told himself to go easy, give in . . . no use fighting anymore. He looked skyward toward a ridge and saw moving phantoms of light. So that was the way it was—ghostly, scanning lights to lead you away into death. Under half-closed eyes, he was experiencing the strangest apparition of bearded men riding four-legged animals, their hooves towering over him, the hooves of apocalyptic beasts. He passed out again.

The foresters leaned over him. One examined for life signs, the other radioed for help.

"One of them's made it, maybe. We can't tell which one. He's in bad shape. Life supports crucial. We'll do what we can."

Tom Lipsky, the metallurgist, didn't need a funeral. He couldn't be found in the burned wreckage. The pilot was lifted from the underbrush, his face twisted in a death grimace. He was removed in a second rescue helicopter. The first one brought out the badly injured, but alive, body of Treading and delivered him to the hospital in Stockton. A staff of doctors got to work on a victim of three compound fractures of the right leg, a large hole in a hip, an injured kidney, plus a severely burned back. They almost didn't know what to do first, or whether what they were doing would save him. The patient was in severe shock. His heart stopped twice as they worked on him.

The first newspaper headline was "Uranium King Dies in Crash"—the assumption of a too-eager reporter who had seen the body of Jesse Simmons being brought into the basement of the hospital. The next day it was "Treading Fights for His Life." The day after that, the stock of Global Materials, Ltd., fell . . . for Maxwell Treading, at the age of fifty-four, had made no provisions for a successor or any other plans predicated on sudden tragedy. Immense as Global Materials was, it reeled from the possibility of its founder's death.

Death, a minute before the crash, had been a word of no meaning to Max. He was in great health; life was extraordinary. A widower for three years—his wife, Sophia, had died of a massive heart attack on their tennis court in Southampton, ending an unhappy marriage of twenty-six years—he was about to marry Hedda Goldsmith, a fashion designer, twenty-two years his junior. *Madly in love* wasn't adequate to describe his feelings. It was more than that. It was going to be a second chance waiting out there for a very lucky man.

Phoebe, his younger daughter, still lived with him when she wasn't in Northampton working on her Ph.D. at the University of Massachusetts. She had graduated from Radcliffe and Max had hoped she would get her advanced degree at Harvard. But, no . . . Harvard was too Establishment, according to Phoebe. The U. Mass. was where *it was at* in radical economics.

Felicitous was the word Max liked to use to describe the apple of his eye. "She's right out of Jane Austen, when she forgets she's a *hippie.*" Since he said it in her presence, Phoebe had to correct him. "Daddy, *hippie* just isn't used anymore, you're showing your age!"

Phoebe loved her father, even though his being so rich was an embarrassment to her. She considered herself a radical, unscathed by her boarding school education. Her mother, Sophia Conan-Walleby, had attended Miss Porter's . . . "And, so shall my daughters." But her younger one cast off being *exclusive* the way pigeon feathers shed water.

Phoebe looked upon her father as one of the rare ones. "A capitalist with a conscience," she would pronounce, with all the seriousness of her absolute, youthful positions. Father and daughter played with ideas like puppies with skeins of wool. He adored her nerve; it seemed to come straight from her grandmother, Martha, though she'd seen her only once in her life. Must have been passed down through the genes, he decided. How come they'd missed Roz, the firstborn?

"Phoebe's a funny little girl," Max once said to Hedda, when they were talking about the daughters she would acquire. "She doesn't miss a trick when it comes to chicanery, that little blond face and bachelor's-button eyes. She's going to have a tough time; on the other hand, she's indomitable, she'll prevail. That used to be my mother's favorite verb—*prevail.* If you're not strong, the word can be a curse. Phoebe thinks that the world is a good place, that truth needs no weapon but itself."

"Don't you?" Hedda asked.

"I *did* at her age, but not as passionately. I didn't have the luxury of a rich father, the luxury to contemplate the state of the world. I wanted to conquer it, not understand it," he laughed.

Max's older daughter, Rosalind, was another matter. She was a cool, self-serving young woman of twenty-eight. Her mother had seen to it that she married well and early—Willard Clyde, only son of the Rhode Island Clydes. Max Treading's freewheeling, liberal, irreverent personality was a continual source of irritation to his older daughter. There were so many things he did that embarrassed her, even wounded her, things never to be forgiven, like what happened at her engagement party at the Pierre. It was so typical, so thoughtless . . . the height of bad manners to forget who you were with, to run on at the mouth just for fun. No, it was malice. What actually happened was that Max was so bored in a roomful of conservative Clydes, humorless stockbrokers, he announced that one of his favorite Americans was Roger Williams, the radical seventeenth-century minister who had founded their state of Rhode Island out of desperation . . . "Because the founding fathers of Massachusetts considered his ideas on toleration intolerable, and banished him. Bless them, but the Puritans of Massachusetts had pokers up their theological asses . . . threw poor Roger out in a blinding snowstorm, and where did he go? South, to found Rhode Island, sanctuary for all the freethinking nuts in the Colonies!" The table at the Pierre went cold as ice. The Clydes and Treadings didn't see each other again until the wedding, and very little after that.

And her father's roots, deep in the dust of Utah—those were best forgotten altogether, according to Roz.

3

Max Treading fought for his life for a week in the Stockton hospital. It wasn't like lying under the tree near Emigrant Basin, hallucinating and trying to hang on. This was different. In that hazy time between feeling pain and being knocked out again, there was a worm of steel in the center of him refusing confinement. It twisted and turned, it pushed against his organs, clanged and belled like an Indian monk walking on a street of nails toward Nirvana. It chanted, "I will not die!"

He woke from the week-long fight and saw his daughter Phoebe sitting in a corner of the room. She had been there all week watching his face, counting the drips of his two intravenous bottles, and praying. The praying would have amused him. She rushed to take his hand and kiss it.

"How are you, Daddy?"

"How am I?" He raised his head and looked around. "Where am I?!"

"You're in a hospital in Stockton, California. You've been out of it for a week. Daddy, you're winning . . ."

He closed his eyes, then opened them again. His mind was

suddenly as clear as the sky on the day of the crash. He remembered instantly.

"The others?"

She shook her head no. He began to cry and turned his face away. The tears became hysterical sobs. Phoebe was alarmed. (How strange, how unlike Daddy!) "Please, you're supposed to be very quiet . . . they'll throw me out." She banged on the patient buzzer for help. Two nurses and a doctor burst in. They decided that his distress was obviously coming from extreme pain. They had been reducing the sedation gradually, but it must have been too soon, so they knocked him out again.

They were wrong. It *wasn't* the physical pain. A tidal wave of terror had rushed through him and broken what he'd always figured was an impregnable dam of courage. That dam was fifty years old, built by his mother and him when his father left them. So late . . . he was crying like a little boy of five. Another tidal wave of thought roared over the first one. Just when he was about to live the best part of his life, he had almost died! He was overcome with panic, not pain. Why were they knocking him out again?

By the end of the day, the sedation had worn off. He sat up for the first time, looked at Phoebe suspiciously, and demanded to know:

"Why isn't Hedda here?"

"She kept calling, Daddy, but you were so knocked out . . ."

"Why wasn't she here watching me be unconscious? What's going on?"

"Daddy . . ."

"Give me the telephone!" He looked at his younger daughter. "And, where is your sister?"

"You know Roz is afraid of flying, Daddy."

"I better arrange to die at home the next time, so it'll be convenient for everybody."

Three doctors walked into the room, delighted to see their patient sitting up, and introduced themselves.

"It took three of you to fix me up? Who was on first?"

"You had us working for eight long hours, Mr. Treading,"

one of the doctors said, unsmiling. "It was quite a game. I took care of your bones." He pointed to his colleagues. "He took care of your kidney, and he's taking care of your burns. You're a very lucky man. The main thing is—you're out of danger, no complications. All you have to do now is lie back and heal, and enjoy the California climate."

"For how long?" Max asked irritably.

The answer came from the burn specialist. "I'd say for weeks, anyway. You're going to need skin grafting on your back. I talked to your doctor about it. He was here until two days ago . . ."

"Hoffstadter, out here?"

"He flew out with your daughter," the doctor said, nodding at Phoebe. "He oversaw us like a hawk."

Max learned the extent of his injuries, but couldn't wait for the doctors to leave. "Will you gentlemen excuse me? I have to make a phone call. Thank you for patching me up." He motioned for Phoebe to give him the telephone. Phoebe was watching him play strong. He motioned her to leave the room.

"Hedda? Where are you? Get yourself out here right away! The big He is giving me back to you with a busted leg and a back that's gonna need some skin grafting. I can't be moved, they say, till they've done a few. Otherwise, I'm almost perfect."

Hedda was crying on the other end. "Oh, Max . . . how wonderful to hear your voice! Phoebe called me every night to report. You're coming out of it now, of course you are, darling, you're giving orders!"

"I almost died, do you know that?"

"I know very well, darling," she said quietly.

"Why aren't you here?"

"Because Roz would be very upset."

"Roz isn't here."

"She might be. Phoebe has been trying to convince her to go, every day. She still might . . . if I'm not there. That was one of the conditions, Max."

"Hedda, what's going on? I won't have Roz dictate conditions for us."

"Darling, I think she's flying out with Willard tomorrow, so there's no point in discussing it."

"I don't want her to come. I'm going to forbid it. I want you!"

"Don't you think I want to be with you? You don't need what happens when Roz and I are in a room together."

"That girl's going to have some growing up to do . . . we're getting married as soon as they say I can be moved, even if it's in a hospital room in New York. Would you say *no* to that?"

"Of course I wouldn't say *no* . . ."

"Then, that settles it." He was exhausted. "Hedda, I've got to be lucky. I always knew I was, but not like this, not this much. I'm alive. The others aren't. That's a tough thing to think about. That fellow upstairs . . . I've mentioned Him twice already . . . I must be getting religion." He was in pain and had to hang up. "Call me every hour on the hour. . . ."

He yelled for Phoebe to come back in. "Get me Alf Barnett on the phone."

"Daddy, you shouldn't be using up any more energy, please . . . Who's Alf Barnett?"

"Damn it, he's my vice-president in charge of Latin America. You should know things like that . . ." He sank back into his pillows, mumbling, "Everything hurts . . . every inch hurts . . . get me Alf."

"Daddy!"

"Christ, you came pretty near to inheriting and you don't even know Alf Barnett. That's my fault. We've got to fix that . . . Christ." He was silent for a moment. "Do you know I don't have an up-to-date will? Dinessen was after me for months, to clean it up after your mother died . . . Now, get me Barnett. I have to talk to him."

Phoebe protested, knowing it wouldn't do any good. She dialed her father's office, hoping a doctor wouldn't walk in, or he'd order the telephone removed. Maybe she should have it disconnected herself. No, he had to be able to talk to Hedda and Roz.

"Alf? I'm fine." Max waited for the delighted response on

the other end. "They say I'm out of the woods. Now, listen
... I hear I've been pretty unconscious for a week. Call President
Portillo in Mexico, not his office, his home. The poor man probably had a heart attack wondering about our deal. I was supposed to let him know if we were going in on the new fields. Tell
him—yes, we are. I promised him the hardware ... How many
points did we fall on the street? Four? Not bad. *I* fell a thousand.
Get out a release. Tell the press I'm fine. Alf, put a conference
call order in for this phone. I want to talk to Rosen and Blunt
about the Emigrant Basin land. It's perfect, what I saw of it."
He groaned, remembering the blue sky and the sudden cracking
sound of the helicopter. "I want to talk to them tomorrow.
Then, I want to see them ... here. Fly them out. I want the jet
here anyway."

Phoebe grabbed the phone. "Mr. Barnett, my father is in no
condition to say another word. He's not going to see anyone
except family, until the doctors say it's all right!"

Roz kept promising Phoebe that she would come, *but she
didn't.* Once it was a sudden virus as an excuse, then a vagueness
about Willard's schedule and when he could accompany her.
Reservations were made and canceled. Her attempts to make it
to Stockton finally trailed off and Phoebe stopped insisting; it
was pointless. Roz's coming and not coming lasted for several
weeks, which meant that Hedda didn't arrive either, since Roz
was always about to fly out to see her father. Hedda was not
going to put herself in the position of being cut dead by Max's
older daughter if they both found themselves in Stockton. Roz
had made it clear that she disliked the very thought of a Hedda
in her father's life. When Max was well, they'd handle it together. The main thing for Hedda was that he was recovering;
she could wait it out.

All of which put Phoebe into a state. She was trapped, with
no one to spell her, and her school semester was going to hell.
Before her father's accident she had been resolutely preparing
for her exams, working like a dog but feeling pretty good about

getting her final credits out of the way—for the coveted Ph.D., finally, finally. She even felt confident she could get through the course she dreaded most—econometrics, that business of trying to quantify *everything*; she hated it and wasn't very good at it. That wasn't how she saw the world, tagged down to the last decimal point. Now, all that was out the window. The only thing to be *quantified* now was her father's health, so she stayed in Stockton, close as she could be, in a hospital room down the hall.

Max would have been delighted by the way his *little one* took over, organized the doctors, commandeered a room for herself. If he hadn't been so injured, he would have been aware of the sacrifice of her staying and would probably have said, "Get the hell back to school, go!" Dangerous illness, though, has a way of negating everything but itself. He just wanted her in the room, he needed her to look at, that lovely face with its broad, open cheeks, huge blue eyes the color of Caribbean water, thick blond hair caught up in a barrette on the back of her head, which she held so straight, like an innocent child unaware of its perfection, an animal without guile. It wasn't until two weeks into his recovery that he realized she had laid away one of the most important times in her young life to be with him, and it made him madder than hell at Roz.

So, Phoebe was there to see his first skin grafts. She watched him get up and walk with half his body in a cast. She listened to him cuss the nurses and yell orders to his office in New York. She read to him, tried to amuse him, but he wasn't about to be amused.

Max was courting very strange moods indeed. The accident had not only shocked his body; he lay there in Stockton, of all places, swamped in introspection, counting his debits and credits. The freedom to think, as he was healing, frightened him. He felt like a racing car driver going two hundred miles an hour and the brakes had jammed on him. Once upon a time, he was a little boy holding his mother's hand and they were walking the desert country in between the mesas and the buttes. Suddenly, he was a middle-aged man who had almost died and he didn't know who he was! He was even courting feelings of failure. He had failed in his marriage. He had failed with his daughter Rosalind.

He kept trying to open the drawers of the past and they kept getting stuck; some were half-open, some couldn't be opened at all; it was exhausting. The past began to seem a giant, stubborn chiffonier with a mind of its own, and he, a weak, healing little figure, pushing, pulling, pounding, coaxing its drawers to open, trying to put them into visual order, at least.

Phoebe was worried. He wouldn't open his eyes for hours at a time and she knew he wasn't sleeping.

She didn't know he was trying to meet himself, a stranger saying: "I'm Max Treading . . ." With closed eyes, it was better, it was easier to see yourself going in and out of rooms and years.

"Hello, I'm Max Treading." He was a bull in a china shop when he walked into the home of Sophia's parents on Park Avenue—a young, tanned, very rich western bull, arriving for dinner at the Roger Wallebys'. Sophia, their daughter, with her pale, Grace Kellyish beauty . . . he couldn't keep his eyes off her. Her mother, an Englishwoman, looked at him with that other-planet smile of the born rich.

It was the week the Treading Mining Company appeared on the stock market for the first time. Roger Walleby, chairman of Walleby Investments (and his father before him and his father's father before *him*), nabbed Max on the observation balcony of the Exchange, introduced himself, and invited him to dinner. One week in town and the door of society opened. (Oh, the venality of the polite, when the chips were down.) Max knew why he was invited. Snare a dark horse, someone who's almost cornered the uranium market, new money, lasso him before the others, curry him, initiate him into the private club. The dues? Wealth.

It wasn't as though he had stormed in with mud on his

boots, not knowing which fork to use. Martha's boy feel ill at ease? Only if a cat could jump without whiskers. His damask napkin didn't quiver on his knees. True, he had never eaten an artichoke before . . .

"What do we have here?" he said. "This looks like it really wants to be unpeeled, and then what?"

Sophia smiled, looked at her mother, then delicately tore off a leaf and showed him how. "Just eat the tender part and throw the rest away."

"Now I know why I never had one. My mother would call it a frivolous vegetable." He repeated the lesson: "Eat the tender part and throw the rest away." Sophia blushed.

Her mother changed the subject. The look on Mrs. Walleby's face was another lesson: "You, young man, rich as you might be, are the commonality. Distinguished families breed with other distinguished families. Being invited to dinner does *not* unlock the door." That look brought the Treading stubbornness boiling up like a squall. Invading the Wallebys for anything but financial connection had been the last thing in his head. Suddenly, there was another possibility: Make *them* uncomfortable. Mrs. Walleby began to question him about his family, where they lived. He dove in, ingenuous and disarming—to shock.

"Martha lives on a passable ranch outside of Moab."

"Martha?" Mrs. Walleby said. "Your wife?"

"My mother, Mrs. Walleby."

"Really . . ."

"I've called her Martha ever since I was a little boy. Everyone around Moab called her that, so I did too."

"And, she allowed it?"

"She must have, she never corrected me."

"How interesting. I'm afraid I disapprove." With a cold little smile Mrs. Walleby went on. "There must be millions of Marthas in this world, but only one to be honored as your mother, don't you think?"

"There's only one Martha Treading around Moab, Mrs. Walleby, and she's honored."

"And your father?" she asked tremulously.

"He was a mining engineer, graduated from the University of Colorado. Might still be a mining engineer, I don't really know. He left us when I was almost five."

"Oh, dear . . ." She was even more tremulous.

"We managed. Or rather, Martha managed. Very well, I might say, or I wouldn't be here. My mother is a do-it-yourself geologist. She's one of the four principal stockholders in Treading Mining," Max said, turning to Roger Walleby. "My mother; Joe Tanner, a grocer in Moab; McGregor, a crazy minister with a long, white beard; and me. *We* are Treading Mining!" Max laughed. "It sounds mighty unorthodox from the outside, but it was all very logical, if you were there."

No one was offering anything better for conversation. He could turn it all around and ask Mrs. Walleby who *her* parents were! And Sophia? She just kept looking at him with a kind of smile, watching her parents' faces, doing nothing to help move the talk. Her big blue eyes showed she knew what he was up to, that the only way for him not to be uncomfortable was to flaunt who he was. That's why he was there, wasn't it?

He proceeded to tell them how Joe Tanner, the grocer, footed their food bills for a year when he and Martha decided to buy acreage between Moab and Grand Junction; Martha had a hunch there was uranium there, and Martha's hunches weren't to be laughed at.

"She hunched two oil wells on our land when I was growing up. They didn't yield much, but enough to keep the cattle going, and a little more . . . for good, experimental irrigation.

"It was after I'd come back from my first job, working in an oil field in Venezuela, that our second well dried up. By then, I was an engineer myself. Before then, I was with the Seabees in the Pacific, during the war . . . got a lot of practical information out there—*that's* an understatement."

"So, you're an engineer?" Mrs. Walleby offered.

"Without a degree. I learned it from my father's books, with Martha's help. As a matter of fact, I used my father's degree to get that job in Venezuela. A little larcenous, I suppose, but

Martha said I knew as much as he did, by then. What difference, if you can deliver?"

Roger Walleby was becoming very interested, and his wife was turning white. Sophia was resting her chin in her hands. (God, she's too much, Max thought. She's what every man dreams of—the beauty that needs nothing to dress it up, not even the string of pearls she's wearing around her neck, or the rose-colored, watery-veined dress . . .)

"Where was I? Joe Tanner, the good-natured grocer. He didn't have a gambling bone in his body, but he found one for Martha and ended up with ten percent of a uranium find." Max paused. "Martha's a very interesting lady." He looked squarely at Mrs. Walleby. She looked back at him, perplexed with this too-direct young man her husband had invited. ("A cowboy," he'd said. "He's made the newest fortune on the Street, if you can bear him. Because Walleby's wants to invest, not only wants to, it's vital to . . .") Well, he was hardly a cowboy, not in the ordinary sense. He was something even stranger.

"Yes, my mother's very special," Max went on. "Rooted and relevant, if you know what I mean." He could see that Mrs. Walleby didn't at all. "And then, there's McGregor, the fourth partner. It could take all night to tell you about old McGregor." Max sniffed. "I can smell him now, just mentioning his name. His white beard was so long, he used to tuck it into his shirt."

"He's dead?" Sophia interrupted.

"Oh, yes, he's very dead."

"Then, there are only three actual partners," her father said.

"That's right."

"Should we leave the table? Unless we want more coffee," Mrs. Walleby offered.

"Oh, Mother, let Max finish his story." Sophia said "Max" so easily. It didn't escape anyone.

"Well, to make it short, when we decided to buy the new land, we sold everything we could, except the ranch. The cattle, the oil riggings, even our small plane—everyone needs a plane out there to get around. But we even sold that, and Martha and

I went to live, if you can believe it, on the new land, in a
heavy-gauge tent. We weren't the only ones. Everyone was out
there looking for uranium, living in shacks, digging wells hoping to find water, praying the winter snows might melt and
reach the valleys. Everyone was out looking for a fortune. Like
the gold rush all over again.

"And, who should appear one day? McGregor, minister of
the gospel when he wasn't busy trying to mine every mineral
known to man. It turned out he knew the land like his own
hand.

"Now, that was 1950," Max said, pointing a finger at
Walleby. "Government men were standing around, ready to
help you, with money to burn. If you hit, you could find a
hundred drifters to work for you. Uranium was a must. The
U.S. *had* to have a superbomb. The Soviets had already test-
exploded theirs. The government men said they were absolutely
sure there weren't any uranium outcroppings where we had
bought. Along comes old McGregor and says the government
surveyors were damn fools, and how come Martha was ornery
enough to buy in the wrong place that was going to turn out to
be the right place! Did we want a hand? he said. It turned out
McGregor knew the geodetic surveys like he knew the Old
Testament. Martha and I were pretty well-versed, too, I might
add, so now we had three evangelical nuts saying the government was wrong. The land we'd bought *hadn't* been fully ex-
plored; not only that, it hadn't begun to be tapped. End of story:
We were right! We struck and Martha gave the old man a partnership. When the mine was in full swing and it looked like we
were on the way to getting pretty rich . . . McGregor abandoned
his twelve or so parishioners who gave him a chicken every
Sunday for his preaching, and from then on, he just sat in front
of the mine, with severe second thoughts, preaching to anyone
who would listen. 'Don't go in,' he'd say. 'It's a mistake. Uranium was given Man by God to destroy himself through
hellfire!' *Why* the old man searched for ore in the first place, no
one could figure. He never used the money, never changed his
clothes or ways, still smelled high and preached to the air. He

died a couple of years later, without heirs. Left his share to Martha. I think she was his secret love. She said he probably died pure . . . pure in heart, she probably meant," Max added, looking at Mrs. Walleby's face. His hostess had the look of a town gossip, her face frozen, bosom heaving.

Roger Walleby also saw his wife's look and suggested they leave the table.

"So, that was the beginning of Treading Mining," Max said to Walleby as they walked into the living room. "After that, we extended our holdings to three more mines in the States, and we're about to buy into Canadian uranium prospects. It probably won't be Treading Mining for much longer. Not with the plans I have to expand. That first strike will seem like a quaint cuckoo clock." He could feel the women rustling behind them. "My mother gave the first mine its name. *The Elephant Mine.*"

"Why?" Sophia murmured at his elbow. Max turned to play with her. "Because, when we went out to live in that tent for a year, she was positive we would make a strike. She used to say, 'If you're looking for elephants, you go to elephant country!' " (If you're looking for Sophias, Max was thinking, you go to Sophia country! He hadn't arrived with that thought in mind. It was being put into his head—wanting what the atmosphere said was forbidden.)

Max was experiencing a terrible anxiety lying in his hospital bed thirty years later. He kept trying to reconstruct Sophia's face, the way it had seemed to him the first time he saw it. Did he fall in love with her because *what* she was would be good for him, open doors, file down the rough edges? Had he wanted to conquer the country of the Wallebys just to win, to prove he was as fine as they were? He was looking at the young man who was himself with a bit of dismay, maybe even disgust. How rough did he feel in the Walleby living room for the first time?

Good God, they were boring as hell . . . all except the tantalizing cloud of rose silk that was Sophia. They talked of nothing but riding, sailing, charities, murmured about people he didn't know, what they said and did at lunch or dinner or at the opera. Mrs. Walleby reminded him of a giraffe, her husband, a chipmunk. And Sophia? Sophia was a gazelle, a creature renowned for incredible, poised beauty. Did Sophia have a brain —to make her an exception in the gazelle species?

Max was recalling the Walleby living room, his first introduction to private opulence—the butler offering brandy, the Oriental rugs, French antiques, the crystal, the portraits of previous Wallebys. He had quipped, "What a wonderful place for women to 'come and go / Talking of Michelangelo,' " and they had just stared at him dumbly for a brow-creased moment. Walleby then steered the conversation back to the only logical reason the young man was in his living room, though *another reason* was growing, unbeknownst even to Max at that moment, like some wild mushroom in an enchanted forest.

"You're very young to be in charge of a company such as yours," Walleby had commented cautiously, and with not some little private amazement about this *family business* that had suddenly sprung up to take its place among the big mining interests in the country. It was almost impossible to imagine this young man as the genius in the woodpile, but that's what he undoubtedly was—a genius of business, with no advisory board but some lawyers in Denver and his mother.

To Mrs. Walleby's horror, Max didn't disappear after that evening. The unthinkable began to happen under her very nose and with the approval of her husband. Max and Sophia were falling violently in love. *Violent* was the only word Mrs. Walleby could find to describe the situation—what she considered a horrible accident.

Two months later, not only had Walleby Investments bought into Treading Mining and its new Canadian uranium interests, but Mrs. Walleby found herself having to plan a wedding. In her own mind, she couldn't accuse Max of being *a fortune hunter*, for he was a very rich young man. That had to pull the teeth of her anger a little but there was something else at work, something even more destructive—her daughter was marrying a man of no background. Not only that, his mother, that Martha Treading, refused to come East for the wedding. The whole situation was entirely undigestible. A ruffian knight from a far-off land had stormed in and grabbed the prized Walleby virgin right out of her bed!

Max lay in his hospital bed thinking—How strange to have gone after one's opposite with such ferocity. Was I as venal, going after Sophia, as her father was, going after Treading Mining? Hadn't we been equally matched in our venality? Hadn't we invaded each other with the relish of lobster eaters?

Why was he forcing himself to pore over the mistakes, the emotional failures? It was all a long time ago, and Sophia was dead. He kept wanting to conjure up her pale, princess face, the way it was when they first married, but he had trouble catching it. Her face of the later years kept intruding, not only her face but the whole of her, tanned, tight as catgut, his tennis-playing, perfect hostess of a wife. How Rosalind resembled her! That was the punishment—to have the unhappiness continue into another generation. He had never thought of it that way. Roz was like the Wallebys and he had not been a good father because of it. He had hurt her. It was his fault she was cold, disdainful, judgmental, neurotic, couldn't even fly out to see her daddy who almost died. He had to push those thoughts away; they were too painful. He wanted Sophia's pale, princess face before him—to justify how much he had loved her in the beginning.

He went into a dream of recreating that first time he brought Sophia to the ranch, how shocked she was by its roughness, its genteel shabbiness. That was the way Martha wanted it, even though they could have afforded anything by then. The potbellied stoves, the Indian rugs, the canning jars and plants all over the place; the smell of horses, pungent flops, wet earth in the garden—just the way it had been as far back as he could remember, except now there was an indoor bathroom, and in Martha's estimation that made the ranch a palace.

His mind anxiously stirred up the sediment of a memory—making love to Sophia in broad daylight at the foot of a butte.

They had been married a month, young animals in love, kissing, sucking, cleaving. The ranch was too small for such delirious noise. They made love outside, anywhere, rode their horses to a *place*, stripped, lay naked in the sun. He was trying to grasp *that* Sophia, excited by the newness, the freedom, sprung loose from Park Avenue. Sophia, the young bride, with the excitement of change all over her flushed face . . . She raced ahead of him on her horse, flung her shirt off, rode bare-breasted till she chose the *place* where they could roll like animals. It was fornicating the sky and earth at the same time, they were so insanely eager to taste, touch each other. Lying on top of her, he had put a smudge of desert earth on her forehead and baptized her a Treading. What a lie. It was a flippant, shallow, society girl on a toot, a Sophia on "a gay, ghastly holiday," playing his game, making believe, suffering his rude beginnings, his crazy mother, waiting to *change* him, mold him, dress him in pinstripes and bigotry.

He felt himself sweating as he desperately tried to create a truth out of the beginning. If there was a truth, it was animal attraction—intense, playful, fleeting, glorious delirium. Rosalind had been conceived during that first visit to the ranch. She should have come out *shining* . . . But she didn't. She might as well have been conceived in his mother-in-law's bed between satin sheets.

Neither he nor Sophia had won. Neither of them had changed the other. They had both been punished for thinking they could. *That* was the truth of it. As a matter of fact, they were natural enemies! There wasn't a thing they agreed on or liked together. After Rosalind was born, Sophia acted as though their sex life had been some sort of aberration, an evil magic he had imposed on her. He was vulgar, liberal, embarrassing, uncouth . . .

He was hurting himself remembering how Sophia and his mother had made believe they liked each other that first visit to the ranch. And, later . . . the open disapproval of Sophia, her not allowing the girls to visit their grandmother lest they be tainted by her unconventionality. Why hadn't he bowed out? Because sharing children meant inviting guests for life? Why had Phoebe been born four years after Rosalind, when the marriage was totally finished? Another of God's tricks! Phoebe came out shining, blond, and beautiful like Sophia, but inside her little being she had been the spittin' image of Martha Treading from the minute she could talk.

He lay twisting and sweating, thinking about the later Sophia, an exact replica of her mother, hawklike, pouncing by nature, hiding it behind icy smiles, perfect manners in public. In private, she could scream like an outraged, drunken whore.

Later, when he used to fly out to see Martha by himself . . . Martha, painting in her old age, going out into the desert with her chair and easel, coming back with the blue sky on canvas, the mesa and butte—the way the landscape looked to her soul and how it had crawled into her veins. Disapprove of Martha? Only a bitch could do that!

He was lying in a pool of sweat, shocked by a truth he hadn't been looking for. He had allowed the Wallebys to win. He had denied Martha her grandchildren, always promising they would come to the ranch, to let her teach them what she had taught him. But there were always Sophia's reasons never to allow it. He had never been strong enough to break her vise. *There was no truth in the beginning,* only the truth of a young bull wanting to own a pale, princess face, seduce the opposition, beat them at their own game, and *they'd* won! No, they hadn't won! He'd become a force to reckon with! Rammed things down their throats! Caused Sophia to flee from his ideas, wind herself so tight, so disdainful, so lacking in love that she just fell down dead one day. He had won.

Max groaned, opened his eyes, and saw Phoebe sitting next to his bed, staring at him.

"Daddy? Are you all right? Were you dreaming? You were twisting from side to side on your poor back . . ."

"I wasn't dreaming, I was thinking."

"You were sound asleep, groaning and carrying on."

"All right, have it your way. I was dreaming."

"About what?"

"And what business is it of yours, Miss Nosy?"

"Oh, I think he's feeling better," she said to the air. "You looked so agitated, Daddy, that's all . . ."

He looked at her curiously intense face, the direct stare of Martha. "I was . . . I was thinking, not dreaming, about your mother and the first time I took her to the ranch to see your Grandmother Treading."

"Were you very much in love, Daddy?"

"Yes, if you must know, Hawkshaw . . . in the beginning."

"But not later on . . ."

"What do you mean?"

"You were the most mismatched pair I've ever met, that's what I mean, Daddy. I'd like to talk about it someday. Promise that you will?"

He was taken aback, but that was Phoebe. "I promise. Before I kick the bucket the next time, remind me." He laughed. It felt good, even though it hurt. "Mismatched? That's the understatement of the century." He was feeling better. "Call Roz and tell her absolutely not to come. I'm getting out of here . . . going home. Call Dr. Hoffstadter. Tell him I want to be in a New York hospital tomorrow!"

"Daddy, you can't be moved yet!"

"Of course I can! They move wounded soldiers, don't they? They can move me. They can release a couple of nurses and doctors to go with me. You know why they will? Because I'm going to give this hospital a great big gift for treating me so well. Call Alf Barnett and have him send the jet out, and I mean it. That's an order."

"Dr. Hoffstadter said he didn't want you moved for two weeks, at least."

"Do you think my brain was injured? I know what I want to do and how I'm going to get well, so that's that."

He was probably right, crazy as it sounded. He needed Hedda.

"Baby, go do what I say."

"Yes, sir! Money can do anything, even convince doctors." She loved to chide him about being so rich and he loved her doing it. Phoebe was probably born to remind him not to "Walleby." God, what a paradox. There she was—looking like her mother and talking like Martha.

"Are you going to marry Hedda, finally?" she said with the directness of a child.

"Yes!"

"Wonderful."

"You mean that, don't you . . ."

"Of course I do. She's good for you."

"You're going to have to convince your sister of that."

"Not me, Daddy. *You're* going to have to do that."

"I know . . . let's leave it alone right now."

Phoebe stood at the door for a moment. "Daddy, I would like to do a lot of talking when you get home . . . about you and Mother." She threatened with a smile, "Parents should talk more than they do . . . to their children . . . before it's too late."

She didn't wait for an answer and left to find the head of the hospital who, whether he liked it or not, was going to have to figure out how to make the transfer of Maxwell Treading, cast, injured kidney, intravenous apparatus, burned back and all.

AN ENTRY IN THE JOURNAL OF DR. HIRAM WESGROVE, MAY 1981

Oh, for the monadic solution to comfort my brain, just one. Will it ever be my fate? The exhausted traveler covered with the dust of experience, spent and filled, eager to go home, finally sees the light in the window from whence he started. How far we've come, in one way, from the English eureka a hundred years ago—that the crap *in chimneys was responsible for the skin cancer of poor chimney sweeps. Then years to isolate the offending chemical in charcoal. Years, years, years. Now we know of a myriad of offending chemicals, we know the vulnerability of cells to numbers of substances and conditions, we chart the course of abnormal cells, we calibrate with modern instrumentation, we are armed with knowledge of the double helix, thank God . . . But still nothing . . . I must be patient! Using an exclamation point means I'm not.*

Working with mice is proving nonproductive; their life span is inadequate to test the rate *of metastasis as it relates to a larger mammal, their bodies too small to compare secondary tumor growth, the probability of. We're not getting even an approximation of human cell behavior when it comes to the secondary growth of tumor after the primary tumor is removed.*

Partial good news from the cryonics lab people today. One of two trained rats was successfully frozen and unfrozen, with its training intact; the other one died. Elusive success is better than none. I am, I must admit, being pulled into an excessive fascination—the progress of cryophysics. I'm even sticking my nose in, suggesting the more sophisticated cat or monkey brain be used, rather than the rat's. If one is foolish enough to want to walk in a forest knowing one will get lost, it might as well be in a grand forest.

I hesitate to share my ruminations with the cryonics folk, who are working so diligently with what they know *and it is the proper way, but I can't help thinking about how to capture the media of exchange* between *the brain cells as well as freezing the matter (brain cells). If a vehicle for the capture of* the nondefined *were to become available . . . I must control my instinct for the big jump, my hunch about some new companion agent when it comes to cooling not only the brain, but the function of the brain. Working with liquid nitrogen—in an attempt to arrest the unknown—is like playing the piano with your knuckles.*

4

Ensconced in a New York hospital, Max was determined to get himself back to where he had been before the crash: a happy, healthy man of fifty-four, at the height of his creative energy, with more plans in his head than two other men would have conceived of in their entire lifetimes. There was no point in ruminating about the past. That activity had built-in hazards. You could sink into a quagmire of *mea culpa;* you could even lose your sense of humor.

The crash had shuffled his priorities. He thanked God for it, at the same time thinking, Come on, it isn't Him at all, but luck, chance, destiny, fate that I'm alive. It's just easier, more economical to thank one word—Him.

The first priority was to marry Hedda right there in the hospital room. To his amazement, she said no, she wasn't going to marry him flat on his back. "I don't want to be accused of kicking you when you're down," she said, trying to make light of his wish. He could see she was serious.

"Max, I'd like to have a real wedding with my mother and cousins and Phoebe and," she paused, "Rosalind . . . the whole world . . . It'll be my first, after all."

"OK, you're right. But I'm still in pain and you're denying me, that's real too."

"I want the longest honeymoon in history, darling, and it can't be in a hospital bed. I want you to walk down an aisle with me, without cast or bandages."

"That can't happen for months, according to Dr. Hoffstadter," Max said forlornly. "Wait . . ."

"But, *in bed* we're gonna do the day I get out of here. Come here . . ." He reached for her and pressed his head against her breasts. "God, that feels good . . ."

"A nurse might come in!"

"All right, I'll make a deal. When I get out of this damn place, you have to move into the apartment with me and the wedding will come when it comes."

Hedda stood up and thought for a moment. He had that Max-look, jaunty and sly at the same time. "I would say yes, why not? But . . . no, darling . . . If everything was fine, the way it is with Phoebe, it would be wonderful, but you have to settle things with Roz first . . . I know you don't need your daughter's approval, but you certainly need her civility. Or, I need it . . . Max, when you were in the Stockton hospital, she was very rude to me. It was during the first week when you were unconscious most of the time. Phoebe called me every night to report, but there was a whole day and night when I didn't hear. I tried to get through, but when they asked me 'Are you family?' I had to say no and they wouldn't give me any information except that you were alive, so I called Roz in Rhode Island to see if she had heard from Phoebe. Do you know what Roz said? 'Please, Miss Goldsmith, I would appreciate your not using me as a conduit to my father. His condition is a matter of family concern and no one else's.' "

"Good God . . ."

"Max, it wasn't pleasant. You're not in any condition to think about it yet, but I had to tell you. Yes! Of course I'd come live with you, it's what we both want, but Roz's anger has to be faced. We don't deserve shadows. There . . . I've said it, I've upset you, I'm sorry . . ."

She had come into the room, all pale orange and purple, she always wore the damnedest, wonderful colors, his little Hedda, round . . . warm . . . juicy . . . black shiny curls . . . He closed his eyes to shut out everything but Hedda, the idea of her. How he loved her. In a way she was another opposite—a good opposite this time. He loved her never-veiled spirit. Hedda, the artist. He was going to have her for the rest of his life. Everything she touched she made beautiful . . . even mushrooms around a fish.

He was recalling the first dinner she had made for him in her apartment, which looked just like her, a riot of color making perfect sense, a kind of bubbling calm. She had only one fault —she wanted everything balanced, reasonable, rational, she worked at it like a prospector looking for gold, sifting, sifting for that precious glint.

"Don't worry," he said weakly, opening his eyes. "I'll handle it. See you tomorrow . . . that's good to say, isn't it?" She bent over to kiss his forehead. The smell of her that he loved, mixed with her perfume, was too strong. She was right. He wasn't in any condition to handle anything. Action was the answer and he would take it . . . later.

He had a mind that could shut out one problem while he tackled another, the ability to wipe his head clear, sleep for ten minutes and wake refreshed. He closed his eyes and quickly slept away the problem Hedda had presented. There were other important things that had to occupy him as he healed. Tomorrow, he was going to feel well enough to have phones connected in his room, to conduct business as usual while he suffered the skin grafts.

At the point of the helicopter crash, Max had been more than exploring the prospect of a new industry. He had acquired the patents and talents of two physicists to build the first solar energy containment plant in the country, a venture with huge ramifications. When the helicopter went down, he had been looking at the land chosen for the virgin project. It would eventually lead to the manufacture of solar cells to be bought in hardware stores and plugged into home outlets like electric bulbs. An oil man do that? Cut his own throat? Crazy! "Not crazy," was Max's answer. "Prescient! Yankee canny! Detroit was too fat and arrogant to retool, make sensible cars and beat the foreign market, and look what happened to the auto people! Hell, if we don't change horses in midstream, dangerous as that might be, we're going to be swept away anyway, 'cause the old horses can't make it to the other side." He was being laughed at; at the same time he was being watched. Treading wants to turn everything upside down too fast, too soon, *they* were saying; he's trying to get the jump and is crazy enough to foot the bill. The biggest fear of the Treading-watchers was that his new venture would work.

It wasn't going to be the first time Max had shifted his interests, confounded his competitors, upset his board of directors, lived up to his reputation as a dangerous foe, a freak. Early in the game he had shaken the uranium market by announcing he could no longer, in good conscience, be involved in the mining and refining of uranium for war purposes.

"If not for war and defense purposes, then what else?" he was challenged.

"For science, for peaceful industry. We'll sell to anyone who wants to move a mountain!" was his retort. "Like China!"

It was more complicated than that. His board of directors were no longer Martha, the grocer, the minister, and a couple of lawyers from Denver. They were careful, dark-suited men like Walleby, men who had invested heavily in the expansion of the Treading Mining Company into Canadian and American deposits of uranium. They weren't interested in war and peace, they were interested in uranium. It was a tricky business for Max, removing himself from personal responsibility, yet remaining a major stockholder; but half a moral loaf was better than none. He used his uranium profits in other ways, delighted with himself and his circuitous games—antinuclear organizations, lobbying in Washington. He began to buy and sell oil leases the way kids exchange marbles, taking special pleasure in the Maracaibo oil field of Venezuela, buying into blocks of land bordering on the best fields and wells, draining them off to the side, and turning his Latin American competitors into mad beasts. That would teach them you couldn't beat up a young Americano engineer and get away with it.

In 1969 the Treading Mining Company had become Global Materials, with holdings in tin, silver, oil, buying heavily in areas of the world that had the metals for high technology, and getting into the innovative business of soybeans—" 'that ingenious legume with by-products from plastics to food . . . to feed the world,' " said Max to his board of directors.

"If Treading is into proteins, you can be sure there's going to be big money in hunger!" a Wall Street observer remarked. Another, who'd watched his manipulations for years, said, "Some jocks need to win so badly, they go into a game with a dislocated disk. Treading goes in with a bleeding heart and it never seems to bother him." Max's response was: "Not a bad image; I'm flattered. Doesn't it belong to their Lord who suffered for their sake?"

The day he was released from the hospital, Phoebe arrived from Northampton for the homecoming. She found him practicing his tennis swings in his bedroom, to prove a man in a cast up to his waist could still hit a pretty passable backhand.

"Sit down, for heaven's sake, Daddy. You'll fall. What are you trying to prove?"

"That I'm indestructible. Is there anything else to prove?"

There was going to be a family dinner that night. Roz and her husband, Willard, were coming in from Rhode Island and staying the night. "A celebration," her father announced. "Everyone in the same place at the same time. Good idea?"

"Are you sure?"

"Of course I'm sure. We'll shove everything into place and make it right my first night at home. I want everyone who means something to me to be here . . ."

"And Hedda?"

"Of course! Hedda most of all! You'll see. It's going to work, because we're going to make it work, you and me, baby, and everyone else will follow."

"Oh Daddy . . ."

"I don't think anyone should forget I almost died, do you?"

"Don't use that too much, Daddy."

"No, I won't . . ." he reflected. "Just a little. For about a year . . . Too long?"

"Does Hedda know the guest list?"

"Certainly! She planned the menu, I think she's in the kitchen supervising. Doesn't that sound good? That's the way it's gonna be from now on—Hedda here!"

"You mean she's moving in before you're married? That's evil," Phoebe said impishly.

"Well, I think I've convinced her; Phoebe, everything has to go well tonight. We're getting married after the cast comes off. That's what I want to announce at the table tonight. I've invited Dr. Hoffstadter and his wife. Thought it might take the edge off a strictly family thing." Max had to sit down. "Funny, the only pain I still have is in the damn leg. One of the breaks isn't healing fast enough. Nothing to worry about, just a damn nuisance. Other than that, I'm just fine . . . Go find Hedda and tell her you're here. She has a present for you."

As Phoebe walked through the apartment she sensed a difference about the rooms, something almost cozy. How could that be? With Mother's antiques like mummies standing upright in a museum? That was it! The furniture had been rearranged! The rosewood tables, the couches, even the French bowlegged chairs, the objets d'art, they had all been put into positions for use, not admiration. The bowls had fruit in them, the vases, flowers. And the curtains weren't drawn. That was it, most of all; the sun was pouring in. Hedda must have done it. It was beautiful.

Phoebe stood in the middle of the Treading living room looking at things she had never noticed before, gazing intently at the formidable collection of modern art her father had acquired over the years, mixed with the ancestral portraits on the Walleby side. She cast her eyes down the long hall out of the living room, with its nineteenth-century seascapes and the Cézanne on the far end, leading to the bedroom wing of the apart-

ment. She had grown up with that sunny, feathery French landscape, wondering sometimes what it had to be happy about.
God, she was thinking, Roz is going to have a fit when she walks
into all these changes.

Phoebe decided she wasn't going to look for Hedda right
away, but go to her bedroom, unpack her bag, and hang up the
skirt she'd wear for dinner. No jeans tonight; she'd surprise
everyone and even put on some makeup.

There was an exquisite cotton lace dress laid out on
Phoebe's bed, with a note attached. "With love. You'll look like
a nineteenth-century doll in this one. Hedda." It was a gift
chosen with tact and affection. Hedda knew Phoebe's radical
distaste for "dresses," her constant uniform of jeans and predi-
lection for coarse, Indian cotton skirts as the height of "dress-
up." A replica of an 1890 garden dress would probably be
accepted because it might have come from a thrift shop. Hedda
was right. Phoebe loved it. She put it on and went into Roz's
bedroom to look at herself in a full-length mirror; there wasn't
one in her room. Roz's room had a whole wall of mirror, installed before her coming-out party. Phoebe had denied her
mother that pleasure. Being a deb was ridiculous, the convention of it, the intention of it. She wasn't going to be made a
potato looking for meat or the other way around. Anyway, she
had been too busy when she was eighteen, writing a paper about
the influence of the unconscious on famous scientists and their
discoveries.

As she stood looking at herself in the mirror, she recalled
the dreadful fight she had had with her mother over not *coming
out*. An emptiness in the pit of her stomach happened when she
thought about her mother. If I knew she was going to die in
three years, would I have fought her on that silly thing? Do you
behave differently when you know someone is going to die? I
loved her but I didn't like her, she said to herself. Why was she
thinking about her? It was the changed apartment, the expung-
ing of her mother's spirit. And, why not? Ghosts had to be laid.
It was Daddy's right to start over . . .

Suddenly she noticed a luscious, green silk dress on Roz's

bed, with acres of material arranged like an open umbrella. What a beautiful color! There was a note. Not too guiltily, she read it. "Dear Rosalind, I designed this—it's a Goldsmith just for you. May this gift be the beginning of a loving friendship. Hedda."

Phoebe hung the dress in a closet, took the note with her to her own room and put it in a drawer. Wrong, dear Hedda; oh, wrong. Roz would consider it the height of presumption. And the "loving friendship"? Her sister would have to be clobbered on the head by a good fairy for that to happen. Hedda had to be protected from her own warm gestures. Let the dress be in the closet, let Roz find it . . . but no note, no plea, no asking for acceptance. If Roz was going to behave herself, it was going to be out of respect for Daddy and protocol, once she learned they were actually going to get married. She'd have to find Hedda right away and tell her what she thought and what she'd done. God! The psychic energy used up in this family. . . . It was always that way.

Phoebe rushed to the kitchen area. On her way, she heard the front door buzzer. She heard the butler greeting Roz and Willard and her father stumping on his crutches to meet them. She continued to the kitchen, not wanting to see Roz's face when she looked around and noticed the changes. Hedda wasn't in the kitchen. Phoebe stood in the pantry hall and heard Hedda greeting them, too. She imagined Roz's face again: What, *you* here? Then, the cold smile.

Roz was saying, "It was a long trip, traffic, I'd like to wash up and nap." (Did she hug Daddy?) Phoebe heard Roz walking down the hall to her bedroom.

"Do you want to wash up too, Willard, or would you like a drink first?" Max asked.

"Drink first, Dad, then I need a snooze. The traffic after Hartford was terrible. The chauffeur is a new one, drove Roz crazy with his foot on the brake too hard, made us both nauseous, as a matter of fact. Where's Phoebe? Is she in yet from Mass.?"

"Yes, she's here somewhere. . . ."

"Well, Dad, you look pretty good for a man who's gone through a crash." Not a word about not seeing him until now, not having visited the hospital. Just . . ."Roz's been worried sick about you, but you know how scared she is of hospitals and all that . . ."

Max responded, "Nothing to worry about, Willard, old boy. I'm just fine. If Roz couldn't, she couldn't . . . each to his own capacity." Phoebe, still listening, thought, how elegant of Daddy to have brushed it all off like that. Roz had called her father every day he was in the hospital in New York, but could never get herself to visit him. Talking about *capacity*, how much capacity for guilt did Roz have? Phoebe leaned against the wall, furious with her sister but beset with feeling: I love her but I don't like her! How can that be? It could very well be, evidently. She belongs to me . . .

The family story was that Roz screamed until she was allowed to hold "the baby" in her lap when they took Phoebe home from the hospital after she was born. Why did she try to push me off every chair I sat on, when I was smart enough to sit? Why is it welling up now? Because this is an important day. Because this family is going through changes. God, let it be a pleasant dinner . . .

Phoebe knocked on her sister's door and went in. Roz had taken off her traveling clothes and was resting on the bed in her underwear. Everything had already been neatly folded, her cosmetics lined up on the dressing table, towel and robe arranged over a chair waiting for her to shower. If it had been Phoebe, everything would have been scattered, certainly the first hour she arrived anywhere. Not Roz. What a beautiful woman she was, shiny and sleek in her satiny chemise. Phoebe was struck: How much time does it take to choose such a thing, with its spidery lace and tiny embroidered flowers? The hours it must take to look the way Roz looked! Roz was utterly beautiful from head to toe, gleaming, cared for, a goddess. It took infinite hours of attention to make a goddess. Well, Roz had learned from an expert, their mother. The mystery was why she, Phoebe, had not learned, or didn't want to, or was constitutionally unable to.

Phoebe brushed her hair away from her face and sat on her sister's bed. She knew that Roz, not having seen her for a while, would look at her the way their mother used to—the scrutiny of a sergeant, the shrug.

Roz sat up and gave her a kiss.

"Hi . . ." said Phoebe. "Daddy looks great, doesn't he, after what he's been through?"

"Yes, he does. What's *she* doing here? I thought this was going to be a family dinner."

"It is. Daddy's going to marry her. He's announcing it tonight."

"To a crowd of thousands?"

"Oh, Roz . . ."

"Well, since you know the good news, then I'm the crowd of thousands."

Phoebe's heart began to beat fast. She tried not to tangle with Roz, it was a waste of time, like getting angry with a hornet; the best you could do was step away. "I probably shouldn't have said anything, Daddy wanted to do it, but maybe it's better you know beforehand, so that . . ."

"So that what?"

"So that you'll behave yourself!"

"I beg your pardon?"

"Oh, Pooh!" Phoebe did what she always did when Roz backed her into a corner—play a bear of very little brain. It was a childhood game. Roz always won.

"That's a quick retreat," Roz said.

"Yes, for the moment. See you later. I'm going to take a shower and get dressed."

"You? Dressed for dinner?"

"I have a very pretty new one. It's an occasion, a celebration. It's making Daddy very happy. Why don't you like her? You don't even know her . . ." She searched her sister's face for clues. Sometimes it was impossible to know what was going through Roz's mind. There was a sudden smile that brightened up her face, like now; you never knew whether it was the front curtain hiding a scheme or just a spontaneous lightening of her features to close off a subject. Mother used to do that—the annoyance and the sudden smile. It was called breeding. It kept you teetering, wondering whether you were being accepted or dispensed with.

On the other hand, there was something so vulnerable, fragile about Roz's face that touched Phoebe, now that she had outgrown being hurt by its coldness. (Oh, you're so sloppy, uncouth, so noisy! Leave me alone, get out of my room, you little worm! Don't touch, don't borrow, it's mine, do you hear? It's mine!) Only when she was in college did Roz stop throwing those sibling epithets. They were still there behind the face, though, all the unfinished business of children. Mother had never tried to help make them friends. Still, there was that crazy sister love, in spite of everything. Sometimes, Roz would put her arms around her, smooth her hair, cluck over her... "My little sister..." when she'd had a few drinks. Roz was always better with a few drinks. Funny, how the lines had been drawn separating the two of them. Roz belonged to Mother and she was Daddy's.

Keep it light, Phoebe admonished herself. (She wanted to say: You bitch! Why didn't you get yourself to the hospital to see him all these weeks? And now you come with all that critical stuff on your face, all the jealousy? Stop it! We almost lost him.)

"Dr. Hoffstadter and his wife are coming" was what she said out loud.

"Oh? That's good. That'll make it easier for Willard. He gets so hopelessly tangled up with Daddy in those silly political harangues."

"I doubt it, tonight. Daddy's head is somewhere else. You'll see . . ."

"It's dress-up? I think I'll wear an old, black Balenciaga of Mother's. So, he's going to marry her. Well, well . . . You didn't have to tell me, I knew. It was the smug look of victory when she was standing next to him at the door."

"Oh, Roz, that isn't fair. She's in a tough position . . . she knows how you feel."

"Yes, I should think she does."

Phoebe couldn't contain what *she* was feeling. "And what

you feel is wrong! To hate someone you don't even know! Take
a nap, damn it!" She left and purposely closed the door very
hard. She opened it again and stuck her head in. "I'm sorry, that
was childish. Daddy's looking forward to our all being under
one roof for a change. Considering what he's been through, let's
make it good, please?"

Roz answered with her slight smile.

Drinks before dinner went rather well. Max sat close to Roz
and held her hand at times. He tactfully caught her and Willard
up on the details of the accident, his stay in Stockton; he joked
about the mistaken headline of his death and, in every way
visible, forgave Roz for her absence, her need to make herself
estranged. Roz drank and smiled and looked magnificently stark
in her inherited Balenciaga; she even commented on how lovely
Phoebe looked in her new dress, all the while casting about the
room, noting the changes, saying nothing. The Hoffstadters
wove themselves very nicely around the chatter. It was all
glassy, fleeting, like a movie or a dream. Thank God for martinis, Phoebe thought, but she was so nervous about everything
going smoothly, her new dress was damp with perspiration.

Then suddenly, Hedda was leading Roz down the hall to
Roz's bedroom.

"How did you like your present?" Hedda had whispered to
Roz a moment before.

"Present?" Thus far, Roz had successfully kept away from
her with a screen of smiles and nods.

"I left it in your room . . ."

"Really?"

"Come, let's go see." Hedda led the way, using the mystery
to establish a kind of intimacy. "It was on the bed with a note,
I don't understand." She opened a closet and found the green
dress. "That's funny . . . Close your eyes, Roz." She laid the dress
on the bed, quickly arranging its folds. "Voilà! I designed it for
you. Oh, dear, I wanted it to be a surprise. How do you like it?"

"It's . . . it's very pretty," Roz said dully.

"Where could the note be? The maid must have come in and put things away . . . well, anyway . . ."

"What did the note say?" Roz asked, uncomfortable with being pulled into a scene she hadn't planned.

Hedda looked at Max's tall, beautiful daughter, with her white skin and long face, long twitching fingers, black shining hair dressed high and severe, a stunning black dress set off by a single strand of pearls . . . everything cruelly black and white as though by plan. Petite, round Hedda, though she was charmingly dressed herself in a gay, chiffon print, her own dark, curly hair framing a flushed, squarish, Mongolian-cheeked face—Roz was making her feel like a peasant! An immigrant off the boat!

(Hedda's grandparents were in the room with them and it was Ellis Island. 'Are you an Italian or a Jew? Sign here! You can't write in English? If you're Italian, you're probably Without Papers, a WOP. Make a cross, that'll do. If you're a Jew, we know you Jews don't like to sign your name with a cross, so make a circle. How do you say *circle* in Yiddish? *Kikel?* OK, kike, sign your name with a circle.')

Hedda took a deep breath, aghast at what facing Roz had allowed to surface. In a faint voice she said, "My note said I hope we can be friends, something like that . . ."

Roz looked directly at her, a tall, impassive statue with a faint smile. "On the assumption that we are not," she said coolly.

"I assume, I feel disapproval . . . yes," Hedda replied. "But I want to try and . . ."

"Buy me with a green dress?"

"What an awful thing to say!" Hedda cried out, unable to contain herself. "How lacking in grace, you ought to be ashamed of yourself. . . ."

"You seem to be assuming the voice of a chastising mother, too. My, you *are* talented in your very new role."

"New role?" Hedda stammered.

"Yes, you've finally nabbed him, acquired him, haven't you!" Roz left the room.

Hedda burst into tears. Roz had been capable of a brilliant

assault with just a few sentences, standing perfectly still. She had never experienced such a withering pain, such a diminution. And what could she tell Max? Nothing. There was no possible way she could sit through the dinner, now. She had to leave . . . How? With suitcases? Most of her things were here . . . Max had finally convinced her to move in. She'd go to her own apartment until they all left . . . until she could talk to him; but first, she had to get out of Roz's room, stop crying. The green of the dress caught her eye. She tore the dress in two and flung it across the room! The crazy strength she had to use to effect the destruction (a Goldsmith creation was made of iron, but not the designer!), the incongruity of her act shocked her into quiet. She went to Phoebe's bedroom, where she sat in a chair in the dark. She couldn't move, she couldn't leave. Her chiffon dress was clammy on her skin. She felt peculiar and swollen, as though she had been bitten by insects.

Before Roz and Willard had arrived, Max, lying in his tub, decided *not* to make his marriage announcement at dinner. He was floating in Epsom salts to help soothe the nerves that were healing. The relaxation was almost creating a state of euphoria. He was home! Hedda was in the house! He had convinced her not to wait. Spring was here. He contemplated his naked body, the half that wasn't in a cast hanging over the side of the tub. It looked good. Good enough to satisfy a young woman for a long time? Damn right, yes. You tell the hormones what to do and they do it! Everything turned out right if you willed it and worked hard with it. It would be better to have a private talk with Roz before they all went to sleep. He would sit on her bed and have a heart-to-heart, walk across that bridge to her, tell her how much he loved her, even talk about her mother, explain things, talk out the differences, the agonies. Reason and love: The magic ingredients. When you escape death, you know it to be true. Reason and love are the magic eyes.

He would have to tell Hedda how he'd decided he wanted to do it.

But he didn't; there wasn't time. The Hoffstadters came,

drinks were served, and they were all together in the living room. He noticed Roz and Hedda walking down the hall. That was a pleasant bit of movement. Good. He looked over at Phoebe, who was noticing too, the little vixen. How beautiful she looked in her dress, like a medieval virgin, which she probably wasn't. What a perplexing thought for a father. Must be the martinis.

Roz was back on the couch now. Max shifted his attention. Good old Dan, wonderful doctor, but kind of a bore outside his office. Well, he was keeping Willard busy. Max looked across the room at his son-in-law. How could anyone so young be so pompous? How could anyone be so pompous and not burst? How could Roz stand it? That was Sophia's doing. The perfect marriage she'd manufactured . . . perfect family, perfect wealth, perfect cardboard ass–conservative twit. *Where was Hedda?*

He whispered to Phoebe to go find her. Dan was telling World War II stories about how his medical unit got special dispensation every so often to go roaring through the French countryside and collect champagne for the general instead of plasma for the wounded. Phoebe came back into the room, trembling, and whispered in his ear, "She's in my room, Daddy, you better go see her!"

Hedda crying because of Roz? Cowering in Phoebe's bedroom, sobbing? Max was in a fury when he was told the terrible scene.

"I want to go home, I can't stay here," Hedda said.

"This is your home!" he said and stormed back to the living room.

"Dinner's going to be late," he announced, trying to hide his fury from the Hoffstadters. "Roz? I want to talk to you, come to my bedroom."

He stood at the windows looking out over Fifth Avenue. Roz sat herself at a dressing table filled with Hedda's bottles and jewelry. It was a room she hadn't been in for a long time. A few objects caught her eye, she picked them up, played with them, put them down.

Max meant to vent his anger, blow sky-high with her, demand that she atone. Yes, atone in the biblical sense, or leave.

The girl had to know how serious he was. He wasn't going to allow anyone to be nasty or hurtful to Hedda.

Staring out the window, he decided—no. That was too dangerous. He might lose Roz. She was as stubborn a Treading as he was. He was going to try and jump across the chasm between them, talk, talk about her feelings. It was going to take every ounce of his willpower to contain his wrath.

"Roz . . . let's talk about what you obviously can't hide. It's important to me . . . how you feel."

"About?"

"About everything. Of course about Hedda, but about me, too. Your disapproval is devastating to her, and to me . . . but less to me, even though I know I'm the one you're after. I can take it better than she can."

Roz looked up with an angry glance, her face suddenly naked.

"Talk to me, Roz, we belong to each other. I must know what you feel."

"It wouldn't seem so, not after the horse is out of the barn." She waited for a second. "If you *do* want to know, I think it's unbearable for my father to marry someone four years older than I am. Are you going to start a new family? Why, you could become a father and grandfather at the same time, think of that!" Her voice was venomous. "She'd probably beat me to it." There was pain on her face. She had been trying to become pregnant for two years without luck.

He wasn't going to be able to handle it. What a direct hit! She was making him feel like a slobbering satyr. It was unbelievable what she was making him feel, what she wanted him to feel —a dirty old man panting for young flesh.

Roz swerved away from it instantly. "Anyway, if you must know, and you said you cared how I feel . . . Well, I feel you're making a fool of yourself. I'd hoped you'd make a more careful choice, someone your own age. After Mother, she's unthinkable . . ."

"Roz, your mother and I had a terrible marriage, don't you know that? I love Hedda. Can't you accept and wish me well?"

She stood up. "I don't think we should continue this, Daddy. It's too unpleasant. As unpleasant as seeing your picture popping up in the news this last year or so, with a young mistress who's always falling out of her clothes."

"That's cruel!"

"It's truthful. You're in a world Mother abhorred. Nouveau riche. After living with Mother, how could you want to replace her with . . ." she stopped.

"Say it," he commanded.

"All right, I'll say it. Replace her with a blowsy little . . . little Jewish peasant who is taking you for a ride!"

Roz was shaking. She knew she had gone too far, but she *wanted* to hurt him.

"If that's the way you feel, I don't want to be with you, not unless you apologize, not only to Hedda, but to me." He wanted to shake her, hit her, God knows what he wanted to do. He began to yell. "I made mistakes with you. I was going to ask for your understanding. I wanted to meet you halfway. But, you're a true Walleby, or is it a Clyde! As for the nouveau riche, you're half nouveau riche, because I'm a whole one! I don't know who you are or where you came from, but you're not mine! Not till you have the humanity to apologize!"

His walk to the door was as excruciating as on a bed of embers, and his heart was breaking. It had been like the fights with Sophia. Sophia had cloned herself inside this girl. This was his daughter, this dark-haired beautiful woman who looked like his mother, but was a monster, her face screwed up tight, a face as cruel and monstrous as those of redneck whites who yelled epithets at little black children.

"There'll be no dinner tonight. You've seen to that!"

When he closed the door, she put her head on the dressing table and burst into tears. The movement made Hedda's bottles fall like a stack of dominoes.

Everyone, including Max, seemed to have forgotten it was his first day home from the hospital. When he came back to the living room, he was dangerously white. Hoffstadter got up and went to him. "Wait a minute, you look as though you ought to be lying down." He took Max's pulse. "I order you to bed. How about calling it 'for drinks'? Elaine and I won't stay for dinner. You should have yours in bed, Max."

No news was more welcome. The Hoffstadters left. The rest was a household topsy-turvy, whispering, rearranging itself as if after a quake. Max went to his room, Phoebe to hers to be with Hedda until she could pull herself together. The only one who could not imagine what had happened and had to be told that demonic forces were working overtime was Willard— dense, impeccable, impenetrable, empty-smiling "Willard, the Clyde," as Phoebe called him behind his back.

"I had an unpleasant exchange with my father," Roz told him. "He asked us to leave! I want to! Right now! Immediately! We'll stay in a hotel and go home tomorrow." They left, saying good-bye to no one except the butler who, naturally, was filled with thoughts of his own, not to mention the cook's —left with a rack of lamb for ten, a chocolate soufflé in the process of being made, and other favorites of Mr. Treading's that she and Miss Goldsmith had spent the entire day planning and making for the homecoming. Lord! Sometimes they certainly lived fast, strange, and thoughtless in this house. It used to be Mrs. Treading running off. Now, it was Roz, just like her mother.

Stand fast, honor their love, and *don't run*. Hedda shoved her shocked, rumpled feelings into a saner design, went to the kitchen to apologize to the cook, which she did with nothing more than raised eyebrows and a wave of the hand (and it was understood); then asked that trays of the gala dinner be brought "to our bedroom." The possessive pronoun was also understood. The staff had known for several weeks that she was to be Mrs. Treading in the near future and had accepted it with approval.

Phoebe was asked to join them and the three dined together, talking little. How pleasant, Phoebe was thinking . . . it feels good, homey. What was the chemical combination in Roz that made it impossible for her to let up, reach out? She looked at her father, who suddenly seemed fragile. He kept watching Hedda with such gratefulness, as though she might disappear if he didn't keep his eyes on her.

"Will you tell us what happened, Daddy?"

"No. Let's just leave it that she thinks I'm too old to marry Hedda. It led to . . . some other things, not good things. I lost my temper, said I didn't want to see her unless she could apologize. I feel like hell, but I'm not going back on what I said. Whatever happened, it was brewing for a long time, and now it's blown. It's gonna be a stalemate with your sister, Phoebe."

Phoebe tried again. "May I call her and say you'd like to see her?"

"If she'd been a man, I might have punched her."

"Daddy . . ."

"Yes, of course, call her, but whatever you say, don't say I forgive her. She's going to have to come here of her own free will."

He looked terribly drained and tired. Phoebe was going to tell Roz that. How could it not affect her—how much she meant to Daddy, how sick it had made him, whatever it was they'd said to each other.

"Life is 'cabbages and kings,' baby. We'll talk about it in the morning. It'll look better then. Go to bed."

Daddy will make everything right, he always did and always will. Like the fights with Mother. Phoebe used to think she had imagined them the next day—the slamming of doors, slamming the air with the terrible things they screamed at each other, and then it went away, everything serene at breakfast, Mother pouring the coffee, Daddy ho-hoing. Maybe Roz would appear at lunch tomorrow, as if nothing had happened.

Phoebe left the bedroom with kisses and hugs good night, a little embarrassed. This was a first—Hedda actually in Daddy's bedroom, the two belonging there together. A new set of parents, declared tonight.

. . .

Max's intention and dream, all those weeks in hospitals, was to make love his first night at home, but they were both too tired. In spite of the awkwardness of his cast, it still felt like silk against the skin, cool grass on hot feet, to have her body tight against his . . . to fall asleep holding her.

The next day, Max shared with Phoebe what the real exchange had been between Roz and himself, including the anti-Semitic slur. He shuddered as he repeated it and made Phoebe swear she would never let Hedda know.

"I've made a painful decision," he said. "No reconciliation, unless Roz can see what she is and try to change, even if it means a break in the family. And, don't speak on my behalf, baby. I think what we'll do when I get out of this cast, is fly to Switzerland and get married there. Hedda can ski and I'll watch." He laughed, trying to dissipate the concern registered on Phoebe's forehead. "Stop squinching up your face, nothing is irrevocable and all things pass, if not sooner, then later. In the meantime, between the sooner and the later, we go about our business . . .

"Time is too precious to be in the grip of anger . . . even though I'd like to take that girl and turn her upside down. Wasn't it way back there in Stockton, you said parents should talk more?" He paused. "I tell you, it was rough last night with Roz. I looked at that tall, removed, beautiful woman as if I didn't know who she was, and I felt guilty as hell. I made mistakes with her. My influence on her was negligible, your mother's paramount, she and the Wallebys with their tight lips. According to them, Roz married brilliantly. According to me, she couldn't have done worse. When you were born, baby . . ." He stopped, deciding you don't *ever* impart certain things to your children, things like 'You were born when your mother and I were going down the drain; you were a mistake on a night of fake reconciliation.'

There were tears in his eyes. "When you were born, I remember picking you up, holding you high in the air and saying to myself, I'm going to be around for this little one, I promise. I think I was, don't you?" he asked tentatively.

"The damnedest thing is—I watched it happen with Roz and didn't do anything about it. Even the way they dressed her. The little white dresses and patent leather shoes. I fought with your mother about what kind of automatic doll she thought she was making, why they didn't let her climb and yell and carry on and who the hell was that English nanny with the horse face bringing up a child of mine?"

"I remember her! She used to spank me."

"With you, it was an entirely different story. You came out ornery from the word go. Your mother never knew what to do with you. You wouldn't even sit still to have your hair combed."

"You remember things like that?"

"Of course I do. I saw them happen, didn't I?"

"Daddy, have you ever thought that we're predestined to be what we are and there's nothing to be done to change it? The Greeks felt that way, didn't they? That the web is woven for us and we're just placed into it; that free will is nothing but the little decisions we make trying to live within the webs the gods created for us . . ."

"Webs, baby? I think we make our own."

"Not even one God?" she teased.

"I doubt it. If there is, He isn't running a weaving factory up There. He's just making and dissolving stars, big bangs and little bangs. No webs. We're the web makers. Don't worry, Phoebe, we'll untangle this one. It might take some time, but Roz will come around. I might even make it easier for her down the road a bit, but not now."

When Phoebe got back to Northampton, she called Roz. There wasn't a mention of anything from either side. It was just like any other call, keeping in touch with that bored family voice. Funny, how we always *do* call each other, Phoebe thought. The boredom was almost comforting. It was a constant —like Greenwich time. After all, she *is* my sister, Phoebe said to herself as she put the receiver down.

FROM THE JOURNAL OF DR. HIRAM WESGROVE, AUGUST 1981

What a peculiar dream I had last night. I very seldom remember my dreams. This one I kept reminding myself to remember even as I dreamed. It was almost a poem; how strange . . . : I am walking into the room wearing my gray suit. / I am walking into the room wearing my gray vest. / I am also all gray inside.

The last line worries me. What does it mean? That I'm getting too old for the fight, the work that might not get finished? Damn it, I say no! Dream or no dream, I'm not too old!

5

Four months later Max wasn't back to jogging before break-fast, but he was walking in the park before going to his office. Buoyant health, one of his targets, was coming back, but now, with a difference—he was living with Hedda and she was forcing him to define himself in ways he had never done before.

He had never known such intimacy with a woman, cer-tainly not with Sophia, hardly in the casual affairs he'd sought to make up for her coldness. He found himself thinking a lot about his mother. She had taught him to let perplexing feel-ings float away like clouds. *Feeling* was an abstraction, and when she needed to express it, she hid behind the poetry of others. Suddenly, Martha Treading's life seemed like a bril-liant deception, as his had been—not one of deceit, perhaps, but omission.

Living with Hedda was definitely uncomfortable. It was mightily strange in his middle life to be experiencing a new mystery. He didn't have to be a good soldier, a rock, a wizard with Hedda, he just had to be himself. And who was that? A man who had made many fortunes never asked, Who am I? He fought, connived, schemed, gambled, he won—that's who he was. He never let things break down inside. He wore armor day and night. He was too busy beating the world and didn't know anything about lying around and talking, sharing fears, dreams, feeling weak and vulnerable. You don't know anything about an endless dialogue with someone you love until you live with Hedda—someone who was there to hear you cry out in pain, walked you to the bathroom like a little boy, lay cheek to cheek with you stroking your forehead, someone who got to know every inch of your body as well as you knew it.

All sorts of disturbing pieces of ideas had floated to the surface in the four months of his healing. Living with Hedda was like walking into a charmed castle every day. New terrors and delights were behind every door.

Not that he wasn't still the old, swaggering cowboy-Max. There was something he had to do when he felt well enough, which he did. Without telling Hedda, he flew out to San Francisco one day and got into a helicopter with a pilot named Elliot. They refueled in Stockton and continued to Emigrant Basin. The pilot was instructed to fly low . . . "Low as you can!" Max sat with maps on his lap; they hovered over the crash site, then headed east to observe the tract of land slated for his solar energy project.

The project had come to a dead stop because of the accident. Looking down at the vast expanse of land, he began to envision with his eyes open—his favorite occupation. Treading dreams? The dream is real. He was going to have to rev up the solar dream again, get the physicists going on the plans for the first solar manufacturing plant in the world with a realistic consumer payoff and benefit, not to mention the final kiss good-bye it would mean for the nuclear energy guys.

Solar energy in Treading cells! Throw your electric bulbs into the garbage cans! Sure, it would take a five-year plan, maybe even ten, but he'd make it happen. Sure, the experiment would cost a fortune, but the end result would be the cheapest energy possible from the most logical source in the world, the source of life itself. It was so logical it could make you laugh, and everyone was trying to hold back the logic. But not he.

The more the pilot made the helicopter hover over the tract, the more Max felt like his old self. He let out a whoop that scared Elliot out of his wits. "Take her up, I've got what I want," Max said. He leaned back in his seat and closed his eyes. The dream realized down there would probably be his last; he'd be sixty-five before it happened, no doubt, but what a way to maneuver Global Materials into the twenty-first century. He liked it, it felt good, it was basic-Max, the game, the trick, the satisfaction—how to make money work the *right* way and not lose it. You had to be some kind of religious nut, straddle Heaven and Hell and ride them both until they were in a lather of exhaustion; you had to combine *greed* and *good*, shake them like dice, pray for a lucky throw. The board of directors of Global Materials couldn't possibly understand, but he'd throttle them into a yes vote, to make his obsession real—how to give back to his beloved land what he had gotten out of it; how to assuage his guilt; how to stop the raping of the rivers and mountains for energy. The secret was solar. The gods knew it . . .

Max opened his eyes. They had risen up, turned around, and were well on their way back to Stockton for more fuel, then on to San Francisco. The Sierras were beneath them. Even with his eyes closed, the mountains made him feel larger than life. He smiled to himself.

Max returned to New York, the same day. He had had to get back on the horse, get into the air, lay the ghost, test his endurance and the body he had trusted for fifty-four years. It was like a child's game of challenge—to see if there *was* a God up There who had planned a death in the desert for him. There wasn't!

Then, there was the problem of Roz that needed solving. How? He'd be damned if he was going to go back on his word that he wouldn't see her unless she apologized.

Hedda kept after him to pick up the phone and break the silence.

"Never!"

"You're going to have to do it, Max. Roz is younger. She has more time for anger."

"No, she doesn't!"

"Yes, she does."

"Oh, stop it, with your wise pronouncements." (It was so good, how they could scrap and not have it mean ruffled feathers.)

"Wise, or no, pride goeth before a fall . . ." Hedda said.

"And other old wives' tales . . ."

"Don't underestimate old wives' tales. A stitch in time saves nine. Think about *that* one. Chicken soup is good for a cold. It's been proved by old ladies for centuries. Even the American Indians knew about 'fowl soup.' Call Roz."

"No!"

"OK, live with an ache."

Hedda was right. It *was* an ache, an active one, like a toothache . . . not mortal, but insidious; it could inflame the sinuses, swell the head, make life intolerable, and who needed it? *He made the call.*

"Roz? Daddy here . . . let's break the sound barrier. Let's apologize to each other simultaneously, like diplomats should and never do."

It was going to be all right; her response was the first half of a suppressed laugh.

"Let's be special," he heard himself saying, not knowing where it was coming from, what with all that pride not wanting to fall. "You're special to me, you're my top daughter, so, one, two, three, I apologize . . ."

She didn't join him, but that was all right.

"Hedda and I are leaving for Switzerland in four weeks . . . we're getting married in Geneva. I want you to know where we'll be. Then we'll be visiting the Williamsons in Gstaad, friends of your mother's and mine. Did you ever meet them?"

"Yes, Daddy," Roz said quietly. "*You* don't remember. Mother and I stayed with the Williamsons when Mother thought I might go to school in Switzerland. We went to look

at one, but then she decided no, it was going to be Miss Porter's . . ."

"Oh, yes, of course . . ." But he hadn't remembered. "Well,"
he said uncomfortably, "just so you know where we are. Listen,
come see us before or after, whatever you like . . ."

"When you get back, Daddy."

All he wanted to hear, really, was Roz saying "Daddy." "All
right. When we get back. Good-bye, love, best to Willard."

Well, he'd done it! He was learning how to breaststroke in
the thick waters. Good Lord! It got up your nose and made you
sweat like a pig! He turned to look at Hedda, who had been
listening.

"Aren't you relieved?" she asked, "picking up that phone
and making the connection, cutting the crap? You look like a
puppy who's just poked his head in a gopher hole and nobody
bit his chin. Oh, am I marrying a mess of stuff . . ."

"Wanna back off?"

"Nope."

"Then, 'nope' it is, for better or worse, lady." Max was
suddenly filled with black humor, maybe even wanting to hit
back a little. "Do Jewish people always feel they have to solve
everything, understand everything? Bring chaos to order . . . just
because they think they invented God?"

"Yes," Hedda answered defiantly, "because if *they* don't
look for solutions, others find a final solution for *them!*"

"Ouch." Max flushed with embarrassment. "How did you
know *that* about Roz?"

"The instinct of the oppressed, my darling."

"Phoebe told you."

"No, she didn't." Hedda paused. "Then I *am* right about
Roz not wanting you to marry a Jew?"

"Yes," he sighed. "But she'll change her mind, with my
help. I'll bet you a million."

"You're on," Hedda said lightly. "But you're going to have
to pay off, if you lose."

"That would be a pleasure, troublemaker. Who needs you?"
He paused. "I do."

⥳

Almost five months to the day, after the crash, he woke feeling oddly unwell, a feeling of weakness and a pain in his back. He didn't mention it to anyone and let a week go by. The pain persisted. A depressing fatigue wouldn't go away. While shaving, he thought he noticed a changed skin tone in his face, almost a pallor. He let a few more days pass. The malaise wouldn't disappear. He gave in and called his friend, Dr. Hoffstadter, casually, "Just for a routine check before we leave for Switzerland. I've got a pain in my back, probably nothing but the nerves healing."

It was turning out to be more than a routine check. Hoffstadter was asking for a million tests.

"What's going on? How am I?" Max asked after the first few.

"I don't know yet," the doctor said evasively. "I want to cover all the bases, try and find out about the fatigue. We'll know by the end of the week, be patient."

What in hell *was* going on? Max hated it. The testing and probings, sitting in cubicles, waiting. He felt reduced to a name on a file card, a pathetic, frightened animal shivering in a ridiculous paper sheet. Hoffstadter was sending him to other doctors, X-ray palaces. Sitting in one of the cubicles, waiting for a nurse to appear, he vowed to start a new company to manufacture elegant, disposable clothes for naked patients. When the nurse stuck her head in, he told her his idea. She looked at him with pity. "Don't look at me that way! You know I'm right. Medicine," he said loudly, "should extol the individual, not make him feel like a rabbit in a warren. I feel like a rabbit!" He tore off the paper sheet and stood stark naked.

"Mr. Treading! For heaven's sake. I have one more test to do on you."

"On me, or with me? Ah, you're shocked. You see a man before you, eh? You thought I was a file card or a rabbit?" (He'd finally raised a little smile out of her.)

"You better put that sheet back on or you'll catch cold." She blushed and turned her back. (The joking didn't help. It couldn't mask a growing apprehension.)

A week later, Hoffstadter asked Max to come in for a talk.

"How are you feeling?"

"How am I feeling? After all those tests, *you* ought to know. I'm just the same, tired as hell. All I want to do is sleep. Dan, does it have something to do with the crash injuries?"

"Let me read you the report. . . ."

"I don't like the way you look," Max said.

Hoffstadter smiled uneasily. There are times when a doctor wishes he were a researcher, not an internist face-to-face with the patient; worse, a patient of many years.

"Well, there are a number of things. . . ." His eyes scanned the report. "There is an overgrowth of plasma cells in your marrow . . . causing pressure. That's the pain in your back; actually, what it is, is referred pain from your right hip. You also have a bacterial infection. That's the fatigue. Your spleen is slightly enlarged. There's also a presence of protein in your urine that reflects a potential dysfunction of the kidneys . . . You're running a low fever, did you know that?"

"Dan, cut the crap? What are you saying? It sounds like I'm falling apart!"

"Max, it's not good. The tests all add up to . . . to a disease."

"Named?"

"Multiple myeloma."

"Multiple *what?*"

"Myeloma. Max, it's cancer."

The word crashed like a bolt of lightning hitting some-where else.

"You must be kidding! How? When? Cancer of what?"

"Cancer of the bone. I'm telling you head-on . . ."

"What's your next word? Incurable?"

"Today, yes. Maybe not tomorrow." Hoffstadter stood up. "I won't be treating you from now on. I'm sending you to a colleague at Cancer Research. Hiram Wesgrove. He's the best in the business."

Max sat immobile. "The best in the business? Why not! The

best is none too good on the way out!" He leaned back and closed his eyes. They weren't talking about him. How could they be? The whole thing was a macabre joke. Hoffstadter was a lousy actor trying to imitate Groucho Marx playing a doctor. Hoffstadter was giving him a lecture on the ailments of an obscure African spider.

"Are you all right? Do you want the nurse to bring you some coffee?"

Max opened his eyes. "Coffee? Hell, I want some scotch!"

"We've got that, too. It's usually for me, not the patient." Since it was the end of the day, Hoffstadter poured them both drinks.

"A tough break, Max, but put this into your head. It's early detected. Your EKG is normal, blood pressure normal . . ."

"Thanks."

"No, listen to me carefully. The disease has invaded a strong constitution. There are things that can be done very successfully for quite a while and you can be sure that Hiram Wesgrove is the one to do them. When the treatment starts with someone you trust, you'll begin to see—you can earn a lot of time. Optimism is the key, Max, it has a curative power that's inestimable . . ."

"Strong enough to cure the incurable?" Max was filling up like a balloon—with anger. In the next second he was going to burst. His heart was beating so hard, it was going to break some ribs, fall out on the gray carpet and splatter it with a waterfall of blood. "Earn some time?" he shouted. "Hedda and I are getting married!"

"I'd put that aside for now, until after you see Wesgrove, anyway."

Max got up. He had to move around. "How do you fellas do it? How do you announce Judgment Day? Tell me again. Did you say 'cancer'? Who in hell is Wesgrove? I wasn't listening . . ."

Hoffstadter fumbled around in a desk drawer. "Here's some sedation, just to level you out . . . don't mix it with liquor . . . Max, sit down and listen. I'm sending you to the most prestigious cancer research place in the world. Wesgrove is its head. He's a scientist, a Nobel Prize winner from Boston, out of Harvard. It's like—if you were suffering from a surfeit of relativity and Einstein, if he were alive, agreed to see you. Wesgrove has agreed to see you. You're lucky."

Max clutched the arms of his chair. "Lucky? You can't sit there and say that to me. What do you think I am, an idiot? You saw me after that fuckin' crash. I lived through *that* to be told what you just told me? Cancer? Bullshit!"

"It's not bullshit . . . it's friggin' real. Max . . . you're a pretty big man yourself." Hoffstadter's professional guard was crumbling.

Max expelled an "Ah . . ." of giving in, understanding the information, where he was and couldn't believe he was. He bit his lip to keep from crying.

"Is your car waiting for you?"

"Yes. Do you want a lift?"

"No, I just thought I'd help you get a cab if your man wasn't waiting. I think you should be with someone."

"Sure, sure . . ." Max said softly, "like the whole world, to say good-bye."

Hoffstadter winced. "Would you like to talk? I'm here for you."

"No. Maybe tomorrow. . . ."

"The secretary will give you Dr. Wesgrove's number. I'm going to be talking with him, but you call him immediately, please. Don't put it off."

Max got up to leave. "Don't worry, Dan, I'll handle it. Forgive me for exploding. The drink helped a little, but the conversation was lousy."

Max told his chauffeur to go on without him. It was dusk and he walked into Central Park across the street from Hoffstadter's office. He kept walking, kicking the October dry leaves, like a boy with a ball. He didn't feel that fatigue anymore. The pain in his back was gone. Hoffstadter had made a mistake! He began to jog defiantly.

He loved where he was running—into the twilight of the

greatest city in the world . . . which he had conquered! All the windows of Fifth Avenue were quivering with light, like pink mercury. The tall buildings were flexing their muscles, boasting, shouting to the sky: "We are full of killers and satisfactions and we belong to you!"

He tried to grab on to how he felt in the deepest part of him, the airy, innocent place that knew the desert and his mother, the earth and sky where he grew. He tried to catch the meaning of his journey as a man . . . who had married Sophia, who was a father of children, who loved Hedda. He was trying to grab on to a line of poetry, a beautiful line of anguish, someone else's words, a line he could melt into—to make what he *felt* be memorable, majestic. He could think of nothing. He was a thin, empty tube with only the wind rushing through it.

He jogged to the Plaza Hotel, where he called Hedda and asked her to meet him.

After two drinks, he told her. She reached over and took his hands in hers. The table between them felt like an altar.

He suddenly remembered the poem that had played hard to get when he was running through the park. The lines came tumbling out. "Because I could not stop for Death / He kindly stopped for me / The Carriage held but just Ourselves / And Immortality. / We slowly drove, He knew no haste / And I had put away / My labor and my leisure too, / For His Civility / We . . ."

Hedda stopped him from finishing. "No! It's not going to be that. It can't!"

He looked at her shocked face. "You know, I couldn't find them when I wanted them, running through the park like a madman. I jogged here, Hedda. Then I called you . . . And here they are, spilling out when I look at you. I love you . . . I love you."

Suddenly he smiled. It was a Max-characteristic that always surprised her—his smile; it did the most extraordinary things to his face, made it so broad, open, devilish, like a little boy with irrepressible secrets.

"Those lines were some of my mother's favorites. She used

to say, 'What does that woman, Emily Dickinson, mean by Immortality!' Martha used to recite them with a little laugh, when she was very tired."

He took one of Hedda's hands, raised it to his lips and kissed it, then placed it back on the table carefully, as though it were made of the thinnest glass. The gesture was so delicate, Hedda felt she wasn't going to be able to contain her tears.

"I think we'd better laugh a little, too, don't you?" Max said.

6

Max made two appointments to see Dr. Hiram Wesgrove and canceled them both at the last minute. How could he go, swamped in melancholy? "Incurable." What was the point?

His body . . . his familiar cover: It was covered with blond down, soft-white until he was five. It hardened and browned; it never mortified itself with pimples; it was never ungainly. It developed long muscles, rode horses, and climbed mountains. It could walk quiet as an Indian on pine needles. It could tango and jive; it could switch to rock and disco when it reached middle age and still look young. It could make love for hours, satisfy a woman, delay its orgasm, because it had always been an erotic athlete. At the age of fifty-four, it was still lean-muscled and long; it let out its water and wastes as easily as light comes with day. If it had been the body of a feudal king, it *still* could have whipped its son for the kingdom. Yes, there were white hairs mixed with the blond-brown on his chest, but they were the honor badges of longevity in the natural sequence of events. As for healing? From the smallest cut when he was a boy, to the massive assault on his body in the helicopter crash, he had always healed, come together miraculously.

There was a lie somewhere.

He had always related himself to other creatures of nature whose lives were a feat of prowess, a mysterious, perfect construction: the pistol fish unerringly catching a flying insect— that unbelievable feat of reaching out of water into the air with staggering precision! *He* was supposed to be the pistol fish, not the insect.

He had been caught midflight by cancer!

He was supposed to be a Jesus Christ lizard (he had seen them in Central America) who runs so fast it looks like it walks on water, cakewalks on the tops of blades of grass.

Max had the arrogance of the gifted. Not in the wildest dream could he imagine he would be felled by a mistake in his body. He didn't die in the War. He didn't die in the crash.

He was going to be shot down by cancer, in slow motion!

That image was as inconceivable as thinking that Canada geese wouldn't be screeching north in the spring, or monarch butterflies wouldn't be catching tail winds to get them south in winter. Of course, there were always those who wouldn't make it, but he was never one of *them.* He remembered watching a butterfly that had lost its way over the dunes in Southampton —its brilliant, orange-black wings finally sinking to the sand, disoriented, its mechanism confused, destiny cut short. Mysterious, perfect construction? That was the human illusion of youth. He had been young until seven days ago.

The third time he made an appointment to see Dr. Wesgrove he was told that if he didn't appear, the doctor could no longer set aside the time; he went, the canny side of him taking over, lest he lose the chance of "Wesgrove has agreed to see you. You're lucky."—Hoffstadter's peculiar definition of luck.

Dr. Hiram Wesgrove was a tiny, slightly plump, white-haired man. Max wasn't prepared for the pixie who greeted him with a sudden smile that went in and out, a lumbering little walk, sharp blue eyes behind glasses half the size of his face. Max wasn't prepared for Wesgrove's office, either—a Dickensian, dusty library, all the more surprising because it was on the eighth floor of the shiny, white, plastic-and-glass Cancer Research Center. He had the disorienting feeling of dropping a century as he crossed the doorsill.

The place smelled of books, as well it might; there were books from floor to ceiling on all the walls. There was an old-red, old-wood color to everything. A long conference table, littered with papers, was at the far end. The other smell was from ashtrays filled with apple cores and orange peel combining to make a curiously sweet, tarty perfume. There were two chairs in front of a fireplace filled with burning logs (another smell). Between the chairs, a half-finished game of chess sat on an old, burled walnut table. In a corner, tucked away, glistened a bar filled with shiny glasses and liquor bottles reflecting the flickering light from the hearth.

Anachronism . . . you must be Wesgrove, Max thought as he walked across the room's frayed Oriental rugs. How could he know that one of Wesgrove's major specifications, when the Center was trying to lure him away from Harvard and his digs in Cambridge, had been that the shiny, new Center comply with his wishes as to office:

"In that ridiculous, modern building you're putting up, I want a sanctuary of real wood and a working fireplace. I can't think without one. I'm used to it. I'll bring my own chairs and no one is to come in and clean!" The response of the poor architect was, "Why doesn't he just work and think at the Harvard Club!" Wesgrove, in his late fifties then, hadn't considered himself crotchety or eccentric. The room in which he did his major thinking had to be to *his* liking, not what an architect envisioned for a man who had received every honor there was in biology and medicine from the time he was twenty-eight. There was no question about the Center's humoring Wesgrove; the architect had to incorporate a flue for a fireplace into his lovely, glass building. That's how itchy the center was to coax Wesgrove away from Harvard.

"Sit down, Mr. Treading. You canceled two appointments, I hear."

"Yes."

"Understandable."

"I've never been afraid in my life, Dr. Wesgrove."

"Are you *on* anything?"

"What do you mean?"

"Did Hoffstadter give you any sedation?"

"Yes, but I didn't take it."

"Would you like some brandy? You must be depressed."

"How do you know that?"

"Because you look it, but that's understandable, too. Depression is the other side of anger, isn't it? If you flip the coin?"

"I've never felt like this in my whole life."

"You've never had cancer before, have you?" Wesgrove added softly, " 'He who can say how he burns, burns little.' "

Max took a deep breath, thinking: What in the world has Hoffstadter sent me to?

"Pain on breathing?" Wesgrove asked casually.

"No, not really."

"Good."

Max sat himself in one of the chairs near the fireplace. "Whose line was that about the burning?"

"Petrarch. And, so true. We're struck dumb with grief and we're expected to respond immediately. Impossible!"

Max leaned forward. "You're right, I'm in shock. I can't decide whether I want to live or die . . . not that I even have that choice, but I can *still* decide how and when. I'm not in control. The most crucial time in my life, and I'm not in control!" Max was very surprised at himself for bursting out. It had something to do with the man's eyes. They had the acuity of a zoom lens; they demanded confidence. Christ, he was going to cry . . . for the first time. He concentrated on trying to keep it a big lump in his throat.

"You're here, aren't you? That was a decision of control. You decided to keep your third appointment."

"You know, Dr. Wesgrove, I'm a nonbeliever, but I went to the Bible this last week. I never read it, except for its poetry. Well, I tell you, the boils of Job gave me no comfort."

"And Aristotle? Did you go to him?" There was a twinkle in Wesgrove's tiny blue eyes.

Max felt a funny kind of relaxation, yet at the same time, warning signals were going up. How could he feel so comfortable with someone he didn't know? "Aristotle? Funny that you should say that. Yes, I did go to him. Ha, he was asked how *he* wanted to be buried. 'As you wish' was *his* answer. I'm not that resigned, not that wise. I don't want to let go, *even after the end* . . . I want to be taken back to Utah where I was born, on a slow train. I want to be buried at the foot of a butte."

Wesgrove clucked a kind of approval. "Not resigned, eh? That makes a good patient . . ."

Max didn't hear it. He had to share something with this man. "I like books, I like to read. I've spent my whole life collecting books. I said, there *has* to be some wisdom there for me . . . *now*. I went from one wise man to another. Do you know what they do? They send you *on!* You open Montaigne. He sends you to Seneca. Do you know what Seneca says about illness? 'Make me lame in hand / lame in foot and thigh / Shake out my loosened teeth / While Life stays, so stay I.' Not for me, never! Loosened teeth and all the rest, just to stay alive? Never!"

"Yet," Wesgrove interposed, "you're not the kind of man to give in easily to the indignity, the fascism of pain, are you?"

"Why do you say that?" Max asked, startled.

"Because I've done my homework, as far as I could go, without meeting you. I know who Maxwell Treading is, from his doctor." Wesgrove paused. "We accept very few patients in this part of the Center . . . I think Hoffstadter must have told you . . . a selected few . . ."

Max interrupted, "It's not a good name for a building. I think I canceled my first two appointments because I didn't want to walk into a place that had the word *cancer* over the door. You *know* when you walk in, you're never coming out."

"Patients whom I treat personally, Mr. Treading, have to *not* want to succumb. They have to be fighters, and stubborn. Do we understand each other?"

"That's a little exclusive, isn't it? What about people who

can't fight and aren't stubborn fools? Are they an inferior breed not worth treating?"

"In this special situation, I'd have to say yes. There is fascism in controlled experiment. It would be a waste of time to try new methods and medicines on a person whose organs were almost destroyed by a disease . . . or someone whose will was weak either from neurosis or lack of character, wouldn't it? It takes a consummate intelligence to want to live, when you've been told you're going to die." Wesgrove noticed the paling of Max's face.

"There's no way we can talk and exchange, sir, without the possibility of death in the footnotes. You'll get used to that. It defines the game, it's the basketball hoop, the goal line . . ."

Max couldn't believe what he was hearing—lines from a Grade B movie. Or was it fiction being stripped away from the truth? Rock-bottom words like Heaven, Hell, God, the Devil— who ever used them in honesty? Those in trouble!

"Mr. Treading . . . I have a patient who's a young woman, beautiful, artistic. She's a writer with a half-finished novel. She's very ill. I'm trying to buy her time to finish her work. But the scales of her person are teetering. She cries constantly, she wails that she hasn't lived yet, she hasn't had a child, she hasn't known enduring love. I've extended her life a year already; however, the unpredictability of her emotions, her negative passions are tipping her scales, cutting her odds.

"I have another patient, a Puerto Rican woman, born on the southern tip of her native country. She was brought up in a shack in the middle of a palm forest, without a day of schooling, but *she* has a light in her. She says she's 'gambling with God' and knows *He doesn't mind.* She's a perfect patient. With her, one doesn't *also* have to combat a chemistry of anger. It's three years since we've begun to treat her.

"Your doctor sent you to me because he said you were an outrageous gambler. So am I. You must feel pretty defenseless right now, like a baby, but pretty soon, we'll be equal, more than equal. You'll be teaching me . . ."

The office began to swim in Max's head. The man was

sounding like a soothsayer, a magician . . . "I don't understand, are you considering me for experiment? Hoffstadter didn't suggest that at all, I . . ."

Wesgrove's tone was impatient for the first time. "Everything in the treatment of cancer is still highly experimental, even the so-called conventional treatment. At least, here, if the convention fails, with your permission, we can try every new avenue that we know of, or invent ourselves. Your life can be extended by our sophistication, Mr. Treading, and you're a good subject; you have a strong constitution; you could help us learn much and in return, perhaps gain some precious time."

"I'm only interested in the quality of that time, Doctor."

Wesgrove's eyes caught him with rays of blue light. "I agree with you. That's the mystery—how well your body takes the assault of chemicals. The gamble is that it might. Think of that. It might!"

Gain time? Of course he wanted to gain time. Max could feel his adrenaline surging. He was suddenly recognizing a train bearing down on him. He had to do something, get off the tracks or die. Run to where? Toward this little man? There was no better choice, evidently; he was the best. (I'll follow him for a while . . . until it gets familiar, this business of dying.)

Wesgrove almost captured the thoughts in Max's mind. "Let me say one final thing. The footnotes, as I said, are going to have to deal with death, but the text will only be concerned with life. *Without a passionate, obstinate heartbeat, medicine is failed magic.* We mustn't feel we're working with potential cadavers . . . only with fighters for life." That last thought struck Max as ruthless. He swallowed hard.

"All right," Max said quietly. Saying the words had the effect of whisking him off the railroad tracks to a bridge overhead. "What now?"

"I want to put you through a series of tests. We don't accept any evaluation but our own. You'll have to endure another round of bloods, X rays. Then, we'll talk about your future when we have all the facts. The next time we meet, Mr. Treading, I'll know as much about you as modern science and medicine can tell me—you, as an organism. But, that's hardly the whole story, is it?"

Wesgrove indicated the visit was over by walking to the door. "Incidentally, one important thing I'd like to know and you can tell me right now. Do you play chess?"

Max burst out laughing. "Rather well, as a matter of fact."

"Good!"

"Does that other patient of yours, the Puerto Rican woman, play chess, too?"

"No," Wesgrove answered with one of his sudden little smiles. "We have other games . . ." He bent over in a kind of bow and came up smiling. It seemed to be a gesture to show his pleasure in acquiring a chess companion, as though what had gone before was only a bad dream.

Max felt something had happened to him during the visit. His grief for himself had been halved by a peculiar infusion. Someone was now standing on the teetering bridge with him— a strange little man, so diminutive as almost to be deformed, with a soft baritone voice coming out of a tiny drum, in a warning: "Do not imagine there is anything small here but what you see."

Max was ready to gamble, down to his last emotional cent . . . for the quality of every second left to him.

7

"Let's go to Southampton for the weekend," Max said. "I feel like walking on the beach, lying around." The tests required by Wesgrove were finished and he had been given a few days off before seeing the doctor again.

Hedda was sitting on the huge, semicircular porch of Max's Southampton house, trying to fix her eyes on the ocean, but the trees on the property kept intruding with their business of shedding. This year, she hated the fall. It used to be her favorite season, with its explosion of color. Her first kudos in the fashion world had come because of her use of leaf tones at their height, in swirling sports clothes. This year she couldn't look at those colors easily; this year, because of Max's illness, fall seemed like the harbinger of death. The lawn leading to the swimming pool was filled with leaves. When a breeze moved the air, branches kept announcing their losses. The skittish movement made her think of fluttering fans and fingers, antebellum ladies, vain silly gestures of ghosts from a dead time . . . *Everything* was vain gesture if Max was going to die.

They had just come back from a walk on the beach. Max had put some music on the stereo before he went upstairs to rest.

The music was rising and falling—someone's piano concerto—forcing blood to her head, making her think and feel too much. She just wanted to look out at the ocean and be calm, while she forced herself to face the fact that life was going to be very different; if there was any child left in her, it was going to have to grow up fast. How stupid of me to break and run down the beach! Of course he'd come running after, catch me, kiss me, fall down laughing, how stupid of us both! He could almost not make it back to the house, he was so exhausted.

What she was trying to squelch in herself was what Max loved about her—the unexpected move, response, the way her dark eyes could suddenly go from serious philosopher to imp, cheeks flushed, her playfulness that surfaced like a swimmer through her basically shy and thoughtful person. It was just that, that would keep him going, he thought, even as he grimly went upstairs to rest. Poor Hedda, he also thought. It's going to be rough. We're in a new place together, if it won't break us apart . . .

Hedda became aware that the lovely music had ended. She burst into tears. For some reason, because the music had just disappeared, it was heartbreaking. Painting or sculpture or the printed word doesn't disappear. Was Max like music? A falling leaf? Her mood began to frighten her. She ran off the porch, down the terraces to the beach, and kept on running until she reached the water.

Max wasn't resting yet, he was upstairs looking at the ocean, startled to see the little figure in its gray sweat suit running, black curls jumping up and down, stopping at the water's edge, lifting arms high, just standing there. He was too far away to hear she was screaming. (Scream, scream, like children do.) Hedda was getting it all out, exhilarated with the sound of her own voice. She screamed till she thought the veins in her neck would pop and what she must have looked like made her burst out laughing. She turned and walked back up the long stretch of beach to the terraces swirling with their dead leaves . . . Looking up for some reason, she saw Max. "Were you spying on me, you sneak?" she yelled, laughing.

"Yes. I love to watch a jiggling behind when it runs," he yelled back.

"Go and rest, you creep!" She blew him a kiss and he closed the window.

Hedda sat herself in a wicker rocker on the porch, rocking and thinking in the same fast rhythm. She felt better. The frightening pessimism was gone. She disliked the house behind her; Sophia was still in it. She had just gone out for the afternoon and would be back for cocktails. Her clothes were still in the master-bedroom closets. Max treated the house, ever since Sophia's death, like a partially wrecked car that he had no intention of repairing. The other times Max had brought her here, they had slept in one of the guest bedrooms. "This place was mostly hers," he'd said. "She used it to run away from me. I never came except for tennis once in a while. Does it bother you?"

It hadn't bothered her. This weekend it did. He was resting up there in the master bedroom "because it looks out over the water," he said. Its closets were still filled with Sophia. She would have to push the things aside to make space for herself. No! She would ask the caretaker's wife to clear the closets once and for all. She had that right! She was going to insist they get married immediately, before any more *falling*. She should have said yes to getting married in a hospital room after the crash. How wrong to imagine one has open-ended time. From now on, they were going to live normally and in sequence. That was her job—to live with him and love him in the hope of another season and a season after that. Spring will come if you will it!

She got up and walked into the house.

Max wasn't resting. He was thinking too—about marriage. He was *not* going to marry Hedda, not with the words *progressive* and *incurable* floating around. Knowing her, he knew she would demand it. Oh, how he loved her . . . but . . . The sicker he got, the more rational he was going to be, he promised himself as he lay there—he was not going to enslave her with his cancer. It was *his* stigmata, not hers. I want you free to walk, whether you choose to, or not . . . he thought. It was going to be hard to withstand her dark eyes filled with determination, her firm little body that reached no higher than his shoulders, insisting that he honor her wishes. No . . . he was not going to honor her wishes, though he knew so painfully what they were and how happy it would make her, for the moment, to have his child. Roz was right. They *had* dreamed of the possibility. Not now! He was not going to leave a widow with a new creature inside her, or out, even if they could extend his life a little with chemicals. What a lucky man he had been, not so long ago—entertaining such a thought—to have a son the second time around. What biblical pleasures . . . to live and live, until old age and a willingness to go brought one down. The injustice of it all was going to make him cry. Cry, damn it, cry . . .

As for loving? He wanted to try tonight. It would be the first time since all the tests, since the pain and fatigue. He couldn't remember a time he hadn't been *ready*, except with Sophia . . . in this bed. He pushed away the anxiety of *can I?* . . . It didn't belong to him.

After dinner . . . and the night turned suddenly warm, as it can in the fall with an unexpected Indian summer, with the windows opened wide and the sound of the ocean breaking gently under the influence of a quarter moon . . .

There was no talk, only his arms enclosing her, only wanting to feel her, slip into her—to float on a salt sea. To forget. He was doing it! He was whole, the person he knew. He was a healthy cat in the garden, springing at a leaf, playing with a shadow in her. He heard his breath expelling with pleasure. He sprang again. The sun was shining on his sleek fur. He was a healthy animal! He made it last and last . . .

Hedda lay on her back, looking into the dark. The old Max had been inside her, the well, tender, strong, playful Max. Now was the time to say it. "Darling, we're going to get married right away. I don't like long engagements, they're unhealthy; it's not good for young people."

He didn't answer.

She touched his back. "Did you hear what I said? You can't say no, you're being proposed to with a shotgun. I didn't wear my diaphragm." He must be asleep or he would sit bolt upright with that one, she thought. "If you're awake, I'll never forgive you for playing possum. I was joking about the diaphragm, darling . . ." Max was lying on his side away from her. She put her arms around his waist and whispered into the skin of his back, "I'll keep on insisting . . . until you either throw me out or marry me, darling."

Max was looking into the dark too, trying to imagine how he was going to be able to stave her off . . . a month at a time.

8

"I agree to become a guinea pig, but with a twist," Max announced to Wesgrove after the Southampton weekend.

Max wanted to make something clear. He had thought it all out, walking on the beach for hours in the abrasive, cold air. Broken shells, fish heads, crab carcasses, dead seaweed and lonely dunes encourage invigorating thoughts about finalities.

"Look, I had always planned to die instantaneously, either by a bolt of lightning or a heart attack in my own car, so I could be driven right to the morgue, quick and neat." Wesgrove smiled. "You don't know me well enough, yet, Doctor. I'm not much on languishing. If what you plan to do, to prolong my life, doesn't work and the quality of my life can't be justified by me . . . then, I intend to take things into my own hands, if you know what I mean. Are you someone who would help in a situation like that?"

"Absolutely not."

"OK. We've put that one away in the right file. I just wanted you to know that I'm not going to allow myself to get so sick from the cure that I won't be able to make a decision on my own behalf. Isn't it true that chemotherapy can turn into a disease in itself and bomb the patient out of his mind?"

"Yes, unfortunately, but usually the patient wants to take that risk. Certain types of cancer *can* be cured, you know that . . ."

"Not mine . . ."

"No. But almost all skin cancer, yes; Hodgkin's disease, eighty-five percent cured in stage one; peripheral cancer of the lung, yes; breast, ovarian cancer in many instances, yes; certain tumors removed in surgery and followed by radiation, chemotherapy; sometimes we can add years to a patient's life. The individual responses to treatment are still mysterious, but getting less so as we learn more."

"Well, I'll submit to anything you've got, but . . . I want a promise from you, Doctor. If you try a chemical or treatment on me and you see it's putting me out of commission—by that, I mean . . . it's turning me into a pathetic sad sack, too weak to say *No!* . . . then, you'll stop it immediately. Do we understand each other?"

Wesgrove shook his head in agreement.

The chemotherapy began—two weeks on drugs, two weeks off. Max's body responded. The signals of multiple myeloma were fading. Endless tests and pictures. The pain in the back stopped. The abnormal production of protein in the blood was checked, the urine cleared. Wesgrove had discovered a spot on Max's right fibula, and that, plus the area of the right hip, showed a cessation of destructive cell activity. By all appearances, Max was having none of the possible adverse "chemo" responses, no loss of hair, nausea, overwhelming fatigue, depression.

Wesgrove's office with its ragged Orientals, chess set, and burning fireplace became an oasis for Max, the one place he felt safe from cancer. Gradually, they began the habit of nighttime visits, since Wesgrove was always working, either in the labs or late at night at the large table with its ashtrays filled with orange rinds and apple cores. The two were becoming fascinated with each other. The scientist and the magnate had a lot to talk about. They were developing the camaraderie of officers in a war.

Max learned that Wesgrove came from a New England family with a doctor in every generation for almost two hundred years; that he wasn't all brain and Nobel Prize, he was an outdoorsman when he could sneak the time—he loved to tramp, fish, and sail off the coast of Maine. Wesgrove smiled in recollection one evening. "I have a big, old family house up there that's been fighting death by salt spray since 1870. It makes for pretty stubborn kids when you spend your summers scrambling around the rockbound coast like sand crabs, and learn how to beat that damn northeast wind in the harbor with a sailboat."

Max knew nothing about sailing, but he understood . . . "If you can handle the wind and use it, every other fight on land is pretty soft." He felt the same way about the mesas and buttes, the canyons of his Utah childhood.

"Active bodies have a better chance," was another thing Wesgrove kept saying. "You've got to work off the toxicity from the drugs."

There was a gym and swimming pool in the Cancer Research Center. Wesgrove would ask Max to join him. It amused Max to see the two of them, he, six-two, and his five-foot companion with the unruly, wispy white hair, lifting weights, climbing ladders. The pixie in his sixties pushed, dared, stretched, sometimes to limits that were hilarious; then, he rushed for a swim, rushed back to his papers, his equations. There was a sense of urgency about Wesgrove, a funny, dear nervousness like that of Alice's rabbit, even when he was patiently sitting over the chessboard, waiting for Max to move.

Max didn't mind anymore walking into the cold, white building with *cancer* in its name, didn't object to the endless needles, machines, technicians, if his visits ended, as they did, in the inner sanctum of Wesgrove. Though the man was only ten years older, Max felt protected as by a father—a safety he had never known or remembered.

October, November, December went by faster than Max could ever remember time going. He was in a kind of ecstasy—

a weird word next to cancer. He slowly realized it was an odd coupling he had felt before—on a Pacific island with Jap bullets whizzing by. The ecstasy of perfect fear. When you thought you were going to get it, but you didn't! When you hit the mud and a second later you were still there. It was the ecstasy of getting up, running again, and everyone around you screaming "Fuck!" Some guys crapped in their pants, ran with erections, some fell flat and wouldn't move, hugging the ground in that moment of perfect terror.

Lately, he had been having nightmares of running, or living in a balloon that burst and dropped him into holes that turned into firing squads, and his body was trying to make one last scream before all its functions exploded.

Dreams of perfect fear would wake him, make him grope for Hedda's waist, thighs, hold on to her breasts—to bring him back to a quieter kind of fear, the sneaky war going on inside him.

He confided to Wesgrove that he seemed to be in a constant state of erection in his head, if not his penis. "Is one of the side effects feeling horny?"

"Not that we've noticed . . ."

"Maybe it's my way of trying to validate myself. Do you think that's it?" Max laughed with embarrassment. He had never talked with a man about such private feelings; it was damn awkward. He *had* to talk about this business of fucking death and screwing life, or was it one and the same when you had cancer? It was excruciatingly important that Wesgrove know what was going on in his head, because if he did, it would make him a better partner, wouldn't it? Max was on a high. Once he opened himself up, he couldn't stop talking. It made him slightly dizzy, letting someone into the inside of his head. Max's axiom for himself had always been: If you can't dope it out for yourself, forget it. Was this how a poor bloke felt on an analyst's couch?

The doctor listened intently while Max confided his dreams, his need for sexual release, but, more important, how it felt to be on chemotherapy . . . for him.

"I'm *willing* it to work, Wesgrove. It's like daring Fate every time they do the bone scans, take my blood, stick that needle in. Do other patients feel that way? I'm daring myself to perform. There's a funny thrill in the challenge, the suspense. The chemicals are beginning to take on a magic quality. It's like a river of potions meandering around inside me and I'm telling it where to go and what to do. I have a picture in my head: a river of sanity is washing away the madness under my skin.

"Is that crazy? Having a board meeting with your cells every day? Cussing them out? Demanding they work right or get fired?"

"Not at all. It's the optimum you could hope for, making the mind and body one."

"I better be careful, Wesgrove, that I don't make you a shaman, a magic man, dispeller of all uncertainty."

"I'm glad you brought that up. It's dangerous to put all your hope in authority. Trust, maybe . . . but not all your hope. It very often makes for bitter disappointment. And, why do you call me Wesgrove? I call you Max."

"Because I want to call you Pop, that's why. 'Wesgrove' gives me the distance I need," Max said shakily.

Hiram Wesgrove was quietly pleased. He had probably found his most perfect patient to date, someone with a constitution so tough he was having no side effects from the drugs as far as could be seen, reactions more dangerous sometimes than the cancer itself. The only spoken-of effect seemed to be a surge of libido. Curious. L-dopa did that, the specific to control Parkinson's disease, but not, to their knowledge, what they were pouring into Max—a combination of very strong conventional chemicals in the treatment of cancer and something new, very new out of his labs, to inspire the immune system to fight back against invasion.

Max's body was pedaling a tandem bike without his knowing. But, why tell him? He hadn't been told that he had, probably, only six months to live *without* chemotherapy. So far, the tandem bike seemed to be making mileage and Wesgrove was keeping his fingers crossed. The something new was influencing the thymus gland, "the Socrates of glands" Wesgrove called the thymus, the gland that offers crucial knowledge, teaches the lymph node cells and spleen how to reject enemies. The new extract hadn't been biochemically tested out, so why tell the patient? Something new could make him too hopeful or too wary and vulnerable; neither state was productive. It was always a mystery—the rate at which cancer cells take over—so why discuss the odds at the start of a game that had no established rules? Still, here it was, Max's constitution accepting a double barrel they'd never tried before.

But Wesgrove was feeling discomfort. The patient was becoming a friend and that was dangerous. It interfered with his clinical approach to a guinea pig. One thing Wesgrove *did* know: He had a long-distance runner on his hands—someone who trusted he could breathe without oxygen for the last few excruciating seconds. To win! The perfect challenger. Yes, Max was dreaming death and talking death, but he was going to run "life" all the way.

Wesgrove was right in suspecting that Max was demanding a special kind of partnership in the war against *the witch*. Max hadn't told Wesgrove about *the witch*, that he'd made cancer a female of extraordinary power. She was all the witches that ever leapt off the pages his mother had read to him when the sun went down. When he was little, it was witches and night. Now, he had *the witch* at sunrise. Max didn't want to think about why he had made cancer a female, or, in reverse, why he viewed Wesgrove's office as the Temple of Athena, symbol of wisdom, reason, civilization.

And, there was that other female. Hedda. The irony made Max ill. Now that he had Hedda to love and share his life, there was *the witch* with her threatening curses in the background. The remission of the cancer would end. Wasn't "incurable" the name of the game? Why was he fooling himself? In a few months he was going to be sick again. Cancer would come to lie between him and Hedda. Cancer would cuckold him! Such was Max's mood a few weeks later.

It didn't go unnoticed. "You're mixing my prescriptions with depression, Max. That's a pharmaceutical mistake," Wesgrove remarked. Max had been unusually quiet the last few visits. He looked drawn and tired, even though the tests had again substantiated the remission and he had been taken off all treatment, to give his body a rest. "Get rid of it, whatever it is. We're not taking pleasure in the successful climb, are we?"

Max was filled with resentment. "We? What do you mean 'we'!" (Suddenly, *the witch* and the healer were one. I hate you, dwarf with your diplomas. You can take your genius and shove it up your ass! It's not going to give me back my life, my voice, my sound!) "Are you married?" Max asked angrily. Funny, he'd never asked him a personal question.

"No. I decided very early that I couldn't burden a good lady with my obsessions."

"Then, you don't know anything about another kind of commitment—children. The grasping arms of more love the minute you conceive." (Where did that come from? He didn't mean it, the way it sounded.)

"Are you worried about your children?"

"Not children, one daughter. It's worse than worry. I don't want to talk about it."

"Whatever it is, you can't afford the energy."

"That's ridiculous! What are you asking for? A noncontaminated cage? What kind of innocent are you? I envy you. You make love to abstractions."

Wesgrove winced. Max saw it but didn't want to stop.

"If abstractions fail you, you find others. Mental peace?" Max exploded, "You're asking for the impossible! Maybe with monkeys and rats, but not with human beings . . . for your precious experiments. You, obviously, have conveniently removed yourself."

"Do you want to talk about what's bothering you? You're very angry."

The patronizing attitude, which was the only way Max could see it, made him even angrier. "No. I do not want to talk about it!"

"Suit yourself. Look, we don't have to see each other for about a month, unless something crops up. Why don't you and Hedda take off for somewhere? A vacation from the ogre."

"And *the witch*," Max mumbled like a little boy.

"The witch?"

"Never mind." Max looked up. "Vacation? You mean Switzerland? Skiing?"

"Why not, if you take it easy and in moderation? As a matter of fact, it's your new prescription."

"You mean, go off as though everything is normal?"

"Absolutely. And there's no reason to think about the *otherwise*. Let me do that, not you . . ."

Max had been sitting in one of the chairs flanking Wesgrove's fireplace. He *did* resent the power this man had over him, but it meant he also had the ability to lift the fog of fear, damn him.

"OK, magic man, look, I'm sorry . . . I lost my temper. You're right, I'm angry. I never needed anyone in my life, except maybe my mother. Now, I need everyone! I need you . . . I need Hedda . . . I need . . . I need to understand one of my daughters, and I can't. I need to understand my mistakes before it's too late. Do you know how uncomfortable that is? Thinking 'before it's too late' after every damn thing you think!"

"Dependency isn't a bad word, you know," Wesgrove said with some hesitance. "It belongs to the strong . . ."

"Bullshit!" Max whispered to himself. He was standing with his hands in the pockets of one of the soft, fine leather jackets he had been wearing lately—elegant cowboy. (Shades of the past, his mother, maybe the desert, back there when all was well and would be forever.)

"I want to know everything," Max said quietly, "everything you haven't told me up to now. I'm in a remission . . . OK, it's not going to last long, I know that . . . but then what? What after it stops?" His voice broke. "How much time do I have to try to know who I am . . . to do what I have to do?" He looked up at the ceiling, the reflection of the fire casting mellow light on his figure, and he listened as Wesgrove explained, projected with no reservations, while Max translated into his own private language what he was hearing.

Wanting to know meant becoming aware that if and when the disease took over, there could be punched-out, bony lesions that might happen, involving his skull, or the danger of fractures of his vertebrae and ribs as the cancer invaded the bone. It meant knowing that anemia could be the bite of the serpent, unexplained infection . . . or a gradual onset of the nephrotic syndrome—kidney disease—the grand bonus from a night at the cancer carnival. And, *the witch* could ultimately create the final burst of fireworks—uremia and finis. Or pneumonia *and* uremia. But how long? Wesgrove had skirted it. Max couldn't bring himself to ask it again—how long?

What a handsome figure of a man that is, Wesgrove had observed, as he talked. Lean-slung, long-boned, not a visible sign of deterioration in the muscle, skin tone. Doesn't even look his age. What a damn shame to know that those fine weight-bearing bones will be quietly eaten away, no matter what. Yes, there was a remission . . . but, what after that? What drug combination could they come up with to cause another remission after this one was finished? Only the most lethal, the last-resort killers. He silently checked his own advice with himself, about the skiing. No, there'd be no danger of any breaks; the bone damage in Max's hip and leg was in an early stage and had been stopped. It was worth the gamble. The man needed to feel normal and get away. Wesgrove was relieved that Max hadn't pinned him to the wall about *time.* He would have lied if he had.

"Wish I could go with you," Wesgrove said.

Max turned to him. "I don't, Wes . . ."

"Ah . . . you found the name."

"What do you mean?"

"Well . . ." The little man began to laugh. "You see how small I am . . ." Max flushed. "Well, you *do* see," Wesgrove insisted.

"What difference does that make, if I do or don't?"

"I have two brothers. I'm the youngest. They're both tall as you are, or were, until lately." His eyes shone impishly.

"They're in their seventies . . . when you shrink a bit; not much though, not them. I was a mistake, born in my mother's menopause. I hated the name Hiram and I refused to be called Hi, 'cause it sounded too small. It was a family joke that I wouldn't answer to Hi or Hiram, so they called me Wesgrove . . . even my teachers in the first years of school. I was born too early, they're having a lot of success now for stunted growth, with hormone therapy . . ." he said, trying to hide a bitter longing with a smile.

"So, this little character became 'Wesgrove' because he wanted an impressive name. In college, it became 'Wes.' By then, I didn't care what I was called. I knew I wanted to be a doctor, it didn't matter of what. My mother died of cancer my first year in medical school. That made up my mind about what kind of doctor. She was a great friend of mine, Agatha Wesgrove. She made it much easier for me to be five feet tall in a family of giants."

"Giants?" Max was surprised at the personal disclosure and wondered why Wesgrove was offering it. It was naked as hell.

"Yes, giants, that's the way it felt. Now, where did *I* come from? What was the joke? The genes were playing ice hockey and forgot their genetic responsibility."

"So you fooled them and became a giant anyway," Max said quietly. It dawned on him what Wesgrove was about, the fox. There were all kinds of journeys, bleeding from the palms. The little man was deadly. He was challenging him with his own pain.

Wesgrove's eyes were moist. He stood there, five feet of defiance, his wisps of white hair a crown of anarchy even more than usual, almost to show the turbulence inside him. His sharp blue eyes were flashing: Look at me! How would you like to have gone through life with my equipment? I've worked hard for humor and vision. Look at me! I know brain isn't all. I know a lot else. I want you to see my vulnerability. I'll force you to see it, to make you feel better.

It was a terrible moment for Wesgrove. He had lost control of his scientific discretion and distance, in the service of a friend.

"Damn your hide, Wes, you give me hope!"

"You said it, I didn't," Wesgrove said, triumphantly.

"*You* said it. Genetic disability, cell disability, the eternal tests. It's all relative, except some tests are longer, some are shorter. I'm not stupid, and you're not that subtle, old man."

"The *use of time* . . ." Wesgrove said quickly. "*That's* not relative, it's crucial. Get out of here. Send me a card from Switzerland."

9

Roz hadn't called her father in four months, nor had he called her again. His call of apology hadn't done much good. Phoebe kept in touch with her when she felt gung ho enough to take the removed voice, the silences. In the awkward spaces, she would keep her sister up to date on their father's illness. Roz never asked about him, but she listened with what Phoebe could only describe as voracious ahs, as though Roz were taking it all down in shorthand.

A few weeks before Christmas, Phoebe had a call from a former college roommate of Roz's, a silly, fluffy girl Phoebe remembered Roz bringing home for weekends; she had had only two things in her head, clothes and Princeton weekends. What on earth was Sally Howard calling her for?

"How did you find my number in Massachusetts?" Phoebe asked.

"I called your father's apartment and a woman answered and gave it to me. Have you seen Roz lately?"

"No, but I talk to her. Why?"

There was a long, "Well . . ." Then, "It's none of my business, but we've met her a few times at a couple of parties in town, and . . ."

"And, what?"

"Oh, then you really haven't seen her, have you!" Sally's high, shrill voice was trying to hide an excited curiosity. "How come?"

"I'm cracking my books. I'm back at school."

"Oh, dear, I know I shouldn't be doing this. John, my husband, you know I married John Phillips . . ."

"Really! A Princeton man?"

Sally had no idea she was being ribbed. "Yes, how did you know? Well . . . John said, 'Don't call,' but I just had to. Roz didn't seem like herself at all, and I just wondered . . ."

"Wondered what, Sally?"

"Wondered what was wrong, that's all . . . if she was ill or something, and if there was anything I could do. You know I'm very fond of Roz."

"Will you please tell me what you want to say?"

"No," said Sally, pulling back. "I think maybe you'd better check it out for yourself." Her voice was fading fast. "How are you, Phoebe?" she added, not wanting to know at all. "What are you doing these days?"

"I'm working for my Ph.D."

"Oh, dear . . ."

"Oh dear, is right. That's just how I feel."

The call ended with a tight little "Bye, bye . . ." from Sally.

That wasn't just a flippity gossip call. It was alarming. There was something wrong. Should she get herself to Newport? It was the worst time; there were two exams coming up. Maybe a call would do.

She called Roz that evening, around eight. A maid answered and said Mrs. Clyde was resting.

"Is she sick?" Phoebe asked. "This is her sister."

"No, ma'am, she's not sick, she's . . ."

"She's what?" Phoebe asked impatiently.

"She's just resting."

"When she stops resting, would you please tell her that her sister is driving down tomorrow late afternoon from Northampton? I don't recognize your voice, are you new?"

"Yes, ma'am."

"If it isn't convenient for her," Phoebe added, "tell her to let me know."

Roz didn't call back by noon the next day, so Phoebe got into her secondhand Volvo, which always needed to be repaired, crossing her fingers that it would make the trip. This time there was something wrong with the gas filter, or it could even be the transmission, for all she knew; she just didn't have the time to get it fixed, or the money. Phoebe was living on a very small, self-imposed allowance. Max said it made him nervous, her driving a piece of junk. He wanted to buy her a brand-new car, but she absolutely refused. She said her fellow students were sweating blood, getting by on student loans or borrowed money, and she had to try and approximate their distress, do it the same way. Well, almost. She didn't need to borrow money, but she was going to keep herself on a tight string. Nothing meant anything, if it came so easy.

"All right, have it your way," Max had shrugged, "but I won't have you driving that car outside the Northampton-Amherst area. When you come to New York, you fly, or I'll send the chauffeur up for you, you hear?"

"Are you mad?" was Phoebe's exasperated reply. "You're purposely not understanding!"

"I understand very well, young lady, but I think it's silly. I worked very hard for my money and there's nothing I like better than to translate it into pleasure. For starters, one of the pleasures is that I can afford a car that won't get me killed, in the name of idealism. You've got things a little mixed up, baby. Maybe I've got it wrong, but I always thought the goal wasn't for everyone to be poor and happy. I thought the goal was for the great day when everyone could be rich, or, at least, have everything they needed and wanted within reason. So, why are you making believe? You're rich, Phoebe Treading. That's not a curse. Enjoy it. What are you cotton-mouthing about?" He was serious and teasing at the same time.

"You're impossible, Daddy. You're purposely not digging me."

"I dig you very well. I'm also suspicious of the too-righteous, the thin-lipped dogmatics, the rigid and the rabid. No, your lips aren't thin, they're gorgeous, but watch out, they might get that way. Look, I'm not offering you an ermine coat. I just want to buy you some new wheels, so you won't die on a highway. Don't look so upset with me. How come you didn't want to study to be a coal miner, so you could get the real feel of the proletariat? Probably would have been safer. The worker saves every damn cent he can, so he can own a decent automobile."

She had won. She was still driving the Volvo and praying it could make Newport without going dead.

Phoebe hadn't been to Newport for almost a year. She hated the place, with its mansions, servants, driveways so long they didn't need *Keep Out!* signs, they practically screamed that there were killer Dobermans lurking in the bushes. Roz and Willard's house was called Greenbriar. The first time Phoebe had visited the Clyde mansion—Willard's family had presented it to the newlyweds—she'd almost got lost in it. It had thirty rooms.

The first floor of Greenbriar was so formal it looked as if it were waiting for a famous dead person to be brought in, to lie in state. On the second floor there were endless family rooms, bedrooms, and bathrooms big enough for six people to wash up in at the same time. At the turn of the century, Phoebe fantasized, it might have been a happy house filled with children. Why else have bathrooms as spacious as nurseries? The feet of the bathtubs were large as real lions' and carved in gold, but from what she knew of the Clydes, Phoebe didn't think it was possible for them ever to have had happy children. The Clydes were as forbidding as their wrought-iron gates. Scotch-Presbyterian mixed well with some German. They'd made their fortunes in railroad cars way back—iron, steel, heavy stuff. Of course, they were new-rich as far as her mother's Walleby family was concerned. The Clydes had arrived in the 1870s, but the Wallebys had had Peter Stuyvesant to dinner.

On that first visit to Greenbriar, a few days before Roz's wedding, which was to take place in the ballroom, she remembered Willard taking her into the cavernous marble room and proudly announcing that his grandfather had given a huge ball for Herbert Hoover after his inauguration. She also remembered wondering what in heaven's name Roz was going to do with herself in Newport, because Willard had announced that he wanted to live there *all year round.* There was no one in Newport all year round. After October, it was dead.

Willard had really meant it. He was weird, it was weird. They stayed in a hotel or his parents' townhouse when they came to New York, which was as often as Roz could make it, and Willard commuted three times a week to the Clyde offices in Manhattan, but there was Roz—on ice, living in a mausoleum. Roz didn't garden. The house was surrounded by flower beds and a park. Roz hated the outdoors, she detested sailing, which was the main subject of conversation between Willard and his friends.

The one thing Phoebe did like about Greenbriar was a large, white, two-story, latticework gazebo, from which you could see the harbor. There *must* have been an imaginative, interesting, hopeless romantic in at least one generation of Clydes. What a wonderful place to read or write. But, Roz didn't like reading much, did she? She also didn't like being in the sun; it was bad if you wanted translucent skin. What *did* Roz like? She married Willard, that's what she must like, and everything that went with him—an undertaker's life full of responsibility.

To Roz's credit, Phoebe observed *this* visit, she had redecorated many of the rooms on the second floor, thrown out the awful, dark, papal-heavy antiques, replaced them with other antiques, no less formal but more beautiful pieces, light, airy, delicately curved—like Grandma Walleby's, like what they had grown up with.

Phoebe could never have anticipated what she walked into. Roz was drinking! She didn't learn how much till later. And Willard, the Dense, was not at all sympathetic. Roz kept making herself martinis and was filled with forced hilarity, as though it

were a cocktail party for twenty. It looked as if the perfect
marriage was crumbling like brittle lace.

Phoebe was almost reduced to tears, the dinner was so filled
with barbs back and forth between Roz and Willard. It was
dizzying, trying to figure out who was more to blame for the
hurting. They behaved as though she weren't there, yet they
were performing for her. They derided people she didn't know,
people she knew slightly; they interspersed their hostile gossip
with private asides: "Do you think you're equipped to pass the
butter?" said Willard. "As equipped as you are *not* to understand
anything," Roz flung back.

Willard excused himself after dinner.

"Why don't you ask where he's going?" Roz said.

"Should I?"

"We *do* have company, don't we?"

"Me?"

"He's going to play bridge."

"There's nothing wrong with that. Is there?"

"Every night there is! Golf, Saturday and Sunday; sailing
all the rest of the time, weather permitting. The entire story of
Willard's mental and physical virtuosity."

Phoebe was going to be very careful. "Nothing wrong with
any of it, if you like it." Roz left the table without answering and
Phoebe sat alone. Willard came back, with his coat on.

"She's been like this ever since that fight with your father.
I can't handle it anymore, I'm fed up. My parents won't visit us
and I don't blame them. I'm glad someone in her family finally
decided to take a look."

Phoebe looked at him—Willard, the impeccable. How
could Roz tolerate him? There was more to her sister than that.
There had to be. She was a Treading, wasn't she?

"My father is a very sick man, in case you haven't heard."

"He's got a sick daughter, too!"

"You mean, she's drinking, Willard?" Phoebe asked coldly.
"Have you tried talking?"

"Talking?"

"Yes, you idiot!"

"I beg your pardon?"

"Talking, like I heard somewhere husbands and wives are supposed to do, or want to do . . ."

"Look, Phoebe, I told her to butt out, it's none of her business what your father does with his life."

"He doesn't have a life. He might have a year!" Willard seemed to choose not to hear that.

"My mother says I have to get her to a doctor, but she won't go," was his reply.

"Your mother says? What do *you* say?"

"I say: I can't handle it. It's like living with Ms. Jekyll and Madame Hyde. She's fine, and then she isn't. The isn'ts are getting too close for my comfort, that's all I have to say."

"In sickness and in health . . ." Phoebe muttered.

"I'll see you at breakfast," Willard said and left.

Phoebe found Roz in an upstairs living room, sitting on a gray velvet Empire sofa, her back straight, all put together, daring anyone to suspect there were six martinis underneath.

"Had a good heart-to-heart with the paragon?" Roz said.

"Roz . . . what's the matter?"

"What's the matter? Nothing! Everything is perfect, can't you see? Don't you know a perfect marriage when you see one? Well, how could you? How could we?"

"It wasn't the pleasantest dinner I've ever had. As a matter of fact, it was pretty lousy."

"Then, why don't you leave?"

"I didn't come to eat. I came down to talk, if we can. I also have some good news to tell you about Daddy."

"What? Is she pregnant? Isn't the Jewess supposed to be exceptionally fecund, darling? If you remember your Bible with all those begats?"

"Are you out of your mind? Daddy's fighting for his life! The good news is that he's in a remission. The cancer has been stopped. Don't you want to know that?" Phoebe tried to figure out the look on her sister's face. It was a mixture of too many things—eyes unrevealing, mouth pursed; there was a kind of terror and defiance at the same time distorting her flushed face. It was like a clown's face deciding which grimace to take.

"Why don't you call Daddy?" Phoebe said quietly.

"I have nothing to call him about. He asked me to leave *his* home and that's it. He called me, yes, but I'll never call him. Never! I'm going to make myself a drink." She moved toward a tray of bottles and glasses a servant had brought into the room while they were talking. Phoebe noted that it didn't seem to bother Roz what was overheard. Halfway across the room, Roz turned around.

"Don't tell me he hasn't told you about our famous fight?"

Phoebe lied. "No, he didn't. He just said you hurt each other very badly."

"Well, *I'll* tell you," Roz said, having gotten herself to the tray of bottles, pouring herself what Phoebe thought an incredible amount of booze. Gin? Vodka? What did it matter. It was horrible.

"I said," Roz went on, " 'How dare you replace Mother with a blowsy little nothing who's taking you for a ride! You're acting like a dirty old man, that's what she's doing to you!' " She stared at Phoebe, waiting for a response.

"How come I don't feel that way?" Phoebe said softly. "How come we're so different? Have you ever thought about that?"

"Of course I have. The answer is: You're Daddy's girl. You always were."

"Oh, God, stop it. If you only knew how much he wants to see you, how upset he is . . ."

"I can't imagine why. We're total strangers, and you know it. Have you ever thought, I just don't like him, I don't approve of him, he was Mother's mistake?"

"Do you approve of me? Am I a stranger too? You're just a poor, little orphan stuck out here in Newport, drinking your head off and making yourself miserable? Is that what you think you are? If you're so removed, Roz, why are you so angry?" Phoebe's face was flushed with her own anger. To her surprise, Roz began to laugh.

"Good point!"

"I'm not playing for points. Why don't you see a doctor?"

"For what?"

"To help you sort out your feelings, that's for what! I'll go with you. Let's go together, to a family therapist or something. I'll ask Dan Hoffstadter to recommend . . ."

Roz laughed again, a light, careless laugh that thinks it's wiping the moment clean. No reply expected. Another laugh. She had learned that laugh well from their mother—sparkle to fill in the senseless, vague spaces in a room. Even drunk, she wasn't forgetting the tools of her society trade.

Whether it was the grim look of Phoebe's face or just plain drunken high jinks, Roz decided to reply, but only after she could tack it on to another cascade of private giggles. "All right, darling girl, with your peasant shawls and loving, good nature. Let's go to the analyst and tell him our troubles. Scene! Doctor's office!" Roz began to move about the room with a theatrical stride, declaiming in an English accent to the imaginary doctor. Phoebe hadn't seen her do this sort of thing since college, when Roz fancied she wanted to be an actress. If what she was doing now wasn't so scary, it might even be funny. Roz did accents very well.

"My sister is veddy much like her father and his side, Doctor. I'm told I resemble my father's mother . . . (she switched to a Yiddish accent) . . . and yet, my sister, underneath, is supposed to be just like my father's mother, but she's the spittin' image of our mother, blond and beautiful. Do you understand, Doctor, what I'm saying? (She shifted to a French accent.) How can you make sense out of that, oh, Doctor? *'Je ne sais quoi?'* Is that all you have to say? You say you don't know about the genes? Then, why are we here? Aha, I've caught you! You know nothing! You're not a fool, you say? Well, neither am I. I'm here only to indulge my sister. Do I love my sister? Of course I love my sister! Who else is there left to love, but my sister! No one! And, she'd better watch her step, too . . ." Roz giggled.

Phoebe thought she would die with the sadness of the revelation hidden behind the accent, the, "Of course I love my sister!" that Roz threw down, making drunken light of it. She

wished the scene would stop, but Roz went on . . . in her own
voice, slightly southern.

"Doctor, yes, I have something to admit. I hired a private
detective to follow my father's mistress. Do you know what he
discovered? Well, my, oh my, my poor father is being cuckolded.
His mistress has a lover. That's rather baroque, isn't it? Or is it
Tennessee Williams?"

"Roz! Stop it!"

The accents were finished. "Oh, yes," Roz flung out. "It's
the truth. Dear Hedda is slinking around corners with someone
else, with her eye on Daddy's money at the same time. Grow up!
Daddy's going to die and she's got her eyes going in every
direction they can."

"I don't believe it!"

"You had better."

"Does Willard know about this?"

"No one knows except me and the man I hired."

Was it truth or fantasy? Phoebe had no way of knowing.
Roz seemed, suddenly, cold sober.

"How could you?" Phoebe said, taking a chance that it was
true.

"I had to."

"For all the wrong reasons."

"Don't judge me, baby!"

Phoebe stood up, waiting for a tantrum, but Roz let go of
the subject as swiftly as she'd exposed it. Maybe it wasn't true,
just a drunk, awful, unconscious play in that imaginary doctor's
office.

"I'm going to check it out, Roz. I won't go back to
Northampton tomorrow, I'll go to New York." She waited for
Roz to laugh or protest that it was a game.

"Do that!" Roz said. "And let me know what the lady says.
'Here comes the lady,' as Othello said." Roz began to giggle.

"If I may be so bold as to remind you, Desdemona was
innocent, and Iago quite mad!" Roz didn't seem to hear her.
She was sitting on the gray couch again, her lips on her glass,
not about to take a swallow, just sort of sucking the rim and

looking out into space. She was absolutely stoned.

Phoebe went to the window. It was raining heavily. She looked at her watch. It was ten o'clock. She couldn't imagine staying overnight. She had to get away from this house, the ice in the rooms, the ice in Roz's glass. She was going to drive right to New York and confront Hedda in the morning. No, that wouldn't be right, she liked her too much. She'd work up to how sick Roz was because she'd said . . . blah, blah, blah about a detective and she was so drunk and maybe she had to be hospitalized if she fantasized such things; maybe they had to tell Daddy, get together as a family to save Roz. Hedda was the only one to talk to out there.

IO

Roz hadn't seemed to care whether she stayed or left, so Phoebe left, driving through rain that turned into sleet, then thick, unforgiving rain again. Should she have stayed?

The driving took four hours of such concentration that it was a blessing not to have to think about anything else, except it kept sneaking into her mind—the possibility her sister was paranoid, too ill to know what she was doing. Her father was dying . . . her mother was dead. Thank God, the Volvo wasn't deciding to conk out on her; if it did, she'd drive up onto an embankment and kick it to death!

Curiously, the least of her worries was losing time to study. A decision came to her, unexpected as someone coming up from behind and grabbing her shoulder. She wasn't going for her Ph.D. this year. To hell with that. There was too much wrong in her world. The world of economics would have to wait. "Wow," she said out loud to the windshield wipers.

The first time she heard the word *economics* was at a dinner party her mother was giving before a charity ball. Phoebe was nine. Why did *she* ask what "charity" meant, when Roz was only interested in the dress Mother chose to wear, the excitement of the diamonds coming out of the vault, the smell of perfume? How come she'd escaped Roz's life? They had the same governesses, lived in a cocoon on Fifth Avenue, a cocoon in Southampton every summer. They both had to learn how to curtsy for Grandmother Walleby, ride horses, play tennis. They both were lonely because Mother was never home when they wanted her, she was always *lunching* and planning charity balls.

"Charity is helping the blind and the deaf," her mother had answered.

"Charity," one of the men at the table said, "means you find out who bought the biggest emeralds this year while you dance to Peter Duchin's tunes, all for a good cause, and when you grow up, maybe you'll be the chairman of a ball, just like your mother."

She remembered her father giving her a particular look, saying, "Phoebe, charity is being kind without expecting anything in return. But, public charity, the rich giving to the poor, to make the rich sleep better at night, that exists only because the economic solutions for most people in the world stink." The dinner table went absolutely quiet and Mother had that annoyed look and Daddy laughed. "Economics makes the world go round, not love. If we can ever get the two together, we'll be in fine shape." Pretty simple, but just right for a nine-year-old.

What a mixed bag of tricks her father was, filling her head with all sorts of things when he saw he had a willing listener. He'd found an old print of the Declaration of Independence in an antique shop and given it to her for her thirteenth birthday. It was very expensive; her mother had thought it was a peculiar present to buy and he had said: "Can't think of anything better to start your teens with: Life, liberty, and the pursuit of happiness!"

By the time Phoebe was ready to go to college, Roz was finishing her last year at Smith and deciding which broker to marry, while Phoebe and her father were talking endlessly about the mysteries of American capitalism, the swings from

conservatism to radicalism that seemed not only the phenomena of politics, but of human nature. Sometimes, she didn't
know whether he was serious or mocking, with his "Everyone
should be able to reach up and tear a banana off the tree,
whether they're smart or not. The trouble, baby, is weather.
Man was messed up a long time ago by climatic changes. He
wasn't meant to live anywhere but in tropical climates. Cold
weather makes Man have to fight too hard for survival. Life
was meant to be lived out under a hot sun, in thick forest, with
cool water and no clothes to speak of. Life was meant to be
idyllic, easy."

She was thinking, as she drove, about how he had shaped
her with his calculated optimism, old-fashioned individualism,
grand feelings, how he had started her on her own search for
answers. She had come home from college demanding to know
why he kept defending capitalism and announced she was a
socialist and dedicated to the class struggle for the rest of her
life. He didn't bat an eye, and said, "I'm *still* defending American capitalism because, as far as I can make out, it's *still* the only
form of society that *still* has enough loopholes in it for some
good to ooze out for the many; and by *good*, baby, I mean free-
doms, not just bananas."

Some of her friends, the radical ones who knew who her
father was, couldn't believe how anyone could amass such
wealth without having exploited everything that had the misfor-
tune to cross his path. It was hard to explain that Maxwell
Treading wasn't like the old robber barons—Vanderbilt, Carne-
gie, Mellon, and Morgan—outstanding crooks in the flowering
of America. Nor was he like the robbers of today, who hid
behind the names of multinational companies. Her daddy liked
nothing better than to make himself visible.

How could she describe who her father was? A billionaire
who was a Jeffersonian Democrat? A child of the gods? Everything he touched turned to gold, and he gave it away so easily.
No one could believe that fairy tale, yet it seemed to be true. He
had begun to confide in her, when she went off to college, about
the extent of his philanthropies. It was staggering. (If she had

known their true extent, she would have been astounded, and her radical friends struck dumb.)

Their only real fights were about "the redistribution of wealth." He didn't think it was humanly possible, without a repressive society, to keep some people from being more "enterprising" than other people, and so, feeling they deserved more "profit."

"And, there you have it," Max said. "They'll sock it away, whether it's legal or not—the old nest egg. What's a nest without an egg? No immortality, no personal stamp."

"Oh, Daddy!" she sputtered. "You're not scrambling metaphors, you're whipping them!"

"Sure, every person on the damn globe should feel free, dignified, valuable, and never know hunger from the day she or he is born. But, there'll always be a ruling class, baby. You're too young and dewy to know that."

She would fight him furiously—about a social system, one day, that would abolish the need for individual wealth.

"Only if we go back to bananas, and the ice caps melt," he laughed. "Maybe we should explore the idea of exploding an atomic bomb at each pole. That'll do it, make it nice an' warm again for a while, until it's all under water, like it was for Noah. You know? That's probably what happened! There was a civilization way back there just as smart as ours, and someone said, 'Let's go back to bananas . . .' "

She got mad at him when he teased her pure idealism. For someone she admired and loved, he could be awfully dumb and dogged. He wouldn't even dream of a classless society.

"You can't change society, except in inches," he said. "And when you get to twelve inches—call it socialism—you're smackbang up against human nature again."

When he talked like that, she'd just say, "You're impossible!"

"No, I'm not. I'm a romantic-realist. Your Daddy's a double negative. With positive intentions." (He wasn't going to share his thought, that if the world had enough Phoebes, maybe human nature *would* change someday, as he hoped. He liked to play crusty with her, the stolid adversary.)

. . .

It was two in the morning by the time she reached the northern tip of Manhattan. The rain had stopped and the Volvo hadn't conked out. She gave the steering wheel a grateful pat. In the distance were the shadows of skyscrapers. The buildings appeared to be larger renditions of endless tombstones. Soaring graveyards. How far from the banana. There was nothing but bad news out there.

Phoebe was doing something old Professor Hardy, one of her favorites, had cautioned his class to stay away from. "Try not to combine personal anguish and public anguish, because then, you'll be a boring injustice collector, unable to calibrate change or weigh good and evil with a cool head. There *are* a few rights in this world, ladies and gentlemen, a few beams of sunshine in this vale of tears, although, admittedly, the repetition of evils can be depressing. Don't compound your view of world politics with the tragedy of a broken love affair."

As she drove crosstown on the black, drying streets, the depressing feeling that nothing was right in the world began to lift. Why should Daddy ever have to know anything from now on, except "a few beams of sunshine"? They weren't unalike, Professor Hardy and Daddy, though Daddy would never make seventy, maybe not even fifty-six. She choked on that thought —the inconceivable fact that he wasn't going to be present and accounted for much longer.

Her decision not to go back to school had become absolutely firm. She was going to live at home, be around to make the most of their time together. The university would have to understand and let her finish her degree later. If not, she'd sic Professor Hardy on her advisers. He'd defend her. Hadn't he begun his first lecture in advanced economics by announcing that society, as far as he was concerned, was the cell of the family multiplied to an unwieldy, incomprehensible degree, and if the cell of the family unit wasn't healthy, what could you expect from innumerable, miserable cells eating away the body?

Watching herself behave in a way that amused her, Phoebe drove up to the apartment house on Fifth Avenue, got out of the battered Volvo, and asked the doorman to park it for her—in that assured, pleasant tone only rich people can elicit for hired help . . . with Daddy's subtext: We're all equal, you're doing your job and I'm doing mine. *Of course* the doorman would park her car at two in the morning. Her father owned the building, didn't he?

The next morning, Max was taken aback but delighted to see Phoebe sitting in the breakfast room having coffee.

"What do we have here?"

"I needed a break, Daddy. Where's Hedda? Is she up yet?"

"She's up and gone."

"Damn."

"What's the matter? You don't look great. Did you drive in the rain last night? With friends? Not in the Volvo, I hope."

Phoebe made a funny face instead of lying.

"In the Volvo," Max translated.

"Yup."

"It made it all the way? It must have, you're here."

"Daddy, where's Hedda's office? Seventh Avenue somewhere? I have to buy a dress or something, maybe she'd go with me."

"If you gave her notice, she would have had it made. You drove half the night in the rain to buy a dress in New York?"

"I said I needed a break . . . There's going to be a party at the dean's house next week, you know, those pre-Christmas things. I thought Hedda could help me pull myself together."

"I'm sure she'd love to, baby. You'll be home for Christmas?"

"Yes, more than that."

"What's the matter with you? You can't fool me."

"Daddy, would you be upset if I didn't finish my Ph.D.?"

"Oh, oh . . . You need a dress because you're going to get married!"

"Don't be ridiculous. That wouldn't stop me from getting my degree. Would you be disappointed in me? Not achieving my goal?" she said, with an ironic challenge to the sound of *goal*.

She watched him trying to hide his response. Of course he'd be disappointed.

"No, I wouldn't be disappointed. I'm way beyond that kind of blackmail. What's going on?"

"My head is tired. Do you realize I've been at school since I was three?"

He just had to look at her face. His little workaholic not wanting to go the whole way? "You're not thinking about me, are you? Because I won't allow it."

"I'm thinking about me, not you."

"Well, if you want a break, take it. Why rush? You have a lifetime to change plans."

"I'll pick it up again next year if I can, but I just feel I don't want to crack another book or my head will burst."

"Anything else in your head to make it crack?"

"Not a thing." She drew a breath; that was settled.

But, he knew "not a thing" was a fabrication. He wasn't going to push. It would come out.

"Do you think Hedda would mind if I came home to live?"

"Mind? This is your home. She would love it. It would feel like family. We haven't had that for a long time." He wanted to choose his words carefully. "Hey, Hedda and I are doing fine. Let me say it this way . . . No, I'm not going to say it any way. You do what you want, and whatever it is, I'll like it, but don't take your own train off the track."

"I'm not taking my train off the track." She looked directly at him. "I want to be with you."

"If you do, pour me some coffee, baby." Max was trying to hide his feelings but he couldn't. "If you're leaving your studies because of this damn cancer, I'll never forgive you!"

"It's not the damn cancer," she jockeyed back. (It was all out in the open, they could still thrust and parry the way they always did, whether it was serious or not.) "Don't be so egocentric. It's for me. I'm going through a big personality change. I want to sleep until noon. I want to be served and go to the theater and . . ."

"And you can have it."

"And, my ma's goodlookin'?" Phoebe grinned. "Gonna get married?"

Max looked startled. "What makes you say that?"

" 'Cause that was top priority, wasn't it, when you were so rudely interrupted?"

"What do you think? Should I?" Max fished.

"I do."

"Given all the givens?"

"Yes."

"Who've you been talking to? Hedda?"

"No, I just know what my father wants, or did want, and I think he should have it. That's what he taught me—'*do* it, if it feels right; trust yourself, don't waste time if your instinct talks.' That's what you said."

"You remember everything I said? Good God, what a responsibility."

"That's right. Daddy, what does the remission really mean?"

"It's a reprieve. The chemotherapy is working."

"I want to know more than that. I want to know everything. Do you? Do you ask the doctor?"

"Do I ask? It's my new business!"

A brown tiger cat walked into the room, jumped on Max's lap, and nudged his head into Max's elbow.

"I don't believe it. What is *that?* A cat? With all the antiques?"

"It's Hedda's," Max said, with mock-apology to the air. "She found it rummaging in a trash can near her office and brought it home. He's about a year old, another success story from rags to riches. The only problem is, he's decided he's mine, not hers. What can I do? Hedda loves cats." She watched his hand abstractedly pat the cat's rump and give it a few gruff thumps. "I prefer horses, of course . . ." he chuckled.

She looked at her father shyly. He was a big handsome animal too. "Cats bring a lot of peace into a room," she said. Her father's presence *filled* a room. She didn't imagine it, that's what everyone who met him said. He looked well. How could he be sick? "Tell me what the doctor's telling you?" she asked.

"It's the damn evil cells. They're *not* multiplying now. When they're doing their dirty work they produce an excessive amount of protein in the blood . . . You really want to hear?"

"Yes!"

"Your bones get destroyed by the pressure from the abnormal cells. My right leg and hip are involved. There's no pain now. The cancer activity has been stopped. My blood count is almost normal. It's good, until further notice."

"And, then?" She needed to ask, but didn't want an answer.

"Let's take it a step at a time. I don't want to know about *further notice* until I'm in it."

"And, you're feeling well, isn't that wonderful?" She got up to hug him and the cat jumped off his lap because of the unexpected movement.

"You scared Rocky to death," Max said.

"Rocky?"

"Yeah. I named him Rocky, for Rocky like in mountains. Rocky like in rocky times."

"And, Hedda? How is she?" Phoebe said tentatively.

"It's hard for me, baby, with Hedda. You're fishing around for it. I can hear it in your voice. I'm not going to marry her. She doesn't know that. I keep putting it off."

"Maybe that's not fair, not so clever?"

"What do you mean 'not so clever'?"

"Nothing, just thinking about how I might feel if I were Hedda. Hey, I want to call her. Give me the number?"

"She'll take you shopping and then you're going back for that party?" He wanted her around, he wanted everything he could gather around him, but would never say it.

"Yes, I'm going to finish the semester, Daddy, tie things up, talk to my adviser and all that stuff. Don't you listen? I said I'm coming home." She stopped. "Oh, oh, one problem. I have a cat! May I bring her?"

"A her? A college cat? Rocky's strictly dees, dem, an' doz."

"That's all right, Red is very liberal."

"Red?"

"She's a red cat," Phoebe giggled.

"That figures. Red an' Rocky. The cook's gonna have a fit. Revolution in the kitchen." He held his arms out and Phoebe rushed into them. Then he held her at arm's length. "Just remember I said this, Phoebe—your father says you bring him joy with or without cat."

Phoebe felt something not easy for youth to come by. Worry and love for someone else make your own life excruciatingly real. Her instinct was right. She *had* to be with him.

When Phoebe woke that morning, she had decided *not* to confront Hedda with Roz's detective story, but after seeing her father, she decided she would. She *had* to know where Hedda stood, how solid his platform was. But, how?

Sitting opposite Hedda in a jam-packed, hysterically noisy restaurant, she decided how. The mood was infectious—there were ten people waiting to be seated; order fast, eat fast, confide fast. It was the wrong place for delicacy.

"Hedda, would you stay with Daddy even if he didn't marry you?" Phoebe sucked in her breath and waited.

Without a moment's pause Hedda answered. "Yes. Why on earth would you ask me that?"

"You mean, no matter how sick he gets, you'll stay . . . like a wife?"

"What's the matter? What are you doing in New York? Do you know something I don't? You're not hiding it very well, you're like your father. Are you trying to tell me Max isn't going to marry me? I know that. He thinks he's keeping the biggest secret. It doesn't matter, darling. I wouldn't give up a minute of being with him . . ."

"Oh, God, am I relieved!"

"Of what?"

"Something Roz told me . . ."

"You've seen her?"

"Last night. I went to Newport to stay overnight. But, I

didn't. She's not in good shape, Hedda. Her marriage is awful."
It came spilling out. "She had six martinis in three hours and
told me something terrible. She said she's had a detective watching you. I couldn't believe it. I had to check it out. Then I didn't
want to check it out. If you were seeing someone else, I didn't
want to know. If she's making it up, I didn't want to know that
either, because that's loony-bin stuff." Phoebe threw up her
hands. "Here I am, checking it out."

"It's true, Phoebe."

"True that you're seeing someone else? I don't understand . . ."

"How could anyone? Max didn't want you to get even a
whiff of it. Not about the someone, but about the detective. This
is what happened. The someone is David Absalt. I almost married him. That was three years ago, before I met your father and
the sky fell in. I left him for Max, I hurt him, but there wasn't
a thing I could do about it. As they say, I fell *madly in love* with
Max Treading . . .

"Anyway, I met David recently in a restaurant, he was
coming in, I was going out. He asked me if I'd have dinner with
him that week, he'd been trying to reach me and didn't know
how, and wasn't it funny to bump into me like that, it must be
fate. David has one trait like your father; he doesn't take no for
an answer very well. There must have been a look on my face,
because he said, 'Girl, I want to see you, I don't like the way you
look . . .' and I said yes. Because David's a wonderful person, a
little crazy, but very good. And, maybe I wanted to talk to
someone . . .

"Well, we had exactly one dinner. I told him about Max's
cancer. I also told him not in a million years would I stop being
with Max, loving him, taking care of him . . . anything, Phoebe,
because in my head, I'm married to Max until death *do us.*

"David had picked me up in the lobby. Max knew where
and why I was going . . ."

"Hedda, you don't have to explain . . ."

"I want to." Hedda continued: "All right, who's David? He
happens to be an assistant district attorney; you know, that

eyes-in-the-back-of-the-head man," Hedda laughed, "just like in the movies. I couldn't believe it when David said he was sure someone had been following us. Someone must have been following me for some time before that and I didn't know it! Before I knew what was happening, David went up to a man in the restaurant and demanded to know if he was a detective and threatened to have him arrested if he didn't explain what he was doing and why. David told him who *he* was. I couldn't imagine what was going on, but I watched that little exchange in the corner of the restaurant. The man's face turned white and he told David who had hired him and that he'd been watching me for a month. That's the ugly little story . . .

"Roz is ill. It's hard for Max to accept. He feels so guilty. I keep trying to get him to call her again. It's the only thing we argue about. I'm sure Roz would like to hear that, she's tried so hard to break us apart. He's teaching her a bad lesson about pride. I think he should extend his hand to her and he'd feel better, but he can't. It might help her, if he made the gesture . . . and I mean more than a phone call . . .

"Where did it all come from, Phoebe—her anger? What did they do to her?" Hedda saw immediately she shouldn't have said that.

"*They*, meaning Mother and Daddy?" Phoebe said defensively. "I'm not the one to ask that." She felt shaky, filled with, surprisingly, loyalty for *both* parents. She didn't want Hedda to judge the past. "I'm sorry, this isn't the pleasantest lunch in the world, is it?" she said, apologetic for her private thoughts.

"No, but I'm glad we're sharing it," said Hedda.

"What can we do?"

"Someone should get her to a psychiatrist."

"She's too proud and locked in."

"Is Willard any help?"

"Are you kidding? He's an idiot. He's just worried about being embarrassed by her in front of his friends and his tight-assed family, and don't think Roz is liking *that* very much, even when she's drunk. She's mortified with herself for losing face, I know it, but she can't control what she does anymore. She's like an iceberg, Hedda . . . and not the kind that will melt. She'd have to be smashed into by another iceberg and maybe she'd crack in two. What an awful image. I don't want Roz to crack."

Hedda felt drained. She wanted desperately to be the wise, older woman for Max's Phoebe, even if there was only an eight-year difference in their ages. "Your father's stubbornness is keeping him alive, but it's also hurting him. He refuses to reach out to her, he just can't deal with it anymore. You're the only line open to Roz; keep it open." Hedda decided to say something else:

"Phoebe, I've had a few years of psychoanalysis myself . . ."

"Really? You've been to a shrink?"

Hedda's eyes flashed. "I don't like that word. It denigrates an art. Knowing and learning more about yourself doesn't mean your head is shrinking, it means your soul is trying to expand."

Phoebe was properly chastened. "You're right, I'm sorry . . ." She had never seen that side of Hedda. It was very sharp.

"I've gone back to see my doctor lately, to ask his advice. Roz is the only shadow between Max and me," Hedda's voice trembled, "except the . . . oh Phoebe! except the ghastly, terrible timetable."

"What did he say?"

"He always has something to say about me," Hedda said ruefully. "About Roz? He said he couldn't diagnose a person he hadn't seen, but it sounded like a serious Oedipal problem."

"What does that mean, Hedda, *really* mean?"

"Oh God, who knows anything about anyone, what made them, what was done to them! The only thing I do know is that she wants me out of her father's bed. Sometimes little girls who have an overpowering, manipulative mother and a disinterested father don't dare to go through a normal phase—the unconscious wish of having Daddy, taking Mama's place, 'cause they'd lose Mama too, the only thing they've got . . . And they spend the rest of their lives fighting for air."

Phoebe was feeling that discomfort and resentment again, about dirty linen and Hedda, the stranger. But she wasn't a stranger, she *wanted* her to be *family!*

"It looks like I became her big opportunity to act it all out.

She can't lose anything by hating *me* out in the open, I'm not her mother." Hedda could see that Phoebe was baffled, that dealing with the mayhem of the unconscious was strange territory for her.

Hedda was trying to censor other feelings . . . Phoebe had that natural, golden calm, the gift of being made right, born right, no dark anguish to ruffle her practical little head. She hadn't been injured in any deep way. On the contrary, she had inherited the best of Max, who adored her, and obviously she had rejected the false notes of her mother. She was like Max. He very seldom considered the unconscious meanings, the spongy layers of Who am I? He could never be a victim. It was just *that*, his ease and sureness, that had attracted Hedda, the mirage of Excalibur under his arm, the Anglo-Saxon hero without fear . . . her opposite. Phoebe gave off similar reverberations. Hedda felt envious, almost resentful. But why should she envy Phoebe? She loved her for those qualities. Poor Phoebe, she had no idea of how to deal with the dark side of the moon. Maybe *that* was to be envied! Who needs shadows and the endless private exercises in your mind and gut, of trying to get rid of shadows?

Hedda didn't feel like talking anymore. The restaurant was hot and noisy and Phoebe was waiting for her to say something wise. She couldn't think of a thing.

"So, what do we do?" Phoebe asked.

"I don't know . . . I guess, just wait an' see."

Phoebe brightened and tapped the table resolutely. "Well, I'm certainly going to tell Roz what the story is. It might just sober her up. I'm also going to give her a piece of my mind; I never really have, you know, but I'm going to, damn it. Daddy doesn't need this shit. Enough is enough. She'll take it from me. I'm the only thing she has. She actually said it! She was drunk, but she said it."

The skepticism and concern on Hedda's face were very apparent.

"Well, I can try, can't I?" Phoebe said with utter simplicity and optimism.

II

[January 1982]

A week in London! Three days in Paris! Then to Switzerland. Max and Hedda were standing on the top of a ski slope in Gstaad. The whole thing was a miracle. It was worth everything to Max to see her look so happy, worth the drugged hell he had tolerated for the last few months.

He took a deep breath. The air was sweet liquor mixed with ozone. Hedda bent over to check a clamp on her ski and he gazed at the spectacular Bernese Oberland, the breathtaking mountain range with its Jungfrau, Eiger, Mönch; he kept turning his head east to west, trying to take in all the arrogant, jutting splendors at once. Are they more magnificent than my Sierras? At that moment, the Alps were the most beautiful mountains on earth. He was cured. He could *almost* convince himself it was true.

No one, not even Wesgrove, knew how tough the first round of chemotherapy had been. They had kept on pouring the stuff into him, making the doses stronger, because he'd said he wasn't having any reactions, wasn't throwing up, wasn't feeling he wanted to die rather than go on. *He had lied.*

Max had changed his mind about how far he could go

before the quality of life made no sense. When his red and white cell counts began to go up and down like yo-yos, it became a game. How far *can* I go? He psyched himself up like a boxer. No matter how much it hurts, think *win*. If the lab tests kept coming back "progress," he wasn't going to say the whole thing made him long for death. He turned on the shower so no one could hear him retching in the bathroom. He walked in Central Park for hours when he felt weak and dizzy. No one can describe that private surge of power that makes for victory. The marathon runner with his arms outstretched in rapture, face screwed up with pain as his chest hits the ribbon of the finish line—no one *knows*, unless he's done it.

Max had reevaluated his breaking point. It wasn't dry mouth, vomiting, headaches, vertigo. He had conquered all of that during the first months on drugs; after that, the symptoms began to disappear. His mind had won.

Here he was, three months later, all systems normal. It wasn't guts, it was deeper, a metaphysical reality. It was the worm of steel again, the same one that kept squirming inside him after the helicopter crash, to rouse him, make him writhe and stay alive. Was it his *mind* that had the power to make the worm of steel, or something that no word could define? He didn't care, he was on a high; he had walked through the shadow of death *without* a shepherd and come out into the sunshine of Gstaad. That was enough.

Hedda stood up. He looked at her with the sun shining on her blue and white ski suit, black curls glinting red, her brown eyes with the sharp, cold light making diamonds in their centers; he grabbed her hand . . . got his skis in position so he could hug her.

The snowy crispness and height were doing strange things to him. "Alive!" he shouted to the snowcapped mountains. "Alive! You old men out there . . . You think you're killers? I've won a round with a bigger one!"

Suddenly, another voice took over, ignoring *his* decision about *breaking point;* it yelled out its own verdict: "If the damn thing challenges me and gallops again, that's it! I'm going to finish it off the Treading way! Quick and neat!" He laughed, drunk with blue sky, ozone, the light, the white.

Hedda was so shocked, she pushed off the slope without him.

"Hey, wait! Wait for me!" Max called out.

It was a steep slope and she wasn't about to stop. She heard her name echoing as she sped down, and Max's laugh, as though they were playing a game and he hadn't blurted out what he had. Did she hear it right? Did he know what he said?

The cancer *was* going to recur. She had gone to see Wesgrove without Max knowing. Is *that* what's going to happen next? Max's suicide?

She got to the bottom of the slope and watched him make his way down, showing off, slaloming around imaginary poles. He was incorrigible.

By the time Max reached her, tears of anger were streaming down her cheeks. "You didn't mean what you said at the top, did you? If you did, I'll never forgive you for saying it that way, so fast, so easy. You're frightening. If you're joking, that's even worse. You level with me, Max, or I can't take it anymore. I can't live with a time bomb."

"I got kind of crazy up there. Let's talk about it later," he said evasively.

"No, here! Right now!"

"All right!" He had to tell her. "This, right here, now, is the quality of life worth living for. Anything less is an obscenity . . . I'm fine now, I feel like myself. The chemotherapy was hell. I'm not going to do it again. If there's a reversal, *I'm* gonna treat it, not the doctors. If you can understand *that,* and you must, it'll be the most important part of making it right."

"God, I love you! You're beautiful." He leaned over to kiss her. "Your nose is freezing cold. Let's go back and get into bed."

She pushed him away, her breath making waves of steam in the cold air. "Fucking! Is that all that's in your head? When the only thing in mine is that you might die or want to die? Damn you!" She skied away, down an incline leading to the chalet where they were staying.

"Yes!" he called after her. "That's all that's on my mind! With you! Until my last breath, damn you!"

They didn't go skiing again, not together. Hedda refused. Max went out alone, up to the top of the slope. It drew him. A perfect place to practice saying good-bye, to the sky, the clouds, the dots of houses nestled into the valley, making them stand-ins for all sky, cloud, house, mountain, valley . . . *This* would be the rare air of leave-taking to remember: Alone, white, blood quiet, going into nothingness. There was no Phoebe up there with him, no Hedda, no Roz, no memory of his mother in her leather dresses, no Utah, no child that he was, no successes or failures, no riches, no history of anything. Only the mountains rising up, timeless for a million more years.

Each time he got to the top of the slope, the decision-voice for suicide *at the proper time* wavered, strengthened, wavered:

He had made her too unhappy. She was sitting in their room down there. It wasn't like her to sulk, use the silent treatment.

How could he leave her, in his right mind?

How could he *not* leave her? He had given her too heavy a trip. He had to release her *and* himself, when *the witch* came again.

He wouldn't be able to. He would hang on to every minute of her face!

From their windows, Hedda could see him coming down the midportion of the slope. There was no mistaking Max's bright, yellow suit, or the figure jauntily practicing the slalom around imaginary markers, testing, testing.

How could she find the words to tell him she understood, when she was so angry, and guilty about being so angry? The terrible thought that she was going to lose Max in one way or another, had finally engulfed her in an avalanche, in Gstaad. She was living Max's death already. It felt like being buried under tons of ice and she couldn't breathe.

She couldn't join him. She had to hide the fear. So, she

watched him from their windows, his yellow figure that looked like a beam of sun playfully making its way down, down. How long could they go on not talking on this supposed honeymoon?

Wesgrove had warned her. "Everything in moderation, if you can keep reminding him." But, there he was for three days, carrying on like a ski bum of twenty.

Max would hold her at night, but they didn't make love. She knew he was waiting for her to say she understood: "Death is in the way but make love to me until it happens." She couldn't say it. Her blood was full of clots. It had to be thinned or she couldn't feel anything but her own pain, the rage of being cheated . . . again. It had happened once before, when her father died.

Hysteria was growing in her—she wasn't going to be able to make it for Max; she was going to get sick again, the unexpected deep depression that had happened after her father's funeral. She had had to go to a doctor to help her analyze her rage and loss away . . . *and it had taken two years!* Max didn't know this part of her, she didn't want him to; there was no time for him to. Her analyst had said *it* wouldn't happen again, but it *was.* Her courage was slipping away and along with it, the romantic notion that she and Max had to be perfect because there wasn't time for stumbling.

They had another week in Gstaad. The taste of the bitter time they were wasting was like a poison. Her stomach went. She began to throw up and feel dizzy from anxiety. She needed time to thin the panic. She could *do* it, if there was time, but there wasn't; there was no place to hide while she wrestled with herself, accepting the shock of recognition: *Max was going to die.*

Max walked into their room, yellow suit, pink, cold cheeks, just off the slope. He went into the bathroom and came out. "Do you have a fever?" he said.

"No . . ."

"But, you're sick, aren't you? Someone's just thrown up in the bathroom."

"Well, what of it? I think I have a virus."

"You don't have a virus. Hedda, I don't want us to end like

this. And, don't interrupt me, let me say it. I've laid too heavy a trip on you. I want you to go back to New York. I'll stay on a few more days by myself." (She couldn't believe what she was hearing.) "No nonsense, either; neither of us needs it. There's no reason on earth why you should understand anything more. Don't make yourself try to. I'm clear in my head now and there's nothing anyone can do or say that will make a difference."

Hedda reeled. Who was this speaking? Not Max!

"There's no artist hidden in me," he went on. "But I do know beginnings and endings. I was pretty brilliant at it. This *is* an ending. I want it that way. So do you! I insist! You're miserable. I don't have to know the chapter and verse. I honor it. I want to go the rest of the way alone. It'll be better for us both. There, I've said it. Pull yourself together and go home."

A fury came out of her like a fire storm. "Who in hell are you? Nothing anyone can do or say will make a difference? Close the door, just like that? How dare you! Who do you think you are? My father? To command me to come or go? That's shit!" It was coming out in extraordinarily loud tones.

"Shhh . . ." Max said. "This doesn't have to be heard by the whole chalet."

"To hell with the chalet. Is that where you're coming from? Self-pity! The martyr! Can't you do any better than that? Is that the great big thing you've come to, standing on the mountain for three days? That's all?"

Max was trying to brace himself against the unexpected heat. This was a pretty wild Hedda. Who was this little woman, her cheeks flaming, her mouth open like a cry from Picasso's *Guernica?* If it weren't such an awful moment, how he wanted to pick her up and tease her, provoke her about how she looked, laugh with her about what anger does to a face . . . her poor little face . . . In one second, with his guard down, he could become a beggar, crying out his needs, pleading for her love. It would undo every resolve he had tried to make on the top of the slope . . . to go white, quiet, impassive as the mountains.

"It *has* to be this way," he said. "You'll see . . . later on . . . that I was right."

"Oh, it seems right, does it? If I were your wife, would it be this way? If I were your wife, would you say, 'OK, leave . . . I want to go it alone because you're miserable, wretched, so forget the marriage, the commitment be damned'? I dare you to say you would, *if I were your wife!* But, the mistress? Tell her to leave in the crunch, that's all right! It's not legal or holy, so it doesn't matter!"

She was screaming. It was almost funny, her depression was lifting by the second. Fight for it. Hers and Max's love. Stand at the door of the cave, tear anything apart that threatens to kill it. *This* was what they needed. It was the next chapter. She was elated, feeling stronger every second. "Max, *you're* not being honest, and it's not *me*, to yell and carry on. What are we charading about? What are we acting out? The word *love?*"

She pushed their lies against the wall and smashed them once and for all—his trying to make believe they didn't need each other to the end, and her fear that she would buckle under the pressure.

Max was shocked, particularly about the "wife" reference. "Please, don't make it harder than it is," he said.

"I'll make it as hard as I can. I'll make it anything I want. I *want* to fight, how about *that*, Max Treading? Say it out, damn it. You need me, you want me, you'll die sooner without me. You love me! Say it!"

"I say it," Max said in a whisper. "But it doesn't change my mind. I want you to leave . . ."

He turned away, to fill an unsure space, and picked up, almost by rote, a little book he had brought along with him; it was lying on the table next to his side of the bed. There was a red leather marker in it and it flipped open to a page where he had underlined something; he had forgotten what it was and looked closer.

"Put that book down," Hedda said. "Don't hide behind it."

He looked up with the most bewildered, sad expression she had ever seen, then he began to read, almost inaudibly, " 'We are put on earth a little space/That we may learn to bear the beams of love."

He walked to the window and looked out at the part of the ski slope that was visible (where Hedda had been watching him for days, and he didn't know). He saw figures whizzing down, small flashes of color, bodies filled with air, the thrill of flying.

" 'A little space,' " Max repeated. "A little space on a slope. A dot on the universe. 'That we may learn to bear . . .' " He choked. "Not pain . . . but, of all things, 'the beams of love.' They're worse than physical pain!"

He turned and looked at her. "I flunk! I can't handle it. I wanted you *not* to see, not to be part of it. I tried . . . I can't go it alone."

"You damn well better not think you could," Hedda said, filled with hilarity. She began to mimic him: "I don't want you around. I want you to go back to New York . . . Who was saying that?"

She went to him, teasing in her own light, round voice, "I want to be alone . . . Go away, love, I dare you to go away. Is that what you're saying?" She put her arms around him. "Is that what you want, you liar? For me to leave? Because I won't. Period."

She put her lips on his and let her tongue trace the shape of his upper lip, as though to press an indelible image into his mouth, to reach his brain and radiate down into every part of him. Enough of talk.

"Whatever bridge there is," she whispered, her saliva mixing with his, "we go over that bridge together."

What could he do? She was smashing the lies.

They stayed the week, determined to make it time in limbo, a new perception of time. It was like casting away Newton's laws in practicality and getting drunk on Einstein's relativity. Even beyond that . . . Could anyone imagine a beyond-that? They made their own time, rolling in white sheets, white snow. The only disquieting thing was that Max was very out of breath when they made love. He gasped for air. It must be the altitude, he thought.

They skied, stood on the top of the slope and looked at the white, killer mountains around them. Everything white, virgin white, a trembling first. Gstaad was a manger with all the trappings of miraculous life. If the other guests in the chalet were too dumb to know, *they* did.

Actually, Max had been trembling most of the week. There was a heaviness, a dull pain in his chest that came and went. He attributed the sensations to too much emotion and air, or charley horse from so much exercise; he said nothing.

The last day, coming off the slope for a final run, Max collapsed. A first-aid crew carried him down on a stretcher. A doctor was called in from the village. Max's blood pressure had made a precipitous dive.

The doctor in his leather cap and embroidered suspenders examined him, then drew Hedda aside, out of earshot. "This man has been skiing? How could he? He's very ill. One of his lungs is filled with liquid. I don't like his color either. His blood count must be alarming, I think he should be moved to a hospital in Geneva."

"No, no! I've chartered a plane to Geneva to catch the next flight to New York. Would it be dangerous?"

"I can't answer that, madame . . ."

Hedda ran to the telephone and called Wesgrove to tell him what had happened. Wesgrove said, "Tell the doctor to start him on antibiotics, broad spectrum; then get him back here . . . on a stretcher, right to me at the Center, from the airport."

It was a very pale Treading who arrived at the Cancer Research Center via the ambulance entrance. The Swiss doctor had given him a tranquilizer to be taken when they boarded the plane in Geneva, and he had slept all the way to New York. He was rested enough to be completely exasperated. Arriving feet first was neither his style nor his plan. And, to be wheeled into a room on a floor filled with sick and dying—a part of the Center he had never seen—was the last straw. The situation had all the smells of *getting caught*.

Wesgrove greeted him with a strong handshake, ignoring everything he saw on Max's face. He had just had a short meeting with Hedda in the corridor.

After listening and thumping Max's back, more listening and thumping, and a quick conference with a technician who had already taken some blood, Wesgrove said, "You have fluid in your right lung. We have to remove it. Nothing drastic, just a single needle going in from the outside of your upper back, local anesthetic . . . a couple of days of watching. You'll be given an antibiotic intravenously. I know you don't want to be here, but you're going to have to stay here. You have a fever of a hundred and one. You were probably running a low-grade fever before that."

"I did feel shivery most of last week," Max admitted.

"Aha . . ."

"Aha what?" Max said.

"You might have picked up a viral pneumonia," Wesgrove said optimistically, weighing in his own mind the alternatives.

"Are you telling me straight?"

"Maybe." Wesgrove was trying for the brusque truth that had delineated their past relationship. "I have to take the fluid out first and see what's in it. If it's bacterial, if it's viral . . . it can go away with antibiotics. If the fever persists and the lung fills up again . . . I would want to go in and do a bronchoscopy, take a piece of tissue from the lung for analysis."

"I won't give you permission for that," Max said.

"I didn't think you would. Anyway, let's not cross bridges before we have to." Wesgrove stopped talking. Max watched him thinking.

"And . . . ?" said Max.

"If it clears up, I want to put you on an immunization drug again."

"I didn't know I was taking one."

"You were, along with two other drugs. The three of them, in concert, brought about the remission. We have a new immunizing agent. I'd like to try it by itself this time."

"Did I read about it in the newspapers?" Max said blandly.

"No, it's too new. It's . . . we'll talk about it later." Cheerful levelness was in his voice, like that of the patient parent wiping the spilled milk of a child. "Collapsed on the slope, did you? No symptoms before that? You were feeling well?"

"Very well . . ."

"But, you overdid it. Skied all day long, like a teenager?"

"Hedda told you?"

"Yes, she did. She also told me a few other things. I'm glad you worked it out between you."

"What do you mean by that?"

"You know what I mean."

"There are no secrets, are there," said Max.

"Not from the interested parties, Max. I'm afraid that's the way it is."

Again, more blood tests, painful bone marrow tests, only this time from a hospital bed. Max didn't like it at all. He was swaying on the outermost strand of the spider's web, about to be pushed to the next strand, the next.

After the fluid was removed from the right lung (with a very long needle, he turned his head away) he felt pretty rotten for a couple of days, with a fever going up and down; but the antibiotic, whatever it was, was working. He didn't want to know its name. All of a sudden he didn't want to know the specifics, the claptrap of scientific words that rendered the layman dumb.

The fourth day, the fever stayed down and he began to walk around the corridors, dragging his intravenous pole behind him. He couldn't stand being part of the scene—patients in every stage of terminal cancer, walking, sitting . . . and the ones attached to machines. There was a low hum of respirators in the air. Outside those rooms sat families in total quiet, looking at one another. Their eyes were their mouths. Max didn't like it at all. His fever was gone but he marched up and down, in sweats, watching everything intently. He began to talk with nurses, a few family members who would share snatches of their tragedies. He peeked into rooms, sat in the visitors' lounge like an interstellar guest invited to observe a special existence on Earth.

A nightmare projection began to form in his head, a slow-moving picture of the last scenes of his life:

The pneumonia wouldn't go away. It wasn't pneumonia, he was being lied to. His white blood count had to be boosted because his immune system had broken down completely. He would be in a room marked *Do not enter without a mask,* lest the breath of another human send him on his way. From now on, he would only see the eyes of people. Days would go by, punctuated by flurries of excitement. Transfusions, infusions. Rising, sinking. Gradually, his kidneys would stop functioning. A catheter would be inserted in his penis. Slow or fast, his lungs would fill with liquid and he wouldn't be able to breathe on his own. He would be moved to that special section where the monitoring machines were, the final ride to death row, the other patients banging on the sides of their beds to say good-bye. He would be attached to a respirator.

He would lie in that special place, hearing everything, knowing everything, suffering the touches and tears from the outside. His eyes, like the soft-slipping hands of a drowning man on floating debris, would clutch at faces. He wouldn't be able to speak because of the tubes in his throat and nose. He would lie listening to the sound of his respirator. The noise would be driving him mad. They would put another tube into him, into his stomach, because it would be bleeding in terror.

He would make a decision *not* to breathe along with the respirator and bells would start to ring. Nurses would come running, scold him for not cooperating with the machine. *They would not allow him to die.* They would advance the respirator's actions, pump more oxygen into him. *That* would make his mind clear as a bell, even more anguished and exquisitely aware that *he could never choose not to breathe, or the bells would ring.* They would keep bringing him back. His privacy had already died. His lips would be dry, his nose caked with blood from the irritation of the tubes in his nostrils. He would look like a wild, mad horse with a cruel bit in his mouth. His eyes would signal a wish for ice, as if it were a gift from the Magi. A nurse would tell him he could have ice on his lips if he was a good boy and cooperated with the machine. Max Treading, age fifty-five, Martha Treading's boy, born between a mesa and a butte, internationally known financier, would be lying like a mortally wounded buck and be scolded by a stranger for not being "a good boy."

Hedda would come into his room. He would writhe in sadness as she approached the bed. Or Phoebe . . . They would stand together, their faces white as monastery monks'. Roz would be there too, not near the bed, but standing at a window, her back to him. He would cry without crying. Somehow, in the middle of one day or night, he would start to slip away . . . too slowly, mortified, going into the darkness, angry, helpless, with grace denied, his eyes not clutching the light anymore.

Lucky again. It was a viral infection. Max went home after twelve days. Wesgrove gave him another week to take it easy. After that, they would start the new round of chemotherapy, he said.

The hospital stay made Max even more determined *never* to get sucked in again. How easy it was to be rushed in, with symptoms to be treated *immediately.* No question, modern medicine was a miracle for some; it could even be God (if there was one) moving in His modern way. The respirator for a heart attack victim (whom God intended to live) was like the touch of Christ. But, to sustain life because one couldn't sustain it by oneself? *Never,* Max concluded. If he ever wavered on *that,* he would just have to recall his fantasy.

It was good to be home . . . with Phoebe, Hedda, the two cats, smiling doormen, the cook wild on fattening him up, a winter Central Park streaming through the windows. He felt a bit weak, but wouldn't anyone after a bout with pneumonia?

Should he go the next round with Wesgrove, make cancer his business again, talk to his cells again? Wesgrove had tried to talk with him a little, but Max didn't want to listen . . . about bodies, antibodies, drugs, radiation, new marrow, old marrow. He refused to tune in. He was going to enjoy his favorite fruit —peaches. Peach Melba. Cornish hen with peaches. Fresh peaches flown in from South America. Phoebe's cheeks. Hedda's breasts.

A subtle change was causing different rhythms even in the most trivial of his actions: where he lay his toothbrush, left his clothes, how he opened a door, sat, stood, walked. There was a looseness about everything; a new consciousness had been transplanted into the cavity of his old one. It was the word *must* removed from his brain. Every act felt inspirational. There was much he had to do, but he was going to do it slowly, like a sleepwalker in a beautiful dream from which he did *not* want to be wakened.

FROM THE JOURNAL OF DR. HIRAM WESGROVE, MARCH 10, 1982

Syzygy—the yoking together, alignment of several celestial bodies —should have occurred today. The planets weren't lined up though, they were scattered. Does the Universe, too, make mistakes, or just mortal astronomers? (!)

May 19, 2161, is the next time a grand syzygy is expected—when eight planets (excluding Pluto) will be found within 69 degrees of each other.

Jeff Gruening, our favorite jokester—biopsychiatrist, put the word on my desk today, to give me a laugh, I suppose, maybe a little perspective, to remind me that all is nothing and nothing is all. The death of two monkeys today has unduly upset me; they had been doing so well, so bravely. Yes, I'm sure they were brave, cooperative, patient. What other choice did they have? Particularly those two, who had been living in the lab so long. I swear I picked up signals that they were proud to be part of the confusion and search. What did they teach us? That general anesthesia in the removal of local tumor increases risk of metastasis, if not done at precisely the proper moment. Why? The operation seems to accelerate release of aberrant cells to build a mass somewhere else immediately. Is there an agent-chemical in anesthesia that acts as a booster, a confuser of the immune system intelligence? Yet another semiotic situation that has to be decoded. You thrust the cells into apathy, you awaken them, they get raving mad to reestablish their arcane identity, their will. I'm going to suggest acupuncture for the next two monkeys waiting in the wings. Let's try not to shock the little ones, the cells with evil intention, so that we may better chart their nefarious courses. Acupuncture on animals? Why not? And see what happens . . .

So much for March 10.

I've been reading ancient Chinese poetry to relax. It's not doing the trick during this period, as we approach the ides of March. What I really need is to get up to Maine and fish.

Worried about Max Treading. The balancing act is becoming too reckless, and without a net underneath.

12

Max's illusion of a sleepwalking dream was over in a matter of weeks. He was back in his office on the top floor of the Treading Building, with its view of two rivers, distant trees and bridges, the harbor to the south, other skyscrapers reflecting fast-moving clouds on their miles of glass. There was no quiet outside or inside Max. The movement, power, irritability, excitement of the city whammed through the windows of his office on shafts of light. Trying to revive his old energies for what he had to do—if he lived the year out—he was having many silent conversations with Phoebe as he pushed to tie up the ends of his huge fortune. (Honey, money is existential, it is and it isn't; it doesn't matter and it matters; it changes character according to whose it is, but good or bad, it is . . . so you better learn about it fast when I'm gone. I'm leaving you a lot of it!)

Max had two fortunes to think about—one from Global Materials, the other his personal wealth. Only his lawyer, Dinessen, had some notion of the latter's immensity and Max's reckless machinations with it. He had investments in most troubled areas of the world, *by plan:* with one hand, making millions in certain countries, doing business with the juntas of every stripe; with the other hand, putting the money back through the rear door—to help foot the bills of those not in power. Dangerous covert games.

The games he played with Global Materials were more careful. A board of directors had to be contended with, not to mention stockholders, even though he owned fifty-four percent of the stock. But he had one more game he still had to convince the board to go for. Not only Global's fist, but its heart had to be in the new age coming—for Phoebe.

Max called a meeting of the board of directors of Global Materials in April. Each member wondered at the broad scope of the agenda: Strategic raw materials and estimated reserves. Copper, bauxite, manganese, chrome, cobalt, columbium. Jamaica, Suriname, Guyana, Haiti, the Dominican Republic, Zaire, Zambia, the Congo. Emigrant Basin. (Boiled down it was —metals for high-tech, and solar.)

What was Max doing? It would take hours, if not days! Was he out of his mind?

Max kept doodling *1982* as he waited for them to arrive: An extraordinary clutch of men, business virtuosi. In the financial journals they were called "the Treading Gang." Pritchard, representative of old man Walleby's investment interests (Sophia's father had died recently at the grand old age of ninety); Barnett, in charge of Latin America; Wilcox, domestic and Canadian holdings; Palmer, responsible for soybeans and the agrobusiness; Boseman, public affairs; Achmeyer, Asian and African resources; Verdolino, banker and treasurer. The men had nothing in common as individuals except the unique success of Global Materials, and their admiration for and trust in the phenomenon of Maxwell Treading, plus a respect for one another's expertise and talents. No one knew that Max had been fighting cancer for the last half a year. They all assumed his bouts with illness were the slow way back from the helicopter crash.

Max jumped right into it. "The Emigrant Basin land, my

friends. It's been sitting there for a year. We have the patents, we have the place, we have the money. What are we waiting for?"

"Too costly to jump right into the main thrust, Max," Barnett responded. "The patents have to be tested first. They're just theory. We're willing to go with a pilot structure in Puerto Rico. It wouldn't be in the limelight; cheap labor, and all around cheaper if it fails."

"Don't agree," Max said. "Rosen and Blunt's blueprints, have they been studied? They looked good to me a year ago, and to you too, Wilcox. They haven't gone bad in a year, have they?"

"You're talking about a new subsidiary of Global when you talk Emigrant Basin," Verdolino, the treasurer, responded.

"That's right. And, won't we be pleased in twenty years?"

Wilcox spoke cautiously. "I think we've held back, Max, because it means getting into the consumer market."

"Damn right. It'll be Global Solar batteries instead of General Electric bulbs. What's wrong with that?"

"Nothing, if Rosen and Blunt are right," said Verdolino.

"Risk," Pritchard, Walleby's man, muttered. If he hadn't said it, Max would have been surprised. That's why Pritchard was there—to say "risk."

"I say—no risk. I say—common sense. We've been there before. You resisted me years ago when I said, 'Buy into the overthrust belt,' and look what we've got now—the biggest reserves of oil and gas in the country. I said then, 'It'll prove out.' Was I wrong? No." Max paused. "I also said: 'Let's get out of the Arab scene in the sixties and concentrate on a big hold of the Western Hemisphere potential, 'cause the Arabs are gonna blow themselves up.' Was I wrong? Have you ever seen such a mess of thieves eating crow, like the OPECs? They're gonna eat themselves alive before they're finished. We've got our own problems, but at least we're closer to them in the Americas. Mexico didn't get out of hand, did it? They nationalize? We service them with the hardware. They're so grateful, they cut us into the resource pie." He paused again. "Let's face it. I've dragged you along every inch of the way, and what's happened?

Global has its eye on the future like no other. I'm saying now
—Global has the capacity to get into *solar* and we're not going
to sit on it. You haven't come up with any impressive counter-
figures to say that Rosen and Blunt aren't right. I'm sure they
are. *They've got it.* I say we go . . . not with a piddling around
in Puerto Rico. I say we go with the whole hog in Emigrant
Basin, even if it costs a hundred million!"

His behavior was unusual, abrasive, urgent. He had always
seduced them into a position, never demanded it. They had no
idea he was fighting against time.

Barnett, the closest to Max of them all, said, "We'll have to
do a search. Who could head up the new company? No one
knows anything about it, except academics. That's not sound
footing. Solar in research is one thing. Solar in business
is . . ."

Max interrupted. "Everyone in this room could manage the
solar business if they had to. What you're saying is: You're afraid
of the giant step." He broke into one of his smiles. "You don't
know what I'm doing for you . . ."

Verdolino responded. "Don't tell me, I know. We'll be roaring our way to the bank!"

"Yes," Max said bemused. He looked around the room.
"Let's put it to a vote, and remember when you're doing it—
Blunt isn't just a physicist, he's an industrial engineer; the plant
blueprints are already done, based on the Rosen theory; they've
worked together for ten years, they trust each other, and we can
always give Blunt an operational manager. Nothing to worry
about, you see . . ."

History had taught the Treading Gang that going down
the primrose path with him usually ended up right. But this
new one? It was like footing the bills for the first shot at the
moon. Yet, they didn't dare *not* take the risk—with a Jew and
a Scot at M.I.T. who'd come up with patents that could push
Global into the twenty-first century. Everyone but Pritchard,
representing the *old money* of Walleby Investments, voted
"Yes."

"Thank you, " Max said. "You can sleep well. Our competitors are buying up the solar patents and tucking them away, trying to stave it off. There isn't a resource business that isn't crouched, wagging its fanny at the start line of solar. The fellows over at Exxon wouldn't have given me the vote today. *If they had the patents of Rosen and Blunt, they'd do it, sure, but they'd do it late* and careful. Global has never been late." He stopped, walked to the west window, and looked out past the gleaming ribbon of the Hudson River. "I want to say something sentimental for a change. Even if I were a dying man, I'd say . . . there's no such thing as death, if you've done something to link yourself into the future . . ." (They looked at one another. What a strange remark. Max's cheeks were flushed, he didn't look like himself.) "And," Max went on, "that's where we'll be, before anyone else . . . *mining* the sun, thanks to Rosen and Blunt, mark my words." This was his last strategy move with Global, he was sure of that, and there was nothing sentimental about it; it was pure irony.

All through April, Max pored over his own portfolios. He arrived home every night exhausted. Trying to hide it from Hedda was futile. They got into the habit of having dinner in their bedroom, so that Max could lie down the minute he got in. It had become a pleasant, though confining ritual, but Hedda made believe it was her wish too, and in a way it was. They had loving, quiet, precious hours; like children sailing in a great big boat that was a bed. They never spoke of it happening, but each knew it was—Max was losing his strength. He was so grateful to her for playing the game of bed, oasis. They watched the evening news; they had a drink; the butler brought them dinner. Afterward, sometimes they played cards or talked while Max had a few brandies. Sometimes they just fell asleep cheek to cheek, or lip to lip. Sometimes he couldn't do more than that, yet she made him feel he had done *everything.*

It was early in May that Hedda dared to say, "What are you doing? I don't think Dr. Wesgrove would approve of your eight-hour day. Can't other people take care of things for now?"

"I'm tying up the private ends," Max said, looking at her directly to see if he could see in her eyes that he was dying.

"You mean you're making out your will? Good for you. Even I have one."

"I'm doing more than a will, baby," Max laughed, shaking his head. "I'm an arrogant son of a bitch. I'm playing around with redemption . . . on earth. Because it sure as hell isn't anywhere else, not that I know of."

They had never talked about money before. Hedda was separate from his work life; he had never shared it with her. She was so new, so young in his old life . . . He began to, he wanted her to know who he was; it relaxed him to tell her who he was. He described the board meeting on solar energy. It was amusing to see her incredulity. "Since Wall Street won't go under unless there's an atomic attack, why not play with it, shock it, manipulate it, drive down energy costs in a few years for *the people*. There are sneaky things one can do and still show corporate profit, I've done it many times . . ." He got a faraway look that was to become familiar to her.

Max was thinking: Does she know she's keeping me going? How can she tolerate a relationship in a splint? She's allowing me to be supremely selfish, like a child. . . . (Actually, Hedda was finding it very difficult. Everything he said was colored in tones of finality, looking back, justification . . .)

"Do you mind my talking about Sophia?" Max asked. "I've been thinking about her, I can't help it, she shared in half my life . . ." He turned his head away so she wouldn't see his expression. "Hedda, I'm wrapping it up, that's what I'm doing, and it hurts like hell . . ."

"You're not wrapping it up, you're living and feeling," Hedda said desperately. "You're doing it with me. We're doing it together . . ." She didn't know whether he heard her because he had to keep on talking, talking.

"I used her. She was so beautiful, it made it easier. A damn lucky ladder her father was for me. I used them and laughed at them—it made her crazy. There was no difference between

Sophia's crowd and Marie Antoinette's except the plumbing
. . . no peeing against walls or squatting over holes *now*, but the
let-'em-eat-cake was still going strong. I kept rubbing their noses
in what they were and they didn't like it . . . They weren't living
a lie, they were just who they were. The narcissism of the rich
is an incredible thing. It's kind of a miracle I didn't fall into that
shit. I didn't yacht-it or whore-it . . ."

"Not even a little?" Hedda teased.

Max didn't think that was funny. "I chose the women I
cheated with very carefully!"

"Me too?"

"When Sophia died, I didn't have to cheat. Anyway, I didn't
choose you, I fell in love with you . . ."

"Thank you, m'lord . . ."

They played the game of king and queen in bed. The king
would overcome the queen, she had no recourse but to give in.
It made Max feel strong, which was what she wanted. Childhood games—they had worked in April, but the beginning of
May brought changes. He began to look fragile, thinner. Wesgrove, in one of the secret meetings Hedda asked for, confided
that Max's chemotherapy had been stopped. It wasn't being
effective so he was receiving placebos to make him think there
was hope for another remission. "We're afraid of trying something new with him because it might lay him low. He made me
promise never to do that. The man is alive on character alone.
Anything to help that mystery is not a lie, so I assuage myself
of guilt."

If the shadows hadn't been gathering, Hedda would have
found it exhilarating—Max's sharing with her the part of him
she had never known: Power and money.

"What to do with it, when you really have it?" Max said.
"You know what I've been doing? Making new grants to universities in science, medicine, engineering—advanced programs
only. If my money's going to mean anything, it's for New
Knowledge. Capital *N*, capital *K*. There aren't enough American students who can afford advanced studies, to become profes-
sors or stay in pure science. Japan's way ahead of us. There also

isn't enough money for academic research or lab equipment
. . . Can you believe that, in the richest country in the world?"
He had been sending off notes to university presidents, notes so
informal, they were shocked, reading what looked like an
interoffice memo, to discover it was a million-dollar gift to set
up a chair in molecular biology, magnetics, physics, chemistry
. . . scribbled in longhand.

In one voice, Max would share with her: "You know what
I did today? I gave a lot of money to some small seacoast countries, so they can vie with and protect themselves from the
conglomerates, including Global!, who'll be mining the ocean
floor like catfish in the 1990s. The manganese, nickel, copper
deposits at the bottom of the sea are limitless!"

In another voice, he'd ask her to lie naked next to him. He
would stroke her, look at her and say, "You know what you are?
A hybrid! A cross between Rubens and Picasso. You're giving
me everything . . ." His fingers played with her hair, touched
the velvet underside of her thighs while he muttered, "I know
the world I'm leaving . . . it's who owns *what*—under the
ground, the water, in the air, Greed . . ." He traced the shape
of her eyes. "The crazy Kewpie doll won't fall down dead in an
atomic blast, I'll bet your sweet life on that . . . Though it might
seem like the end, the fight between the haves and have-nots is
gonna get so hot . . ." He rolled toward her, put his arms around
her and whispered . . . "I love you . . ." He couldn't turn the
world off. In the next breath it was, "No, it's gonna be a slow-
rolling revolution in human behavior that's gonna do it . . . Too
many people on earth know too much now . . . Man is gonna
have to change if he wants to keep on hugging the beautiful
blue-green planet . . ." He had leaned away from her, into his
pillows, and was staring at the ceiling.

Hedda felt she was living a nightmare, forced to eat a banana split of *everything*, because in the next minute he was making love, not in the old vigorous way, but in the new way—slow
and sad; not with physical passion but with almost a psychic
sexuality. It made her love him in an excruciatingly painful way.
Sometimes she felt she was in him, not he in her.

. . .

Three months had gone by, with Max playing his own brand of Monopoly—with real money. Great fun . . . if it weren't for the pains in his back and leg, the crippling weakness. The thought that he wouldn't be around to see the fruits of his activity was like the buzz of a solitary fly blown into a room against its will.

The buzz had become a roar. He knew things were very wrong again. Not in his head. Inside his cheating body.

By the end of May, Wesgrove was looking at Max's charts with grave apprehension. Max was running a low-grade fever again. Wesgrove had only to look at Max to see that the pains had returned full force, that his patient had been pushing himself for weeks before uttering a word.

Wesgrove observed the pallor, the shrinking, tightening aspects of a cancer victim about to enter the crucial stages of the fight—a slender tree bracing itself. It could survive if there were juice and resilience inside. The cancer victim was getting hollow, dry, anything could topple it, snap the trunk and expose the eaten-away pulp.

Max broke down and confided that there was a new discomfort—pain when he urinated. Pain in the bones was easier. You could imagine it to be neuralgia, the weather, a twisted muscle. But, when you didn't pee right . . . then, *what you were,* from all the time you could remember, *wasn't anymore* and there was no returning. Your body was leaving you. He knew he was galloping into darkness before Wesgrove had to tell him.

"How long have you been hugging these lousy secrets?"

"Three weeks."

"That wasn't fair, was it?"

"I had too much to do."

"I see . . ."

"Do you?"

"Well," said Wesgrove, "now that we both know there are sharp reversals . . . not that we didn't expect them . . ." (He didn't quite know how to proceed.)

"What's the kidney thing all about?" Max asked, as though it weren't his.

"Too much protein excreted, infection, eventual kidney damage—the initial stage of what's known as the myeloma kidney. In the advanced state, the tubes get blocked."

"How long do I have and under what conditions, since I'm not going to let you do anything else?"

Wesgrove took a deep, thinking breath. "Maybe a few months."

This time, Max couldn't hide his shock. "That's all?"

"Knowing you, it could be more."

"In pain?"

"Yes. Weakness, pain, then probably pneumonia because your immune system is breaking down."

"Then, this is it," Max said firmly.

"Yes, if you don't permit me to experiment with new agents and use what knowledge we have. I need your permission."

"No, Wes, not for me." Max paused. "How *much* pain in the next months?"

"We'd make you comfortable."

"At home?"

"If that's the way you want it."

"This is it, isn't it?" Max said faintly.

"Yes, if we do it your way. You'll probably die of a stubborn viral pneumonia, not cancer."

"Suffocating in my own water."

"We could put a small respirator in your room. You can afford it. Others can't." There was an uncharacteristic edginess in Wesgrove's voice. He was suppressing anger. No one had ever rejected his judgments before or challenged his Hippocratic oath to heal till death. "Max, if I told you we have a new serum and we need to experiment with it . . . would you be interested, in the name of science?"

"No!"

"Then, that's it. I can do nothing but make you comfortable." He looked at Max squarely. "There's no other way to talk now, we're playing by your rules. I'll respect them and tell you what's happening as it happens."

"You mean, watch me die a natural death?"

"Yes, a natural death." Wesgrove allowed himself a cynical smile. "Illustrious men in their days—before serum and antisepsis—died of earache, kidney stones, even tooth decay. Ignominious, but natural."

Max looked at him closely. "You're with me, I'm grateful for that, believe me, I am. I'm making you go against your grain, I . . ."

Wesgrove interrupted, "Would you like to know a speculation of mine? My suspicion—your body held fast for years, but you contracted cancer way back when you were a young man, from too much radiation in that first uranium mine of yours, when everyone was sloshing around in the waste and didn't know what in hell they were up to. I think your immune system was so strong, it fought off the disease for half your life. The shock of the helicopter crash just might have been responsible for giving the cancer cells their chance to take over in a traumatized and weakened body. What is it, thirty years ago—the stories you told me about your mother and the old minister?"

"Hell, I was up to my ass in uranium, with the Elephant Mine."

"You should see the figures coming in thirty years later, on American Indians who either lived near or worked in the mines. There's no mistaking the connection. Cancer, cancer, cancer. The medical literature on it is piling up, if you know where to look. And it's still being denied officially. Cancer from job radiation gets raked under shockingly easy, too. The incidences are like pieces of sea glass buried in a beach of two hundred million people. Only the medical profession can find them. Sometimes, they take thirty years to uncover."

Max was alert, slightly stunned. He was thinking of McGregor, the old minister, turning his back on uranium—

"God's punishment for the evil in Man"—and saying, "You have to have a moral payoff, boy, or you're in league with the Devil." If McGregor was right, his cancer was the payoff for the Elephant Mine and the beginning of Fortune.

"So, I'm a piece of sea glass, eh?" Max began to laugh. "Wes, you know I'm not going to die a 'natural death.' Let's stop avoiding it. You know I'm going to commit suicide. The only question is: How? What's the most efficient way? I've saved up enough pills to fell an elephant, I think." He came up close to a shaken Wesgrove. "You're my friend and doctor. Isn't that the best way? Two hundred pills should do it, don't you think? With no slipup? I used to be a two-hundred-pounder. I'm down to one-sixty."

"Where did you get two hundred pills and what kind?" It was asked with as little emotion as Wesgrove could manage.

"Demerol. Where I got it is my business."

"It could become my business *and the law's.*"

"Don't worry. I'll write a letter to be attached to my will, absolving my personal physician, Hoffstadter, and you from any involvement. Just tell me, is two hundred enough? Mixed with a lot of brandy?"

"What's the strength of the Demerol?"

"One hundred milligrams. Give me a straight answer."

"You've got enough to kill, a baby elephant. Forty pills would be more than enough for you."

"I'm home free."

Wesgrove's mind was working like greased lightning. He took Max completely by surprise. "How would you like to join me for a few days in Maine, see the old family house I talked about, do a little sailing?"

"Are you crazy? In my condition?"

Wesgrove paid no attention. "I'll show you how good I am with the wind. We've never done anything together except in this office and this building. The pine forests are a momentary cure in themselves. I think you're up to it . . ."

Max was taken aback. "You haven't been listening to me at all!"

"I have. I'm inviting you to join me in the woods. May's a great month for sailing . . . spring winds."

"Are you mad? You know I'm running a low-grade fever and I'm not peeing very well, and the pain in my back is . . ."

"Do you feel *very* bad?"

"I can take pain."

"You're accepting my invitation? You alone, you understand, not with Hedda."

"You wouldn't be planning a sailing accident, would you, to get me off the hook?" Max quipped. "Patient drowns on vacation with doctor." Wesgrove kept his face unreadable. "OK, Wes, maybe I should be a little flattered that you want to share free time with me before it's over. I *am* flattered, man." Max hesitated. "You're not planning to dissuade me, are you? It won't work. I've made up my mind. But why Maine? Why don't you just come visit at the apartment, like an ordinary friend? You never have . . . You've done your best, I know that, and I also know that I *have* made up my mind."

"I see you have, I'm respecting it more than you know. I need to get away and I'd like you to join me, let's call it my last prescription. *Will* you join me? I need to breathe in some nature and it would be good for you too." What Wesgrove said next Max interpreted as a funny kind of challenge and didn't know why. "You're still on your feet, you can take it . . . I want to share some special time with you, is that asking too much?"

"No, not after what you did for me this year, it's not too much . . . Maybe it wouldn't be a bad idea to walk in the woods," Max said reflectively. "OK, I'll go . . ."

Wesgrove suddenly changed into all business. He smashed his hands together, saying "Good!", then picked up a phone, adding, "I'm calling the lab upstairs. I'm going to give you something that might relieve the kidney problem . . . we don't want anything to go wrong with your kidneys while we're away. They haven't been invaded too much yet."

Wesgrove was doing something far afield from himself, and yet he knew he *had* to. He had never done anything underhanded professionally in his life, yet he was doing it for the first time and not even apologizing to himself. He also had never faced a patient intent upon suicide and not to be dissuaded. He had just given an order that Max receive a first dose of a new serum, one that had been deadly on one monkey and successful on another. In the light of what he had been planning for the past few months, *anticipating* Max's announcement of suicide, it was crucial to try anything to delay further deterioration in Max's body. He would share his thoughts and plan with Max . . . later. In the green woods of his childhood, in the house with memories of his parents, all that had fashioned and influenced him . . . *he had to do it there, where he knew himself best.* Because he was becoming someone he almost didn't know—reckless, fanciful. But revolution was never achieved by a conservative! Max was someone who could savor that premise and agree. Max was the only one who could help him in what could be the most unusual experiment of his life, a wild experiment for a friend who was about to die one way or another.

13

Max's jet was waiting for them at La Guardia Airport; it transported them, in what seemed like a few minutes, to Bangor, Maine . . . where a helicopter waited to pick them up and deposit them on a low-tide beach below the weathered clapboard Wesgrove family home, twenty miles up the coast from Bar Harbor.

Wesgrove was bemused, being snatched up in the style of Max's life outside the Cancer Research Center. The extraordinarily rich evidently transport themselves in the wink of an eye, on imaginary red carpets. Luggage is delivered by magic, unpacked by a genie—Max's man, Jeff. Why a valet for an old gray house in the woods? Wesgrove needn't have worried about the intrusion. The man disappeared to stay in a motel ten miles away, until called for.

Max laughed when Wesgrove commented: "Do you always travel as though you were meeting Churchill at Yalta?"

"Always. It's one of the dividends of having too much. Disconnect from the trivial and your mind is in top form for anything. I got used to it a long time ago, traveling like a king, not worrying about underwear and where to put it. My excesses have been small. Don't accuse me of vulgarity. Your face looks like a New England conscience."

"I'm envious, I suppose. I waste a lot of time looking for socks, hailing cabs, and standing in line for tickets."

"Nobel Prize winners should have private jets and valets, old man . . . and I'm going to see to it that you do."

"Ridiculous," Wesgrove spurted. "I've always had all the money I ever needed, maybe more." He was frightened by Max's implication of a personal windfall. "It's not I who need funding, it's the whole field of cancer research."

"I know that, and I intend to do something about it."

"Max, I would rather you wouldn't share such thoughts with me, not now, at any rate. Definitely not now."

"You mean not in this room, not for the next two days?"

"Yes, if you please." Wesgrove's response was almost severe.

Max looked about at the large, friendly living room of the old house, with its gray wicker chairs, ancient pillows on window seats facing the ocean, the books and bric-a-brac of generations, the worn floor and doorsills thinned by children's feet, and their children's feet, on and on for a hundred years. Permanency struck his heart, the immutable nest where little boys snuggered down on window seats looking at the immutable ocean, the water vying with the house as to which would outlive the other, and both winning, it seemed.

It was Max's turn to be envious. It made him think of his mother and the ranch. Both were ghosts. He felt like crying. He felt as random as desert grass growing just to get trampled by hooves racing somewhere else. How he would have liked being embraced by a clapboard house, its continuing history, an ocean that repelled strangers and welcomed its own. His mesas and buttes, the only landscape of his heart, were aloof cats, always keeping proper distance. He had dug into them like a hungry beast, mining the land, clawing the surface, making tunnels, extricating riches—to make up for the loneliness. He began to see himself in a strange perspective. He was the West, the strong, angry, greedy pioneer. Wesgrove was the East—civilized, protected, contained, connected. Martha was a tree planted by a madman (his father) in the desert. She had dared the desert to blow a wind big enough to fell her. Instead, the West had grasped her with its arms and thighs, entwined itself with her spirit. *That* was *his* inheritance.

Why has he brought me here? What difference, that I know what is his and what he loves? The little man obviously loved where they were—his family pictures glinting in their dusty gold and silver frames, his trees, house, ocean, coast. What is this man to me, that I could say yes? Max answered himself. This man has given me an extra year of my life, therefore he towers over every other man I have known. *That's* why I'm here. I owe him! Another thought perplexed him. This man has something up his sleeve, his time is too precious for a weekend with no meaning.

Ever since they arrived, Wesgrove tried to observe Max without his being aware; he watched for a shaking, a tremor, even disorientation, convulsion—some of the responses of certain monkeys to the new serum; *yet, with others,* there had been a shrinking of blockage and tumor in the cancer-affected areas.

So far, so good. It was almost twenty-four hours since the first injection. With Max's history of tolerance, Wesgrove prayed he would respond like one of the successful monkey experiments. If not, he had brought the means to stop negative reaction, or, at least, the antidote that worked on monkeys, God help him. He would have to confess to Max later what he had done . . . after they had their talk . . . which was why they were here.

They dined on frankfurters and beans, efficiently cooked up by Wesgrove. They talked very little through the supper, each looking out at the darkening ocean. The water pulsed like molten blue metal heated from fathoms below; on the surface, it was being colored by jumping patches of silver and orange, from the setting sun. Max began to feel it was a brilliant idea of Wesgrove's, a last drug—woods and the ocean.

Then, the order from Wesgrove: "Early to bed." Up the creaky staircase . . .

As Max started to climb into his brass four-poster he was overcome with a fit of shaking. He held on to one of the bedposts. God, what now? The franks? Violent indigestion? It wasn't his stomach, his whole body was shaking and wouldn't stop. He rested his head on the cold metal post and called out before he hit the floor.

Wesgrove came running, observed the seizure, ran out and came back with a hypodermic. In a matter of seconds it was over. Max lay on the floor in a pool of sweat and looked up. "What in hell was that?"

A guilty Wesgrove answered, "You'll be all right. It's my fault. It was the injection you got yesterday—the new serum you said 'no' to—to see if we could stave off blockage in your kidneys. If it worked for a while, as it's done in some of our animals, it would give us more time to . . ."

"To what, man!"

"To plan an alternative . . . before your organs are destroyed," Wesgrove said apologetically. "I've never done such a thing—used a human without his knowing. I *must* make you understand, but not now, not tonight." He left the bedroom before Max could catch his breath or explode with outrage . . . "What alternative?!"

Max lay in the bed, an old comforter strewn with faded red stars pulled up to his neck. The night air of the old house was uncomfortable, damp, acrid-smelling. It was unbearable! It came from the ocean. It came from the bully-smell of heavy green forest, mixed with salt and eons of fish, dead and alive. It was nauseating. He would leave in the morning. Enough of Wesgrove.

The man had no place in his life now, he had done something unforgivable. He had given him an injection of a dangerous chemical without telling him. That was not to be forgiven. As he tried to make himself go to sleep, Max began to think of his first negative impressions of Wesgrove . . . the magic man, shaman, salesman of medical voodoo, the victimizer, the fascist who pulled the strings of the helpless sick doll.

Max felt feverish. Well, that wasn't something new, he'd

been feverish for a long time. A pain in his back suddenly shot up like fire and then put itself out. That wasn't new, either. He'd lived with that for a long time. What had Wesgrove really given him? A fat, big, horrible almost-year. It would soon be over, if he had the strength to get out of bed and call Jeff at the motel . . . who would get the helicopter . . . that would meet the jet . . . that would get him to his own bed . . . and then . . . Sleep. How he would relish the eternal sleep! The phrase came out like a shocker. *Eternal sleep.* He had never used it in his whole life . . .

Max was astonished when he woke the next morning. He had actually fallen asleep during the night, despite the terrible smells, and had awakened free from pain. Was it the injection? No, the mysterious witch had her way of pressing against him and disappearing.

Wesgrove's dishonorable act had depressed him terribly. He'd had every intention of telling him, but woke without that feeling or intention. He woke curiously quiet. Wesgrove had turned into a stumbling human—like everyone else—because of his deceit. He wouldn't challenge him, but he'd stay the weekend. Just by being silent, he would force him to admit to the personal betrayal. He didn't call Jeff at the motel to come and get him.

Hot coffee and oatmeal swimming with heavy cream and scotch were waiting when Max came downstairs. The old house was freezing but the wood stove in the kitchen crackled hot and the sun poured in from every window. If Max hadn't been feeling so dour and removed, he might have enjoyed the scene —the little man bustling around in an apron, saying, "Oatmeal and scotch, *a must* on a brisk morning, according to my mother, and it works!" He jabbered away about the fine weather, the names of the people in the dusty, gold and silver frames, anecdotes about Cousin This and Great-Aunt That . . . as though there were nothing else on his mind. Max hated oatmeal but he ate it dutifully, like a little boy, having to admit silently that it warmed you from the inside out. Then suddenly Wesgrove announced, "We're going sailing. Take a slicker from one of the hooks in the back entry," and he was out the door before Max could say "No!"

Why am I following him? Max said to himself as he made his way down the stony path to the dock. The man is mad, or he's got me hypnotized! Wesgrove was already standing in a fine, little sailboat with the name *DNA* emblazoned on its stern.

"Hop in! The weather's perfect!"

They were caught in the wind immediately. "Would you like to take the tiller when I get us out of the cove?" Wesgrove shouted.

"No," Max said, huddled down in the old slicker, which was so stiff and gnarled from countless sails, it could have steered the boat itself. "I don't know anything about sailing and I'm not going to start now!" Water wasn't where Max wanted to be, he felt chilled to the bone, paranoid. The oatmeal wasn't working because he was sick unto death and Wesgrove *knew* that! He was making him catch pneumonia so he could rush him back to the Center, pump him full of chemicals against his will —to have the last word and control.

There was nothing to do but hunch down, wait it out, and pray, with salt in his eyes, salt in his mouth . . . and listen to a crazy little man shouting in the wind about what a brilliant day it was. The man was going to kill him one way or another, he was sure of that.

Back up the coast against the wind, it wasn't so easy. They kept going out into the ocean and coming back. They were standing still, going nowhere. Large swells kept coming at them from the ocean side. They were going to capsize, drown! "Christ, why can't we go in a straight line?" Max finally screamed out in panic.

"Ah!" Wesgrove called out. "You don't want to die! Wonderful! Neither do I!"

Max burst out laughing. The situation was totally ludicrous. Here he was, hanging on to the side of a boat for dear life, afraid of drowning, when his only wish was to be in his bed, take pills, and have done with it. If he wasn't so terrified of the swells that threatened to sweep over them, he would have kept on laughing.

"Don't worry," Wesgrove yelled back to him. "We'll fool the kit an' caboodle, sly devils! Wind and water! You go right when they think you're going left! That's the fun of it!"

"Sailing's a cheating game," Max yelled back. "Get us off this thing. Do you know what you're doing?"

Max couldn't see it, but there was a little smile on Wesgrove's face, busy as he was, tacking in and out, making careful, sure triangles out of their course up the coast. He was a grand sailor. There was nothing to worry about, not for one moment, though Wesgrove did say, as they walked up the cliff path to the house, "There'll be a storm by tonight, it always starts with those sneaky swells. Didn't check with the Coast Guard this morning, probably should have . . . But it cleared my head. You didn't enjoy it, did you?"

"No!"

"I'm sorry. We'll keep you on land for the rest . . . I'll go out myself tomorrow morning. I get up here so seldom." He looked at a very dislocated Max. "I'm truly sorry, it frightened you . . ."

"My sport was riding. I never met a horse that could make me sick, scared, cold, and pickled in brine. Wes, I'm being very patient with you. Why did you invite me here? I'm not up to this. You, of all people, ought to know that!"

"You're very angry with me, I know—for giving you that injection. Why don't you take a nap? I'll make lunch and if you're up to a walk, we'll go to a lake on the property this afternoon, do a little fishing . . . and I'll try to explain. Not now."

It was Wesgrove of the Cancer Research Center speaking, not Mickey Rooney at the tiller. His eyes had their piercing, zoom lens look. Max went to his room and slept for an hour.

Giant, pungent pine groves led to the lake. A mammoth boulder threatening to plunge into it greeted them. There was an ancient rowboat tied to a crumbling dock. Around the boulder was new spring growth, wild strawberry, Indian paint, clover. Sunlight flashed up from the quiet water. "Row to the middle or sit on the rock?" Wesgrove asked.

"Definitely rock," said Max. "What a beautiful spot. What are we fishing for?"

"Bass, if we're lucky." Wesgrove sat himself cross-legged on the huge rock and slowly unreeled his line. Max found a crevice lower down and slightly to the right, almost a natural seat for a tall man. Silence, haloed by the warm sun, surrounded them.

"We're on the Wesgrove Gethsemane rock," the older man said lightly. "We used to settle the unsettleable here. Naughty boys were dragged off here to repent in reason. We weren't a touching family. We were a talking family. Did you come from a touching family?"

"There was no family except my mother. My father? I don't remember . . . Yes, I do. He would lift me into the saddle when I was too small to mount by myself. I was about four. I was five when he disappeared . . ."

"Let's talk, Max."

"OK."

"About suicide."

"Oh, no . . . Wes, don't do that!"

"I must."

"You know my mind is made up." Max was terribly irritated. He stood up. "That's why you invited me to the Maine woods, man?"

"Yes. To explore the subject with you."

"That's damn stupid, there's nothing to explore. When it's done, it's done . . . and, hopefully, done well."

"There are many ways for it to be done . . ." Wesgrove said, with a riddle-sound to him.

"We already talked about my way. Pills! You agreed it was the best. What more is there to say? This is cruel, Wes, what you're doing. I'm a man with very little time . . . and furthermore, that injection you had them give me at the Center . . . what was that all about? What did you think you were doing? You had no right, knowing my mind is set . . . if you were honoring my mind!"

"I ordered the injection to try and save your kidneys for a while."

"Why, for God's sake? What difference would it make?"

"A big difference, if your organs are intact."

"For what? Cremation?"

"Do you know anything about the history of suicide?" Wesgrove asked. He was looking at the lake, talking to it, not to the man standing behind him. "It's a fascinating subject."

"It hasn't been one of my serious interests until lately," Max said angrily. "I can't believe you want to lecture me on the chapter and verse of suicide. It's ghoulish . . ."

"Only as a preamble."

"Going where? What could be important to me now?"

"In your case? Everything."

"Wes, I've had enough of this. Stop fishing! You said you were sitting on the Wesgrove talking-rock? Talk! Don't beat around!"

Wesgrove veered away from the assault—"My father, you know, was a wonderful doctor. To the end of his days, he quaked like a young intern, feeling he knew nothing or was just beginning to learn. Bear with me. I learned how to think here, sitting with him.

"I want to help you die well . . . but it's even more than that, that has captured my mind, it's . . ."

"What?" Max said, almost rude.

"I don't know where to begin. It's a most unusual subject —suicide. To know the history of something is . . . is comforting; you start with the known, then jump into danger, a little more fortified."

"Is it my imagination, or are you getting more devious by the minute?"

"Imagination . . . that's the word." Wesgrove turned to look up at Max. "Sit down. Don't tower over me." He went on in a heedful, professorial tone as Max sat next to him.

"We have the historic suicide account by Sophocles—poor Jocasta, guilty of incest. Even the land of Thebes turned barren and blighted because of it. Poor woman, her distress was so great, there was no other way but to take her own life, die for the dishonor. What a dreadful story. It must have happened—

reality first, myth afterward. Like the Bible . . .

"There was Aegeus, the grand old king. He killed himself in grief, threw himself into the sea when he heard that his beloved son had been killed by the Minotaur. It was false news; poor Aegeus . . ."

Wesgrove stopped fishing. He dabbled his pole in the water, making rings within rings. The rings created bubbles that sailed out on the surface of the lake. Microcosmic, ancient secrets lay under each rainbow dome, otherwise, why were the two men looking at the bubbles so intently?

"And there's Valhalla," Wesgrove went on . . . "final resting place, no . . . living place, for those who died violently in battle, or took their lives if they were defeated. They killed themselves to join Odin, the supreme Viking god, bravest of the brave. And there were the primitive tribes in Africa, who felt a violent death against one's enemy was a sure ticket into their imagined paradise. The bloody old Romans made self-murder an art. Suicide is a modern word."

"What are you doing, Wes, for God's sake . . ."

"Back to the Greeks," Wesgrove said, as if Max hadn't spoken. "The Stoics felt—if Life was not in pleasing tandem with Nature, what could be more rational than to end Life?

"Then the gentle Christians came along. Life is God's gift to Man! You kill God if you kill yourself! Self-murder became a felony. And those poor creatures who bungled the act? Hanged! They had stakes banged into their hearts as though they were vampires. The gentle Christians buried a suicide far away from a town, at a crossroad, so the Devil in him wouldn't infect anyone else. Suicide? A mortal sin." He paused . . .

"And then, there's *modern* man with his sophisticated psychology: The poor wretch who wants to take his own life is disturbed, he must be *treated,* made whole, sane, free from depression; suicide is anger turned inward; heal him, for there is only life on earth . . . Another *modern* approach: A person who doesn't want to live has the right to make a decision of intellect, it is his ultimate right to *choose* death . . .

"It's a fascinating subject, Max, from the Druids right

down to you, who are about to take your own life."

Max was furious. "I repeat, Wes, what are you doing? You dragged me here to give a lecture on suicide? Your betrayal, the injection without my permission is what I want to talk about! And as for *suicide,* none of it applies to me, old man, except maybe the Stoics. If you're not in tune with Nature, then what the hell! That's it for me, it's *that* simple. I have no anger turned inward, bullshit! I just want to die, damn it, intact, in control to the end of the time that's mine, and I resent like hell your trying to interfere. The subject is closed. You can't change my mind."

Angrily, Max left the rock and scrambled up the grassy incline behind it. "I never should have told you! It was a mistake to burden you, but I expected a friend to accept and understand," he said looking down on Wesgrove. "I wish there were another word for suicide, it has a terrible sound, but not for me anymore . . ."

"There *is* another word. There are a lot of words. There could be for you." Wesgrove got up and faced Max.

"I'm walking back to the house, if I can find my way. No more riddles. The subject is closed." Max suddenly felt ghastly, not in his body but deep in his soul, because Wesgrove, his friend, looked destroyed. A rush of feeling came out . . . "I've never felt as close to a man as I have to you. I have to thank you for what you've done, through the lousiest of times a man could ever live through—a slow death, that's what it is. You walked with me, my doctor, my friend . . . I know that, but the rest of the way is alone, Wes."

"A friend has a better offer," Wesgrove said gruffly. "You haven't let me finish. I'm not trying to talk you out of it. *I want to help you do it another way.* Be quiet, please, and listen! Because I'm going to make a plea, an unusual experience for me . . . You're right, we're not only doctor and patient, we're friend to friend. These could be the most important minutes in both our lives.

"Ever since you said you were going to take things into your own hands, if the cancer galloped again, I've been over-

whelmed with an idea, a plan. The injection you're angry about
has to do with my plan—to save your kidneys as long as possible,
and any other part of your body that might be invaded by the
cancer. Why?" He paused. "I almost feel too old for this, but I
must.

"Max, a lot is going on at the Center, not only in cancer.
The Center has, under its roof, the finest scientists in the world.
We're cross-fertilizing our ideas, bouncing up and down on high
rafters. The investigation of cell life is taking us in so many
directions . . . We feel like children learning to sit, walk, and
jump at the same time. Science is fact *and* imagination and
trying to put a bit into the mouth of nature, to harness the
random which is all. What tells what to do what? How? When?
Why? The cells of the brain, the nerve cell, the sick cell, the
molecular makeup of the cell in aging, disease . . . everything!
We're into the investigation of everything because of my insistence that we all be under one roof—to investigate together,
neurobiologists, behavioralists, biochemists, physicists, medical
doctors." Wesgrove exploded. "There will be a cure for cancer
as surely as I'm on this rock! Max, you're a brave man, die for
a reason! Not by your own hand, by mine! Before the disease
kills you, allow yourself to be frozen, give me permission to
perform a cryonic suspension. I'm asking you to consider this,
instead of suicide."

He looked at an incredulous Max. "You would have to
think of yourself as a guinea pig, that's all. One day, perhaps
sooner than we think, there would be a body to experiment with
—yours. In the eventuality of a cancer cure, a human body to
test with—frozen cells, frozen brain." Wesgrove continued in
almost a whisper, "It's my way to help you die rather than have
you fall like an elephant on your pills, my friend . . . To this
moment, I have been a rational scientist."

The good doctor had just stepped across the threshold of
medical taboo. He was shaking. "I dare to talk like this because
I'm convinced you *will* take your life. I don't blame you, I would
do the same, knowing the kind of death you face. You might as
well die for a grand purpose, it suits you better, and I can help
you. By injection."

Max was nonplussed. "If I didn't know who was talking, I'd swear it was a Baptist preacher selling snake oil on the side. Wes, in a nutshell, say it again. I'm not sure I understand, or maybe I do and I can't believe it . . ."

"Give yourself to science. Die *before* your organs are permanently damaged. A painless death. By injection."

"When?"

Wesgrove took a deep breath. "Within the month . . . the latest by the end of June. It would have to be an absolute secret, nothing to Hedda, your daughters, no one. Only two of my colleagues will know, I'll need them, I trust them, and they're extraordinary scientists, former students. As far as your family and the world are concerned, you will have died a natural death from cancer, do you see? A faked death will have to take place. It must appear that you chose to be frozen *after* death, instead of being buried or cremated . . . another eccentric who bought a bill of goods about getting himself reanimated, that's what it should appear. The others, poor devils, died ravaged by their diseases. If they ever could be unfrozen in the future, they wouldn't stand a chance in hell to be revived *or* cured; let alone that their cryonic procedures were infantile, primitive."

"Are you offering me a glimmer of a second chance?"

"Absolutely not. That glimmer has as much chance of becoming light as we have of understanding the human brain with its some trillion nerve cells and their connections, astronomical in number. I'd be a damn-fool scientist if I answered you anything but 'Absolutely not,' what with the precarious ifs, Max, the ifs that fog up and surround giant steps, experiment after bloody experiment."

"By the end of June," Max repeated to himself out loud.

"Yes. You're a very sick man, but you've not been consumed yet. You have an amazing constitution, a very strong heart, a brilliant heart. The civil war going on inside you would have killed someone else a long time ago. If you weren't planning to kill yourself, you could keep on dying for some time. But you've gotten a taste of the pain and seen the sights and you've convinced me that you don't want that. You'd be a fine experiment for us . . . but time is crucial.

"I ask you to think about it. That's why I dragged you up here, where I'm more comfortable than anywhere else in the world—to ask you to be the first guinea pig in history, like no other."

Wesgrove had exhausted himself. "Don't give me your answer now, this weekend. When you've made up your mind, and if it's yes, we'll talk further, but . . ."

"I'm going for a walk," Max said. He looked around and pointed to an unusually dense growth of pine behind the boulder. "I'm going in there. You'll have my answer when I come back. I don't like delayed decisions."

Out of sight of the boulder, Max leaned against a pine tree. He looked up to find its top, but couldn't, it soared so high, mingling and waving with other tree crowns. He breathed in the damp perfume of pine forest. It had sickened him the night before. In the open, it was a mad elixir.

The end of June . . . He repeated it. Tears poured down his cheeks. Of course you couldn't kill yourself, you'd hang on until the last minute like everyone else. You'd never take pills. Where would the courage come from—to close off the air? You lie if you say you can! He wavered in debate. Remember the machines, you coward, the eyes in the cancer faces. He's giving you an out, crazy as it sounds, you lucky bastard. Now, you'll never know if you had the guts to do it by yourself.

A decision was coming fast. What an astounding idea! To die—taking chances. A sudden breeze came up. He shook with a longing to be connected to *everything*. I don't want to die! God, I don't want to die! Voluptuous life, defiant, pumping, luxuriant, disintegrating, self-resurrecting life was all around him. His eyes clawed at the forms. Shelves of petrified mushrooms the size of footballs clung to their host cadavers—dead pines. Giant tree trunks axed by lightning hadn't given in, either. They *were growing* scabrous moss on their bodies!

And where the bark behemoths had fallen was gentle greensward, dappled light swinging free of the shadows, a green tippling song. The will to live was laughing. Green grass grew the minute a tree died. Everything was going into death, coming out of death, there was no death. The mysterious place was filled with answers.

"Pick one," he ordered himself.

Goddamn you, Treading, you're gonna make a deal. You'll go like you lived. Gambling. What a last big laugh. He drew in his breath with a gasp. Decide now, this minute, this second! He stamped his foot. Now!

"Yes!"

Max walked slowly back to the boulder, stood behind Wesgrove and said, "I'll be a part of the making of an answer, won't I . . ."

"Yes, a large part."

"Then, I agree."

Wesgrove stood up and they faced each other. The older man said, "Yes, that's it—the making of an answer. You're understanding completely. I thought you would."

Max put out a hand. Wesgrove's small one trembled in his firm grip.

Max threw his head back and laughed. "I never went to college, but it looks like I'm going to die for pure science. Isn't that worth an honorary degree from Harvard?" As he laughed, a familiar pain flashed from his spine to his head. Rage on, witch, he said silently, we won't be together much longer. I can take anything you dish out . . . till the end of June.

Wesgrove then said, almost shyly, "Would you mind if I stayed and fished awhile? You can find your way back to the house."

"If you don't mind, I think I'd like to stay . . . and watch the light go."

Max sat on the rock next to his companion and stared into the water as Wesgrove began to fish again. They were sharing the quiet as if they were ordinary men enjoying ordinary time. Suddenly, a yank, then another . . . a whoop from Wesgrove . . . and a big, fat, shiny bass came catapulting out of the lake with a look of wild surprise, the look of a smart fish with a hook caught in its mouth.

"Wow! That's a big one," Max exclaimed. "He's not a lie."

"Hardly," Wesgrove said, reeling in slowly. "Mature, handsome, survived many winters . . ." he stopped, guiltily.

Max finished the thought: "To be caught, midlife, in the spring, poor bastard."

He laughed, Wesgrove didn't. "When do we talk more about the plan?" Max asked.

"Tomorrow. I'd like you to sleep on it."

They decided to get roaring drunk that night and save the cooking of the fish until breakfast. Ham sandwiches and brandy, more and more brandy, a few games of chess, until they could hardly make out the board. Two men in mackinaws and boots sat on a porch, with the sound of the Atlantic binding them.

Wesgrove woke up petrified the next morning. With Max's agreement, he would be taking a life. *Before* the cryonic suspension he would have to stop Max's life. *Kill* was the word, not *stop*.

In the early morning light, Max's answer was still yes. Wesgrove was cooking the bass for breakfast out-of-doors, over an old fireplace of piled-up stones. "What about this freezing business?" Max asked. "And how are you going to use me? Part of me wants to know and part of me doesn't. I agree to everything, remember that . . ."

A prankish thought showed on Wesgrove's face before he spoke it. "You're going to be my favorite monkey and no one will know about it, if ever. How are you going to be used? Good question." He fixed his attention on the bass and went silent, making Max feel that his saying "Good question" was answer enough. Wesgrove was trying to harness and simplify a response. "We're very close, Max, to unlocking many secrets of the cell, the gene. *Close* in science can sometimes mean a lifetime. We're beginning to really understand the life of a cell, how it's programmed, what makes it healthy or diseased, how an intrusion of a substance, a chemical can change the fate of a cell. We know that certain cells are programmed to migrate and others to stay where they are. We know that a long time can pass before cancer occurs to upset the applecart and throw certain cells into confusion. We know, we know and we don't know . . . We know that the ammunition a cell uses to penetrate the blood vessel wall of an organ is a protein strong enough to puncture. We're beginning to isolate and understand cancer genes that have a substance in them seemingly normal and so are accepted by a normal cell, but the cancer gene is a deceptor, it comes in protein disguise, making believe it's normal—a double agent. We're seeing that a normal cell has inviolate protein, supposedly, around it so that it can't be invaded, and yet it *can* be invaded by the double agent, a protein that's deficient, a spoiler armed with wrong signals, it fools the normal structure . . . and gains entrance. Cops and robbers . . .

"Yes, all life, Max, mirrors itself into Infinity, the good and the bad; we didn't make it up, it surrounds us, reproducing itself —Good and Evil. It makes one wonder, indeed it does, from the cell to the heavens . . .

"The fish will burn if I don't stop talking, but I haven't answered your question yet, how you will be used."

"Take the pan off the fire; the fish can wait, I can't. It's all unbelievable even if I could understand it. But keep on talking, give me more, more to hang on to."

"All right, all right . . ." Wesgrove set aside the pan. "Fish is ticklish, don't blame me if it's spoiled."

"I won't blame you for anything except silence. Come on, where does Treading come in? My cells, my brain, my what?"

Wesgrove had a curious look and blinked his eyes. Like a child, Max had a crazy impulse to say what he was thinking. "You look like a mad owl!"

Wesgrove accepted the outburst gently. The time was hardly normal, demanding of the usual graces. "I feel more like Hansel and Gretel in the forest, my friend." He paused. "We're getting close to the magic of how the body immunizes itself, but it isn't magic, it's chemistry, it's the language of the gene, the wonder of DNA, protein, acid. I've already used you in an immunization experiment, you and a few monkeys. There are keys and keys to turn and unlock the staggering, innumerable doors . . . but I'm beginning to feel that the biggest key that will open the most formidable door is going to be the one into the room of the brain, a place of connections and instructions as myriad as stars in the sky; and all the other keys that open the doors to the molecule, the gene, the cell, the chemistry of life, are as pupils to the teacher . . . that is, in human life. Which sets us apart in the Universe—to maybe even discover how to teach the teacher, the human brain!"

Looking at Max, Wesgrove was finding it almost impossible to protect himself from *feeling*. He must protect himself *with fact*.

"Back to the more realistic keys, Max, as difficult to turn as they are. At the Research Center we're not confined solely to the phenomenon of cancer, we're also committed to investigation in the field of cryobiology, the behavior of matter when submitted to cold, the preserving of cells and organs, trying to break the code of *cold*, successful methods of freezing to ensure successful transplants in the future. We've been working with small mammals, mice, cats, monkeys, working even toward a suspension of a human body with the use of cold; we're analyzing the chemistry of hibernating animals. I've fostered and encouraged cryogenic research along with finding the explanation of cancer because . . ." He stopped. "Because they both have to do with the promise of continued life, healthy life, even to the transplant of the brain, one day . . . in the very distant future.

"You? You will be our first human body to undergo a cryonic suspension under the optimum of clinical procedure; we'll have the chance to test new chemicals, cryoprotective liquid agents that coat the cells and help them fight damage from cold; we'll be testing a new tempo of freezing with your body, because we've had a few successes on some monkeys. The trick is how *not* to injure the brain . . ." He placed the fish back on the fire.

(*My* brain, not *the* brain! Max reacted silently.)

The fish was sizzling red and silver in the frying pan. Wesgrove turned it carefully, tenderly. He prodded the fish's succulent body into position with knife and fork. He could have been pinning a rare butterfly. Max watched him with equal attention, thinking: That man would approach anything with the delicacy of a da Vinci putting paint to the face of a Virgin, a man to be trusted with the final statement of *anything.*

"What about the moment of death, Wes? Play it like a cerebral game, it's the only way we can handle it, please . . ."

Wesgrove looked up from the fish. "You will be numbed first by acupuncture, then an injection to cause oblivion so swiftly, you will not even be aware that it has happened. That too will be a new experiment," he said almost inaudibly. "I'm finding this talk very difficult. I can't adequately explain it to you . . .

"I'm skirting around reams of figures and numbers on a page, endless experiment and years of thought. We've made big strides at the Center and they haven't been published or talked about yet, but they could be strides with phenomenal future meaning."

Wesgrove went into the house and brought out a pot of hot coffee, the last of the brandy from the night before, which he poured into the pot, and a loaf of bread. The two men sat on tree stumps beside the fire as the rising sun began to take the chill off the spring morning and shimmer on the Atlantic below them.

"What do you mean by 'future meaning,' Wes?"

Wesgrove was about to censor himself but the enthusiasm of the artist in him prevailed. "Impossible to define and probably even arrogant to say, but you will be part of it, you know. You're giving me the rarest of gifts—the chance to exercise my intuition to the fullest. By giving me your body, you might be making," he laughed, "my Sistine Chapel more than a dream. The chance to test not only painstaking work but scientific intuition on a human being. What can I give you in return? What could equal such an offering?" Wesgrove was filled with emotion, the fish lay cold on his plate.

"A second chance for my immortal soul?" Max said guardedly.

"No, no, no, don't even think that. Let's go back to the

beginning of this. *I came up with an alternative for suicide, that's all,* a death with honor that would please the Greeks. You could say —what's the point of honor if no one will know? The only place you'll be honored is with the gods, if there are any."

"The end of June?"

Wesgrove nodded yes. He looked drained; the usually benign, owlish face was lined with shadows, his huge glasses askew on his nose from rubbing his temples nervously while he had been talking. "That's if . . . you continue to refuse further chemotherapy when you get back to where you do your serious thinking."

"I did my 'most serious' yesterday in that pine grove of yours near the lake. You know my answer. Don't ask me again." Max took him by the shoulders, almost throwing the startled Wesgrove off-balance. "No guilt," Max said. "I will go willingly, sane and very grateful. I thank you." He released his grip. "Don't look so scared. Look what you're offering me, I'll go out of this world thinking: This isn't death, it's gambling! Let's make it three weeks . . . the twenty-first of June." (He had picked the number out of the air.) Max's hand went to his head. "Jesus, I have a headache."

"Probably the brandy."

"For the next three weeks, Wes, what do I do about the kidney, and those sharp pains that shoot up my back and down the thigh? They're pretty awful . . ."

"I'm going to continue with the serum I gave you. You didn't have an outrageous reaction. The monkeys who could tolerate it had your first response—the shaking—but it disappeared with the next series of injections . . .

"I'll also put you on some sedation, not enough to make you feel out of it, just comfortable . . . enough to allow you to do what you have to, then get into bed and make believe you're sinking the last week."

"I'm going to be a very busy man," Max said. He closed his eyes. He was thinking of Hedda.

How would he say good-bye?

14

That same weekend, the manager of the Sherry-Netherland Hotel was at his wits' end with a very drunk young woman. She had wreaked havoc in every public room, tongue-lashed every waiter, bartender, and unsuspecting male in her path. She sat at the bar, being amusing, caustic, turning furious with strangers. She would disappear into the ladies' room and return all witty and revived, then get drunker and drunker ... An observer in the bar remarked, "Who *is* that woman? She's absolutely marvelous. She's out to crucify someone, if she can't crucify herself."

In one of the passing-out scenes of the performance, the manager searched the woman's purse for a name to call before asking the police to remove her. She was too beautiful and elegantly dressed to be treated roughly. At the first number, a maid with a foreign accent answered, not understanding. The second number had a Fifth Avenue address under it and the name *Maxwell Treading: Father.* "Oh boy," the manager said to himself. He thanked his lucky stars that his judgment about drunken thoroughbreds was as superior as it was, from years of observation. The special people had to be protected. Maxwell

Treading's daughter! Even so, there were limits . . . He made it clear to the person answering the phone that the young lady had to be removed immediately.

It was Phoebe who took the call. She ran.

Roz had just come back from one of her forays into the ladies' room. She was sitting at the bar in Le Petit Café. The manager stood next to her. Roz was stony, staring him down, her spine straight—and that meant outrage. She was holding on to the rim of the bar, so as not to fall. That's all she wanted was to wish away whatever was going on, to start erasing her own brilliant performance, talented dialects, other actors who had to be silenced; they were saying their lines so stupidly, daring to be snide, how dare they snub her! And now, who in hell let Phoebe in? Straight back, Roz! straight back, you fool . . . How in hell can Phoebe still look like the pink-bottomed baby Nurse used to lift out of the tub?

"How long have you been in town?" Phoebe asked her.

Roz didn't answer, she wouldn't *ever* answer!

"Two days, Miss," the manager answered. "Miss . . . ?"

"Treading," Phoebe replied.

"Her sister . . ." the manager said with relief.

"Yes."

"We're sorry for this, but she's made it impossible for the staff to serve her, you understand."

"Don't believe a word he says," Roz interjected, trying not to slur her words. "This hotel is ridiculous. It's run like a cross-country diner." She swayed on her seat and caught herself, looking at Phoebe with large, vacant eyes. Behind the drunk vacancy was fear—what am I doing here? why are you here? who is he? Behind the fear was a glimmer of amusement. She was watching herself and finding it hilariously macabre, whatever was going on.

The manager mopped his face with his white, immaculate handkerchief. "Please remove her before it starts again. She's had enough to sink a battleship."

That she had. It had started with: Enough of Willard! Enough Newport! the exile to Rhode Island! Enough! What was it called? Marriage? She had gotten herself tanked up enough to leave Greenbriar *forever* . . . to live in a hotel *forever.* Alone. But now, she had to get back to her own bedroom. At least she could keep her door locked against invaders . . . meals would be brought by well-trained, frightened mice . . . she would have her own things around her. She *needed* her gray and mauve velvet comforter, the blue vase with gold flowers on her dressing table . . . the casement windows with branches of red oak brushing up against them. She wanted to go home. It was the end of Willard, *but she wouldn't let anyone know it was.* She had to go back. It was her only place. She'd never go back to Daddy's . . .

"Let's go home, Roz," Phoebe said calmly.

"All right . . . on a train," Roz mumbled.

"It's too late at night for a train. I didn't mean Greenbriar, I meant let's go home to Daddy's. We'll take care of you, darling."

"No!" Roz raised her eyebrows and giggled. "A train. The good thing about a train is, if you're worried about something, you don't have to do anything about it—until you get into a station."

"We've got to get out of *here.* Let's go to your room and I'll pack your things."

Roz laughed. "I'm not unpacked, silly."

"Let's go up and see."

"Oh, look at you! Aren't you the clever one, with your pretty little basket all full, and I'm still picking my blueberries off the bush one . . . at . . . a . . . time."

Phoebe took her firmly by the arm. "We're leaving, and right now!" Roz allowed herself to be eased off the bar stool, into an elevator.

Phoebe was thunderstruck. The hotel room was strewn with Roz's belongings, underwear on the floor where she'd stepped out of it, clothes everywhere, food trays she wouldn't allow removed, cigarettes stomped into the rug, the odor of dirty whiskey glasses.

Roz sat in a chair and made believe she was a visitor as she watched her sister pack the mess of a slob, a stranger.

"Disgusting!" she said out loud.

"No, it's heartbreaking," Phoebe said, closing a suitcase.

"I beg your pardon?" Roz reacted through a cold haze. She was moving through a dizzy time in her head, into a tight-jawed recovery-room chamber, in preparation for the drink she was going to order as soon as Phoebe left.

"Get out, thank you," Roz commanded.

"The hell you say, lady. You're coming with me. Now!" Phoebe called for a bellhop. "If you don't come with me, the manager is going to call the police. Do you understand?"

Roz got up, walked gingerly to the bathroom, banged the door shut, and threw up the last four hours of binge. She returned with a spine of steel, picked up her handbag, and walked out to the elevator, refusing to look at her sister. Phoebe, following with the suitcase, kept trying to force eye contact in the hope that the ludicrous scene would make them laugh rather than cry. If she could catch Roz's eyes, the porcelain face might dissolve into something human. But, Roz hung on to the fallen-queen look, strode through the lobby, her head high, hailed a cab, got in, banged the door in Phoebe's face, and Phoebe heard her say "Newport" to a disbelieving cabdriver.

"There ain't no such place."

"Newport, Rhode Island, stupid!"

"Are you crazy, lady?"

Roz didn't move. "I said Newport. You have to take me. If you don't, I'll see that your license is taken away." She sat waiting. So did the cabdriver. Phoebe opened the car door.

"Roz, come out. I'll drive you to Greenbriar."

"Get out, bitch," the driver snarled.

"Hey, wait a minute . . ." Phoebe yelled, sticking her face into the front window of the cab. "Who do you think you're talking to?"

"Get that drunk out of my cab, that's what I'm saying, or I will." He came around, opened Roz's door and grabbed her by the arm. Phoebe was furious; she kicked him in the shin, screaming, "How dare you!" . . . pulled at a dazed Roz, who slid out by herself and none too soon, because the driver had run around to his door, jumped in, and raced off.

Roz stood on the sidewalk, still porcelain and steel, not looking at Phoebe, but tears of mortification were falling down her still perfectly made-up face. Phoebe took her sister's face in her hands. They stood there for a moment in the middle of Fifth Avenue, at one in the morning. "What do I do with you?" Phoebe whispered, with tears in her own eyes. She was terrified, not knowing what Roz would do next. "Listen, Daddy's away for the weekend, sleep at the apartment and leave in the morning. Hedda sleeps late on Sunday, she won't even know you've been there. I don't know what else to do. Please, Roz, let's get another cab and go home . . . please, for me?"

Roz obeyed meekly, went back to the apartment with Phoebe, climbed into her white-ruffled bed, and fell asleep like an innocent child. Phoebe, agitated and wild-eyed with concern, called Willard. She talked to him in a way she had never spoken to anyone in her life. She screamed, called him emotionally bankrupt, demanded he tune in to his wife and stop being a stuffed animal, or there would be a tragedy; if not a divorce, something worse—Roz's sanity.

"She's your wife, damn it, and if she does go down the drain, it's your fault as well as hers. And, another thing, Willard, sick as my father is, if I tell him how miserable Roz is and you're just standing by and watching, not doing anything or caring for her . . . he'll ruin you financially, make a monkey out of the Clyde name." (What was she saying? Daddy would never do a thing like that.) She could feel Willard believing her. He was sputtering, trying to calm her down, promising to do something about the disaster happening under his nose.

"And, another thing . . ." She wasn't quite finished. "You get yourself and Roz into New York before my father gets too sick to know you're there, or . . . or you'll be a murderer too, the two of you. He'll die sooner than he should . . ." It was three in the morning when she hung up.

The Clyde chauffeur drove half the night and was waiting for Roz early the next morning. Phoebe woke her, brought her some coffee from the kitchen, sat and watched her dress and apply her makeup. Roz left without a word, maybe a faint, regal smile as she went out the door, trying to make believe that nothing had happened. A queen demands forgetfulness from her subjects. *Thank-you* to a little sister isn't necessary. A fall from grace is a figment of someone else's imagination.

15

What does it feel like to stand in a cemetery and look at your own tombstone with *all* the dates carved in? How many know the day they're going to die? He did! Except there wasn't going to be an epitaph in stone.

Max lay in bed luxuriously mourning his own demise. The time between Born-and-Died . . . What was it? The center of him felt like jelly. Be strong, he commanded; no looking backward. It was no use; his thoughts kept sliding.

A sudden memory. A stray dog. A boy of eight or nine, already tall, dirty-blond hair capping his head like an inverted tulip. (Martha didn't believe in haircuts too often. "Keeps the sun off," she said.) He could recite Wordsworth, and ranch like a man already. Who was that boy?

The dog had been wandering on the edges of the ranch for days. No one could get near him or convince him to come into the house; he just kept moving, paws swollen from ceaseless walking, looking for his master, sniffing every horse and vehicle that went by. Everyone decided he must have fallen off a truck, or, more likely, been pushed off—a beagle too old to hunt any-more. There was no doubt a cruelty had been done, or someone would have come back to find him; the dog was trying to find *someone*. It made everyone on the ranch restless, angry, made Max go to sleep crying.

Max was remembering so completely, he forgot he was fifty-five and dying. He was a boy, foot on a fence, watching the beagle, the lost one, and trying to will it, with unspoken thoughts, that the dog allow himself to be saved. Then, on the fifth day of wandering, the beagle came up to Max as though he had made a life or death decision—"I'm too tired, I've had it, I want to live. I'm finished looking for someone who doesn't deserve it!" Max picked up the exhausted dog, brought him into the house, put him down next to the stove in the kitchen with its smells of Martha's herbs and flowers, coffee ready for the ranch hands, the iron pot simmering, heavy with stew. The dog sighed and went to sleep. He woke up, looked at Max with relief, and put his head down again. He had obviously found paradise and the world was not mad, though loving was too painful. Being loyal (which his former master was not) was a torturous journey that could kill you—even if one had tried to be the best sort of animal most of one's life. The dog knew all *that*. He told the boy *that*, with his soft, old eyes and proud head.

Max smiled; half of him still there, in Martha's kitchen. He was remembering that when the dog finally had slept enough, he ate ravenously and lived on with them for six years, assuming ownership of the entire ranch and its occupants as though he had never lived anywhere else. Max could still smell the dust of the land, hear the scurry of rabbits and gophers, feel the heat of the sun on his eyelids. Way behind his eyes was the figure of his mother in her leather dress, bending over the dog, whispering, "Lucky little old devil, you. Do you know you're living a second chance? Of course you do, I can see it in your eyes." And the dog licked the fringes of her skirt, which smelled of horse, wild grass, lavender, and boot polish. The memory brought unexpected tears and a yell inside him. "I demand to start over! I demand a second chance . . . like (What was the dog's name?) Like Bo!" That's what Martha had named him, short for *bobo*.

. . .

He was leaving the ranch to Phoebe, with the proviso that she visit it at least once a year, as he had done. If she didn't, it was to be burned to the ground. He would say that in a codicil to his will. No stranger was to live in Martha's place. Eccentric? Why the hell not! He had just a few weeks more to do any damn thing he pleased!

He lay there thinking: *Hobo.* A nineteen-thirties word. What was the forties? *Atom? Beatnik*—the fifties? What was the sixties? *Yippies? Love children? Draft dodgers?* He had lived through many words that defined his five and a half decades . . . Oh, could he think of words! *Dust bowl. Roosevelt. Cole Porter. Hiroshima. Iron curtain. Cold war. Charlie Chaplin. Sputnik.* What a game to fall asleep by . . .

The stern of Wesgrove's sailboat with the letters *DNA* came to mind. What a shame to miss what was going to happen with all of that. He would be leaving without knowing what it was like to have grandchildren. Would Phoebe marry? Of course she would! But there would be no more Treadings by name. Roz? Would she and Willard "beget"? Fat chance, those two . . .

He made an instant decision. There could be no other kind from now on. Call Roz! Why be stubborn? Pride had no meaning now. He'd be an ass if pride had any part of it now.

He also had to call Dinessen.

Wait a minute . . . He'll ask Dinessen to call Roz. His lawyer's voice would have the official tone to bring her back for a family conference. There had to be a family get-together . . . to prepare for the death scene.

"You're still an ass, you won't call her," he muttered to himself as another part of him picked up the phone and dialed Newport.

Roz answered. How many months was it that he hadn't heard her voice?

It was the old Roz voice—careful and cool. Little did he know of the trip it had taken in the past week—to get back to itself. He had not been told about Roz's bizarre weekend at the Sherry-Netherland.

"Daddy here . . ." His voice trembled. "How are you, darling? I'd like you to come in . . . it's rather important. I'm not well . . . As a matter of fact, not well at all. There are family things to talk about . . ."

"Of course we'll come. When?"

"How about Saturday for lunch? Dinessen, my lawyer, will join us. You remember him?"

"Of course I do," she said evenly, but quickly calculating the seriousness of the exchange.

"Are you all right, baby?"

"Yes, fine, Daddy."

"And Willard?"

"Just fine."

"And the weather's fine," he added with a laugh.

"Very fine out here. See you on Saturday, then. Take care, Daddy . . ." That sounded right, just enough to reach out and not have to say anything else.

It was easier than he thought. "Not well at all . . ." —obviously a magic phrase.

It was going to be a family affair, a solid front, that's how he had to leave. It would be the first good-bye. He put Roz back carefully in her special drawer in his head. He was too tired for more innings. It was too late. Civility and allegiance were all he wanted and he would have them. He was leaving fortunes to be remembered by. That was the bottom line.

He hated the way he was thinking, but he shrugged it off, got dressed, and went looking for Hedda, to tell her he had made contact with Roz. That would please her. She'd been at him for months. How did she say it? "Give in to love . . ." What an incurable romantic, the darling. He wasn't giving in to anything anymore, except efficiency. Love took too much time . . . He went from strong to mush to strong, as he called out for Hedda. He didn't know himself too well anymore. It was getting very difficult.

The Roz he had talked with hadn't been drinking for a week. She was so glad to be back at Greenbriar—it was like being saved from drowning. The Sherry-Netherland scenes were so bizarre, they didn't belong to her. She *wanted* to be Mrs. Willard Clyde. It was the Treading part of her that had gone crazy, not the Walleby part. It would never happen again.

Willard was being wonderful, no recrimination, no door slamming, he just took her in his arms and welcomed her home.

"Poor baby, you certainly made a mess of your weekend," he said. "Let's just forget it." Special handling wasn't Willard's forte; it embarrassed him, but he was trying. She'd been careening around for months, threatening to go off the deep end. Why, it could have ended up in the newspapers if Phoebe hadn't extricated her. His parents would have died from the exposure. Here was his wife, his beautiful, half-Walleby . . . almost booked for drunkenness, but for the smarts of a hotel manager. (Willard had gone in a few days later, to hand the man a check.)

The tongue-lashing he got from Phoebe had penetrated. Willard was trying very hard. He mentioned to Roz that it would be a good idea for them to see her father. "We'll feel awful, sweets, if we don't. Phoebe says he's not good at all, might not last the year out. The fences should be mended," he said solemnly. (He was thinking of inheritance, but trying to make it seem the last notion in his head.)

Roz had *other feelings* about her father not lasting the year out; they made a terror that rolled like a fiery ball from her head to her feet. It wasn't wise to wish your father dead and have it happen. A sly voice was talking to her through that nameless terror. She didn't wish him dead. The day Max called, she was deciding to call him.

Roz couldn't believe it when she heard "Daddy here . . ." When she hung up, she wanted to have a drink, but *didn't*. She was trembling so, it was ridiculous. It felt like being madly in love, but how did she even know that? She had never been in love . . . like Anna Karenina.

She allowed Willard to make love to her. It upset him—the way she clung to him. She had to be coddled and stroked too long before anything could happen. Roz wasn't good in bed, even in the beginning, but she was an outstanding beauty with a Walleby blood line, the future mother of their children. How

many men were lucky enough to have that around? So he sac-
rificed a lot and it made him feel good.

Hedda found Max suddenly different after his weekend in
Maine, and stranger, he wouldn't even talk about the weekend.
It wasn't a sicker body she snuggled against when they fell
asleep, it was a body building armor, closing doors against her.
He did look more pale . . .

She had a terrible premonition that these were their last
days and should be force-fed like a French goose. And now, Roz
was coming for lunch. She dreaded it, but would try to keep
everything gracious, including her face. Max seemed in high
spirits as he paced the apartment waiting for Roz and Willard
to arrive. When they did, he embraced Roz and held her for a
long time. He even embraced Willard.

To Hedda, time seemed like a pancake being flipped over,
slow motion. There was an exchange of looks between Phoebe
and Roz that Hedda didn't understand either—a raising of Roz's
eyebrows, a hand gesture that waved away a need for words.
The two girls grabbed each other and Phoebe flushed with pleasure. Hedda didn't know about Roz's drunken weekend, nor
could she have known what Phoebe was thinking now: "My
God, you've straightened out!" Hedda had no idea what anything meant anymore, she felt like a stranger.

The lunch was carrot soup, lobster, and peach Melba—
Max's favorites. Max and Willard talked the stock market. Roz
surprised everyone by running on about the gardens of Greenbriar, the early roses coming up. She announced she was playing a lot of tennis and Willard had a new boat, and she loved
going out while he fished . . . " 'Course, I'm covered with number 15 sunscreen, but I adore lying on deck just reading; Henry
James's *The Awkward Age*, Daddy . . . You must come out,
Phoebe, and sit in the gazebo and get revived from this dreadful city. How can you stand it for more than a few days at a
time?"

Phoebe couldn't believe what she was hearing. *Roz was acting.*

Hedda sat at the foot of the table opposite Max. She had nothing to say because no one spoke to her. Dinessen smiled at her, though. He seemed like a nice man and rather bored with the market talk that was keeping Willard busy. Phoebe was so preoccupied watching her father and sister, she forgot about Hedda.

Max pushed his chair away from the table. Hedda caught his eye. He returned her look with a smile and sent her a kiss. Did she imagine it? Had she been sitting there, a victim of her own making? She blushed.

Max cleared his throat, trying to find an easy voice. (The pain in his back was terrible.) "Meeting come to order . . . I want to talk about Israel's air strikes over Lebanon this morning. What do you think about it, Dinessen?" He didn't wait for a reply. "I'm with Prime Minister Begin. Israel's intelligence is the best in the world, it has to be. There are still PLO in Lebanon, why shouldn't they go in and prove it to the world?"

"I don't agree," Willard said quickly. Roz's face tightened —Daddy with his political talk and Willard falling right into the trap again.

"Very special case—Israel," Max said. (He wanted to keep on talking about the world . . . delay the other subject—himself.) "A case of morality. We're gonna make her negotiate eventually, or we'll all drown with her, the Arabs are so crazy . . ." He stopped for a cough. "Don't worry, Roz, darling, I'm not gonna talk politics. I have to talk about another invasion . . . the one in me."

He looked around the table. "I love you all . . . I love my daughters, each in a different way . . ." (They were stunned by the switch. What was he doing now?) "I love this guy here." Max patted Dinessen, sitting on his left. "He's taken a lot of nonsense from me for twenty years, protected me not only legally, but with his friendship."

Dinessen blushed. He was a stocky Scandinavian with deep lifelines on his cheeks and forehead, topped by a mane of silver hair. It was an intelligent, square, kind face but could tighten like a killer's if it had to. He had stood behind Max in some of the most outlandish situations a lawyer could ever dream of—

Max's global shenanigans—and had won most of the time; it was not to be believed what he and Max had done together.

This was Dinessen's first visit to the apartment since Sophia's death. As close as they were, he and Max had never spent much social time together, only work time. Dinessen was thinking about that, and also how much he hadn't liked Sophia. Through lunch he had looked at Hedda occasionally and thought, So this is the woman Max finally loves, I like her face, she has deep, dark lovely eyes, but she looks under stress and why not . . . He wished he were sitting next to her to pat her hand. Damn, life can be so beastly unfair and short! Max had honored him with the confidence when they were redrafting his will—"I would have married her . . ." Damn, Dinessen said to himself again as Max went on:

"And I love Hedda the most. You have to understand what I mean by that. My other loves are not more or less, it's just that my love for Hedda is more crucial. I'm a man who found his true companion, his other side. That doesn't negate the other loves, one should have them all! I've been a lucky man.

"I loved the mother of my children . . ." It was said so firmly, Dinessen was confounded. Why the summing up in front of an audience? Where in hell was Max going now?

"Well . . ." Max continued, looking at no one in particular, "the cancer has finally taken over. I'm stopping all treatment because it's useless. I intend to die at home with dignity, not in a hospital, attached to tubes and machines."

Had they heard right? Hedda's stomach convulsed as if it had been hit. He hadn't given her any warning!

"There's no point," Max went on, "wriggling on the end of a line with a hook in my mouth. I've never been a victim, I don't intend to be one in the last few . . . It'll be soon, the doctor says . . . very soon, if they're not pouring chemicals into me just to stave it off. I've opted for an old-fashioned death, with those who love me, I hope, near me . . ."

He got up, walked around the table, sat next to Hedda and took her hand. "There will be no funeral. I'm giving my body to science. It will be frozen immediately after my death, put into a capsule and stored in a laboratory for future use someday . . ."

He went on quickly so there wouldn't be room for a word from anyone. "Also, I'm giving permission for live cells to be taken before death—for experiments in space, where the lack of gravity makes it easier to isolate properties . . . I'll be whirling around in the heavens, a small bit of me, even though I'll be in a state of cryonic suspension on earth. Frozen: like in orange juice. So, there'll be no funeral."

It was the bland way in which he announced it all . . . The feeling around the table, including Hedda, was that the cancer might have affected his brain. Roz leaned over and whispered to Willard, "Someone's gotten hold of his sanity. He sounds like Frankenstein. What shall we do?"

"Nothing," Willard whispered back. "Absolutely nothing."

"Daddy?" Phoebe's voice was so tremulous and tiny, she almost couldn't get out the words. "What do you mean 'soon'?"

"Don't know . . . It depends on how fast the cancer takes over, how soon it causes pneumonia or kidney failure . . ." His tone was schoolteacherish. He looked around. "How shocked you all seem because I want a natural death, as though it were outrageous to let the body go in its own way, its own time, with no outside interference. They've tried everything. Dr. Wesgrove gave me a year more of life than I would have had. From now on, it would be torture. I don't want that. And, lest you think otherwise," he looked around, "I'm of sane mind, if not body." He looked at Dinessen, "You an' I have some work to do. The will stands, but there are some codicils we have to add." He came up with a wan little smile. "Let's look at it this way—no one's going to have to wear black for me, no veils, no stranger mumbling words from the pulpit."

Phoebe couldn't stand it anymore. She got up and left.

Max was exhausted from trying to be matter-of-fact; holding back the heartbreak had drained him. He wanted to share Wesgrove's plan with Hedda, but he couldn't. Wesgrove had to be protected. How he wanted to tell Phoebe he was going out in a blaze of challenge. And how he wanted to plead with Roz to be proud of him, ask her forgiveness for the mistakes he'd

made. Later, he'd tell Hedda he wanted only one thing after he
was gone, for her to be happy, marry, have children . . . Forgetting was as healthy and natural as breathing. Boy, you're a crazy
son of a gun, he said to himself.

"Daddy, what do you want us to do now?" Roz said getting
up. Willard followed with alacrity, the two standing straight as
boards. "Is there anything Willard can do? Should we . . ." She
wanted to say—*tell anyone* . . . is it a secret? It was horrible! How
could she tell anyone about the freezing business? Who ever
heard of such a thing? Leave it to him to do something everyone
would be talking about. The Clydes would be aghast, everyone
she knew. ("No normal funeral, *my* father is in a laboratory,
frozen!") She looked at the man who was her enemy her whole
life. He's going to die . . . Her knees began to quiver, she was
getting dizzy. A wave of nausea was rising up, it was starting,
that *thing* that had been happening lately—wanting to faint, a
surge of anger that started at the back of her neck like the blow
of an ax. She would *not* let it happen, not here, not in front of
Hedda.

Max saw his daughter's chest heave with hard breathing.
He went over and put his arms around her, held her so tightly
that the shock of the closeness made her burst into tears. Willard
moved back like a man caught in cross fire. Roz's symptoms
dissolved in a storm of sobbing on her father's chest.

(Relief couldn't be *that* simple, a dazed voice said inside her.
The ax didn't hit; she felt disembodied, floating, free . . . in his
arms. No, she was suffocating!) She wrenched herself away from
Max, grabbed her purse, and left. Willard followed after a hurried handshake with Dinessen, an awkward grasp of Max's elbow.

That's it? That's all? Max reacted to the leave-taking. He
remembered Wesgrove saying, "We weren't a touching family,
we were a talking family." What was *this* family? A running-out-
the-door family? He felt Hedda's clammy hand in his. She
wasn't running yet. Maybe there came a time when it didn't
make sense to hang on, be connected . . . the living had to protect
themselves. Maybe his announcement had made his death before he died and he would have to watch them as if he *were* dead,
good Lord . . .

. . .

That was on the fifth of June. He spent the next day with Dinessen working out the final version of his will. When they finished, Dinessen went home and got drunk. Among other things, the good lawyer learned that he had to oversee what Max insisted upon calling "my *Re-animation Fund.*" When Max introduced the idea, he said, "I want to put a million away, in my own name."

"I don't understand," Dinessen said.

"Allow me a joke, I want it done."

"You can't create a trust forever, Max, there's something called a rule against perpetuities. Banks don't like the word *forever,* or governments either. Relatives in the distant future could end up owning the world with the interest accruing, and no cutoff . . ."

"Interesting idea," Max said, amused with Dinessen's seriousness. "So, how long can I put a million away for?"

"The maximum time is the extent of two lives *in being* at the time the trust begins, plus twenty-one years; in other words, Phoebe's or Roz's life span plus twenty-one, whoever lives the longest of the two."

"Do it," Max said. "And I don't want it mentioned in the will. It's my business."

"It's an expensive joke, Max, but I'll talk to the bank. They'll call it a 'contingency fund.' "

"Let them call it what they want. I'll send you some stock to sell for it in the morning. I'd do it myself, George, but I feel punk, very . . . my energy has a few inches left.

"Anyway, finishing up a will is depressing. It's like sending up smoke signals to the angels of death, isn't it?"

On June 8, Max took to his bed after a long day with Wesgrove at the Cancer Research Center. He submitted, for the last time, to a workup of his entire body. He gave specimens of everything from sputum to semen to feces. Left at the Center was every possible knowledge of the physiobiology and chemistry of a Maxwell Treading.

Through all of it, Max felt very weak, but he tolerated the day like a faithful draft horse. The end of the day was amusing, if one could assume it was shared by two sane men. They plotted the design of Max's supposed death in his bed. Death by pneumonia, a total breakdown of his immune system . . . (for the coroner's report). The lungs would fill up with fluid, breathing would be difficult. Wesgrove coached Max on the appropriate sounds, facial expressions, even to fool a real nurse in attendance; he was going to need one to authenticate the scene. Death would come fast—a slightly open mouth, a few long gasps, a shudder of the chest. Max would be taken mercifully, it would be said by those who watched.

"I'll come to see you every day until it happens, Max," Wesgrove said. "Never made a house call in my life, never left a lab or hospital in my whole career." Wesgrove stopped to think. "Look, I'm going to put you on something to keep you pain-free and happy."

"Happy?"

"You're going to feel it, if I don't mask the disease. I don't know what you're made of. You must be in a great deal of pain, but I don't want to use an overwhelming drug, a total depressant like morphine. The tests today show an invaded fibula and a kidney in not good shape. It's the kidneys I'm worried about . . . A man can live with one . . ."

"I don't believe you, Wes, you're mad, that's what I think! You're calculating as though this whole thing is going to mean something in the future! I'm not!"

Wesgrove looked at him above his glasses, which had slipped, as usual, to the bottom of his nose. He made no response.

Mad old owl, Max said to himself. It doesn't matter. He's helping me die, bless him; let him have his dream; he, too, will die someday soon and it won't matter to him anymore, whether his dream failed or not. It certainly won't matter to me very soon.

"Max," Wesgrove said quietly, almost reading Max's mind, "Don't judge. Keep your mind open . . . to the last; that's a medicine in itself. Look . . . I'm going to put you on mescaline.

It's going to make you very happy, a little separated from what's going on. It's an old Indian drug to induce trance. You won't be getting enough of it for that, just a small draught, mixed with a muscle relaxant used for asthma and pregnant women who go into labor too soon. We have to keep your *whole* system relaxed but not depressed. We're fighting for time against cancer cells running riot . . .

"I don't want an invasion of any other organ, but you do need several weeks at home, to make it appear a normal expiration." He looked at his calendar. "That will bring us up to the twenty-third of June."

"I thought we decided on the twenty-first," Max said anxiously. He had become used to "the twenty-first" . . . He'd kept saying it to himself ever since he had picked the number in the Maine woods.

"No, the twenty-third." Wesgrove said definitely, and closed his calendar. "However, no later than that."

16

The combination of drugs—to keep him free from anxiety and pain—was working, but Max's mind felt like a broken kaleidoscope. Glittering, alarming pieces were flying around like geometric birds. He wasn't used to cutouts slipping around in his head. It was hard to remember who he was . . . No, he *did* remember. He was between life and death. It was a peculiar place of glittering pieces. He was lending his soul to Wesgrove, that's who he was.

He was still Max, he knew that, but he could change his bedroom into marble halls with dancing statues, grinning satyrs, vases that kept cracking and healing, vases with arms and legs running down the halls looking for their pieces, finding them, losing them. There was a real vase on his bureau, filled with flowers. He could change the flowers into ten times their size, until they filled the room from floor to ceiling. He could stop it whenever he wished . . . whenever he pushed, bore down into the center of himself and repeated his name over and over.

The drugs helped him play another game. He could be stillness itself, face his death with such clarity that he became an Easter Island monolith looking out on Vast Time. Time disappearing, reshaping, disappearing. In the quiet pools of Time, he felt his right to die so beautiful, death had no terror. He was giving up *the will to live,* ending the destruction of his body, that was all . . . Terror came only between the drug doses. Then he felt like a raccoon caught in a leg trap, in a Vast Forest where he was the only animal.

Wesgrove lessened the dose of mescaline when Max confided the strange places his mind was traveling. Wesgrove didn't want him to be taken over by hallucination, he just wanted him quiet, relatively free from pain; he wanted Max's mind to be the one he'd lived with, not the phantasmagoria of a drug freak. Max agreed, otherwise he wouldn't be able to control his death scene . . . he would be a victim and Wesgrove would be guilty of manipulation. That must never be suspected by those who were watching.

During the days Max had been getting too much mescaline, not only his bedroom was awhirl. Hedda and Phoebe were in a spiral of dumb anxiety. Hedda had moved into Roz's bedroom because Max was so disconnected and restless. She detested the room, with its tiers of lavender and white ruffles everywhere; there was no relief from them, the room was mirrored. It all reeked of Sophia and the fairyland she had designed for a virgin *coming-out* daughter. Hedda had to take Valium to knock herself out at night, she was so grief-stricken and disconnected herself.

The kitchen was another spiral of anxious whisperings. Mr. Treading is very sick . . . shhh . . . keep the cats out of the hall to his room. Then a nurse arrived, a tall, horse-faced woman with popping eyes, who dared to tell Cook what to make for Mr. Treading after twenty years of service in his kitchen. Fair is fair, the kitchen said, after she was fired in one day by Mr. Treading himself.

"I will not have a pop-eyed wretch in my room watching me die! If I can't have a beautiful nurse, I won't have any, damn it! All I want is a woman who can smile, whether she means it or not."

It wasn't the poor woman's face, it was what she had said that got her thrown out. When she began to lecture Hedda and

Max about how difficult it was going to be to care for him at home as well as she could in a hospital, because he was probably going to need a catheter inserted, and an oxygen mask, but she would manage as well as she could under the circumstances . . . Imagine her surprise when Max said, "Get out!" She huffed her way to the door, throwing over her shoulder to Hedda . . . "He'll not do very well, I'll tell you that, if he doesn't have a specially trained person like myself. I specialize in terminal patients."

Hedda found the *beautiful nurse* by that afternoon. It was the day after Wesgrove had cut the mescaline dose in half. When Max realized that Hedda had moved into Roz's room, he insisted she come back where she was supposed to be—with him, if she could and wanted to. "Of course I want to! But, with a nurse around . . ."

"We'll kick her out when we feel like it. If I'm lousy, she'll come back. I want you here in the good hours, I want to hold you . . . I don't think I can make it anymore," he said, bereft, "but we can make believe, can't we?" He stretched out his arms and she crawled into bed, fully dressed.

He slowly unbuttoned her blouse.

"What are you doing?"

"I'm helping you get undressed, what do you think I'm doing?"

He unfastened her bra, kissing each breast as it became free. "Take off the damn skirt, darling," he whispered.

"Max? What are you doing?" She wriggled out of the skirt.

"Not doing, *trying* to do . . ." He stroked her belly, sighing as he rolled down her lace bikini . . . so slowly, with a sense of wonder, it seemed like the first time.

Hedda felt his erection against her. Could they? Should he? Max lay back, pale. How he wanted to be inside her one last time, feel that glorious shudder *once more,* more mind-blowing than all the mescaline visions of violent-colored flowers.

Her head was on his chest. She stroked him up and down, thinking, it was *his* skin, *his* muscle, but underneath were the devils that were going to take him away. She rubbed her face against the blond-gray hairs. Underneath was a nightmare. And there was a new smell, the smell of illness, a dusty smell of a body gathering cobwebs, mixed with a vague odor of rubbing alcohol. Damn the nurse, he should be rubbed with his cologne, the one he liked most, or a new one! She stirred and his erection was still there pushing against her. She pressed her body into it like a mountain climber hugging his peak after a treacherous climb. They must, they would, she would make it happen . . . She climbed on top of him, trying to keep her full weight away, and guided him into her. She closed her eyes and willed it to happen—the erotic energy of two Indian goddesses—if she could!

"We have to come together," Max whispered, the thrusting and pushing of Hedda accelerating for them both. "Tell me when . . . it has to be together this time." His voice was hoarse, almost inaudible. Hedda kept her eyes closed. She couldn't look at his face; she used to love to, when he exploded inside her. This was madness . . .

No, it wasn't! It was stopping the cells! It was wading through a dance-of-death parade of grinning black cells wearing skull masks. *Because of what she was doing,* the black, dancing cells were routed, running away . . . their masks fell off. Impostors! They ran naked, screaming with anger, vanquished. They were running away . . . far away . . . from the atom sick-cell-smasher in their victim's penis.

Hedda slid onto her side. They held each other. Max was soaking wet. "That has to be the fuck to end all . . ." he mumbled with his old irreverence. Hedda looked up. He wasn't smiling. His face was waxy white and staring off into space—that far-away look.

He stroked her hair. "Thank you . . ." He lay silent. "I want to say good-bye *now.* I love you . . . I want you to be happy . . . Remember that I said that. Fall in love again or I'll haunt you. There are a million ways . . . I don't want to admit it . . . but there are a million ways out there . . ."

She got up to look for a robe. He watched her small, naked body, slightly pink and moist. "The only other animal as beautiful as a naked horse, is a naked Hedda," he said.

She turned around. "No, any woman a man loves . . ." She came to the foot of the bed. "Thank you, Max, for making me feel beautiful." She just stood there crying. This was good-bye. There was nothing else to say. It wasn't good what they'd done. Not the way he looked. She found the robe and put it on. "I don't think I'd better stay in here, do you?"

"Maybe you're right," he said, turning on his left side, away from a pain that was threatening to engulf him and make him scream. He closed his eyes and the image of a raccoon caught in a leg trap came back to hurt him further, but, in spite of it, he sank into a deep snoring sleep.

That was on June 21, in the late afternoon. Max woke feeling better, he couldn't believe it . . . (the crazy witch). Wesgrove came to see him in the evening and examined him.

"How am I?"

"Not bad, considering. Your pressure is up a bit, what did you do, run a mile today?"

Max blushed. Wesgrove knew. How could he know? (There were no secrets anymore.)

"Is the answer still yes, Max? It doesn't have to be. No notion is that fixed that it can't be stopped, except . . ."

"Except the Universe."

"Nothing has to continue," Wesgrove protested. "You can go out like this, slow, easy, up and down."

"The answer is still yes!" Max said heatedly, annoyed with Wesgrove for continuing the debate of yes or no. "Don't ask me again, damn it. You're a coward and a bastard, if you do."

The new nurse walked in and right behind her, Rocky, the cat. Behind him was Phoebe's cat, Red. There was a quick hissing and turbulence on the doorsill and Red was banished by Rocky. Max's room was Rocky's domain. Ever since Max had taken to his bed, the cat would sneak in to stand watch or sleep watch, a scruffy tiger with big green eyes, and Max didn't say no.

The new nurse giggled as Rocky slipped through her legs. His tail was high, saying: You stop me, an' you're gonna get yours.

"Cats allowed, Mr. Treading?" the pretty face asked.

"Cats allowed, you gorgeous creature . . ."

"Why, thank you, Mr. Treading, my goodness . . ."

"Don't mention it."

Hedda followed Wesgrove to the door as he was leaving. Her eyes asked and he answered. "Not very good."

She wanted desperately to say: "How *not good?* How long do we have him?" But she didn't want to know, not yet.

He patted her arm. "It's hard to watch, but so much better here than in a hospital. Get some rest yourself, my dear. Be the best you can for him, that's all one should expect in this dreadful business of watching. This afternoon could never have happened in a hospital . . . it buys time."

(Hedda was shocked. How did he know?)

He held her arm tightly for a moment. "It's going to be easier for him than for us, I promise you that." He released his grip. (He had to make believe the end was near.) "I've taken a blood sample, I'll let you know tomorrow about his blood gases. That's the telling. If he were in a hospital situation, we would be legally responsible to transfuse him; but here, he's the only one responsible." He looked at her questioningly. "Would his daughters, if it came to that, countermand his wishes? If he were to lapse into a coma?"

"No. I don't think so," Hedda said shakily. "No . . . he made his wishes very clear to everyone." (Would I, if I were his legal wife, to keep him longer?)

She knows nothing, Wesgrove thought, as he bowed and left. Max was exceptional, without a doubt. It was so human to clutch someone you love and share your deepest secret. No, Max understood there was no such thing as a secret, once told to even the most trusted.

That night, Max had two dreams: A gray mourning dove wearing large glasses flew into his line of vision, so close he could smell its feathers. It landed at his feet and disappeared into a dark-purple clump of bushes, singing its four-note dirge as it went.

He woke (he dreamed) trembling. His heart felt like the flutter of gray wings and he thought that Wesgrove was standing at the foot of the bed, holding a vial of purple blood and pointing to it, saying, "It's time, you see . . . it's time."

The other dream had the perspective of a medieval painting, its sight lines stretching into Infinity. From that point of Infinity, tan cows appeared, walking slowly toward him. As they approached from what appeared a rise in land, they were the most handsome, gentle-faced cows he had ever seen. Lean, proud, they walked in a stately gait, two abreast, lifting their legs in a half-prance, like the inspired walk of dancers or exquisitely drilled soldiers in dress parade, or like gods disguised as cows. A mysterious beauty stirred in front of them as they moved toward him, a disembodied *feeling* beauty unrelated to anything human, like nothing he had ever experienced with his eyes.

It was early the morning of June 22 that he woke with the unearthly rhythm of the cows lingering. He felt peaceful, as he had never felt in his whole life.

Things were getting mixed up. He had to remind himself that the cancer *was* racing and he *was* dying. He could tolerate the way it was—spurts of weak, spurts of clinging to relief with the help of drugs. He had to remind himself—it was *his* decision to hurry the dying, to stop the pain that was definitely there and wouldn't go away. He would never be able to walk out of the apartment again on his own steam, much less jog in morning air; he would never be able to function as head of Global Materials; never make love with Hedda again. So, what was the point? Two days, two weeks, two months. *It was over.*

That afternoon, Wesgrove phoned Hedda to tell her that the blood sample showed dangerous signs, total loss of immunization, and there was a pneumonia virus. He added, "If he were in a hospital, no one could enter his room without a mask." (It *could* be true in a few months, but not on June 22.)

Later that afternoon, according to plan, Max began to show difficulty breathing. The beautiful nurse called Wesgrove to report the change and ask permission to order an oxygen tank.

Wesgrove's response was, "No. I might as well tell you now, this is an unusual case. The patient insists upon no aids to delay the end. There's nothing we can do about it. We must abide by Mr. Treading's wishes—no masks, no machinery in his room. Do you understand?"

"Yes, Doctor." She was overwhelmed by receiving orders from the famous Dr. Wesgrove, as though he were an ordinary doctor.

A few hours later, Wesgrove arrived.

"Should the cat be removed from the room?" the nurse asked. "The dander might not be good for him."

Rocky pricked up his ears at the foot of the bed. Max was shaking his head no.

"I don't think it matters one way or the other, now," Wesgrove said. Then, with a confidential, making-her-an-equal tone, "We haven't witnessed a natural death without life supports for a long time, have we . . ."

She smiled knowingly, thinking how interesting it all was —a great doctor in the room of a famous millionaire, a cat at the foot of the bed. All this top-level stuff and it was so unflashy, almost cozy, no airs at all. She sighed and puffed up Max's pillow before walking out the door with the famous Dr. Wesgrove, perhaps to get more orders out of earshot of the patient. But there were none, so she went back to sit next to Max, take his hand, smooth his brow, and smile.

It was just what Max wanted—a smiling, pretty woman who smelled like spring flowers. He couldn't handle Hedda's presence anymore. A pretty nurse and a cat. There was a lot of peace in the room, no sadness.

The next morning, June 23, it was raining. The word must have leaked out that he was dying. People came to break the peace. The board of directors of Global Materials, Max's secretaries, Dr. Hoffstadter and his wife. The special people were allowed into Max's room to say good-bye. The phone didn't stop ringing—tennis partners, bank presidents, Wall Street cronies, even members of Sophia's family he had rarely seen when they were married. Max could hear the constant movement and bells, they began to agitate him. The phones were unplugged. Dinessen came late in the day, took his hand for a minute, pressed it hard, began to cry and had to leave. (How soft, like newborns, people made themselves in a death room, Max noted.)

Roz came. He had already imagined what that would be like. She stood at the windows, looking out. Phoebe had been in the room most of the day, ushering people in and out. When she wasn't, she sat next to him and held his hand. Hedda came in, placed her cheek next to his and left. She must have done that twenty times all day.

By evening, Max began to gasp a little. The nurse called Wesgrove: "The patient is breathing with great discomfort." He told her he would come immediately. When he arrived, he examined the patient, announced he would stay, and Phoebe took him to Max's library, rather than the living room, where Roz and Willard were sitting. He was grateful for that. He wanted to be alone, away from questioning eyes.

Max wondered whether he was doing it well. There was no chance to discuss it with Wesgrove, to go over the climax of the performance. *He was on his own.*

At 10:30, the nurse went swiftly to the library and said the patient was extremely restless and having great difficulty breathing.

Wesgrove, followed by Roz and Willard, came into Max's room. Hedda was in a chair at the foot of the bed, resting her head on his feet, not looking at anyone and crying softly. Phoebe was in her bedroom and was called. Wesgrove stood in a corner, after taking Max's pulse and listening to his chest. Rocky hugged his corner of the foot of the bed as though a hurricane wouldn't have the nerve to remove him.

Phoebe entered as her father was making terrifying noises that ended in gasps. She stood at the door, struck dumb. It wasn't Daddy, it was someone dying in a movie. It couldn't be happening in Daddy's bedroom! Death rattle! A sound not to be imagined until heard! She steeled herself and inched along the wall facing the bed, bracing herself against the bureau that held Daddy's clothes . . . it didn't make sense . . . it was all Through-the-Looking-Glass crazy . . . a capricious decision that her invulnerable, glorious Daddy die.

The gasps from the bed were subsiding into shudders. Some rasps followed, or were they croaks? Phoebe found herself remembering, in spite of the moment, the sound of frogs in the pond near the Southampton house, the cacophony she and Roz used to delight in, if Mother let them take a walk after dinner. "The frog symphony" they used to call it. A fat frog would start the first movement. It must have been fat, it made such a deep, commanding sound that started all the other frogs. And then, the counterpoint that followed was hysterical, always ending in a small croak from a young member of the orchestra who was way off in its own mud, allowed to sing just one note and that's all. The rasp-croak coming from Daddy's bed was the allowed one note of the little frog. How awful of her to think of such a thing, when her father's eyes were opened in such a wild stare, an elbow jumping up in an awkward little spasm.

Suddenly, the room was quiet. The wild eyes were half-closing. She had to! She had to run to the bed, kiss the face.

"Daddy . . . Daddy . . . Daddy . . ." She would stop the madness if she stayed there, bending over him. She looked up at Wesgrove, who had rushed over. He moved her away gently, bent over Max, looked up and shook his head.

"He's gone."

"Oh God," Phoebe pleaded.

Roz turned from the window.

Hedda lifted her head from the foot of the bed. Looking at no one, she rose, went to kiss Max's lips, whispered "I love you," and left the room.

"He's gone," Phoebe repeated, looking at her sister. Roz's face was dead white. The nurse sat her down and put her head between her legs, whereupon Roz pushed the nurse away, sat up, her cheeks flaming, and ran from the room.

Wesgrove continued to bend over the body to shield Max from view. They hadn't rehearsed this part, much less anticipated the movement and reaction of others; how stupid of them. The nurse stood waiting for an order, perhaps to cover the face. Wesgrove began to issue commands. Willard, Phoebe, and the nurse were startled.

"Everyone, please leave the room. The body must be prepared for cryonic procedure immediately. Not a moment is to be lost. Out! I must remind you, this is the wish of the deceased.

"Nurse, call downstairs to the lobby. Tell the doorman to get the men waiting in a van up here as fast as possible. Call this number." He fished in his pocket for a piece of paper and handed it to her. Tell them the body will be arriving in three hours." He threw off his jacket and began to strip the body. They left in shocked confusion, and none too soon.

Max thought he was going to die from holding his breath. One more second, he felt, and all would be over. Why hadn't he thought of *that* as a way out?

He opened his eyes. "It was all right, wasn't it? It worked."

"So far, but stay the way you are, with your eyes closed," Wesgrove said anxiously. "The nurse can come back in, anyone can walk in . . . they're upset. They might want to take one last look, it's natural, under ordinary circumstances; it's the family's right to . . ."

Max opened his eyes again, struck with the "one last look." He had been too busy acting to consider its effect.

"You've just expired, remember?" Wesgrove scolded. "We must continue as if it were true. Behave! I'm going to make believe I'm injecting you." He took a large needle from his bag. "It's hardly the first step for a cryonic suspension, but who would know? My assistants are on their way up, Dr. Arthur Lewisohn and Dr. Jeff Gruening—the only other people on this earth who know what we are doing." Beads of sweat had broken out on the poor man's face. "Their presence will make it official, participants in a procedure, strange as it might seem. If anyone should ask, I'll explain they're here to remove your blood and inject you with a fluid for slow freezing . . . so, please continue to play dead, it's crucial." He stared at Max for an ineffable second. "We're in it. There's no going back, God help us."

A funny little smile suffused Max's face. "Moral quaver, Dr. Wesgrove? Do I see shattering second thoughts?"

"Shattering, cosmic second thoughts, my friend."

"How did I do the scene? You can tell me that. It felt right
. . . I was almost convincing myself."

"The rattle was too strong." Wesgrove's worried face relieved itself with a grimace.

Someone was quietly opening the door. Wesgrove turned
about. Phoebe stood in the doorway. What she saw was Wesgrove still leaning over her father with a needle in his hand.

"I want to see him once more. I don't care what you're
doing or what I'll see. He's my father . . . I want to be with him,
be a part of what he wanted to happen to him . . ."

Wesgrove tried to hide his hysteria. "It's too unpleasant,
what will have to be done to him now. My colleagues are on their
way up to help me. Your father would not want you to witness
what has to be done. Yes, I understand, my dear . . . Come in and
say good-bye again, but please do it fast. There is no time to
waste, or the cryonic procedure will be destroyed." He pulled the
sheet up over Max as she resolutely walked to the bed.

One of Max's hands had not been covered. She took it,
kissed it, held it to her cheek. "It's so warm," she whispered.

She began to cry. "I don't know anything about death. I
don't understand about anything . . ." In a wild, little move, she
pulled the sheet from his face. Max held his breath in terror, as
she implored, "You've cheated me, Daddy, that's how it feels. So
soon . . . so fast . . . why this horrible freezing?"

Wesgrove's colleagues, Lewisohn and Gruening, entered
the room. Phoebe looked at them blankly. Dazed, she turned to
look at her father once more and walked out.

"Wes, go after her and tell her! I want her to know. She
must know," Max whispered frantically.

"No," Wesgrove protested. "No one else should have the
burden of knowing. It's not safe."

"She'll keep how I wanted to die locked in her, I swear. Do
it! I will *not* cheat her."

Max quickly explained where Phoebe's room was and Wesgrove, a drawn little man looking like a tiny doll in a tempest,
went down the hall, his white hair on end with apprehension,
his heart beating too fast. This is what happens when you for-
sake abstraction for emotion. God, God . . . He felt like a

plumber in the theater being asked to take the place of an actor who had suddenly become ill.

"My dear . . . my dear . . ." He sat on her bed, patted her blond hair, looked into her blue eyes that had the shape of her father's—wide, intelligent eyes, their capillaries swollen with tears and questions. He spoke as bravely as he could, trying to remember his lines, plumber that he was. "I don't know you very well, but it seems to be my place to tell you a most extraordinary secret for a young person to know and keep. Your father isn't dead and he wants to see you."

"I knew it!" Phoebe jumped up, almost knocking him over. "I know his eyes. There was a look in them and they weren't dying! I thought I was losing my mind." She started to rush out. He took her firmly by an arm.

"Please sit down, I must talk to you first. Your father has asked me to." He proceeded to tell her of her father's determination to commit suicide and his own dissuading him from that course, in the name of science. "It's much for you to comprehend at your age—the pain of a terminal illness, a man wanting to die in his own way. You were right. Death is very far away from you, as it should be. And, you must try to understand my role, I beg of you. This whole plan is utterly dangerous for me." He paused. "Your father insists I trust you. I will, because you are his daughter. We had to make it appear like a natural death here. Now you see . . . now you know . . . and I hope you understand."

Phoebe shook her head yes and stood up. "May I see him now?"

"Yes, but quickly and quietly, please." He stayed where he was, to give them a few minutes alone.

The two other doctors were standing on either side of Max's door as she rushed by them.

"I might have known you weren't going to die without some kind of fireworks," Phoebe exploded as quietly as she could.

"This is the real good-bye, baby, I couldn't leave without it. It all looks and feels crazy, but it isn't. It's rational. I would have taken pills otherwise, remember that. Wesgrove explained everything?"

"Yes."

"Listen to me, baby, I would have done it, be sure of that . . . when I felt my dignity going. But, that's a hard moment to know, I see that now. Just hang on to it—that your daddy tried to die well. Don't lose track of Wesgrove. I've given myself to him.

"Oh, I love you, little one. You're myself. I have pride in myself. Don't I sound like a bag of wind . . ." He felt tears wanting to break loose like all hell, but this was no time for tears.

"Watch over your sister, even though you're the younger, Phoebe. And, don't lose touch with Hedda. She loves you, too. Hang on to love. She's going to feel pretty lousy for a while. She got a bum deal, so did I . . ." He looked at the little face that was so like Sophia's, except that it wasn't cold and tight, showing its wretchedness in every feature. Phoebe's, with the same genetic combination, was clear, loving, listening beauty.

"Make some man good and happy someday," he said softly. "This is a big trip for you, isn't it . . . a lot of responsibility. I'm asking you to protect Wesgrove's genius and reputation, as you would protect me with your life. No one must ever know he helped me die, not even the man you're going to marry someday. Now, walk out the door like we're going to see each other tomorrow . . . that's the only way."

They embraced. She started to leave. She wanted to turn, run back, plead with him not to do it, plead with him to hang on, stay alive as long as humanly possible; she would convince him, rage, cry, scream, tear the whole place apart—to be able to have him in his bed, alive, tomorrow!

It was almost as though he had read her mind from the look of her back. She heard him whisper.

"If not tomorrow, how about someday, baby?"

She wanted to turn around, but she didn't trust herself. Instead she said it to the door. "It's going to be very quiet without you."

"You'll get used to it. That's an order" were Max's final words and she left. Closing the door felt like trying to turn off the sun. It was a physical impossibility, yet she did it!

Hedda was in Roz's room, rocking back and forth in a chair that didn't rock, looking out the window onto Central Park, watching a man walking home, unhurried, *as though there were all the time in the world;* watching couples in taxis going home. She had never felt so excruciatingly lonely in her whole life.

Wesgrove rejoined his two colleagues in Max's room. It was 1:30 in the morning. Roz and Willard had left to stay in a hotel.

The servants were still sitting in the kitchen observing a kind of wake, not wanting to see it, but waiting for the removal of Mr. Treading. Except the butler, who stood rigidly at the front door, ready to open it for the last time for the best employer he had ever had. Shortly after 2:00, he watched Dr. Wesgrove approach, and the two men he had let in with a stretcher earlier. Now, on the stretcher was a body bag. He sucked in his sadness. It was like you see it on television after a fire or an accident—a body bag. It just didn't seem right or proper, a big, fine man like that going out, not in a fine bronze coffin . . . just a body bag. He opened the door for Mr. Treading.

(Actually, it was a body bag with tiny holes, to allow Max to breathe until he was placed in the waiting van.)

They drove in silence in the back, a driver up front who thought he was taking a corpse to a laboratory in Long Island.

Not until they were crossing the Triborough Bridge did he feel hands slipping the bag off him. Wesgrove introduced the two men for the first time: "Dr. Arthur Lewisohn, Maxwell Treading. Dr. Jeff Gruening, Maxwell Treading."

They drove in silence. Max sat up and accepted a cup of coffee from Dr. Lewisohn, a youngish man with a serious, round face, shock of red hair, tired blue eyes, and the pallor of a hospital resident, but the kind of skin that turned pink from the least excitement. Just handing the cup to Max flushed his cheeks. There was a concentrated physicality about Lewisohn, like that of a deadly purposeful mountain climber. Max liked the look of him. Jeff Gruening, the other one, was another matter—a tall man with everything about him dark, lean and sour, a shadow of a beard no matter when he last shaved his thin cheeks, a tall white forehead with a head of curly black hair that came to a widow's peak almost feminine in its curve; the severe portrait-face of an Italian Renaissance nobleman, not evil but definitely exacting, predatory. The three of them, Max, Gruening, Lewisohn, filled the back of the van with their presences, three big men. Wesgrove was almost not to be found. Each was lost in his own grim thoughts.

As they made their way, Max looked out the small back window at the fading skyline of New York. They still had not spoken. Max wanted to laugh about the weirdest adventure of his life, but he saw his companions were not in a mood to join him. They were protecting themselves from contact; they couldn't accept him as alive—that was too much to ask of three scientists schooled in objectivity. Almost an hour went by.

Max *didn't* want to be silent. "It's not the twenty-third of June anymore, Wes, it's the morning of the twenty-fourth."

Lewisohn and Gruening were startled by his referring to their mentor as "Wes." No one had heard him called anything but a reverential "Dr. Wesgrove." They looked at each other. The silence was broken.

"The day after Midsummer Eve," Jeff Gruening, the dour biopsychiatrist said, with a cutting edge to his voice. "The night to go mad, burn fires, make insane love, push the evil spirits away for another year. An unholy, mad, glorious time was had by all." He looked at Max with dark-gray, clear, inquisitive eyes, wanting to ask questions, probe the man who was allowing them his body . . . but he decided against it. It was beyond the time for metaphysical questions. Yet, this man Treading looked like he might be up to questions. Gruening checked himself and remained silent.

"Hey, you guys," Max said to both young men, in a voice

he might have used to address his metallurgist and pilot a moment before the helicopter crash. "What do you think? What are
the chances?"

"What do we think?" Lewisohn said uneasily.

"Yes . . . I don't understand why we're all so quiet when
there's so much to say, isn't that funny? What do you think of
my chances for a second time around, is the question. Any
takers?"

"At the moment, none," said Lewisohn.

"But in the future?" Gruening chided his colleague. "How
can you say 'none'? Such humility. Give the man hope, I dare
you."

"I do *not* dare. You're out of order, Jeff."

"No, he isn't," Max corrected. "He's on the beam, for me
anyway. If you can't laugh when it's the worst, then you've lost
your ticket."

"Ticket?" Gruening asked.

"Ticket to life, damn you all."

Max caught the silent censure of Wesgrove: Guinea pigs
don't play with time. This was the time to be nothing. He felt
like talking till Hell froze.

Gruening had several retorts on his lips but he didn't dare.
The boss looked like death warmed over.

An hour later, Max was looking at the dawn coming up
slow and easy.

They neared their destination—a long, white building with
a small, discreet metal plaque, CRC Affiliate, over its entrance.
Max was enclosed in the body bag again, lifted onto the
stretcher, and carried to a room with a hospital bed in it. He was
aware of aggravated activity, bodies moving around him.

The personnel of the Cancer Research Center Affiliate were
receiving what was thought to be their first dead human to be
frozen and placed next to the cryonicized bodies and organs of
the lower animals they had been experimenting on for some
time. This was a most special specimen, the body of Maxwell
Treading, who had died of cancer and had willed his remains to
the Center. The procedure was to be done by the three bosses,

Wesgrove, Gruening, and Lewisohn. It was going to be a day to remember. Everything was ready. The call had come in at midnight. What a wild night . . . they'd been running around like lunatics. The only thing missing was a full moon.

Hedda's door opened at five in the morning. She was in bed, not asleep, just staring at the tops of the trees in Central Park that could be seen from the bed. The dark green was slowly being touched with dawn light.

"May I crawl into bed with you? I'm frightened . . ."

"Of course, darling." Hedda held her arms out to Phoebe. They clung to each other and wept. It felt the way a funeral should be—unabashed, exhausting grief. They both fell asleep . . . about the same time as Max was being settled in his room in the Cancer Research Center Affiliate building.

The time had come.

It was seven o'clock on the morning of the twenty-fourth. Max was light-headed from lack of sleep. He hadn't eaten anything for twenty-four hours. A dying man isn't supposed to eat. He was ravenous, but there was a clarity in his head, a sense of purge. Everything had the sharpness of a hard-edge painting, including himself. He was sitting up in bed signing papers that would authorize Wesgrove to perform a cryonic suspension on his body, providing also for perpetual care in a cold storage laboratory. It wasn't cheap. No wonder rich eccentrics were the only ones to indulge themselves in a vision of reanimation. Max predated his signature. The document was to be delivered to Dinessen with an apology from Wesgrove; it should have been sent when Max decided almost a month ago, but it had slipped Wesgrove's mind.

Oh, how he wanted some good, hot coffee with *schlag* in it, like Cook often made, knowing he loved it so—dark, brown Colombian coffee peaked with whipped cream. He fought the wish, it was affecting his clarity. Then, he did a peculiar thing, he thought. He reached out with his hands to grab the air, made funny little gestures like a child grabbing at butterflies.

He put aside the papers he'd signed, leaned back with nothing on his mind that he could describe, no concrete thought, no image, just a feeling of nothingness . . . It was so total, it was *everything*. At that very moment, the sun came into the room and lit up the floor in front of the window. He watched the yellow light announcing "Day" on the dark-grained wood.

If Hedda had been in the room, she would have thought that he looked like a John Singer Sargent portrait. He was caught in a suspended moment, every feature delineated in a sharp front light, expressing itself without a secret held back— handsome, broad, American, strong, proud, vulnerable features caught in a crucial moment. His eyes held their deepest look, his cheeks their nakedest, the broad mouth ready to speak. A lock of his blond-gray hair had fallen over his forehead. It was catching the reflection of the sun coming in. Altogether, the most handsome, dramatic man she had ever known or would hope to meet for the rest of her life. A man who had *done* something, and *felt* something. It was all over his face, a face Sargent would have *had* to capture if he had seen it.

That's what Wesgrove saw when he walked in—a portrait of peace in action. It was very disturbing. Begin, he commanded himself. Without a word, he inserted acupuncture needles to numb Max's neck and head. Still no word between them. Then suddenly, the two men embraced in an awkward way. Wesgrove's eyeglasses were on the end of his nose. Max lifted them gently to the bridge of the nose—a tender gesture of son to father. They disengaged themselves from the brutal nearness. Wesgrove turned away to reach for a hypodermic. Each silently resolved not to say good-bye. That would have been unbearable.

Max, to his surprise, began to recite the prayer of his childhood . . . "Now I lay me down to sleep . . ." It brought a little smile to his lips.

Wesgrove waited.

Max refused to look away as the needle was inserted into his jugular vein . . . a needle with a silvery drip, a magic tear hanging from its point. That point was to enter his body, catch his *being* instantaneously and cause him to die with the speed of light.

And, it did.

Maxwell Treading, born between a mesa and a butte, son of Martha Ackers and Jonathan Treading, husband of Sophia Walleby, father of Rosalind and Phoebe, was now legally *and* clinically dead.

Wesgrove stood there, his eyes ignoring his command; he had no way to stop their behavior. He was crying.

He had just shut down a man's power to think, reason, and feel. There was nothing to fortify himself with, except the echo of Max's words in Maine, coming back from his walk into the pine grove: Max's "Yes . . ." . . . "I'll be a part of the making of an answer, won't I?"

He had seen many die, but this was the most overwhelming death. He had caused it! Caused the brain systems associated with the eye-ear intricacies, the chemicals that allowed Max to experience fear and anger, the hormones, enzymes, the cells, the love, creativity, music, word, philosophy, humor, bravery, invention of a man, the myriads of astounding biological connections . . . he had caused them all to stop! It had *all* ended in an infinitesimal space of time, because of the liquid in the hypodermic needle—*never* before used on a human being, a liquid so powerful it was capable of killing with the speed of light. Max had said yes to it all, he had to remind himself again, trying to regain his calm.

"I apologize for not having been able to cure you," he said out loud, with heartbreaking humility. "Now, nothing but to take the next steps on a long journey . . ."

Wesgrove braced himself. The rest of the freezing procedure had to begin immediately. He walked swiftly to the door and let in Lewisohn and Gruening.

Equipment had been made ready in the room, waiting for that moment after death.

Max's chest was slit open and his body attached to a heart-lung apparatus by Wesgrove's two colleagues, to prolong organ functioning and oxygen intake as long as possible. The procedure seemed to be happening in a split second for Wesgrove, not long enough to adjust his view away from the body of Max to the body of a guinea pig in an experiment. He silently thanked God for the help of his colleagues.

There was a sense of urgency but not hysteria, from then on. Wesgrove forced himself into the transition.

The blood was drained off at the same time as the chilling agent and the cryoprotectant substance were injected *simultaneously*. This was Wesgrove's demand—the simultaneity. The enzyme-laden cryoprotectant must *get there* first, as in a race; it was to coat and prevent injury to the cells as they froze slowly, drop by drop, in perfectly timed sequence with the blood leaving the body. Slowly, slowly . . . As they worked to achieve the exact rhythms, Wesgrove's concentration was distracted by an image —under a microscope this would look like a dance of exits and entrances.

One of his targets was to experiment with the suppression of all physical and biochemical changes under the trauma of freezing. As the outer layers cooled, his young colleague Dr. Lewisohn removed the heart-lung apparatus and sewed up the open chest delicately. He was satisfied. The other colleague, Dr. Gruening, a physiologist *and* biopsychiatrist, was busy monitoring a salt-and-potassium-balance controller that expressed itself with a needle protruding from the body's right thigh. Slow cooling was the intention, slow enough to let the cryoprotectant take over only in a ratio compatible with cell stabilization. That meant—sneak up on the living cells; for cells can be severely injured by salt concentration as body liquid is withdrawn in the freezing process, causing the cells to shrink.

Wesgrove was beginning to feel comfortable in the event. It was working well. He had sworn his colleagues into a holy confidence after Max had given his yes to *this* use of his body.

They had talked for weeks about the new methods they were going to use; even the cryonics section of the Cancer Research Center had not approached them. Lewisohn's and Gruening's attitude was: This is the old man's ball game and we'd go with him no matter what. For weeks they had talked and prepsyched the present like athletes preparing for the overstretch that could break a record.

Yes, it was going well. Wesgrove even voiced it with a grunt that the other two knew so well as his way of saying "Not bad . . ." He added to the grunt. "I don't think we have to be afraid of ice crystals either, the way this thing is working."

They were learning and computing invaluable information about the new cryoprotectant that was being used for the first time on a whole human body, plus testing the cellular response to the slow-freeze injections, which was being recorded and interpreted by the computer attached to the chilling agent. Wesgrove was thinking: Max's gift of his body might pay off in full.

As the three men leaned over the slow-freezing body, intensely observing and balancing the procedures, their sweat drops fell, joining the cold that was embracing it from the outside in . . . down to twenty-eight degrees, Fahrenheit.

The body was then wheeled to another section of the cryonics laboratory and other technicians took over. It was placed in a container of dry ice to continue the freezing downward. It was wrapped in a tissuelike foil made of lithium (another experimental product of the Center, achieved with the help of Dow Chemical), secured to a stretcher, and placed in a container inside a steel capsule filled with liquid nitrogen, where the body would move downward into a solid state, achieve and maintain a temperature of minus three hundred and twenty degrees, Fahrenheit. The liquid nitrogen would be replaced from time to time as it evaporated or boiled off.

The capsule was wheeled into a facility where organs and animals could be preserved forever . . . barring a cataclysmic event that could cut off the generators of the building and their three back-up systems.

TWO

17

Dr. Roy Candleman had a solid career behind him in the academic world, culminating in a lectureship at Harvard. It had been a long, careful trip to Cambridge, one that had allowed no interference, no marriage, no children. He had published scientific papers of some interest, yearly, in his field of molecular biology, making his name very familiar to colleagues in the same area.

Candleman had an enviable talent—he was able to beat out his competitors when it came to getting funds and grants for whatever project he was pursuing; he was so adept at raising money that some of his associates along the way wondered why he remained in academia and didn't join with industry to make himself a fortune. They didn't realize that what he wanted most was to earn his place in that special ivory tower *class* that used to be the domain of the Wasp and a few genius gate-crashers.

He had done it. The kid from Brooklyn had turned himself into an obsessively neat, dapper, dedicated, very inventive, even talented lecturer and research scientist in molecular biology.

In his academic circle, Roy Candleman was known as a "hardware man." He always seemed to be in a project with offshoots that could turn into commodities—a new tool to be used in the lab, a finding that could be utilized by a pharmaceutical company or a medical supplier. Though he wanted to be part of it, there was nothing *ivory tower* about Candleman. He could extrapolate from work that was still trembling with birth trauma in the lab and make it seem that the answer to the mystery of life was just around the corner. His was an open, easy way of making incomprehensible scientific information seem like the next movie coming out. He was close to *the know* and made you believe you could understand not only his field and work in the mystery of the cell, but anyone else's work on any subject, from clouds to the unknown power of aspirin. He was a strange combination of the careful drone bee and the careless visionary—an unusual duality, to say the least.

Perhaps the biggest mistake of his meticulously planned life was to have maneuvered himself into the atmosphere of the great Hiram Wesgrove at Harvard.

On the basis of several papers he had written, and a humble meeting he had arranged with Wesgrove, in Candleman's own words: "To get the star's reaction to *my* work in relation to *his*, with the cancer cell . . . we hit it off like gangbusters and he invited me to come on board."

But, what a shock for Candleman, to be at Harvard and under the thumb of Wesgrove. Scientific papers were not allowed to be sent to medical journals, much less daily papers. The rule out of Wesgrove's department was: Put away a successful experiment, a new finding, let it simmer, let it season; cross it with the findings of others, and the results of many minds will be published, not the work of one, no matter how interesting for the moment.

It was an unbearable atmosphere for Candleman the hustler. But Candleman the scientist, knew he had to be where he was, at the center of class thought. He had to submerge his natural *entrepreneurial* talents. He had to reason: This was a time to lie back, cap the lid. He dreamed of heading his own department of research in some illustrious setting—a respected scientist who had the talent of combining the worlds of finance and science. How else could theoretical science flower, if not for men like him? No humble pie, but a smartness—to be temporarily humble—made him willing to wait, delay his dream. After all, wasn't he a *wunderkind* himself? Thirty-five, and look where he was already!

When Hiram Wesgrove was persuaded to leave Harvard and head the Cancer Research Center in New York, Roy Candleman was asked to join him and readily agreed. Wesgrove had learned to lean heavily on Candleman, if not for his original thinking, then for his exact contribution, when it came to testing and follow-through. But Candleman anguished. He hadn't written an original paper for years. Anything that did reach publication was always under the name of the Center. A plan began to take shape that would free him, make him his own man again. He asked Wesgrove's permission to tackle some independent research at the Center in the hormone field. His reasoning? If it came to anything, his position there would change first, and then he would move on. It was crucial for him to do some original work on his own or he was heading for oblivion. He was also beginning to see that he wasn't exactly in Wesgrove's inner circle . . . and it included Lewisohn and Gruening. Wesgrove gave him permission for some independent work.

In May of 1982, Candleman presented the results of a study having to do with the cells of women cancer patients in menopause. It was interesting research, doubly so because it came up with conclusions diametrically opposed to those of a project Wesgrove had done many years before. Candleman knew nothing about that project *because it had never been published.* In effect, his figures challenged those of the master, and the master, being who he was, was willing to admit to mistake.

Wesgrove asked an impartial group to check out Candleman's findings. They discovered that the results of Candleman's work were based on manipulated material. He had falsified curves and charts—everything was an ingenious, creative lie.

It was one of the most upsetting private talks Wesgrove ever had. Candleman broke down and cried and asked his forgiveness. He asked for a leave of absence. Obviously, what he had done was so reprehensible, there was no excuse; he must be suffering from mental and physical fatigue to have so betrayed his position, his moral and ethical senses. Candleman pleaded for another chance, a vacation of several months, promised to see a psychiatrist and get himself well. He hoped Wesgrove would do him the honor of being quiet about his aberration; otherwise, his whole career was finished.

Much to his shock, Candleman was fired. He thought he had pleaded his case poignantly and well. He hadn't lied. He *didn't* know the part of him that had falsified information and results. It was strange but human. His aspirations had tripped him, his impatience, cupidity—all so human. He was a first offender. Couldn't Wesgrove forgive something that had never happened before and would never happen again?

Wesgrove refused to back down on the firing. He promised to keep the reason for Candleman's leaving the Center a secret, if possible; there were others who had reviewed the falsified material, but he would do his best not to have "the crime" known in other places. Candleman winced under the word.

Wesgrove went on: Candleman should think about himself as a man of science in search of truth, think long and hard about whether it was the wrong field for him to be in, not only for himself, but for his unsuspecting fellow men . . . a crime in science was a crime against humanity!

Candleman was more upset at being lectured to by the righteous guru than by being fired. Wesgrove's holier-than-thou attitude, his unwillingness to forgive the fallibilities in the best of men, his refusing to allow a person a *second chance*—it was unbearable, unfair to the extreme.

Candleman left the Center without cleaning out his desk. He went off for a vacation in the Caribbean; he needed rest and time to face himself. When he came back, he thought confidently, he would tackle Wesgrove again, with time the healer.

By late June, he had tried three times to make an appointment to see Wesgrove, without success. He had to admit that the door was shut. He went to his office at night, when he would have to meet as few people as possible, to collect his papers and belongings. He had expected to find them already boxed, but they weren't. His office was unused and intact. Wesgrove, the puritan-guru, must be transmitting another lesson: *Remove your own bed, the one you can't lie in anymore.* Candleman felt sick to his stomach. There was only one thing to do—clear out, and fast. He heard movement in the corridor as he sat at his desk, then activity next door in Arthur Lewisohn's office. He heard doors open and shut and muffled voices. He debated whether to open his door, see what was going on after hours, maybe even talk to Arthur, if that's who it was . . . They'd worked so long together and Arthur was a straight, level guy, close to Wesgrove. Maybe he'd help him open up his options again with the old man.

As he sat there listening and thinking, he sensed something in the air, that special something at the Center when someone had broken through with new findings and there would be a coffee klatch, a sharing of information. He was going to miss it, that sharing . . . He was going to miss Wesgrove's genius, which permeated every floor of the building, even though the air could be annoyingly modest, Quakerish, too religious.

Sure, he revered a Wesgrove kind of man, but he, Candleman, had a spark of his own, not to be undervalued. He decided not to make contact with Lewisohn and grovel. He began packing. Though he tried hard to ignore it, he had a worthless, expelled-boy feeling and resented it . . . and couldn't help thinking about the irony of the whole thing . . . Wesgrove's modesty. (If he had published, I never would have gotten into trouble . . . His modesty hung my ambition. Quick, get out of the nightmare . . . you did a dumb, stupid thing.)

Instead of *quick* . . . he sat down at his desk to pull himself together. He opened the newspaper he had brought with him and glanced at the headlines. At the bottom was: "Treading, financier, dead from cancer." He read on: "The billionaire uranium king, after a year's fight with cancer died yesterday at his home on Fifth Avenue at the age of fifty-five. According to a release from Global Materials, Ltd., the international corporation of which he was founder and head until his death, his body will undergo freezing rather than conventional burial and he has willed his remains to be used for scientific purposes at the Cancer Research Center, headed by the illustrious Nobel Prize recipient, Dr. Hiram Wesgrove. . . . Cont. Section B, Page 8."

He turned the pages quickly. (Treading had been under the care of the boss. But, cryonic suspension?) He continued to read a two-column obituary of the life and times of Treading, his position in the international world of natural resources, his liberalism, outspokenness. There would be no memorial service, and members of his family were unavailable for comment, nor was any statement forthcoming from Dr. Wesgrove, according to a spokesperson at the Cancer Research Center. The story ended with a brief explanation of *cryonic suspension.* It was rumored to be the form of burial chosen by Walt Disney, as well as some unfortunates, recently, whose families were defrauded in a certain burial *scam;* frozen bodies were found in distressing states of decomposition because of neglect or amateurish procedures that had promised "perpetual care" in a frozen state.

A bell began to toll in Candleman's head: You were so far out of the inner circle, you didn't even know what *they* were doing . . . Obviously Wesgrove has come up with something important in cryonics, or he wouldn't want a dead human to work with. *That's* what the special air around here was all about!

The voices in Lewisohn's office were still there. He tried to close them out; burning with resentment, he swept his desk clean, went down the hall to a service room to collect some cartons, returned, filled them with the years of work. He left a note on his desk asking for the cartons to be delivered to his apartment, turned the lights out, and left. He had bumped into no one, thank God.

Cryonic suspension, after the obituary in the newspaper, was the subject of dinner table conversation for the next week, as well as the "quirky" Treading himself, his wife's heart attack on the tennis court, his attachment to Hedda Goldsmith, the designer, his billions, "his friendship with Fidel Castro." Wall

Street cronies remembered or *thought* they remembered that "Treading was one of the first, if not the only American to be allowed a tour of the Russian space program, and might even have been selling the USSR forbidden materials." The stories grew more fanciful as the week wore on—about Treading's secret trip to have an audience with Chairman Mao before he died; Treading's fight with Henry Kissinger over the Vietnam war and how Sophia Treading got up from the table and left the apartment, leaving all the guests agape. (That one was true.) On and on about . . . there must have been a Mafia tie somewhere, or how could such wealth be accumulated so fast in the beginning? Gossip, wonderful gossip, tales of a Paul Bunyan or a Dracula. He was a bleeding heart and everyone in conservative circles knew bleeding hearts were fit for hanging. Everyone, in those circles, also *knew* Treading had a connection with the infamous Kennedys, had shared women with Jack and state secrets with Bobby.

Max would have gotten quite a kick out of the afterwave of his death . . . before he got mad as hell. He thought he'd lived a neat, careful game for a maverick. He had no idea so many were watching and ready to pounce. "Me, fit for hanging?" Max would have exploded. "The idea of Freedom? The idea of the individual? American! We invented it. If I was anything, I was American, and I really tried. Hang me for it? You can't—I'm frozen!"

"The good leave too soon, no matter how long they've been around." *Some* did say that about him.

Roz was in a state of collapse from the notoriety. She was hiding out at Greenbriar. Still, the stories hovered over Newport and were retold to her by Willard, who got them from his parents, who felt impelled to pass them along as they heard them from well-wishers, commiserating about the name of Clyde having to be connected with that of Treading. Their daughter-in-law ought to *know* what was being said about her father, they owed it to her. Poor Roz, with the burden of having her mother's sterling name of Walleby dragged in the mud, as well as theirs. It was important for her to know what she must face when the ruckus died down and she went out into the world again—with a clear eye. The mote had been removed. The only saving grace of the mote was that it had left an incredible fortune.

Dinessen allowed a week to go by before he arranged a reading of the will at the apartment. Roz would remember she wore black. Hedda wouldn't remember what she wore. Phoebe knew she must have been wearing jeans because she and Hedda were busy putting her father's things away. It was a week of astonishment for Hedda and Phoebe as they went through Max's papers, the thank-you notes from universities and students all over the world—for the endowments and trusts he had set up. And the condolence mail, waves of it. Phoebe was determined to answer everything. Verdolino and Barnett, representing the board of Global Materials, came to hear the will. They were in Brooks Brothers suits and school ties. It was raining and they left black umbrellas at the door.

The first paragraph of Max's will disclosed that he had bequeathed one million dollars a year for ten years to Hedda; the same amount—ten million dollars—to Roz.

("I want Hedda to be free of me," he had said to Dinessen, "but I'm vain, I want to be the one to make her feel independent in a way she doesn't know. As for Roz, she's got a trust from her mother, she's married to the damn Clyde money, she doesn't need mine, but I want to leave her just what I'm leaving Hedda.")

The assembled then heard that Max's share of Global Materials—fifty-four percent—was to be handed down "to my daughter Phoebe, who must also assume my position as chairman. If she does not agree to this bequest and directive, my stock is to be sold in the open market and the proceeds given in equal gifts to the treasuries of the countries of Israel, Mexico, Cuba, and Zimbabwe." Dinessen read on . . . "I direct that monies derived from the sale of stock registered in my name, other than those of Global Materials, be used to create the Treading Foundation. The purpose of this foundation shall be for the advancement and enlightenment of the human race in the arts. The above-described foundation shall be guided by my daughters, Phoebe and Rosalind, who shall alternate annually as president and vice-president. Each shall appoint three members of the board of directors."

Verdolino and Barnett, the only Global board members present, almost fell off their chairs. A little girl in jeans would be the head of an international company, and they would have to vote her in!

Dinessen remembered that he hadn't been able to contain himself when he and Max were working out the will. "Max, what are you doing? She's twenty-four years old! And do you mean to say—if she refuses to become chairman of Global, she'll receive no inheritance?" Max had answered: "I know my little girl, George . . . I'm giving her the chance of a lifetime. My little one is a radical, you know. Down with capitalism, she says. Since it's the only system available to her in America, and if she can see I'm challenging her, she might learn what you *can* do with it, when you have it—profit, that damnable word. I want her to learn firsthand, like I did: In the course of making profit is the inevitability of producing social value . . ."

Dinessen responded, "Max, aren't you playing with her and Global as if they were toys? What if she says no?"

"I'd respect that . . . I just want to give her a chance to take her thinking to the end of the line, the way I did; I want her to know me, be me, improve on me. She's a special young one."

"She's not a son, Max," Dinessen said cautiously. That remark took Max a little aback. Dinessen then said, "What makes you think the board will go along with it, if she says yes?"

Max had a ready answer: "They'll have to. If my shares have to be sold in the open market, it'll depress everyone else's, and more than that, only a consortium could afford to buy in. My gang wouldn't like that. They'll vote her in to maintain the

balance, they're not gonna let go, they've worked too hard to
help build Global. They'll run it until she grows up . . . and
you'll be there, her adviser, my executor. Global will go down
the drain if she doesn't say yes. I'm asking her to honor my life's
work. You're going to have to explain it all to her . . ."

"Thanks a lot, my friend," Dinessen remembered saying.

The last paragraph of the will stated: "I bequeath the re-
mainder of my personal assets—one hundred million dollars,
consisting of gold and bonds—to the Cancer Research Center,
to be used at the total discretion of Dr. Hiram Wesgrove in his
pursuit of the cure for cancer and any other research he deems
worthy under his direction . . ."

They had just heard the largest bequest by an individual to
any scientific institution. The only contents of the will that had
not caused emotional reverberation and shock were Max's be-
quests, handsome as they were, "to my employees for their
respect, loyalty, and good work . . ."—his cook, butler, valet,
chauffeur, a maid, and two favorite secretaries.

When they all could leave the living room gracefully, how
could they not wonder if Max had been sane? It was even
Phoebe's thought. Roz's face was a mask. What she was hiding
was something else. Justification for anger was a tonic. She had
always been right—he hated her! What a relief. He had done
what she expected—given everything to Phoebe, as he had done
in life. She *did* know her father, she hadn't been wrong, she had
fantasized nothing. The will was almost a cathartic.

(The intentions—bittersweet, sad, and optimistic—behind
Max's directive for a Treading Foundation, to keep his two
daughters bonded for life in public philanthropy, hadn't penetrated either Phoebe or Roz, there was so much else to react to.)

Phoebe was numb. Hedda suggested they all stay for a
drink. Roz and Willard excused themselves. "I have to talk with
you," Dinessen said quietly to Phoebe. She took him into the
library. Verdolino and Barnett stayed out of respect for Max,
and because they both needed hard liquor fast. Hedda joined
them for an uncomfortable fifteen minutes of silence, then wandered off and the butler saw them out.

. . .

Phoebe flung herself into a chair, looked around the library (Max's favorite room) filled with her father's books and memorabilia, and burst into tears.

"Phoebe, listen to me carefully . . ." Dinessen said.

"I want to live my own life, not his!" she cried. "I will not do it, I'm not equipped or interested. He can't shape my life, I won't let him!"

"Your father was a genius, you know . . ."

Phoebe looked up. "I know that . . ."

"You're also aware he did some unusual things with his money?"

"Yes . . . Hedda and I have been going over his papers . . ."

"They're not the decisions of an ordinary man, all those grants and trusts, you agree?"

"Yes . . ."

"You agree with the spirit behind his decisions?"

Phoebe stopped crying. "Of course I do!"

"Then, our problem is—how can we preserve that spirit?" He knew she was listening and he wanted to take advantage of it; he became hard. "Fathers have a way of indulging their little girls. Dead fathers make their little girls grow up. He asked me to explain it to you; he knew it wasn't going to be easy, what he hoped for—the business to go on in his image, not just to amass millions, but to benefit people, if capitalism could . . . He said you were very serious about studying it in books. Did you ever talk figures with your father, the reality of what he's done?"

"We only talked philosophy and we disagreed . . ."

"Funny . . ." Dinessen purposely mused with irony, "the shoemaker's child goes without shoes. You're a student of economics; under your nose are learning tools and you never used them." He pressed on, she was definitely listening. "Why is Global also in the agrobusiness? Food, protein, the problem of hunger. Why was the last effort of your father the start of a solar energy plant? To prove that nuclear energy was not necessary; to pioneer in making energy as cheap as possible one day. You can be sure that the first thing to happen if there's a change in management of Global Materials, will be the stopping of the solar energy plant. Do you agree that his commitments have to be preserved? *He willed you an important vote.* I ask you to look at it with all the wisdom you have, for someone so young. Another thing, Phoebe, do you realize that Global has thousands of employees and their families around the world? What would happen to them if Global got rocked by the sale of your father's stock and a change of policy? He made a big mistake by not preparing you for this, but we have to forgive him, he didn't know he was going to be struck down by cancer . . ." Dinessen paused for breath. (What am I doing? he said to himself. I'm flailing the poor little thing, she looks like a waif. Max has infected me with his arrogance; he has no right to manipulate her with his life, with his death . . .)

"No more, please," Phoebe said weakly.

"Forgive me . . . I promised your father I'd plead his case. I've done it the best I could, not good enough for you or him, I suppose . . . My dear, think it over, we have decisions to make, you and I. Max trusted his board, but people do curious things in a crisis. We can't keep the situation off-balance . . . If it will be any help to you in your thinking, the company can run very well as long as there's no big quake it has to withstand . . . while you're growing up." He smiled weakly.

Hours later, Phoebe was saying, "Hedda, I want to run, I'm *going* to, back to school . . . maybe even out to Berkeley, as far away as I can get . . . I have a friend out there. Daddy's still talking to us, it's freaking me out."

"Who's the friend?"

"A nice guy, he stayed with me for a while in Northampton. He sent me a beautiful letter when he heard about Daddy . . ."

"No loves, Phoebe?"

"No . . . it hasn't happened to me, not the kind you mean," Phoebe said defensively. "Not like you and Daddy. Anyway, I'm not ready to sink . . ."

"Sink?"

"Into someone else. I've watched friends do it, marry, get pregnant, juggle two careers. It's a terrible struggle. And the other way—my mother getting Roz ready for marriage, that wasn't exactly something to get excited about. I didn't have the best role models for love, did I . . . ?"

"Max is a hard act to follow, I should imagine," Hedda said.

"Yeah . . ." Phoebe wrinkled her forehead, maybe with a little shock of recognition, Hedda thought.

"You're very rich, Phoebe, you're going to have a special kind of life."

"I'm a fraud. I don't know where I fit. It feels like nowhere. I want to go back to where it was . . ."

"A little girl in blue jeans, eh? Getting straight A's and making believe some day she wasn't going to have to think about a tremendous fortune to handle?"

"Don't do that! I don't have to handle it. I don't want to! I'm not eighteen, I'm twenty-four!"

"Exactly."

"Meaning what?" Phoebe was getting angry.

"Meaning, you're old enough to put the pieces together."

"My pieces, not his!"

"Both, darling, his and yours. Or don't you value his? That sounds rough, I didn't mean it that way. I mean you're not dumb enough to think you're a seed in the wind. You're Max Treading's daughter. You worked your head off getting your A's for him, didn't you . . . How come in economics? How come not in another field? You were going to show him. But you weren't doing something you didn't want to do . . . He was very proud of your being a social animal. Your father was an outrageous dreamer. He left you a ladder of dreams. You add steps of your own. Isn't that the way? A continuity of dreams, or am I crazy?" (Tears came to Hedda's eyes. Max was in the room listening. So was Hedda's father, who had left his own small ladder of dreams and they were still hers.) "You can't make believe you're Jane Doe."

"That hurts," Phoebe said softly.

Hedda wiped her eyes and smiled quickly to ease the tension. "I'm eight years older than you, you better listen."

"You're a heavy trip, lady."

"I know. That's what your father used to say."

"Daddy loved you . . ."

Hedda put her arms around Phoebe and held her—a living piece of Max. She couldn't keep back her own thoughts—thank you, Max, for that outrageous gift, I don't need it, it will remind me of you year after year. Was that your plan for me?

"Hedda, please stay with me?"

"You have yourself and your sister. You'll make it happen, if she can't. I'm moving back to my own apartment. Thank God I kept it. Max didn't know that . . ."

"Not right away!"

"Don't look like that, darling, I'm not disappearing. I have to leave and start over. I'll stay with you, don't worry, until we've got everything settled." Hedda was wondering if being a mother felt like this—you put your own life on hold for someone else's growing time. The next two days, she helped Phoebe put things in boxes, watched her sniff a sweater of her father's, finger a tie. They put away pairs of jogging shoes, the soft leather suits he liked wearing the last winter of his life. Phoebe tucked away talismans, and so did she—Max's old bathrobe he wouldn't throw away, his silver brushes, an evening scarf.

Dinessen came for dinner two days later. Phoebe seemed more settled down and at ease with him. The three of them talked about Max, his life. Dinessen told them anecdotes and Phoebe learned, for the first time, how her father had used his personal fortunes from time to time—to help foot the bills of certain revolutions he saw as worthy. Dinessen laughed. "He once said to me, 'It's an American tradition, only we keep forgetting it. What would we have done without France? There wouldn't have been a USA if she hadn't helped foot the bill.'"

"My father was a glorious nut, wasn't he . . . I used to call him my favorite capitalist. Huh . . ." Phoebe grunted, with some sort of private thought going on.

"He scared me out of my wits," Dinessen said, "trying to keep him out of trouble, but you know, it was an amazing thing, it was as if Someone were watching. Whenever I'd open a newspaper and read about a country changing hands, I'd shake. I knew Max had had a hand in it somehow, if not guns, then money for trade."

"Did Daddy believe in God, I wonder?" Phoebe said, looking at Hedda. "Now it's too late to ask . . ." For some reason, Phoebe found that funny. "There are a lot of things I'll never know."

"I asked him," Dinessen said with a twinkle. "His answer was a Max-answer. 'Absolutely no, I believe in myself.'"

"Have you made your decision, Phoebe?" Dinessen's voice was hard and definite, comforting to her in a way, but she didn't want to admit it.

"I'm too young."

"He said you were obstinate like his mother, but worth challenging. He also said you'd enjoy the game he did—borrowing from Paul to pay Peter, or was it the other way around?"

"He was wrong," Phoebe said.

"He also said you were ornery . . ."

Hedda watched Phoebe squirming with fear and indecision. Damn Max, did he think he knew what was good for everyone? There was so much she should have said to him and didn't, demanded and didn't. The grief would have been easier as Mrs. Max Treading. There would have been a structure for the grief. This way, she had no social license to mourn. What a difference between *loving wife* and *loving mistress.*

Phoebe sat with her chin in her hands. "I think I'm going back to school and get the damn degree." She looked at Dinessen. "I could write my dissertation in New York, that'll take another year at least, if I ever do it. I already had my subject chosen when Daddy got so sick . . . and I left." There was a gleam in her eye. "He would have gotten a kick out of it. It will concern," she continued in a mock-serious academic tone, "the tax structures of countries emerging from colonialism in the twentieth century, to independence, and their relationship to

modern economic growth and development. The apple don't
fall far from the tree, does it, Hedda? Can Global run smoothly
if its *chairperson* isn't around?"

Dinessen and Hedda looked at each other with amazement.
She was going to take it on! Like Max—a decision in a second,
or so it seemed.

"The company will run very well until then. It's the way
your father wanted it." Dinessen was satisfied.

Hedda receded into herself for a moment. Well, that's done
—the way he wanted it. She sighed. Suddenly Phoebe looked all
firmed up, just like her father. But *she* was a wreck. "You grapple
with life too much," he used to tease her. If knowing Max had
taught her anything—aside from a terrible love—watching him
die had given her a terrible knowledge of time. "Is that all?" Max
would probably say, laughing. No that's not all . . . Watching
him she had witnessed a wonderful arrogance. Max would say,
"You gotta grab time, throw it off-balance, surprise it, seduce it,
make it work for you—not you, *it*. That's the trick." Maybe
Phoebe inherited that too.

At Greenbriar, Roz had a delayed reaction. She blew her
stack. No liquor, no depression, just plain outrage. One day
Dinessen was the culprit; the next day it was Wesgrove in ca-
hoots with Dinessen. Her father was obviously out of his mind
the last month of his life. She'd challenge the will. Her father
must have been in the grip of Hiram Wesgrove. Why else leave
such an outrageous bequest to a stranger? It wasn't the amount,
it was the principle of the thing. Willard was terrified she would
open it up to public scrutiny and embarrass them all. He needn't
have worried. It wasn't a drunk Roz letting off steam, it was Roz
mourning in her way—in anger. It took a few weeks, then she
calmed down. She and Willard talked a lot about the will. He
reminded her the nightmare was over. They were both surprised that the bequest to Hedda hadn't been more. As for Roz
feeling disinherited, that was kind of funny, and Daddy *had* left
her the Southampton house, the ranch to Phoebe. That was the

most sensible part of the will. (The house had been Mother's haven—was Roz's private thought. So would it be for her, a haven from Willard when she needed it.) The apartment was Phoebe's, that was fine, Hedda had made it rotten. Roz never wanted to walk through that door again, if she didn't have to. She'd see Phoebe, of course . . . little Phoebe, head of Global Materials. She and Willard laughed about that; it wouldn't last a year.

She felt almost freed, even almost happy. There was no huge figure to fight anymore. The man who had ruined her mother's life was dead. The hurt was live, but that would go away. The gossip would go away . . . she would face that with grace. She had always been Mother's girl, and Phoebe, Daddy's. She hugged a thought that she wouldn't share with Willard, about the will. When she thought about it, it was a secret balm, a pleasant flush. Daddy wanted it—she and Phoebe, "my daughters" . . . "The Treading Foundation" . . . "dedicated to the advancement and enlightenment of the human race . . ." She secretly read it over and over. It felt like an embrace, like the moment he had held her so tight, the day he told them he was going to die.

18

Hiram Wesgrove had asked for a closed-mouth attitude from those who had reviewed the Candleman "falsified experiment."

"Otherwise," he ordered, "a valuable career could be killed; if I dare to speculate about human nature, the man will never do it again. We must give him that benefit, as we would want it ourselves, if we had been as misguided by our ambition. He's a good cell man, a fine administrator. We need all there are around the country, to be working."

So, there wasn't a conspiracy to keep Roy Candleman from finding a new place for himself in the field of molecular biology.

But, he thought there was. Yale and the University of California had both said they would be happy to consider an appointment for the following year. He was sure they were sluff-offs, he mistook the atmosphere as hostile and was certain that word of his transgression at the Cancer Research Center had been spread abroad.

By mid-September, his mind had reached an unhealthy state. He sat in his apartment ruminating, reviewing the humiliation of his last meeting with Wesgrove, playing it back over and over, rewriting what he could have said in his own defense, furious with himself that he couldn't have made it come out differently. Mixed with his humiliation was a buildup of pressure to vindicate himself. Wesgrove had promised to keep it quiet and he hadn't! The pious son of a bitch had decided to ruin his career and there was nothing left, no door to open. He was finished in science.

He spent a lot of time looking in the mirror and was sure his face was changing into a tight, hungry one. He hated the look, it reminded him of his father—the anxious, harassed, gray look of a factory pieceworker! You look like your father, he said to himself at least once a day, and he was filled with revulsion.

Actually, Candleman was an attractive man, balding, but his cheeks had an open, ruddy, tight-skinned, young look . . . and probably would for years to come; broad, Slavic cheeks last a long time. Above them were large, hazel eyes, unusually heavy-lashed; his receding hairline made for a broad, intelligent forehead; his chin had a shadow of a small cleft. A cleft in a man's chin has the same appeal as a dimple in a woman's cheek. All of his attributes were still there, but he was seeing them wrong. Maybe it was the lack of exercise in the last few months of worry. He had made himself into an excellent tennis player, and lately, squash. He missed the workout. He used to play with Lewisohn and Gruening, they'd break away from the lab and get it all out.

There hadn't been any sex either in the last few months, since the debacle. Maybe that would help. He flipped through his address book, looking for the name of someone he remembered as intelligent, someone who'd be grateful for a long-overdue lay. No good. He wasn't in any shape to fake an evening that would end in bed; he was too preoccupied, too exhausted. He felt too small. What's the matter with you, Roy? You're five inches taller than your father was!

His silent talking to the mirror was getting to be dangerous and he was smart enough to know it. He had never wasted time on negatives. Everything had always been a positive molding toward positive goals.

Everything. He dressed carefully, his only extravagance—
classic, beautifully tailored clothes with an English cut. He successfully rid himself of the New York accent and acquired a
cultivated, deep-voiced speech. He learned to modulate his tones
as a lecturer and taught with deep, emotional resonance. He
captivated his students, male and female. Candleman was "a
good talker." As a matter of fact, he talked incessantly, but he
was so good to listen to, whether on the mysteries of science or
his other passion, music, that he was never boring. There was
too much energy and intelligence. He had worked hard to perfect himself.

Candleman was also a great whistler. He could whistle
whole movements of concerti, like a solo instrument. The
fidelity and accuracy of his whistling was a virtuoso performance. *Con brio, andante cantabile;* or bop it, zing it down an' dirty,
blues it. The serious molecular biologist could be quite a surprise at a party when he soared with Mozart, rendered the
intricacies of a Bach Goldberg Variation like a whistling tightrope walker, and ended with an imitation of Fats Waller or
Ellington, including the instrumental accompaniment.

It had all collapsed like a stabbed balloon. He couldn't face
what he had done. There was no other way, but to vindicate
himself. *He* had been wronged. He didn't deserve to be black-
listed, denied his right to work because of *one* mistake. He was
too valuable to be set aside! He kept reviewing the last day he
had gone to the Center to clear out his office. The voices . . . he
should have listened better, he with his talent for almost perfect
audio recall.

It was Lewisohn's voice, of course! And Gruening's voice.
He went over that hour of packing in his office, trying, as he
packed, to block out the voices because they were the enemy.
They could have defended him against the old man, they could
have argued for him, but they hadn't.

(Actually, they had.)

What *were* they talking about. He hadn't wanted to listen.
They had turned their backs, men he'd worked with and played
with for two years, like brothers, warriors in battle.

His thoughts whirled in self-pity. The more he ruminated, the more wronged he felt, and the more devastatingly poignant and epic was his condition—a hero in a classic tale of good-turned-to-evil that could have become a resurrection, if but one person had come forward, forgiven him, and offered that *second chance.* They owed it to him to ridicule the old man into a Christ-posture of forgiveness. He would have done it for them if the shoe had been on the other foot, he damn well would have.

The other thing Candleman couldn't let go of was the cryonic business, the amazing disclosure that Wesgrove was adding the first human cadaver to the frozen library out there in the Long Island lab. And then, weeks later, reading about the hundred million dollars for research in the newspaper account of Treading's will! The work on the cell would go like a house afire now, and he, Candleman, wasn't there! When he thought about that, his agitation was almost too much to bear.

He sat for hours trying to figure out what forward movement had been made that he hadn't caught a smell of. What had the old man come up with about mammal cell suspension that they didn't already know from their work with mice and monkeys? Suspension for a dead human: Did Lewisohn and Gruening know? What were the hushed, excited voices saying? It was the day after Treading died. The atmosphere of breakthrough was in the halls of the Center, he could swear to that.

He kept clawing through his mind to remember that last time he was in his office. It was like driving in dense fog, through familiar landscape . . . you knew every foot of the road, but you couldn't find your way . . . you had to inch ahead slowly, with your brights turned off, maybe even your head out the window.

He sat with his eyes closed, listening to the sounds in his head—the sounds that had been put away because he had heard them under stress—and, suddenly, his audio memory rewarded him. The voices of Lewisohn and Gruening began to merge into remembered phrases. They were so clear, it felt like sodium pentothal coursing through his veins . . .

And he began to whistle.

❧

The man didn't look like a kook or behave like one; on the contrary, he looked highly professional, serious, and visibly pained by what he had just disclosed to David Absalt, assistant district attorney for the county of New York.

Dr. Roy Candleman was ending his statement . . . "I had no choice, as a member of the scientific community."

Absalt had just heard a suspicion strong enough, according to Candleman, to warrant investigation: That Dr. Hiram Wesgrove had *hurried* the death of his famous patient and perhaps administered a fatal drug to Maxwell Treading in order to test a new cryonic process, *before* cancer had thoroughly invaded the patient's organs. Moreover, Treading must not have been of sound mind by June. Because, though he, Candleman, was no longer affiliated with the Cancer Research Center, since he had left it in May, he had, at that time, observed the rapid rate of cancer in the patient; "and by June, Mr. Treading must have been too ill to know what was going on."

How was Candleman acquainted with the rapid rate of cancer in the patient?

Because he had done infinite tests on the cellular structure of the patient, at the request of Dr. Wesgrove; at the time he had thought the investigation rather excessive, if not unwarranted, and had laid it down to the importance of Treading, nothing more.

Absalt had just heard what Candleman said he *overheard*. If you added it all up, though the man had not used the word, Dr. Hiram Wesgrove was being accused of murder.

"Drs. Lewisohn and Gruening might be able to shed more light on the matter," Candleman was saying.

Absalt stood up. "Thank you for coming forward, Doctor. We'll get back to you as soon as we've done our own checking. I advise you to say nothing to anyone else, for your own legal position."

When Candleman left, Absalt sat for a few minutes,

stunned. The Treadings again! First, it was Roz Treading trailing him and Hedda last year, trying to prove Hedda had cheated on her father. Now, this . . . not just a lousy detective to corner in a restaurant and scare the hell out of. This could be as serious as Dr. Roy Candleman looked. Or *was* he a kook?

That evening, Absalt called Hedda and told her the strange story, the creepy coincidence. She, of all people, would know the condition of Max Treading before he died. He wanted to see her; would she have dinner with him?

Hedda was so dazed, she said yes. David had called her several times after Max died, but her answer had been "No, not yet, David, I'm not ready to see anyone."

He got a painfully recounted description from Hedda of Max's last hours. "I was there every minute until the end. Dr. Wesgrove was in and out of the room. Max was pronounced dead." Her eyes welled up. "I kissed him. His two daughters were there, a nurse was there. This man Candleman must be sick in the head. I never heard of him, don't know who he is, and I don't want to talk about it, please . . ."

But, David gently got her to talk about the movements in the apartment afterward. She could offer nothing because she had been in a bedroom by herself and joined by Phoebe much later; and Roz, he certainly knew who she was! . . . had already left with her husband. "Why are you pressing me to go through it again? This man's story is the tale of a madman. Why, Max called a family meeting at least a month before he died. He told us he wasn't going to allow any more chemotherapy, he was going to die at home and had decided to give his body to science, be frozen . . . It was shocking, it wasn't exactly conventional, but Max wasn't conventional, he was extraordinary." Her eyes were moist. David reached out to take her hand.

She drew it away. "Please, no . . . I'm all right. I just need to get over the fact that he's dead. Are you going to do anything about this nonsense, this man?"

"I'm not sure, I'll let the boss decide. Sometimes, it's better to do nothing; rumors have a way of dying by themselves. The man *was* connected with the Cancer Research Center. We did a little checking late this afternoon, with the personnel office of the Center. Candleman told the truth. He left the place in May, they said, to go back to a possible professorship in the fall. He sounds pretty reputable. You never heard Treading mention his name?"

"Never."

"He seemed to know a lot about the progress of your friend's cancer."

Hedda was furious. "My friend, David? He wasn't my friend, he was the man I would have married!"

David apologized. He had slipped into his work habit of interrogating and had forgotten it was Hedda. The Treading affair had certainly rocked her—not the rumor, the man himself. "I'm jealous as hell," he said softly.

"Of Max? Someone who's not here anymore?"

"Jealous of what he made you feel."

"Don't be. It's all pain."

"What does one say? It will go away . . ."

"I know. But I don't know where to begin."

This time, he took both her hands in his and she didn't pull away immediately. It was good to feel a strong clasp.

The next afternoon, one of the New York newspapers ran an item: "A reliable source suspects foul play and doctor involvement in the death of financier Maxwell Treading. An investigation is possible."

David Absalt called Candleman, who vowed he had spoken to no one. Absalt didn't believe him. It was now necessary to check out the Candleman story further, if only to kill it or nail the man as disturbed. Maybe the doctors he had mentioned could shed some light; maybe there was a professional jealousy or vendetta. The district attorney's office got hundreds of calls from wives, husbands, lovers, business partners—there were lots of people out there cooking up tales about someone they wanted *to get, the enemy.* Nine-tenths of the accusations faded into the woodwork where they came from. But, this one had hit the papers and big names were involved. It had to be checked out. Reluctantly, Absalt called Drs. Lewisohn and Gruening.

In Absalt's office, Lewisohn and Gruening froze into an impenetrable line of defense. Not if they were hung by their thumbs would they open a crack of light into the Treading story. Candleman, the fink, had blown his lid and they were going to jam it back on, if it took a ten-ton weight to do it.

Clearly, with just the right tone of patience needed when talking to a layman, they described the cryonic suspension as performed by them and Dr. Wesgrove on the body of Max Treading at the Cancer Research Affiliate building. They described the death and cause of death of Treading, as told to them by their superior, Wesgrove, who was attending till the end. It was not an unusual death—as a matter of fact, very usual, except that Treading had willed his entire body to be used in scientific experiment.

What kind of experiment could be performed on a frozen body? Would they venture some answer, since they were evidently so closely involved with Wesgrove's work?

Yes, they would venture to say that scientific experiment is best not discussed until results are forthcoming, but it was common knowledge that the space program was especially interested in the behavior of the human cell in a weightless state for long periods of time.

As for Roy Candleman, of course they were familiar with him. He had been a member of their staff until . . . Lewisohn turned to Gruening, "What was it, Jeff? May? That he decided he wanted to get back into lecturing?"

"Yes, I think it was May," Gruening affirmed.

As for what Candleman thought he overheard from one office to another, they had no idea what his motive might be, where he was, or how he was . . . except to say that whoever had been in the vicinity of the Center a day after Treading died . . . there was a lot of excitement. Would you expect it any other way, when a man of vision had willed his body to one of the most illustrious scientists alive today?

It was Absalt's turn. "We've looked into Candleman. He's a reputable person in his field, is he not?"

"Absolutely," Lewisohn said quickly.

"Can you imagine any reason for his coming to us with his story of what he thought he overheard? His suspicion?"

"None," said Gruening.

"Let's go back two questions. If he *is* reputable, would you say he should be listened to? Fast forward. Would you consider him your professional equal?"

"In a manner of speaking," Gruening answered coolly.

"What do you mean by that? Would you elaborate?"

"He'd been under some stress this past summer."

"Personal stress?"

"Everyone was aware of it at the Center, I'm afraid." Gruening lifted a finger to correct himself. "Not everyone, just a few of us."

"Your field is psychiatry, Dr. Gruening? Would you care to take a guess—why Candleman was under stress? Not, would you care to, I'm asking you to."

(Gruening looked at Lewisohn. Here it was, they weren't going to be able to keep it simple, like they'd planned in the taxi coming down, *Keep it simple, stupid.*)

"Candleman was fired, sir, by Dr. Wesgrove, for good and sufficient reason, in May. It's not my place to say why. You'll have to go elsewhere for that, maybe to Candleman. But, he *was* fired. In my estimation, his reprehensible accusation . . ." he paused, "is the sting of the spurned. That's all I have to say."

Lewisohn jumped in. "This is an informal talk, I presume, Mr. Absalt?"

He got a pursed-lip nod.

"Then, we're not obliged to help you with a motive for Candleman's behavior. I don't have to remind you that the medical profession is notorious when it comes to protecting the reputations of its members, sometimes even against themselves. You'll have to get it from somewhere else."

"From Dr. Wesgrove, then?" Absalt asked.

"I can't speak for him," Lewisohn said curtly.

"Maybe it won't be necessary," Absalt said lightly. "Thank you for coming in."

His sudden relaxation surprised them. For a moment there, he had been pressing hard. He hadn't meant to, it was force of habit when questions were being fenced. Absalt was actually relieved when they wouldn't come forward about Candleman. There probably wasn't a whole lot behind the thing, except what was said—a man under stress. He probably needed protection from himself (which they had given him nicely).

Absalt was deciding then and there not to move any further on it. "You understand why I had to check things out, two important names involved . . . The start of a rumor is unpleasant enough, but there are people out there who get paid to fan it. We'll let this one die right here. I don't think this office has to know why Dr. Candleman was fired. If he wants anyone to know, he'll have to tell them."

"Absolutely," Gruening agreed. "But he might, and it won't have anything to do with his fantastic story, it'll have to do with his own death wish. That's my professional opinion about the poor guy . . ." Then he added sourly but casually, "Anyone who would come up with anything so bizarre as to suggest that Dr. Wesgrove is a villain, is hell-bent to hang himself."

On their way back to the Center, Lewisohn and Gruening agreed not to tell "the old man" about their meeting or Candleman's concoction. The thing was dead. Wesgrove probably didn't even know of the existence of the afternoon rag that had printed the story. If he read any paper, it was the *Christian Science Monitor* a month after it came out. There were stacks of them in his office. Gruening laughed.

"The old man once said he preferred to read his news of the human comedy 'cold.' It gave him a calmer perspective about the repetitive theme of man's inhumanity to man—greed, lust, and murder."

19

Hiram Wesgrove might not have been a reader of the afternoon rag, but Roz's roommate from college certainly was. It was Sally Howard again—she of the doom calls of friendship.

With a swiftness that would have impressed her father, Roz arranged to be sitting in the office of an assistant district attorney named Absalt.

So, there she was, one of the sleekest, most gorgeous women he had ever seen, polite, imperious, demanding to know what his office was going to do about a rumor that her father had been a victim of foul play. Did they know the origin of the rumor? If not, were they going to find out? She insisted upon knowing. He had no choice but to tell her—about Candleman, about having interviewed the two doctors from the Cancer Research Center. He had to admit he hadn't followed it up with Dr. Wesgrove himself.

"Why not?"

Because he and they were convinced the rumor came from the mind of a disturbed individual.

Roz, in perfect control, was asking logical, itchy questions. Why had he not contacted the attending doctor immediately, to disprove Dr. Candleman's story? If only to protect the family. It had had enough discomfort over the death of her father. Perhaps the man, Candleman, was dangerous? Wasn't it the duty of this office to protect from mischief and harm?

Not unless there was evidence of a crime, and a rumor was not a crime committed, though it might seem that way sometimes, Absalt replied. She kept insisting on the details of his conversation with the two doctors, particularly their description of her father's death and dying. Absalt felt the only way to stop her was to shock her. He told her that the name of her father was not unfamiliar to him, nor, for that matter, was hers. "I'm an old friend of Hedda Goldsmith's, Mrs. Clyde—the friend who had a detective follow *me* at your request."

There was a moment of silence, but Roz wasn't fazed. "I was an unhappy, disturbed person then, Mr. Absalt," she said with alacrity. "Please accept my apology. I'm a very different person now, I can assure you."

"Then, you see how things have a way of settling down, if you leave them alone," he said, surprised he had not shaken her. She was playing with a handsome scarf around her neck and leaned forward confidentially.

"I understand why you just did what you did, and I appreciate your reason—you're trying to diffuse something, protect me and my sister, even if it meant you were going to embarrass me. But, I must tell you something now . . . I've had upsetting thoughts of my own about the death of my father. I've tried to put them away, as you would like to put this Candleman story away, but I can't.

"My father's death was too quick, too strange. Everything about it was peculiar. He failed too fast. About two weeks before he died, he seemed to be on a high, on a drug of some kind; and then, suddenly we were told he had pneumonia. The next day he died. Just like that. I asked several doctors about it afterward, socially, not professionally. I asked them to describe the last weeks or months of a multiple myeloma patient—that was the type of cancer my father had. There were mystified looks on their faces when I described my father's last days. You know how doctors don't like to comment on a case that isn't theirs, but I saw the surprise about how quickly he'd died." She paused. "There was something strange about the whole thing, from the moment he announced to us at lunch one day that he wanted to die at home, he was refusing chemotherapy; and when he died, his wish to be . . . to be frozen."

He watched her take a breath. "My father was an unusual man. We were like oil and water, Mr. Absalt, but we loved each other. No one could take advantage of him *unless* he were out of control . . . which I think he was!" Her voice became very quiet. "And the will . . . his leaving so much money—I'm sure you read about it—to Dr. Wesgrove. Wouldn't you, an outsider, think about that twice? It's quite astounding, isn't it? How could one help but wonder about negative influence on a very sick man?"

The white, beautiful face with its large eyes fastened on his. She went on in almost a plea: "What do I do *now,* with my own feelings and suspicions . . . when something pops up out of the blue, another suspicion, not just from limbo, but from someone connected with Dr. Wesgrove? Forget it? Or, does one try to get to the bottom of it? Does one ask Dr. Wesgrove, if only to vindicate him? Does one ask for the medical reports? I'm asking for your help—to sort it out." She stopped. "I would like to meet this Dr. Candleman, hear his story with my own ears."

"The only way—is to let it die, Mrs. Clyde," Absalt said as patiently as he could. "But that doesn't seem to be what you want."

"That is exactly what I want," Roz said angrily. "To stop him. I want to meet Dr. Candleman in this office, if you don't mind. With my sister . . ."

"Does she know anything about your feelings?"

"I don't think so, but I'm going to tell her. Don't you think I should? I do."

There was no stopping it after that. Hedda had to hear from David about it. Phoebe had to accompany Roz and they both had to meet Roy Candleman in David's office. It was a crazy game

—four people playing with four different aims in four different languages. Phoebe, who knew the truth, watched the game unfold like a tree snake slithering up into a nest of fledglings.

After the meeting, Phoebe left for Northampton to get away as fast and far as she could, her hands, figuratively, on her ears, praying for someone with a wand to make it all go away.

But, it wouldn't. Candleman insisted upon being put under hypnosis—to get a more accurate recall of the conversation between Lewisohn and Gruening. Under the hypnotic state, the phrase *final injection* surfaced. What final injection? Why was it final and where was it given?

Questions had to have answers. Absalt asked Lewisohn and Gruening to come in again.

They knew nothing about the phrase *final injection*, they said, and gave him another lecture on the fine points of a cryonic suspension as perfected by Dr. Wesgrove and the research going on at the Center. They also repeated for Absalt the fact that Treading had given his approval for a procedure that involved a number of injections to be performed after his death.

When Lewisohn and Gruening left Absalt's office, they were beginning to feel they were standing in an open field, watching a small black speck in the sky getting larger and larger, threatening to turn into a blazing hot meteor, large enough to destroy Manhattan.

A mistake had been made. The old man, and they, too, had counted on the ignorance of the layman and the arrogance of their profession. They had never thought, for one moment, that someone might ask: How do you perform a cryonic suspension on a dead body? What's the timing? The steps? Maybe it was time to tell Wesgrove what was going on. Or, should they just keep looking at the speck in the sky and hope it would change its mind, go back where it came from—to another galaxy, if they were lucky.

David Absalt waited too. But he interviewed the nurse in attendance the last days of Treading's life, and the servants, who had nothing to offer, except the butler, who described his last view of his employer being carried out in a body bag. The driver of the van was talked with. Again the body bag and three doctors who accompanied it. Was there a glass partition between the front of the van and the back? Absalt inquired. No, a solid partition, the driver said.

The unusualness of the cryonic procedure, instead of normal treatment of a corpse, kept intruding in Absalt's thoughts, justifying the behavior of three scientists. There didn't seem to be anything out of order, if one went along with what one didn't know a damn thing about.

Absalt called in the lawyer, George Dinessen. He wanted to see the will of Maxwell Treading, the dates, signatures. Attached to the will were the papers allowing for cryonic suspension. Both dates were the same, although Dinessen said the latter had come in almost a month later than the date of the will, from Dr. Wesgrove, with an apology.

Had Dinessen seen Treading at the very end, too? Had he noticed anything out of the ordinary, as to the state of the dying man?

Of course not.

Had he found the huge bequest to Wesgrove anything to question?

No. It was surprising, but not anything to question, if one knew his client as he knew him. Dinessen responded firmly.

Absalt waited some more. It might have been Hedda's influence that made him move like a snail before he called Dr. Wesgrove to come in and have a chat. Hedda was adamant that a man Max loved and respected should not be embarrassed by the horrors of innuendo. The whole thing was insane.

"The body wasn't removed all that quickly," David said to her, "not according to the time on the death certificate and the time remembered by the butler or the van driver. The body . . ."

"The body! The body! The body was Max!" Hedda said in exasperation. "What are you doing? I don't understand."

"I don't understand, either," David had to admit. There were things that didn't jibe, maybe because of his layman's ignorance. How much could you grasp, standing on the sidelines like a ninny and asking a brain surgeon—"What are you doing now? Why did you cut there and not here?" You'd get a bop on the head! That was the way he'd felt with Gruening and Lewisohn—their annoyance, condescension, not-so-veiled impatience with stupid questions.

Someone else was learning about cryonics—firsthand. Roz and Roy Candleman were meeting, dining together; after two or three times, they found each other's company very pleasant. She was leaving Greenbriar on any pretext, coming into New York to meet him in little Italian restaurants; she was filled with excitement about every thought and turn of his mind . . . the delight in being conspiratorial . . . in search of the truth . . . having a kind of partner; she felt fresh, seductive, like a new book with a rich binding to be opened slowly, slowly. Roy savored her, he respected her feelings; he was so *all there*, his voice, his look, he was so comfortable with himself; he made her feel comfortable. She almost wanted to reach out and touch him, but, of course, she *wouldn't*. She just secretly enjoyed the wanting to, it sent a little tremor through her, startled her. There was nothing wrong with people finding each other attractive. It was a plus, when they'd been thrown together in "a common cause —truth and justice." Roy put it so neatly. He was an exceedingly brilliant man. She had never known anyone like him.

Life was strange, wasn't it, they both agreed, over lunches and dinners, and finally, for the first time, in Roy's apartment. (Oh, it's not what you think at all! Roz would have said. We're friends, we have a common cause, the chauffeur brings me and takes me; it's not a secret, but Willard couldn't possibly understand.)

Her attraction to him went against her every instinct. She preferred tall, blond men; she'd almost found it repellent to be touched by a dark-haired male. There was no mistaking the fact that Roy was Jewish. He told her about his family, his father, and how far he had come from his beginnings. It was an exotic story as told by a kind of hero . . . like her father, in a way, she admitted to Roy. Max's beginnings on the ranch in Utah took on a different color for her because it pleased Roy to hear about the rise of Treading from the dust (according to Roz), though he didn't have the handicap of being Jewish too. Roy was careful to point that out, and all that *that* meant when you rose to the top and *still* had certain doors closed to you. "Anti-Semitism is like a pilot light on a stove. It's always there, ready to be turned on to a flame. The gas is always there . . ." Roy's hazel eyes, with their incredibly long lashes, flashed, and his broad, Slavic cheeks flushed. "Do *you* know what I mean?" he challenged.

Of course she did.

Roz had to admit it, and she did it with candor: Willard belonged to a private club that excluded Jews. It *was* unjust, yes it was. She was enjoying her turnaround, it made her feel light-headed.

Roy relished watching the enemy fall away . . . a beautiful enemy . . . who *might* become an acquisition if he played it right, let it happen slowly, trawled for ten times as long as it usually took to get a woman in bed. Because she wasn't usual. She was extraordinary. Silk, platinum, porcelain, cloth of gold, one of a kind, she was top of the heap, the wife he should have been looking for and had never had the guts to. Here she was— bespoke!

He didn't say that to himself. It was a visceral response, uncluttered with words. It was something *immediate* that he felt when they were together, when their eyes met, when he watched her flower under his eyes. *What had been done to her?* She was so cold and wary in the beginning. But look at her now, flushing and changing. They were listening to a Beethoven quartet, and he was explaining the theme, subtheme, the repetition, the coming together of two disparate themes, that no one in his right mind could imagine coming together, or make happen . . . except a genius. (It was like *them,* he noted to himself, two disparate themes, brought together by a genius. He smiled privately. They had been brought together by the genius of Wesgrove.)

As the quartet played on, Roy went deeper into his private

thoughts. *He deserved the princess.* Or, if he'd come upon her late,
he deserved the queen that belonged to someone else. Willard
sounded like a prick, a Wasp who couldn't tell the difference
between a pea and a diamond, a woman faking and a woman
satisfied. She needed *him,* fucking rabbi that he was. She needed
him and he was going to try! And, wasn't she going to learn
what else there was in the world besides cotton batting! She had
a problem, no question, it oozed out of her . . . stories of her
father. She made him sound like a myth. Maybe he was . . . with
all that money. This Willard couldn't match the myth. Could
he? Roy wished he'd known Maxwell Treading.

Oh, did he want to touch her, get her into bed, but he
wouldn't. It had to move excruciatingly into the inevitable
blending of two wild, disparate themes sucked into one sound
of grand recognition.

20

"Do what you can to bury the thing. Neither the Treading family nor the board of directors of his company need a *National Enquirer* type of story to contend with," Dinessen said as he left David Absalt's office. He had gone over Max's will with Absalt, who knew very well that he was sitting with one of the most prestigious lawyers in the city. Dinessen had sworn that Max Treading was nothing if not sane when the will had been prepared, and he hadn't hidden his outrage that it could have been thought otherwise.

Dinessen returned to his own office and asked his secretary to put the will back in the Treading file. She returned a few minutes later with an envelope marked *Personal.* "It was in the *W* section but should be under *P.* Do you want to see it?" He looked at it and remembered—Max had given it to him one day, saying, "Put this in with the will, but no one may open it except me, after my death." Dinessen also remembered shrugging off the order, with the same incredulity he had felt about Max's Re-animation Fund. Another Max-joke in the face of Fate.

He fingered the envelope. Prank or no, it had better be opened, just to be on top of everything.

He paled as he read:

"I, Maxwell Treading, of sound mind, if not body, had every intention of taking my own life to shorten the horror of a lingering death. This is to absolve Dr. Hiram Wesgrove of any responsibility in the way I died or when I died. It was I who convinced him to accept me as a guinea pig in the service of science. The manner in which he will use my live or dead body will be at his discretion and with my cooperation. Let it be set down here that I am eternally grateful not to have had a senseless death." (Signed) "Maxwell Treading. May 30, 1982."

Dinessen reread it and stared, in shock. Max had been planning to commit suicide! But, he didn't! "Every intention of taking my own life" . . . it was clear as a bell. Then what? Wesgrove had dissuaded him? Would help him die? It wasn't *that* clear . . . yet what other conclusion could be drawn? "The manner in which he will use my live or dead body . . ." It was *more* than inference.

Dinessen stared and stared. His was a crafty legal mind, but he was a moral man. The letter was not a legal document; no one had witnessed it. Was it his duty to present it to Mr. Absalt? Damn, damn, damn. Dinessen was trembling. What a dumb thing! Max had done dangerous things, but not dumb things. This was both. Why write it at all? And, if it was a prank, it might be one joke too many. *The letter had to be presented.* He immediately called Phoebe in Northampton and demanded she charter a plane and come to his office that day. "It has to do with your father's papers . . . No, we can't discuss it on the phone. It's that important, or I wouldn't ask it of you."

She was in his office by late that day. "It's Roz, isn't it? She's trying to break the will?"

"No . . . not Roz. Sit down." He handed her the letter.

She read it and looked up. (Daddy had sworn her to say nothing. She had to lie, even to Dinessen. Let it come out if it had to . . . but *not from her.*)

"Did your father ever intimate he wanted to kill himself?"

"Never."

"Do you think Hedda might know something?"

"No," she said emphatically and too quickly.

"Phoebe, I have to bring this forward." He looked at her, upset and perplexed. "You didn't tell me you were in Mr. Absalt's office with Roz and a Roy Candleman. I think you should have told me . . ."

"I should have, but I didn't," she said sheepishly. "I wanted to get back to school and I thought it would blow over. I didn't want to mess up my mind. It's not good to let the bad vibes sneak in. If you walk away from them, they sometimes disappear."

"With this letter, there seems to be more than what you call 'bad vibes,' Phoebe." She was behaving in a very casual manner. Did she understand the implication in the letter?

"You wouldn't just want to tear it up?" Phoebe suggested boldly. "No one knows it exists except us, do they?"

Dinessen flushed. The same thought had occurred to him earlier.

"No, Phoebe. There could be a copy somewhere else. Who knows what your father might have done without legal counsel! I can't tear it up."

"You're sure?"

"Yes, I'm sure. I've spent the whole damn afternoon deciding that I can't. I'd like to tear into your father, that's what I'd like to do." He saw his criticism of Max not well-taken. "We'd all like him to be here, to talk to, I know, my dear . . . I know . . ." He paused. "Don't ever write what even smacks of an official letter without showing it to me first . . . as long as I'm your lawyer. That's the lesson we learn from this. What your father has done, with the best of intentions, and we'll never know what they were . . . is going to make one hell of a mess."

There wasn't much choice anymore. Absalt had to call in Dr. Wesgrove for questioning. The whole Treading thing was beginning to feel like a free-fall. It could land anywhere—it could fall on Times Square or to the bottom of the sea. Wesgrove was the only one who could tell them where.

. . .

This was the famous Dr. Wesgrove, one of the most venerated scientists in the country? He looked like a midget, Absalt thought, with his glasses falling to the end of his nose, his white hair waving as if there were a wind in the room. Wesgrove was leaning forward, listening, ingesting the information with "Yes, yes . . . go on . . ." as Absalt unfolded the series of events that had led to the necessity of calling him in. And so, Wesgrove heard about Lewisohn and Gruening's sessions in the same office, the role of Roy Candleman, Roz Treading's disquieting feelings about her father's death; then, the hypnotist who had pulled out of Candleman the phrase *final injection.*

There was a growing frown on Wesgrove's face as he listened. His head nodded as it received, digested, and evaluated what it was hearing. Absalt had kept Max's letter to the last. He was about to hand it to Wesgrove to read for himself and then ask for an interpretation. But, what happened next almost took Absalt's breath away.

Wesgrove put his hands on Absalt's desk, looked at him, and lifted his hands in a gesture of no-need-to-go-on.

"I helped Max Treading die, because he asked me to. He was going to kill himself. I offered him a more sane and worthy way. There were no witnesses to the fact. There is no one else to be involved. I take total responsibility."

"I didn't hear what you just said," Absalt said quietly.

"Have you had complaints of deafness before?"

"You shouldn't have said what you did, without legal counsel."

"Could someone else tell me what to say, better than myself?"

"Legally better, Dr. Wesgrove." Absalt felt *he* was the one taking the free-fall. There was no one in the room except a detective sitting in a corner. He should have had someone taking down the exchange, but who would have thought what had happened would be so simple! It didn't make any sense. Everyone connected with this Treading thing seemed to be quite mad, including the illustrious doctor.

"May I read what you were about to offer me?" Wesgrove said.

The letter was handed to him. He read it, looked up, and smiled weakly. "You see? It's just as I said it, isn't it? He was trying to protect me . . ."

"Dr. Wesgrove, the rumor would have died in this office, if he hadn't written that letter. Why did he?"

"I don't know . . . in great trust, I suppose . . . trust in a future time, future knowledge. We might never know . . ." Wesgrove stood up. "May I leave now? You know where to reach me . . . to let me know what is to happen next."

Absalt was trying to think as Wesgrove stood there watching him.

"Would you tell me why you fired Dr. Candleman?"

"No, I don't think so."

"You would do so under oath?"

"Of course." And, Wesgrove walked out the door.

Under normal circumstances, an ordinary person would have been detained. Absalt couldn't believe he had let the man walk out. He looked over at the detective, who was also stunned. The confession had come so simply and easily, it seemed as if it hadn't happened. Absalt had to say something. "You heard it. Let's give him a couple of hours. We'll have to go get him, bring him back down, and do this all over again. Damn it! He's guilty and he agreed, just like that. My God, what a scandal!"

Absalt tried to unboggle his mind. Candleman was right, the bastard. Right about what? Wesgrove was guilty of murder? Or was he guilty of euthanasia? Euthanasia: A plea like falling into a well of molasses. A ton of feathers was going to fall on everyone, prosecution and defense alike. What do you do with a holy admission of guilt from a man of stature? Until the letter, there hadn't been a shadow of a case, nothing but innuendo, no facts, no witnesses, no nothing. What kind of cockamamie head did Treading have on his body? Why in hell had the man written it? It was going to be Hiram Wesgrove's undoing. Absalt was catching a strong dose of bias. He was thinking, what a challenge to be lawyer for the defense. Christ, Wesgrove could have

slipped through any noose Candleman had thought he'd made
. . . a man of Wesgrove's stature . . . if it hadn't been for a dead
man's letter. But no . . . wait . . . Wesgrove had confessed even
before he read the letter!

A confession was a confession.

So fast. Wesgrove had no idea justice possessed such wingèd
feet. Who would have thought it? Weighed down under her
voluminous folds and heavy scales was swiftness.

He was back in his office no more than a few hours when
two uniformed men arrived, not in togas or sandals with gold
feathers . . . just two New York City detectives, young, firm,
polite . . . to bring him back to Absalt's office.

He was ushered down the halls of the Cancer Research
Center, taken down in an elevator and into a waiting police car.
The place was stunned.

He needed a lawyer, he was told. Did he have a lawyer?

Not really, just an old friend in Boston who took care of
family matters.

Did he know a lawyer in New York?

Of course he did, a bevy of them, the Cancer Research
Center had an army of lawyers.

"I've even cured a few lawyers," Wesgrove said. "But, I
think I'd like to see Maxwell Treading's lawyer. Would you call
him?" he asked Absalt. His sound might have been weary, but
it was the request of a superior. Wesgrove sat himself down on
the nearest chair without anyone saying he shouldn't. He sat
there like an owl waiting for morning light to give him the right
to sleep.

Dinessen arrived an hour later, with Phoebe. She had not
gone back to school, but (again) had thrown her resolve to study
for her degree into the air like a cast-off ribbon. How could she
go back? The vibes around her were booming, becoming more
horrifying by the minute.

She threw her arms around a startled Wesgrove. Dinessen
was shocked to hear what she was saying. She had *lied* to him

in his office! She was telling Wesgrove she was the perfect witness to her father's wishes. It was his life and he had the right
to commit suicide any way he chose. It was noble, courageous,
and beautiful—what Wesgrove and her father had chosen to do
together. Her father was not insane; she, of all people, knew *that!*
Her father was not manipulated. Who could manipulate Max
Treading?

Wesgrove shook his head. "Noble, courageous, and beautiful is not legal, my dear. Not according to the medical profession
and the laws that govern it today. Laws must be abided by, until
new ones are made. Max and I gambled and it looks like we lost.
I don't feel I committed an immoral act but I'm guilty, nonethe-
less. There's nothing to win or convince. I'm guilty and will be
set up as an example . . . for now. It's only for now . . ."

Phoebe was not to be gainsaid. She sounded like Max. Dinessen tried to shut her up; there were people listening. "Daddy
was not insane, he was not manipulated or coerced. No one will
stop me from fighting that, otherwise the will will go down the
drain."

"Phoebe," Dinessen tried to say quietly, "this has nothing
to do with the will, it has to do with murder . . ."

"Others will continue, with or without your father's
money," Wesgrove said. "It will just take longer."

"This has nothing to do with the will," Dinessen whispered
angrily. "Don't mention it again, either of you!"

"It was your genius he trusted," Phoebe said, concentrating
on Wesgrove and grabbing his arm. "He told me."

Wesgrove looked drained, morose even, for the first time.
The failure of his plan was too much to bear.

Phoebe turned to Dinessen. "You'll help us, won't you?"

"It's going to take a very imaginative criminal lawyer.
That's not my expertise. I'd have to hire a lulu."

"But you *will*, you'll manage it all," Phoebe translated with
optimism.

"Wait a minute. I didn't say that."

"You did, and I'll pay for it! Daddy would want me to, in
his place . . . and you know it."

Dinessen made a rueful grunt. "Damn Max, he's still trying to make a Clarence Darrow out of me. The man just won't die."

Dinessen extended his hand to Wesgrove. "I'll do my best, Dr. Wesgrove. Max and I always did fight about just how far morality, conscience, and individual freedom should go."

Absalt informed them that since the alleged murder had taken place in Long Island, he was about to call the district attorney in Riverhead, Suffolk County. "The problem," he referred to it gently, "will be out of our jurisdiction. A grand jury out there will have to hear the case, subpoena Dr. Wesgrove . . . and others."

Justice wasn't that winged. It was going to have to walk heavy-footed across the Triborough Bridge to Long Island.

FROM THE JOURNAL OF DR. HIRAM WESGROVE, OCTOBER 1982

Came across a poem by an emperor named Yao. Smart man, Yao. He, too, must have known a Candleman thousands of years ago in ancient China. Maybe there were a host of Candlemans—to warrant the old boy sitting down to write a poem of warning:

"Tremble, be fearful," says Emperor Yao. "Night and day be careful. / Men do not trip over mountains: / They fall over earth mounds."

I beg to differ with Emperor Yao a little. I have tripped over many mountains and enjoyed it. I have picked myself up from such falls and started again. But, he is right about the "earth mounds." When one's head is in the clouds, one can never anticipate the smallness that can topple everything.

I am tired to the bone from this turn of events. I cannot let it destroy me. I wish I could believe myself as I write it—I cannot let it destroy me.

21

In the beginning, Roz had found it such a relief—Willard's charming indifference, the careful, elegant Clydes. Life wasn't a wheel always threatening to fly off its axis—like her mother's and father's. Life should run on Rolls-Royce bearings. Even making love was the way she wanted it—just the obligatory "Ah . . ." when it was over, like "good shot, great sail." It was peaceful.

Slowly—or was it suddenly, she couldn't remember—everything changed. It was after her mother died. Willard's charming indifference became for her either stupidity or boredom, or both. He couldn't even talk about grief. The new game between them was—How many ways can I winnow you down, my love? She was a papier-mâché doll coming undone. The paste was flaking off; pieces tore if you touched them. What was inside the doll terrified her. She was losing. To win, every word out of Willard's mouth had to be seized, attacked, throttled. She also had to keep a terrible secret: he was an idiot without feeling. He had no more clue as to who she was than a minnow, a tiger. Not that she had ever had a clue to what her unhappiness was about—what made her want Hedda dead, what possessed her to fight her father with silence, what made her go icy when he died, or *now,* what made her want vengeance for his death. There was a snake inside her that someone had made her swallow when she was little, that was all she knew. It grew as she grew; it died and grew again, bigger. Liquor killed it; it grew again. The snake had to be killed once more. Roy could help her do it. She could talk to him; he listened. She could be all her selves with him; beautiful, intelligent, haughty, Walleby and Treading together, even unpredictable and quixotic as her father. Roy made her feel she was amazing. He even made her wonder if she wouldn't like him to make love to her, passionate, needy love. She had never felt that kind of love.

She teetered. But she *had* to have Willard and Greenbriar as a safe harbor; life had become frightening again.

She tottered. She would knock on Roy's door. "Here I am!" And fall down a fascinating hole . . . with a man who never stopped talking, like Daddy . . . A man who was a Jew, like Hedda . . . It wouldn't be as frightening as what was going on with her and Willard now. Hiram Wesgrove had been arrested. It was a week of hell as stories leaked out. She and Roy had made it happen. She was glad. The man had confessed. She had not been paranoid, with her suspicions.

Willard was in a fury. Reporters were parked outside the gates of Greenbriar and wouldn't go away. They were prisoners. He commanded her not to make any statement or in any way implicate *his* name. White-faced, his parents came through the cordon of reporters and repeated Willard's orders. She and Willard must go away, they said, remove themselves from the notoriety. Not a word, not another connection with the Clyde family must happen . . . with this mess and their lives.

Willard had another side to his stupidity and boredom. He was abusive. "If you hadn't opened your Goddamn mouth, none of this would have happened! You and this creep, Candleman, whoever he is! Who in hell cares how your father died? He was going to die anyway. You're sick, that's what *you* are! My parents will never get over it. You'll kill them too, you're so interested in murder. Don't sit there saying nothing . . . like a zombie.

We have to get out of here, sneak out like thieves, for Christ's sake! If you want to know the truth, I've had Treading up to here!"

She began to scream back. "My father was murdered! As for my 'Goddamn mouth' . . . isn't that lovely coming from you. Go to hell, you idiot, you and your parents!"

"You're a psychotic bitch!"

She hit him hard on the cheek and walked to the door to get out. He picked up a chair and flung it across the room. It almost hit her. Her heart was beating so fast and she didn't know whether it was out of joy or fear. It was wonderful to see him crack wide open!

"I'm leaving, whether you like it or not," she said, suddenly cool.

"If you do, you better not open your mouth or drag my name into it, or I'll . . ."

"You'll what?"

"I'll divorce you!"

"Wonderful! Your name disgusts me." She made a throwing gesture toward him. "Here! Take your name, you boring bastard!"

Rosalind Treading. No more Clyde, she'd just thrown that across the room. No mother, no father. I have a sister named Phoebe, she reminded herself as she called for her car to be made ready, packed a few things, walked through the gates of Greenbriar and the reporters, without a word. Not one tear. You don't cry in an earthquake, you're too busy saving your life. Where should she go?

The chauffeur was looking at her in the rearview mirror. "Where do I drive you, Mrs. Clyde?"

"The Plaza," she said off the top of her head. "Then take the car back, please."

He noted how she looked—that gorgeous, tight, rich look. How did they get it? Were they born with it? He was going to be asked by the reporters when he got back—"How did she look?" He'd say, "She looked tired, a little nervous, and I drove her to New York." He wouldn't say "The Plaza" or he'd get fired. He also wouldn't say he'd heard yelling, a knock-down-drag-out upstairs.

"You will, please, not tell *anyone* where you drove me," Roz ordered.

"Yes, Mrs. Clyde."

"Not Mrs. Clyde, Miss Treading!" There it was, to a chauffeur, of all people. Willard would be furious. That's what she wanted.

It was a long, numb trip to the Plaza. She felt like a body leaving one planet and being delivered to another. The first thing she did was try to call Phoebe in Northampton. No answer. Her heart dropped. Why hadn't Phoebe called her all week? Wasn't she shocked by Wesgrove's confession? Wasn't her own behavior vindicated? It unsettled her that Phoebe hadn't called. There was no one to tell, no one to whom it would matter that she wasn't Roz Clyde any more. Phoebe would stretch her hand out, if she knew. Roz was sure of that.

There was no one to tell but Roy, but she wasn't going to, not yet . . . She would call him, though, and tell him she was in town.

Roy suggested they meet at a Turkish restaurant. "One of my new finds."

"I don't have the car."

"Shall I come for you?"

"No, I'll take a taxi and meet you there."

"I'll be there fifteen minutes early, waiting," he said, knowing how spoiled she was, a little nervous about getting around by herself.

She knew he knew. To make light of it, she said, "How will I know you?"

"I'll be wearing a red carnation. Don't worry, it's only twenty blocks from the Plaza, a little west, but not in the river. Come slum with me, lady."

His voice sounded different, light, airy. In the beginning,

there had been reasons for their being together—the business of justice being done. Later, if the reasons weren't apparent, they made them up. There was absolutely no reason tonight, except to be together . . . In the taxi, she was thinking she shouldn't have sent the car back. She felt safer with it waiting for her; she could leave anywhere, anybody, quickly, if the car was outside. Not having the chauffeur's familiar face waiting made her uneasy.

The dirty, noisy street frightened her. It looked like a Casbah. There he was, rushing to the curb, beaming, dark jacket and brass buttons—a familiar face. She gave him a radiant smile, looking marvelous, much too elegant for the scruffy street, in her beige suit with its little sable collar. People turned to look. Roy ushered his prize into the restaurant and away from the gawkers.

There was a reserved table against a wall. Cymbals, drums, and a melody on a reed instrument filled the dark room.

"Why here?" she whispered, as a waiter in a red turban seated them.

"Why not? This is a celebration . . . we've won haven't we? Would you like a drink? Do you know ouzo?"

"No."

"It's milky white when you mix it with water and it sneaks up on you."

"Why not," she replied, leaning back, and suddenly noticed what the music was doing—playing for a belly dancer, a large, fleshy woman with long black hair, breasts undulating, hips gyrating, and enormous flashing eyes lined with kohl. The atmosphere was charged, like a country road with fireflies. "Good heavens," came out of Roz involuntarily. She rested her chin in her hands and looked, while Roy ordered.

"She's wonderful, isn't she?" he said.

"I don't know, I never saw one in person." Roz flashed a smile and went back to her looking, trying to feign a critical air, as though it were a concert hall. Otherwise, she would have to admit that the place was whirling intimacy and instant sex, and how obvious of Roy to have brought her.

The ouzo came. They clinked glasses. Roz kept her eyes on

the dancer as Roy began to lecture quietly in her ear: The art of belly dancing in the Middle East, the significance of the gestures, the architecture of harems—the high walls around women in ordinary households . . . it wasn't *all* bad, they certainly knew who they were, managers of the household, crucibles for men, mothers chosen as carefully as faceted diamonds, willing mistresses . . .

"I can't believe what you're saying," Roz whispered back. "They couldn't be *willing* . . ." But on Roy went about the research and writings on the sexual behavior of Arabs as observed by Richard Burton, not Liz Taylor's Burton, the *original* Burton, the one who went looking for the source of the Nile. A complicated, mystifying man was the original Burton, with a fire for strange, sexual facts in his Anglo-Saxon breast, with an amazing wife who stood by him, not losing an inch of her own splendor or independence, hormonally in love with her opposite. So much for the *women's libbers* trying to solve the mystery of freedom, he added. There is no freedom. A man or woman in love is both free and slave. Bravo biology compounded with the mystery of emotion . . .

A convention of words was being whispered into Roz's ear. On and on it went. The difference between the philosophical, aesthetic, and biological approaches to love, vis-à-vis the Arab and the Hebrew. Oh, the Hebrew was exacting as to result. The foreplay could be kinky as anyone could imagine, but the final position of the act of love *had* to be the missionary position, like Ruth and Boaz—the position for assured procreation, so that the sperm and ovum meet in as confluent a state as possible, as ordained by God, the God of the Old Testament . . . And wasn't it all amazing, Salome's Dance of the Seven Veils, the genius of femaleness . . .

It was all said in the same modulated voice he used when he lectured to her about Beethoven's last quartets.

The ouzo was beginning to take care of everything. She felt herself giving in to the incredible flying breasts of the dancer, the gleaming belly with a piece of colored glass in its navel, the bells on her ankles, the incessant drums, the smiles of the dark-skinned men around them, their fingers drumming on the tables, impatient for more . . . Their throaty "ah's" of approval . . .

The woman was ending her performance on the floor, on her back, with the most amazing hip movements to an imaginary partner. And, her dance was finished.

Their food came, none too soon. Roz was feeling uncomfortable in the silence. How to diffuse the air, now that the dancer was gone? Roy was still drumming his fingers on the table. "How do you know so much about it?" she asked casually.

"Research," he grinned. "This dancer is one of the greats, from Egypt. She's fifty years old, can you imagine? And, just beginning a national tour."

Roz laughed. "In a shabby little place like this?"

"Not shabby, special." He was hurt by her remark, but being very patient with her. "If you were looking for the best flamenco music in Spain, you couldn't find it. You know why? Because it's in a dark, little cellar that looks like a thieves' den. No one knows how to get there but the *aficionados.* I was taken to one of those dens by a young Spanish doctor who studied with me at Harvard." He paused.

"I brought one queen to see another. Don't raise your eyebrows. You *are* a queen . . ."

"You're getting drunk?"

"A little. Aren't you?"

"A little . . ." Roz agreed.

"And, why not?" Roy said. "We're celebrating. When are you going back? Tomorrow?"

"Not for a while," she said cautiously. But, the ouzo was allowing her to look at him deeply, in a most personal way. She saw his eyes with their long lashes, the broad, gleaming forehead, the carefully clipped sideburns a little too long, but interesting against the baldness, his trim shoulders in their English jacket . . . rather distinctive, all in all. She had never been this close to the ruddy, fine skin of his cheeks . . .

"Bridges burned?" he asked, meeting her gaze.

"No comment," she said, not taking her eyes away.

He returned her look with hope. It *could* happen. Hadn't it been moving that way for weeks? Or was he crazy? He had observed her with infinite care, like an endangered species . . . and she was. Garbo shot through gauze, encased in ice. Why did it attract him? Bringing her here was an inspiration—Garbo in the Sahara. First, she would be uncomfortable, then amused, then disarmed. She needed him. He was surprised it had happened so fast.

He *knew* her. He had put under a microscope her every movement and gesture. He had compiled a lexicon of information on the way she used her lips, carried her head; her irises— their rate of expansion and contraction. Everything about her was a contradiction. She walked with a stride and sat like a virgin. Her rib cage was contracted, tight, yet her breasts flared. The spine was too straight and lean to the waist, but below were succulent buttocks. Her fingernails were long female talons; she wore no polish to call attention, yet they shone like pink quartz. Her eyes were beautiful lakes of green, and fish were dying in them. God, what contradictions. He had never seen her wear the same pair of shoes twice; there wasn't the slightest intimation of foot shape in the expensive leather, but he knew she wriggled her toes and her feet wanted to be naked, massaged, and kissed; he could swear to it. Everything about her said "Touch me" and "Don't touch me" at the same time. Oh, he had researched her well, everything except a living cell.

"Too bad, in a way . . . about Wesgrove," he said, to remind her of the subject that bound them.

"I don't want to talk about that tonight," she said.

"Did you and Willard have a thing?"

"What makes you think so?"

"You can tell a woman's had a fight with her husband. She looks . . ."

Their heads were almost touching.

"Looks how?"

"Looks new . . ."

She had taken off her jacket and was wearing a sleeveless blouse so exquisitely shirred and embroidered, it *had* to cost, he

didn't dare to think *how much.* A professor out of work? In a
cloud of ouzo, his mind was jumping like a gazelle. His society
wife. How could he do it? Cool it, too fast, Roy, too fast.

He let a finger run up and down the inside of her arm. It
was the first time he had ever touched her. He knew it! She was
made of silk. He felt her shiver. Tonight was a foregone conclusion, he wasn't worried about it. He was thinking of the long
haul.

Neither felt like eating much. The belly dancer was back in
a blaze of classic bumps and grinds, the likes of which would
have put the untalented into traction for life. Roz began to
giggle. "I'm getting seasick."

"Shall we go?" Roy suggested.

"Yes."

"To my apartment?"

She didn't say no.

He paid the bill, took her cool hand in his, and they glided
out to the street. They kissed in the taxi. His snow princess was
melting down to *real.*

Roz sat in a chair, a little dizzy. Roy's living room was
beige, gray and brown, meticulous, like a doctor's office, except
for the walls lined with books and records. Roy was in the
bathroom. He was going to come out and examine her . . . she
was going to be defenseless, naked, her privacy invaded. Ridiculous! He was going to make love and she had come willingly—
to find out what it would be like. But, suddenly, it was an awful
little place and she felt lost. There had always been Greenbriar
and Willard to go back to, the other times she had been here.
Who was Roy? She didn't know whether she liked anything
about him except his voice and the way he listened. No, it was
a good room, they had planned and schemed here, and they'd
won. She had even cried in this room, talking about Daddy and
Hedda, her mother, even about Willard. Roy was keen, sympathetic; he wasn't a stranger, he was one of the closest friends
she'd ever had . . . but it was all going to turn into something

else, the minute he opened the door of the bathroom . . .

Roy sat on the floor next to her. He took her hand and kissed it, slowly, over and over. (How delicate, thoughtful, and courtly, she thought.) She leaned back and closed her eyes.

Suddenly he was kissing her shoulder, burying his head against her breasts, making it hard for her to breathe, murmuring "Darling . . . darling . . ." She had to stand up. He pulled her to the couch and kept on kissing her, wild, frantic, wet kisses. He was going to eat her! She pulled away with a violent jerk, she was going to be sick! He was like a baby rooting for a nipple.

"No! I'm sorry, don't!" she cried.

"What do you mean 'no'? You want it, I know you do."

He kept on kissing her lips, her neck.

"I don't," she said in as ugly and cruel a voice as she could, and pushed him away. "I said no. You misunderstood."

"I did not!"

He pushed her down on the couch, refusing to admit failure, pressing himself against her, words coming out of his mouth, his body insisting she give in. "Relax . . . you want it . . . it's happy time, I have to teach you that . . . teach you how to give in . . . slowly, slowly . . ." he whispered, rotating himself against her. "Doesn't that feel good? Let's go into the bedroom, it shouldn't be like this. Let me undress you, touch you, massage you . . ." He was raising her skirt, finding her thighs, trying to open them to excite her. He had to prove she would accept him willingly, after the nos. They were just the crazy contradictions in her that had to be broken down. His hand reached her silky underwear, the silky triangle, the silky door. It was moist. She was aroused, of course she was, she couldn't help it. His mind was aflame with all the wrong signals. He began to hum the insidious little drumbeats of the belly dancer's music, pressing against Roz in the rhythm. Suddenly, his shoulders were pushed with such force, he almost fell off the couch.

"Are you mad?" Roz's voice was so removed, it was almost more shocking than her push. "I'm leaving. Would you be good enough to put me in a taxi." (Not a question, a command.)

He somehow managed to extricate himself from his ridiculous position and stood up. He was destroyed. He knew how he looked—wild-eyed, hurt, stunned with embarrassment, and a damn flying buttress in his pants. She was laughing at him. The bitch had humbled him. He wished he were capable of raping her. Come swim with me, the bitch said, only there wasn't any water. The princess was his? Fuck yourself, Candleman, you must have been out of your mind! You've been had!

"Put yourself in a taxi, damn it," he said in a fury, went into his bedroom and slammed the door.

Roz got herself back to the Plaza very well indeed. She was so angry, she strode through dark streets for several minutes without being afraid, before she found a taxi.

Into a hot tub. Wash it all off—his saliva, real or imagined. She had forgotten who she was. He had existed only to serve her purpose—from the first day she met him in the district attorney's office. Poor wretched, panting, hungry thing. Catfish.

She was still feeling the effects of the ouzo. Catfish clean up the bottom of the tank. She was a dolphin. She stroked herself with the warm water, remembering the tremors she had felt when he began to touch her in that terrible, Turkish, cheap, tinsel place. A disturbing picture came to her: Hedda, with her head at the foot of Daddy's bed, Phoebe holding his hand . . . but *she* was standing at the window, alone, separate. Was that her fault? No! It was theirs, everyone's. Her thoughts leaped. She was going to live in Europe, anywhere she wanted . . . she'd start in Italy, be mistress of herself, her income. There wasn't going to be any Willard to take care of it. She would, she needed no one. She was going to hire a lawyer and get a divorce. She would buy a villa.

Roz got out of the tub feeling brave, pure, and utterly alone in the world.

Early in the morning the phone rang. She sat up in panic. No one knew where she was, except Roy! She wouldn't answer, she'd let it ring. It kept ringing. What was wrong with the desk?

Couldn't they see she wasn't going to answer? She grabbed it to make it stop.

"Yes?"

"Darling?"

(Willard!)

"How did you know I was here?" Her voice sounded trembly.

"The chauffeur told me, and he damn well better have. Aren't you glad?"

She sank back into the pillows. "Where are you?"

"At home in bed, where should I be. It's seven o'clock . . . there's someone missing." He sounded soft, almost unfamiliar. "Darling, I'm coming in to get you. Will you forgive me? We're all getting too upset about what's going on. I have to take care of you, Roz. Stay right where you are, I'm coming in. We'll have a wingding, anything you want. We'll face everything together . . . Are you there?"

She drew a thoughtful "yes" out of herself.

"We have to forget the lousy things we said, sweetie." He paused. "I didn't sleep very well, did you?"

"Not really . . ."

The hesitancy in her voice relieved him. "What did you do all by yourself last night? See anyone we know?"

"Good heavens, no! I went to see a horrible little film." All of a sudden, *last night* fell away, seemed almost amusing. She stretched and yawned with relief. "It was about a belly dancer and a vampire . . ."

"I called you until midnight, then I must have fallen asleep. I called you again at two . . ."

"I was in a tub. I took a very long bath after the movie."

She was a master of self-hypnosis, almost to the point of inducing amnesia. It was as though Roy had never existed when she got back to Greenbriar.

22

The day after Wesgrove's arrest, reporters were in Phoebe's lobby. They were pushed out to the sidewalk on both sides of Fifth Avenue. She was a prisoner, unless she wanted to take them on. She couldn't . . . She could do nothing but look out the windows and cry, no one to commiserate with except the servants. Hedda didn't dare come because she would have to walk the gauntlet; her name was splattered all over the papers . . . "thought to be Treading's very special friend and with him before he died, it is said . . ." Who said? Who was telling the press anything?

Phoebe was so angry with Roz, she couldn't imagine ever forgiving her, yet she'd *have* to someday, Daddy wanted it that way. Roz's name was splattered all over the place too . . . "Older daughter's suspicions were partly responsible for the investigation into her father's death . . ." She wasn't going to call Roz for a long time! Most of what had happened was her fault. How come Roz hadn't called to gloat? Maybe the Clydes had her locked up in a bedroom. Should she call Willard? Maybe Roz needed her . . . Her feelings always flip-flopped when it came to Roz. What a last living relative! How had everything gotten so crazy?

Phoebe had other thoughts that made her even more sad
and wondering. Daddy hadn't been fair. He should have taken
Roz into his confidence too, loved her enough to tell her his last
wishes about how he had to die. And, Hedda too. He was only
a hero with big gestures *outside,* inside he was *small.* She couldn't
stand what she was feeling. She had to contradict herself. But
he did love Roz! He had to protect Wesgrove, he said so. Roz was
theirs! Flip-flop . . . all she could do was look out the windows
and cry, and imagine what she would say if she had the guts to
go down to the street to the waiting newspeople and say . . .
"You're finks in the capitalist world, carrion hunters! Get your
noses out of my ass!" That would make them part like the Red
Sea and she could escape . . .

Dinessen came by to see her. He suggested that she come
and stay with him and his wife for a while. News stories like this
usually fade in a week, he said. But for some reason she couldn't
explain, she said she had to stay where she was, she had to hold
the fort even though there was no one in it but herself and the
servants. He said he'd also come to tell her that he had hired a
brilliant defense attorney for Dr. Wesgrove . . . "someone courageous enough to take on a euthanasia plea. You understood I
wouldn't be handling the case since I don't practice criminal
law, but I'll be advising . . ." Dinessen thought maybe she should
go up to Northampton if she wouldn't come home with him, but
Phoebe said her friends had told her reporters were waiting for
her there, too. "How do they know I have an apartment in
Massachusetts? The world is like one big mouth." He responded
that it was pretty easy to find out anything about anyone, if you
were paid to do it.

Dinessen sighed. It was one of many sighs since Max's
death. Max had left *some* weight on his shoulders—a murder
trial and trying to settle the estate at the same time. His entire
staff was doing nothing else. Max, who had thought he was on
top of everything his whole life, had left a turmoil of problems
for other people to solve, one hell of a mess of laundry. He
stayed on for a few minutes, had her sign some papers having
to do with Global Materials business, suggested, with kind

amusement in his eyes, that she could call him "Uncle George" if she liked, kissed her on the top of her head, and left.

She felt better . . . OK! Get out of here, get yourself to Mass., practice saying "No comment!", have Daddy's car and chauffeur ready and drive off! (She couldn't do it, that wasn't her style.)

Phoebe hadn't let any of the servants go, she couldn't get herself to fire anyone. They were all there waiting for the other shoe to fall. It never would, but they and she didn't know that in October of 1982.

You're losing your marbles, she said to herself. Call the garage, have them bring the old Volvo around, go downstairs, say "Fuck off!" to anyone who gets within a foot of you, drive off, and never come back! To that, she added another defiant thought: and let good old Dinessen pick up the pieces. She sat down and began to cry again.

The doorman rang from downstairs. "A Mr. Simon and a *Mzzz* Wilkerson are here . . . and someone named Skip, won't give his last name, Miss Treading. Don't know if they're reporters or not . . ."

"Send them up!" she screamed into the intercom. Northampton was coming to her! Thank God! Amy had probably made a fuss with the doorman about being announced Ms. or Miss, which accounted for the doorman's exasperated "Mzzz."

"Oh, am I glad to see you!" Phoebe exclaimed to the tall, red-bearded Bill Simon, frizzy-banged Amy, and a young black man, Skip Washington, all U. Mass. graduate students in economics.

"We thought you'd be," Amy said. They stood there in their padded jackets, jeans, and sneakers. "That's why we came. God, how are you handling it?"

"I'm not, I'm afraid to go out, I don't know what to do. I thought I was losing touch with reality . . . I wish I were a million miles away . . . but aren't you wonderful to come . . . oh my." Phoebe burst into tears, protesting, "I'm so nervous, forget it, just keep on talking . . ." Phoebe couldn't stop crying . . . "I don't know what to do."

"We do. Listen, Phoebe," Bill said, "we came down to get you out of here. You have to move yourself away from what's happening and not stay holed up like a victim." Bill knew very well about Phoebe's conflicts—being the daughter of a famous financier and her own ideals, choice of life-style; they'd talked about it a lot. He felt there might be a little sharpness needed now. "You know, you're going to have to face the fact that you're not Phoebe Treading at U. Mass. anymore. You're something else, and you told me you agreed to it—you're the potential head of a very big organization. Sure, you'll do it, when you're ready, in your own way, and sure, what's just happened is pretty wild; but you're going to handle it, 'cause you're you, you have friends, and you're going to weather it, you hear? So, of course, the damn press wants to get a look at you, talk to you, but you don't have to, and you don't have to hide in a corner either . . ."

Phoebe had taken them into the library while Bill talked, blowing her nose and not being able to stop the tears. Amy had an arm around Phoebe but Skip couldn't keep his eyes off the books. "What a fantastic collection!" he exclaimed.

"My father's," Phoebe sobbed. "This was his favorite room. God, what's the matter with me? I can't stop."

"Yes you can, because we're hungry. Is there anything to eat in this house?" Skip said turning from the books.

"Of course there is! I'll get the . . ." Phoebe paused. "No, I'll go and see . . ."

"Number two, before you go, the reason we came is to take you down to *The Clearwater* and get you out of here. How about that for street smarts?" Skip added.

"She's docked at the South Street Seaport," Amy added. "Isn't that luck? She could have been up in Kingston. We'll drive you down and then head back for Mass., we've all got classes tomorrow."

"*The Clearwater!*" Phoebe cried. "What a wonderful idea. Why didn't I think of that?"

"Yeah . . ." Skip said. "The perfect hideout." He made a subtle finger snap. "Would the purveyors of violence and sex hiding behind 'the right of the public to know' ever think of looking for the daughter of M. Treading on an environmental watchdog sloop schlumping around in da dirty water of da Hudson?"

"If they knew her, they would," Bill said with a smile.

"*The Clearwater*'s starting up the Hudson tomorrow, Phoebe," Amy added.

"How do you know there's room for me?"

"We've checked it out. Someone on the volunteer crew got sick."

"You mean it's all arranged?" Phoebe's tears welled up again.

"What are friends for, lady? Just to sit around and drink beer and discuss definitions and taxes?" Bill joked.

"And whether capitalism panders to the worst in human nature?" Amy quipped. "And *is* it built on greed, anxiety, and the exploitation of poverty?" They were trying to do a comedy act for her.

"I'm hungry," Skip said.

"Find your way to the living room," Phoebe said. "I'll get us some sandwiches. Eating's not allowed in Daddy's library."

"I'd like to spend a month in this library," Skip said, holding a volume of original Lincoln letters for the year 1863 that Max had collected and bound. "Is everything *original* here?"

"Yes, it is," Phoebe said solemnly. "It was my father's hobby; no, that's not right, it was his passion—American history."

While they talked and ate in the living room, Phoebe was thinking that such nice sounds hadn't been in the room since her father died. She was overwhelmed by their gesture, the three of them rushing down to help her, busy as they were with their studies and the *real* work that was an obligatory passion and commitment for some economics students—going out to communities, talking to workers, making them politically conscious, informing them how *the system* works. That capitalism was a

failure was never talked about, *that was the given.* How to change
it and correct the failure was where the energy should go. Students of the system should be teaching, talking, organizing with
the people who suffered most from the failure. Or what was the
point of devoting your life to economics? If you couldn't be part
of economic change. Radical change.

Phoebe learned that her friend Amy had just, finally,
bought her own car, "a secondhand GM compact, I'll probably
get killed in it, but I can't go to a union meeting driving a
foreign car, can I? No way . . ." And she sat quietly listening to
Bill and Skip talk about their favorite injustice of the year, the
creeping-up existence of workfare, a government-backed procedure that allowed cities to force welfare people to take any job
available to pay off their welfare checks, and work side by side
with union laborers who earned four times as much in the same
jobs. The welfare people were caught; the unions wouldn't take
them in and the city governments were happily getting cheap
labor. And how could *the poor* fight the psychosis of poverty, if
no one was going to help them handle the apathy, the depression? "It's going to take years to undo what's happening. How
do you organize the apathetic? They look at you with vacant
eyes . . . You don't take no for an answer," Bill said quietly. "You
keep making contact, talking, exposing, holding out a hand,
breaking down doors . . ."

Phoebe began to cry again. Her dear, dear friends . . . that's
where she wanted to be, had planned to be, living the way they
lived, would probably live for the rest of their lives.

How could she have thought her life wouldn't change?
Make believe she was a poor student, or if not poor, just gen-
teelly getting along like the rest of them, running around in the
old Volvo, looking for teaching jobs after the precious degree
was finally earned? How could she have thought she could re-
main the same after Daddy died? Hadn't she agreed to be
Daddy's daughter in front of Dinessen and Hedda? Daddy had
left her power—the power Bill, Skip, and Amy were going to
try and make some sense out of *and not only for themselves* . . . All
at once she felt like Alice eating the cake that would make her

grow abnormally fast, gross, too big for the room. She was separating from them. It hurt!

"How stupid of us," Amy said. "Phoebe doesn't need this nonsense, we're all so smart! Let's get her out of here, that's why we came, and it's getting late."

In a few minutes, Phoebe had a duffel packed. Her mood was changing. Bill was right. She *had* to face it, be herself doing it . . . Phoebe had been on *The Clearwater* many times before. She knew what she needed. They were out the door by midnight. Bill's VW was parked right at the entrance and evidently the doorman hadn't said a peep. (Of course he hadn't. They were going up to see Miss Treading and she owned the building, didn't she?)

Skip looked up at the no-parking sign and laughed. "Boy, you can break a lot of rules if you know the right people." The other two looked at him with disgust. It was an unwritten rule not to talk about *rich* in front of Phoebe.

"Shut up, Skip," Phoebe said with good humor. "It's not my fault, like it's not your fault you're black!" She gave him a kiss to make up for the stupidity of both their remarks.

"My love, get closer . . ." the car radio played softly. Bill drove so fast, they almost reached the deserted dock streets of lower Manhattan by the time the song ended. He clicked off the radio and they drove the rest of the way in silence, looking at the lights on the bridges over the East River, the harbor lights, the ominous, gorgeous mass of half-lit skyscrapers as they approached the tip of the island, dark-glinting glass and reflecting steel. "God, what a powerful town," Skip mumbled to himself. "You keep forgetting when you're away from it . . . Man's idea of who he thinks he is . . . it's too much, it's all here . . ."

They parked on a cobblestoned street, stumbled through puddles, walked down a long dock toward a lone mast-light on a little schooner that looked like a delicate but defiant anomaly in the soaring steel landscape that loomed just a few blocks away.

Phoebe hugged them a silent good-bye. Someone came on deck with a flashlight. A hand reached out to help her jump over a foot of black water. "First bunk on the right," the voice of the young woman captain whispered. "See you in the morning."

Phoebe climbed down the galley ladder to the main cabin. She curled up without getting undressed and went off to sleep like a top, with the smells of boat wood and harbor water, old sneakers, wool, wet gear, soap, fish, sleeping bodies . . . in her nose.

23

It was all Max's fault—Phoebe having to run away somewhere.

If he had had to prescribe where, he probably would have said: You're in a good place where you are. You'll be sleeping with someone's knee in your back! You'll be in a nest 106 feet long (including the bowsprit), having breakfast with sixteen people. You'll be cooking zucchini soup for them today, you've done it before, you know how. (Closeness, common purpose, sails unfurling . . . up the Hudson on a cool October day.) And, baby, you won't be alone in the apartment with the world crashing in.

Max had never been on *The Clearwater* except at its launching, but the idea had appealed to him immensely and he had contributed to its being built. In 1969 Pete Seeger, the folksinger, and some friends realized that the Hudson River was dying from pollution and decided to try to help clean it up. Alert the people. A beautiful sailing vessel was built in Maine, an almost exact replica of nineteenth-century packet boats. Max liked the idea of the centuries shaking hands to honor history—"a continuity of dreams . . ."

The Clearwater had become a floating conscience in the thirteen years since it had been built; an environmental schoolroom-workboat going up and down the river to tell and teach the people along the banks that their river would die if they didn't do something about it; its hundreds of species of fish, its marshlands, its birds . . . The same river that caused Henry Hudson to say, the first time he cast eyes on the beautiful ribbon, that there was no more life-giving awesome water in the world. Yet now, the river was getting too hot, too dirty for life. Tell the people to keep industrial waste from being spilled, raw sewage from being dumped, and even nuclear plants from being built along its banks.

Alexander Hamilton had written one of his Federalist Papers on a sloop such as *The Clearwater,* on his way to Poughkeepsie . . . which was just where they were heading, and by the end of the week, Albany. Hamilton had sat at a scarred wooden table just like the one Phoebe was scrubbing the next morning. This wasn't the first time she had spit-an'-polished the tiny galley. Her first trip as a "volunteer crew" was a present from Max the year she graduated from Miss Porter's. He was always figuring out ways to counteract his wife's influence on "the little one" and not have her follow in Roz's footsteps. There was a mood on the sloop that he wanted his daughter to know—trust in others, theirs in you, communal life, dedication to a purpose.

This was Phoebe's fourth trip, and she had always loved it. You lived cramped, busy, friendly, and tough. You learned about knots, sails, wind, and storm. You scrubbed decks and cleaned the heads when it came your turn. You worried about the brine barrel needing fixing. You learned how to take water samples and you skeined for life signs. At night, you went on deck and observed a moment of silence, to listen to the sound of a sailing vessel making its way; then you sang songs and talked. You heard everything from "Eleanor Rigby" to Bach on the classical guitar.

She was just where she was supposed to be, this trip, more than she ever could have imagined.

Dreading the moment of introductions the next morning, Phoebe was relieved and surprised that no one on board said, "Oh, you're . . . ?" Everyone had been prepared for her arrival and asked to say nothing about the story that had been in the papers all week.

The other volunteers were a nuclear physicist of sixty-five; a female anthropologist who had just returned from New Guinea; a lawyer and his twelve-year-old son, who were on for the first time; a young man who said he was a writer, "whatever that means . . ." It was his first time on *The Clearwater* too. Sam Russell was from Montana and admitted he'd never been on a boat before, much less a sailing vessel. He was on board to write a story for a San Francisco magazine about the administration's loosening up on environmental controls and how it might affect the progress of "cleaning up the rivers of America." Why did he pick the Hudson, why not a river out West? "Because the Hudson has *The Clearwater*," he said.

Sam was all thumbs. He didn't do well learning knot making or the timing of putting up and taking down sails. By the second day, he was relegated to helping in the galley, and let him write his article, if he could. He was also slightly seasick. He took more than his share of turns cleaning up the heads, saying, "My due, for being a landlubber klutz." The rest of the time he either sat at the big table in the main cabin, writing, or tried to tuck himself away on deck in the tiny space behind the anchor line. It was hard for Sam to tuck himself away. He had six feet, two inches to make unobtrusive, a shock of blond hair with beard to match, and a Lincolnesque face that made him look too serious and old for his twenty-seven years, until he grinned; and then he looked like a farmboy.

"Except, a farm in Montana isn't exactly that. It's a ranch of at least a thousand acres, if you plan to make any kind of living with steer. They need lots of room, an' so do you," Sam said to Phoebe, helping her spit-an'-polish the galley. "Lots of room," he smiled. "Maybe that's why I'm not doing too well here."

He admitted to being a damn good rider, pretty good with the tractor and planting machine, bringing in the cows off the range, rounding them up in the worst of snows. But, getting the hang of a sail up? Couldn't dig it, wasn't that peculiar?

What had he done between bringing in the cows and now? she asked. Oh, he said offhandedly, he'd gone to the University of Iowa, majored in journalism, got restless, landed in San Francisco, begun to write articles, short stories . . . Sam grinned in a shy but confident way. "Sold 'em all . . . Social criticism, mainly. Almost got to Lebanon last month, but it didn't work out. The magazine I write for couldn't dig up the money. You really learn your trade if you're reporting a war . . .

"So, I'm looking for social wars, I guess. I came up with the idea of the rivers—history of, beauty of, use of, pollution of. I'm starting with the Hudson. I'm gonna do as many as I can, East to West. Rivers an' people . . . I'll be seaworthy by the time I'm finished, I guarantee . . . an' that includes going down the Colorado in a rubber raft . . ."

"And you?" he asked shyly. "Where are you, may I ask?"

"Well, you know who I am, I guess . . . everyone seems to, 'cause they're giving me my room."

"I mean *you,* not who made you."

"Oh . . . me!"

"Yeah, you!"

It was said so ingenuously. They exchanged credentials. Phoebe told him about her aims for a Ph.D., maybe wanting to teach. She laughed. "What am I saying? I'm in limbo. I'll probably never do anything like that. My life's in a shambles at the moment."

"But you're still you, shambles or no."

"It's not that simple."

"If you did get your degree, what kind of economist would you be? Conservative or radical?"

"Jeffersonian Democrat," she shot back, surprising herself; that was Daddy speaking. "I'm not responsible for anything I say. Don't take that down."

"I don't have to take it down, I remember everything I've heard," Sam kidded. "It's an asset for a reporter."

She went into a tailspin. What a neat concealment behind

that western drawl. Everything about him said *truth*, and it wasn't! He was on board to get a story about her!

She pushed him up against the stove. "You're here to do a fucking story about me, aren't you! How awful! How sneaking awful! Who told you I was coming on? Someone must have told you!"

Sam was so upset at being misread—the lovely, tense little face in front of him was so angry—he didn't answer.

Because he said nothing, she was sure she was right and ran on deck.

Where to go and hide it, when you're midstream with sixteen people crammed into a wooden womb? She felt paranoid —everyone had conspired against her, Bill, Amy, Skip, the crew! Conspired to help someone get a story out of her. Not just the reporters hanging out in front of the apartment, *everyone* was a carrion feeder.

She had bumped into that moment of silence observed on board before someone started to sing or play music after dinner. She held on to the railing to steady herself. A guitar began to be strummed, a voice singing something about . . . "Oh, love, be like a river, watercress and foam . . . / Oh, love, be like a river, be my Gothic dome . . . /" On and on, it went with its "Oh, love, you be the river . . . I will be the sea" She felt so alone, she thought her heart would stop. She went below and curled up in her bunk.

Sam had followed her on deck, wondering how to approach her without making a fuss. He went below after her. "What's the matter, for God's sake? What did I say?"

"You're a swindler. You're a reporter and you want a story. It's like rape, you know, or don't you know?"

"You're wrong!" he protested.

"I'm not wrong, you're a liar; you're like all the others, except that you're worse, you with your phony story—you're gonna write an article about rivers? Bullshit! I'm getting off this damn boat tomorrow, so it won't matter."

"Don't do that, please don't . . . You've got it all wrong. Yes, I am a reporter, but I didn't know you were going to be on.

Yes, we were told the night you came, but that is *not* why I'm . . ."

"I don't believe you."

"Then, there's nothing I can do about that, is there?" He couldn't seem to get through to her, so he left.

Everyone was having a fine old time, throwing their voices into the wind. He paced back and forth along the deck. Phoebe Treading's unreasonable behavior didn't have anything to do with him, it wasn't his fault . . . They were strangers. Funny little thing . . . the way she had of looking right into you, with big, blue eyes opened wide, like she'd known you for a long time; or like she didn't know anything and had to know right away what was inside you.

Everyone finally went to sleep. Phoebe was wide awake, suffocating from claustrophobia, experiencing symptoms she had never known in her life. She rolled out of bed quietly and crept up the galley ladder to the deck.

They were anchored at Poughkeepsie. Tomorrow, she would get off and take a train back to New York. She stood at the railing and looked up at a sky full of stars. Daddy, Daddy . . . I thought I was strong . . . I'm not . . . I can't handle what you left me.

Sam was standing behind her.

"Hey . . . let's talk."

"Stay away from me," Phoebe said without turning around.

"Aren't you overreacting?"

"Yes, but it's none of your business."

She brushed past him and went for the ratlines, the rope ladder going up to the crosstrees—beams you could sit on three-quarters of the way up the mast.

"Hey! Where are you goin'?"

"As far away as I can get."

She had climbed to the crosstrees before, but never at night. Sam began to follow her. She looked down. "Don't try it, you don't know how!"

"To hell with knowing how, you're upset an' I wanna talk."

There was Sam coming up, rung by rung. Maybe the darkness kept him from fainting dead away, he was so scared. How could she not talk to him after that? That was exactly his point. No one had ever called him a liar. If he had to climb a mast to refute it, he damn well would; did!

Phoebe whispered, anxiously, "If the captain knew what you just did, she'd be very angry. No one's supposed to climb up the ratlines without instruction, it's very dangerous."

"To hell with the captain, you've broken a rule in my book. No one calls me a liar without debate. You're not gonna get away with it."

"What are you going to do? Push me overboard?"

"No, just insist that you apologize."

"How did you get yourself up here?" she said with just the smallest bit of admiration.

"Anger . . . and some sympathy for you, believe it or not. I really am who I said I was. Trust me, let's forget it. Throw the bomb away. I'm too young to die, so are you." Sam looked around and down for the first time. "Christ? Now what do I do?"

He had disarmed her but she wasn't going to admit it. "What do you do? You don't look down, that's for sure."

"I don't look down, I look at you. Then what?"

"Then I guess I have to apologize," she smiled.

"You'd be a rotter if you didn't, because I'm going to die. There's no way I'll get down in one piece, no way . . ." he gasped. "I'm terrified of heights. The last time I did anything this crazy was when I climbed up a Mayan temple, hundreds of tiny steps . . . the Mayans had tiny feet. I got to the top and collapsed. Nothing was going to make me go down. A helicopter was going to have to come and get me off that stone slab."

"How *did* you get off?"

"I crawled down backward on my hands and knees . . . pushing widows and orphans who were coming up the steps out of my way. I flailed my arms and screamed, 'Out of my way! dying man! out of my way!' . . . all the way down."

They burst into laughter and had to shush themselves. "No kidding, Phoebe, I won't be able to get down from here at all."

"Look up at the sky," Phoebe said softly.

Sam obeyed. "Star-studded . . . What else shall I look at, since I'm never going down?"

"I think we should."

"Why rush? I'll just sit here and look at your face." He paused. "I like your face."

"Why?"

"It's . . . I've lost my similes up here."

Phoebe reached out her hand. "I've changed my mind. You're not a liar, you're crazy."

"I was worried about you."

"Why should you be? You don't know me."

"That's what's crazy." He looked at her. "You look like a daisy, that's what you look like." He looked up at the sky. "Cast your eyes about the night . . . Extraordinary. Precarious, but extraordinary."

They were still holding hands. "All right," Phoebe said, "I'll start down first. When I get halfway, you begin. Hang on, don't look down; backward all the way, it's just another ladder. Look up at the stars, sing *Twinkle, Twinkle* . . ." She started down, one rung, two rungs, three rungs. Sam followed. He stopped halfway and dared to look down. "We haven't had our talk, we've just started, Daisy."

When Sam finally felt his feet on the deck, he put his hands lightly on her waist. "That wasn't just your ordinary, everyday thing up there. Was it, Sam Russell?" he asked himself out loud. "No, I don't think it was," he joked, as though she weren't there. He had to bend way down to reach her forehead and kiss it. "Good night, see you in the morning, all wounds healed . . . except," he looked at his hands, "they're raw with rope burn."

Phoebe tiptoed down the galley ladder and into her bunk. Sam stood on deck for quite a while, thinking about what had just happened . . . very high up. Not definable, but definitely something, he'd bet his life on that. He just had! He looked up at the crosstrees and mumbled "Christ!"

. . .

By the time they reached Kingston, all the others on board knew something was happening. Phoebe and Sam had their heads together every free minute. They just couldn't stop talking.

The farther they'd come up the river, the clearer, colder was the air, the more beautiful the fall riot of changing leaves. The slopes and palisades on both sides of the magnificent Hudson were aflame with raucous reds, yellows, and oranges, to the palest mauve of an old lady's lace. Sam had never witnessed the turning of the leaves in the East. There wasn't a phenomenon like it anywhere else in the world. "Good God, how can death be so beautiful!"

For the first time since Max's death, Phoebe was quiet enough to mourn him, at the same time, happier than she could remember. By the time *The Clearwater* reached Albany, Sam and Phoebe were falling in love. "An interesting pair," the female anthropologist commented. "They're walking around with eyelids of opal . . ." (She had a very intense way of talking about *anything*.) "They're the long and the short of it, aren't they? He could put her in his pocket . . . very dear, mythic, very beautiful." The nuclear physicist had lost his wife recently and had no children. Watching Phoebe and Sam made him very soft, nostalgic. "It's an amazing thing to see, isn't it?" he said. "One forgets the power of the quiet explosion."

The female anthropologist was right. There was something beautiful about them—tall Sam with his blond beard and serious face; Phoebe with her bachelor's-button eyes, as Max used to say, her face getting brighter by the minute, their arms about each other's waist. They didn't have that closed-door feeling of —leave us alone, we're exploring each other. Well, they couldn't do *that* on *The Clearwater*, not very well on the crosstrees. No, they emanated a kind of light that flickered around everyone else as well. It was very old-fashioned, very . . . affecting.

The only place for intimate talk was the crosstrees. Much to Sam's amazement, he was getting adept at climbing up the ratlines. If he had been after a story, he was getting it—from the

dust of Utah to the death scene in Max's bedroom. Up high on
a mast, somewhere on the Hudson, Phoebe broke her promise
to Max (except for Dinessen's knowledge). She told Sam the ruse
of her father's death, shared with him the reanimation implica-
tions of Wesgrove's experiment with her father as guinea pig.
They talked about Hedda, Roz, her mother. They defined love
for themselves, as if they were the first to define it. It was a
drunken high on crosstrees, up a mast. Fate, magic, coincidence.
It was *everything*.

Phoebe heard about growing up in Montana. She could
have brought the cows in off the range herself by the time Sam
had filled in his own biography. How different from hers. His
parents were *there*, alive . . . There was a kitchen, a garden, a
soup kettle on all the time for the ranch hands. There was
normal childhood, no death or anger. There was a sister he
loved, she'd married a rancher and lived close to his parents.
They laughed a lot, they worked hard. Sure, there was a lot
unsaid, like in most families. No one imparts enough secrets to
give one a real clue . . . Some people want to know more than
what is said. He had to leave the ranch, get interested in words,
people who'd never come across his path. But there *was* continuity, family . . . passionate belonging.

Phoebe made a connection between Max's Utah and Sam's
Montana. She bonded them—Max and Sam. Tall, gentle-on-the-
outside men, seething inside. Their seething was different.
Sam's was more elusive, hard to describe, but it was there. He
was going to do something with it, she was sure of that. Anyway, who in her right mind would want a Max-seething to live
with for the rest of her life?

Of course, they talked about what it meant to be ungodly
rich. Sam was so intrigued with the notion of "the responsibility
of wealth," it began to remind her of Max, his expiation for
having amassed so much.

"And it's all mine now, isn't that terrifying?"

Sam laughed so hard, he almost fell off the crosstrees.

"What's so funny?" she asked.

"Falling in love with you, Daisy."

"I know."

"It's happened, hasn't it?"

"I think so."

"The next test is not going back West. I'm going to try and get a job at the bottom of the *New York Times.*"

"Daddy knew one of the editors very well."

"Are you kidding? I'm not gonna do it that way."

"Why not? What's wrong with favoritism, if there's talent?" The practical, assured tone of her voice surprised him a little.

"You've never read anything I've written."

"I'd bet on it, Sam." *Sam*—a new name on her lips. It was the strangest thing that had ever happened to her, meeting Sam, except her father's death, and that wasn't over yet, might never be.

After a week of nonstop talking, they fell silent.

"Well . . ." Sam said quietly, breathing in the winy air, the October light crashing with color on the riverbanks. "Fall isn't the death of things. It's nature preparing for the sleep of a lion." He let out a roar and kissed her. They stayed that way for a long time, high on the crosstrees.

24

The Clearwater had made its way back from Albany to Poughkeepsie, where it was going to be docked for a few days. Sam had gotten his story about the Hudson, but it looked as if he wasn't going to investigate any other rivers.

He was going to New York with Phoebe to look for a job. It was only supposed to happen in novels—that you found yourself switched about in midstream, mythically met and bound to a course as illogical as ". . . Why the sea is boiling hot—/ And whether pigs have wings"! His life from the moment he set eyes on Phoebe Treading had taken on the same illogicality, yet perfect sense.

A week after Sam found himself in New York and staying with Phoebe, he felt like a psychoanalyst invited to a party by his patient, to meet everyone he had heard about *in depth*, everyone except Max Treading, absent because of death, but oh, still there. Even the doorman would say, "Read the paper this morning, Miss Treading? Your father would have said . . ."

Sam's little galley girl in blue jeans and tousled hair turned into someone with a butler, cook, maid, and chauffeur. She was also the head of an empire. Her bedroom was filled with books on economics—Marx, Engels, Keynes; there was a huge Declaration of Independence on one wall, a collection of rare teddy bears on another. Her father's ghost was everywhere, and the people around her behaved as if the floors would cave if they didn't walk lightly. They were all going to have to appear, one at a time, before a grand jury sitting in a place called Riverhead, Long Island, and testify for or against the alleged murderer— Dr. Hiram Wesgrove.

Sam Russell didn't come from Montana for nothing. He knew how to handle himself in a stiff wind. He couldn't have come into Phoebe's life at a better time, with what he had to give —the essence of what he was or hoped to be: direct, spontaneous, dependable, words chosen carefully, simplicity the aim, at least on the surface. No feints or foolery. What you saw is what you got—a tall, serious young man with an easy quiet about him; a straight elegance like that of a tree that had been well-planted in the right place.

There weren't many shadows around Sam. He had learned his ways from *steady folk*, hard-working ranching people with a little dour Scottish in their blood, mixed with some Irish and English and a deep, dry humor about the ways of things— wrestling with Montana winters that could kill, springs of beauty that sent you reeling, and summers sometimes so dry there didn't seem much point to it all. One thing you learned very quickly was how to hold your own in the unexpected.

Sam's father always faced a difficult situation with a "Well, let's see . . ." and in his tone was the promise that things would work out if they could, particularly if you impressed *your* will on them. If they didn't work out it wouldn't be for the lack of trying or *seeing*.

Sam had inherited some of his father's unruffled quiet, but he wasn't going to end up wrestling with the Montana earth and seasons, rather with "the intolerable wrestle with words and meanings"—the work of a writer. Sometimes that seemed harder than walking into the snow wind of a blinding storm, your eyelids caked with ice, your breath coming short and scary.

The Russells could boast an American heritage as long as

Phoebe's on her mother's side (the Wallebys) . . . but those
Wallebys would surely have thought the Russells didn't 'mount
to much, just farmers from New England who went west to
Pennsylvania, west to Illinois, west to Montana. Liberal, stand-
fast people all the way from dumping tea in Boston Harbor to
"Hey, we ain't got no truck with slavery . . ." to Sam's father
saying: "We have no right to be sending our boys to Vietnam,
someone else's civil war; get them the hell out; and if he doesn't,
get the president out!"

Sam's father was the first college-bred Russell in eight
generations. Sam was the second. He was going to have a more
quixotic nature, be guilty of doing unexpected things—like
finding himself in New York, right in the middle of what was
going to be one of the more curious murder cases in a long
time. No sex overtones, no violence, vengeance, greed, drugs,
passion. *Just murder by moral intention.* He itched to write about
it, but he couldn't. He was sleeping with the daughter of "the
victim."

Sam was glad to be in New York *by chance.* He believed in
Chance. Chance made life exciting, unpredictable, maybe even
preordained. Chance took over some of the heavy work of life,
made it more than a dull ceremony of days; there was no question about that. He had been brought there so Phoebe wouldn't
have to do it alone.

Max would have approved of Sam Russell. Hedda said that
to herself the first time she met him. It was outside the Criminal
Division of the Supreme Court in Riverhead, Long Island. She
had been called to testify in the morning. Phoebe was called for
the early afternoon.

The grand jury had already been in session for three days.
Dinessen had come to the apartment to prepare Phoebe as well
as he could. She was determined to say nothing about her
knowledge of the fake death scene in her father's bedroom. Let
the chips fall where they may; *she* was not going to be a part of
deciding Wesgrove's fate, except to say that whatever her father
had wished to do, it was his right to do it, and he was the sanest

man in the world when he drew his last breath, as far as she was concerned. The jury was to hear a very contradictory account from Rosalind Clyde the next day, shored up by Dr. Roy Candleman's testimony the day after. Drs. Lewisohn and Gruening had stood on their constitutional rights under the Fifth Amendment and refused to testify, and they would continue to, till hell froze over—their original intention way back, from the first time in Absalt's office.

The horror had begun for all of them. The very nature of the grand jury is secret, dark, ominous. At least, in an open trial the truth and the lie have their ways of being tested in the public air.

Actually, the district attorney felt he had a shaky case. There was almost no corroborating evidence except Treading's letter and Candleman's statements as to what he *overheard* and what was brought out under hypnosis. Such information wasn't the strongest evidence you could get; it was psychological hearsay. Everything depended upon what Dr. Wesgrove would say and do.

Wesgrove stood fast. He denied nothing. If there was any deception in the little man, it was for what he felt a just cause —to keep his colleagues free from involvement.

There *was* a final injection; *he* administered it. (Wesgrove was determined to keep it that way. He needed Lewisohn and Gruening to continue his work, take over . . . if the worst should happen.)

As for the cryonic process itself and the two doctors right there in the apartment while the "hoax" was going on . . . didn't they *know*, if they were his colleagues, that the usual way of preparing a corpse for freezing was not being adhered to?

No, Wesgrove testified, because the usual way was not being performed. The grand jury was told by Wesgrove that *as far as his colleagues knew*, he was testing a new form of slow freezing, with an injection *immediately upon death in Treading's bedroom*. Lewisohn and Gruening saw only a body in a bag, which they helped remove. *He* alone was responsible for whatever took place the evening of the twenty-third of June and the morning of the twenty-fourth. (Sometimes, it's important to lie

and pray history will absolve one, Wesgrove said to himself as
he lied through his teeth.)

The beacon of his confession couldn't be turned off. It was
not the grand jury's work to decide on the right or wrong of
Wesgrove's empathy, philosophy, morality. In the state of New
York, even assisting in a suicide was a crime, and Wesgrove had
not only assisted, he had *done* it! It was murder. And so, the jury
handed down its indictment.

Pro forma, bail was set at one hundred thousand dollars,
though such an outstanding citizen was not about to run away.

Riverhead, Long Island, was going to have a big case for
such a little place. The court reporter would probably become
a rich man, feeding the daily proceedings to the world press.
The trial date could have been set almost immediately since the
docket in Riverhead wasn't exactly jammed up, but Wesgrove
asked for time to complete certain projects and clean up his
affairs the best he could. His request was granted. The trial was
set to begin the last week of January 1983.

Who will we get? Some baggypants judge in Suffolk
County? And what kind of jury to be the peers of a Dr. Wesgrove anywhere? Those were the worries of Dinessen and the
criminal defense lawyer he had hired to plead the case.

The district attorney was glad of the time to gather as many
experts as he could—to testify on the subject of euthanasia. He'd
have to find damn good doctors to refute someone as highly
respected as Wesgrove. He'd have to base his case on "coercion
of a dying man." If the jury ended up sympathetic (and who
wouldn't be, who'd had a member of his family die of cancer;
and what family hadn't!) . . . then, there was the chance that the
case could fall apart and wind up making new law! He was going
to do everything in his power to keep that from happening.
Euthanasia: Like standing in tar. You get one foot free and the
other one sinks in.

The first time Phoebe saw Roz after the grand jury started
was the day the indictment came down. Dinessen insisted the

family get together and stick together, make peace, talk about the will, and prepare a common face for the world before the trial. He had a plan that he had discussed with Phoebe first and she had agreed to it: Involve Roz in the Treading Foundation *now*. Give her power, dignity, make her feel indispensable; the Treading name was hers. It might change her testimony in the trial, her my-father-was-too-ill-to-know-what-he-was-doing. The plan worked. Roz and Willard came to the apartment for dinner and Sam met them for the first time. Phoebe was right about them, Sam thought. Roz was gorgeous and had the most un-categorizable green eyes he had ever seen. He couldn't get over Roz's eyes. They had some kind of wacked-up light in them that flashed love and hate without warning, so you didn't know whether to go or stop. And, Willard *was* pompous and irritating.

Roz and Phoebe had been in Roz's bedroom for a little while before dinner; they must have behaved like sisters making up, catching up, because at dinner, Roz seemed to know every-thing about *The Clearwater* and Sam. Roz was charming with Sam. She always knew Phoebe would end up with someone like him—intelligent, handsome, poor. But, what did that matter? Nothing much mattered anymore, except to have a heart that didn't beat too fast. It was so obvious that Phoebe and Sam were in love. Roz, the elder, was almost playing the role of the-moth-er-who-wasn't-there. Who else was there to welcome Sam into the family—if that was the way it was going to be? "We're go-ing to live together for a year and see," Phoebe had told her.

Not a word was mentioned about the indictment, but they all knew they would be spending a lot of time together when the trial started. The dinner was a trial run—a pun in action, Sam was thinking.

Dinessen was so pleased with his plan working that he almost dared to think Roz might show a different face when called to testify. Then Wesgrove would be burdened by nothing more than Candleman's accusations—which wouldn't hold much water (as to a dying man being coerced), not when the jury learned Candleman had been fired and for what reason. *That* would finally come out under oath and from Wesgrove, no less.

Dinessen was thinking optimistically: If light kept shedding itself in the right places, who knows? The jury might be sympathetic enough to come in with a verdict of manslaughter . . . or original and brave enough, God help them, to make it "Not guilty" altogether. Dinessen was daring to hope.

Willard was the only one at the table who was bored. He didn't understand about the dust settling around him, the cessation of hostilities, the trial run.

Roz helped him a little. "Do you play tennis, Sam? Willard's very good . . ." (The difference between the two men was so marked, it made one want to do anything not to acknowledge it.)

"Sorry, I don't," Sam apologized. "Played a little soccer in college, that's about all."

"And, he's a lousy sailor," Phoebe added.

"I wouldn't say so," Roz said playfully. "He can sit on crosstrees very well, I hear."

Willard was derisive. "In a bathtub?"

"One-hundred-and-six-foot mast, Willard," Phoebe said with a straight face.

"What were you doing? Looking for Moby Dick?" Dinessen joined in.

"Looking for a Phoebe," Sam said.

Willard was becoming annoyed. "You're welcome to come out and sail . . ."

"Thank you, but never . . . I'll never sail again," Sam laughed. "I have to look for a job, that's what I have to do."

"Doing what?" Willard asked, not really caring for a reply.

"There's nothing duller than a writer out of work," Sam said.

"A writer? Well, all you have to do is come out with a best-seller, then we can talk about investments . . ." Willard didn't mean it as a joke totally. There wasn't anything he had to say to this Sam, whoever he was, but he was trying.

"Wrong department. I'm a journalist, or will be, before I'm through."

"Are you good?" Roz kidded.

"Very. Can't you see it all over me?"

"Yes," she said, in the nicest voice Phoebe had heard her use for a long time. Roz liked Sam, Phoebe could see that, and knew why. There was something about him . . . A very young Daddy, sitting in that chair . . . Phoebe voiced it to herself consciously, for the first time.

That night, Phoebe found a note on her pillow: "Let's make haste slowly, love. The love is mine. The 'Let's make haste slowly' is in the dictionary. It's my favorite oxymoron. Look it up, dummy."

Phoebe ran into the library and found Sam looking at Max's collection of books and pamphlets.

"What makes you think I don't know what *that* word means!"

"Well, do you?"

"No, I don't! I used to, but I've forgotten."

"Then, look it up."

"I intend to," Phoebe said making a little-girl face. "What are you doing, Professor?"

"I'm looking at your father's collection. It seems like he's got everything that's ever been printed about dissent in America."

"*Successful* dissent," Phoebe corrected him. "Daddy was only interested in success."

"He's got everything here from Roger Williams in Salem, in the 1630s . . . to Martin Luther King's 'We shall overcome' speech. Some of the things should have been left to a museum; they're originals."

"He left them to me," Phoebe said, leafing through the dictionary. "Here it is: oxymoron. 'A figure of speech by which a locution produces . . .' Oh, God, the people who write these things, really . . ." She went on " '. . . produces an effect by a seeming self-contradiction as in *cruel kindness* or *make haste slowly*.' " She looked up. "So, what does that mean on my pillow?"

"It means . . . you've got about three months before the trial. It means I have to look for a job. It means it'll be good for you to get away from here, get your head straight, mine too. A lot's happened very fast. There are things I want to do very fast, but slowly. And there isn't much time, but they should be done carefully . . . See what I mean?"

"Not really . . ."

"Let's go to Montana. I want you to meet my family. A letter wouldn't be fair—telling them I'll be living in New York and why and who and what and when and where it all happened . . ."

She surprised him with a swift response that made him shake his head. "Let's go to Utah first! It's on the way, isn't it?"

"Utah?"

"Yes, Daddy's ranch. It's in the will that I'm supposed to visit it once a year. We could do that first," she said excitedly. "I want to see it, I haven't been there since I was little. I want you to see it with me . . ."

"Why not?" he teased. "Utah's right next to Montana, everyone knows that." He took her in his arms. "Let's take two weeks off. Then, I have to find myself a job and you have to think about your degree, remember that?"

"I've dropped that idea for good," she said quietly.

"That's why you need a break, you see? To decide about things. You shouldn't dump an almost Ph.D.; that would be dopey. Give it room, Phoebe. You don't want to lose a whole year."

"I think I was doing it for Daddy, not me. It was something he wanted . . . and I had to prove I could do it . . ." She looked around. "It upsets me to be in here. Daddy was in this room a lot."

"It's a wonderful room, filled with amazing things. My God, the stuff he picked up and thought valuable. Come on, turn it around . . ." Sam went to a shelf, pulled out something, and waved it in the air. "Do you know he's even collected a flyer passed out by the Yippies in the presidential election of 1968? What kind of a nut would consider having *that* share the air with original Lincoln letters? A wonderful nut," he added reflectively. (He had been thinking about it before she came in.) "Someone trying to define the American spirit and doing a damn good job of it . . . There's a lot of love in this room."

She burst into tears.

"Cry fast," he whispered in her ear and hugged her tightly. "Let's leave tomorrow."

"Tomorrow?"

"How long does it take to pack pants and boots? I gotta get back an' look for work, lady."

If Sam only knew that Phoebe had already called Max's friend, one of the editors of the *Times,* and told him of Sam's existence . . . (He'd known her since she was little. Sam must be someone special for her to make the call. Of course he'd see him.) she and Sam would probably have had their first fight. Phoebe had made the call without hesitation, even though she knew Sam had a too-innocent misconception about *doing it alone.* Her father would have made the call. Sam deserved it and would prove himself, so why not?

Actually, Phoebe was a little surprised with herself; how easily she'd picked up the phone—for two reasons: She was so certain of Sam's worth; moreover, she had a growing sense of her own power. With Max's willing *his* place, power, and influence to her, she had started to put on the outer garments of it. She had asked Dinessen to send her material on the history and organizational structure of Global Materials, to study, dope out, and get a handle on what was hers. She was surprised that it fascinated her, that maybe learning about real business and finance was going to be *her* Ph.D., not the ivory tower one. She wasn't going to say anything to Sam about it because she didn't quite know herself. Was she changing? Was Max's bullheaded will making her into something she wasn't? The only thing she was sure of was that she loved Sam. His arms around her in Daddy's library felt like a strong bridge between the past and now, a growing-up bridge all their own, a beautiful swaying span.

Sam was holding her, rocking her side to side. "Are you going to stop crying? Or we'll be standing in a river."

They flew to Moab the next day. The way they flew did cause their first fight. Phoebe was supposed to have made reservations the night before. They were driven to Kennedy Airport by the chauffeur, to the section of the airport where private planes took off. While Sam was saying "Hey, wait a minute . . ." he saw a large jet with *Global Materials* written on its side, waiting for them. "No, Phoebe, I don't like it, it doesn't feel good." He stopped dead. "The limo is one thing, but this is too much. I don't want to go this way!" He was furious.

Phoebe was very upset. "They're waiting for us, please, there's a takeoff time, we have to get in." Sam stormed off in front of her and ran up the ramp without saying hello to the pilot and copilot, who were smiling a greeting at the bottom of the steps. He sat in a seat, looked out the window, and glowered. Phoebe slipped in beside him. "I'm sorry, I didn't think it through . . . I didn't realize . . ."

He didn't want to face her with the thoughts in his head, starting at dinner the night before, about Willard, stupid snob, vacant, pompous bastard—because of money. Only money gave airs. Only money made pompous asses. He turned to her sharply. "It's swollen horseshit! It's not my style, lady. Is it yours? If it is, we've got some things to talk about . . ."

"You might as well have slapped my face, Sam. Please answer your own question. Am I horseshit?"

He looked at her, in her old jeans, a wool plaid jacket, and old boots with thick soles, on the verge of tears.

"No, of course not, but what are you doing?"

"You said 'Make haste slowly,' didn't you? Well, I couldn't make connections to Moab for today. Tomorrow, yes, but not today. The damn plane's just sitting here doing nothing. How stupid not to use it. It's mine . . . I thought we'd break up laughing about it, not fighting. Sam . . ." She took his hand and put it to her lips. "I'm very rich . . . richer than Willard."

"What's he got to do with this?"

"I'm smart, that's what. You hated him last night. You were uncomfortable. He has a way of making anyone who isn't a member of his club feel worthless, gooking, gawking . . . and he doesn't have a thought in his head except who he is . . . because of money. Daddy wasn't that way. He was the exact opposite. He flew around in this thing, laughing. You know who my father was, you said so last night in his library . . ." she paused. "It's gonna be a test for us, isn't it, the money, money, money?"

"Not for me, it isn't. How about you?" he said curtly.

"Cut the crap, Sam, you're hurting me, if you don't know who I am yet." She dug her nails into his hand. "Do you?"

"Ouch! Stop it, what are you doing?"

They hadn't even noticed that they were taxiing down a runway. The pilot's voice was saying, "Miss Treading, seat belts, please, we're about to take off."

Up, up, through a cloud bank into the sun. Sam looked around the cabin. "Two people to Moab? It's obscene . . ." and he began to laugh. "All right, love—Moab *this* way, but we're going to Montana *my* way, like ordinary people. This beauty goes back to New York when we get to Utah."

"OK, OK, but you will admit it's fun, isn't it?" She had her tongue in her cheek, but her eyes were serious.

"Are you changing, or am I seeing things?"

"Maybe a little bit. Trying to put the pieces together, facing who I am, not some dream of voluntary poverty. You have to help me. You can give me hell sometimes, but not too much. I'm an orphan . . ."

Sam unfastened his seat belt and crawled over her to stand up. "I'm going to say hello to the captain. I didn't look very friendly when we got on, did I?"

"You certainly didn't. You looked like a fundamentalist walking into a whorehouse . . ."

"No, I looked like Willard," Sam quipped as he walked forward, "sitting opposite Fidel Castro at dinner!"

. . .

They rented a car and drove to the ranch. The door was
open for them. Max had had a caretaker from Moab come in
once a week, ever since his mother died. Phoebe had contacted
him. She'd really planned it . . . from the jet to the open door.
Sam was beginning to see how much it meant to her—a homecoming and a funeral at the same time. She walked into the
house, came out, looked at the desert, and said she wished she
had Daddy's ashes, to put them where he belonged . . . she
wanted to find Martha Treading's stone the next day . . . maybe
one of the neighbors could tell them. The house was just as
Martha had left it the day she died . . . all except the smell of
lemon geraniums in the kitchen. The caretaker wasn't going to
keep them going for years, even though Mr. Treading said
"Keep it just like it was . . ." (Going on to ten years ago, that
didn't make sense, did it?) But, the beds were made and the
kitchen stove was ready for a match.

"It's eerie, isn't it?" Phoebe said. "Daddy's . . . kind of fetish
. . . like a memorial. It's just as eerie 'cause I feel I'm home, but
I don't want to sleep in the beds, I don't want to disturb anything."

"What a wonderful place to write!" Sam exclaimed. "The
silence is incredible. Are you going to keep it up?"

"Of course I am! It's in the will. If I don't come here once
a year, Daddy said it had to be burned down."

"Wow. He must have had an incredible love for the
place . . ."

"Yes, very . . ." She was looking at the pictures of herself
and Roz, her mother, Max . . . silver frames, young faces, baby
faces. "Can you imagine my mother not allowing us to come and
visit her?" She was looking at a picture of Martha Treading, her
arm through Max's, both standing in front of an opening in the
ground with a sign over it—*Elephant Mine;* looking into each
others' faces and laughing. She held it up for Sam to see. "If that
isn't Roz in a leather-fringe dress, and happy, I don't know who
it is, my God." Phoebe sat down with the picture in her lap. "My
mother denied Granny her grandchildren and her son . . . isn't

that awful? Daddy used to come here by himself to see her. He brought Roz and me once. I don't remember it, I was too small . . . I don't *think* I remember it."

"Do you know why your mother did what she did?"

"Of course I know. I heard the fights. Mother said Granny would tell us bad things, she'd let us run free, we could go naked if we wanted to! Evidently, the one time Daddy did take us out here, Martha took one look at us, took our clothes off, and said 'Get those children out in the sun, they look like Chinese tea-cups fit for breaking.' Daddy told me that . . . I don't remember, it's hearsay evidence."

Sam could see her mind was going in wide circles. It had all started here, in this house. He wanted to help her sort it out, but he couldn't. She'd have to do it by herself. Obviously, Max Treading was an exceptional man, who had come from here and gone to there, in a kind of genius arc. Amassing a fortune was a kind of genius. If what was in his library was the true man, he had done it and laughed at it. What a mixed bag. Phoebe had inherited the bag and the arc.

"This place is filled with bright spirit," Sam said quietly. "I love it."

"I knew you would. Please kiss me and remind me who I am. Me . . ." She looked at him with pleading, huge eyes. "Me, come from them . . . but me."

He put his arms around her.

"Phoebe, we're here together, I'm holding you and it's kind of a miracle, isn't it? To feel we're the children of children . . . Your Martha and her son, they were mixed with *wonderful*, obviously, because here you are!" He held her at arms' length. "With your blue eyes, sweet head—what should we do with it?" (He was trying to make her smile.) "Too big to put in a bread-box, too small to pay attention to, except for Sam Russell, who loves you very much."

The place was filled with death and dreams. You had to shout the fact of your living. It must be the desert, he thought. He'd never been in a desert. It made small things smaller, big things bigger. *You had to testify for yourself . . .* in such an expanse.

He was beginning to understand Martha Treading and her son, a little bit.

The next day, they hiked the land, met neighbors; the older ones were delighted to see a Treading back. A leather-faced man in his eighties talked about Max as a boy . . . "Tough an' soft at the same time, never saw anything like it in a kid. Would wrastle an' cry in the same five minutes . . . got himself all upset about a stray dog once . . . had us all walkin' around with lanterns, like fools, tryin' to pin the critter down an' get 'im into a warm place. His mom never put any brakes on 'im, let 'im do an' feel what he wanted. No one around like Martha, an' never will be. She, for sure, put gumption an' real, good manure in that boy, didn't she? Look what he did with his life, your dad. You proud, girl? What ya' gonna do? Sell? Some rich fella gonna put up a lotta damn houses 'round us? Progress comin' to this stretch o' nothin'?"

Phoebe assured the old man her land would never be sold, not in her lifetime, anyway.

"What are ya doin'? Walkin'? Wanna borrow some horses an' ride around? Ya' can, if ya' wanna." He looked at Phoebe like an art critic in a museum. "Ya' don' look like none of 'em. Who do ya favor, little girl?"

Phoebe told him she *favored* her mother, but her older sister looked like Martha Treading, her daddy always said.

"Then, she's a mighty handsome girl, your sis. Your grandma had the biggest, greenest eyes, outside of a jungle critter, ya ever saw. An' bossy, oh, she was. If things didn' go like she planned, those eyes could dig ya a grave. But, God help her, where she is now, if anyone is. She was always right, that Martha."

Sam watched Phoebe. She was loving it—an oasis of connections in the desert.

They took the old man up on his offer of horses. Phoebe had a little trouble with the Western saddle. Sam kidded her about "fancy ladies from the East an' their fancy English bottoms." How could he have known that Max had said something similar to Sophia?

They rode out to get closer to the buttes, the mesas in the distance rising up like astral burial grounds. They rode for an hour until they got to a particularly towering butte, and stopped.

It was a cold day. The sky almost looked like snow coming, but the sun was brilliant and fighting off the clouds. They stopped at a protected, cavelike indentation at the foot of the butte, got off their horses, clasped each other, took their clothes off, and made love, feeling no cold.

Phoebe knew they were sealing their love in a bond that would never rip open. They were being married in the bride's land, as it *should* be. Daddy and his mother were there to witness the ceremony. She knew it as surely as Sam was slipping inside her, and she, wide open and ready to receive—it was their wedding—his soft beard against her breasts, her lips on his forehead, her hands pushing, pushing his head to her, harder . . . harder . . . a perfect bond! Bare-assed! Wind blowing! It was cold! They were crazy!

They rolled over and laughed.

When they got to Montana, it had already had its first snow. A big one. Phoebe watched Sam. Like a pianist who hadn't played for a long time, he was finding his reflexes. With a whoop and a cry, he went out to bring hay to the slopes, talking about the pregnant ones and whether they should be brought in. Soup kettles boiling, breath steaming. Sam's family treated her as if she had a halo over her head. She felt like a very little bear, fallen from a high place into a pot of honey. Sam's family embraced her in its warmth. She wasn't used to it, had never had it . . .

"You're the only one I ever brought home for them to meet. You're *it*, don't you know that?"

"Then why don't we get married?" (She couldn't have surprised him more.)

"Here?"

"Yes . . ."

"You're sure, now . . ." Sam said very carefully.

"Yes." She said it just as carefully.

"Mom asked me if the thought was in my head. She comes right out with things. I said it's been in my head for a long time, about a month. Is that long enough, Phoebe?"

"I think so . . . for us."

The wedding was in the Russell living room, a long, homey room with chintz and petit point and windows looking out over snow slopes as far as you could see, blending into hills and patches of evergreens. A judge who was a friend of the family officiated . . . because both Sam and Phoebe wanted a civil ceremony. The Russells didn't mind; they seldom went to church except for weddings and funerals . . . and the second snowstorm of the week had just started. Home was the only place to be. It was all very simple. No one gave the bride away, no bridesmaids, flower girls, no best man, no fountains of champagne and Duchin's orchestra; not the way it was in the ballroom of Greenbriar (where Roz was married), with two hundred people whirling about.

Phoebe had packed only one dress in her duffel bag the night they decided to take the trip to Utah and Montana—with a vague, but definitely a feminine, prescient, idea. Pack a dress, you might need it!

She stood in front of the judge, looking past his shoulder at the snowy landscape outside, as she half-listened to his words. He was saying more than a judge would have in his chambers; he had known Sam since he was born. She was wearing the dress Hedda had given her (the beige lace that made her look like a medieval virgin, according to Max). Of course she'd packed it. She *knew* she and Sam were going to be married.

Her eyes were fastened on the snowy slopes. There were indentations of footsteps out there, delicate shadows of feet going toward the big red barn. More indentations trailed down and over and up to the pastures where the cows were standing —too far away to see—but she knew they were there, the snow coming down on them. Sam's father had explained the tough rituals of winter on the ranch, the strong ones making it, the weak ones not, but you did your best *and then some*—to second-guess nature. Her eyes rested on the trails of caring footsteps, tractor designs in the snow, meaning hard work, love, attention, pride. She and Sam were going to be as solid together as all the symbols and intentions behind those patterns on the land.

Sam was kissing her. They were married.

25

Who would make up the Wesgrove jury was so crucial to the case, George Dinessen was reminded repeatedly of Clarence Darrow's advice to lawyers on picking a jury: Don't choose a Presbyterian. "He's cold and grave; he knows right from wrong, although he seldom finds anything right. He believes in John Calvin and eternal punishment. Get rid of him before he contaminates the others." As for Baptists? "They are more hopeless than the Presbyterians. The Methodists are worth considering . . . their religious emotions can be transmuted into love and charity." A Catholic? "He must be emotional, and will want to help you; give him a chance." But, "Beware of Lutherans, especially a Scandinavian, they are almost always sure to convict . . . A person who disobeys must be sent to Hell; he has God's word for that. As to Unitarians, Universalists, Congregationalists, Jews and agnostics, don't ask them too many questions, but keep them." As for women, according to Darrow . . . "Women still take their new privilege seriously. They are all puffed up with the importance of the part they feel they play and are sure they represent a great step forward in the world."

It took three weeks for Jay Markham to fight for the jury
he wanted, with Dinessen sitting on the sidelines. They had a
little of everything, except a Lutheran; hoped that the two Jews,
with their skepticism and habits of questioning, their superim-
posed or imagined guilts, might make them work harder in
search of the truth; and that the two Catholics might be the kind
capable of understanding the *taking down off the cross*, the cessation of pain; *that* was Wesgrove's primary intention toward
Max, which they planned to prove without a doubt, laws of the
state notwithstanding. What other intention could a man of
Wesgrove's caliber have?

The trial itself lasted one week.

Jay Markham—tall, lean, nervous, with a long list of Not
Guilties in highly controversial cases, with a sureness that usually withered the opposition by a perfectly seamed preparation,
wit, and intelligence—presented everyone who had had anything to do with Max Treading in the last six months of his life
—to attest to his control and sanity. The saner the Max, the
more challenging the search for the truth of this case. He even
put Dinessen on the stand . . . "one of the most trusted and
impeccable legal minds in the state of New York."

The prosecution was to bring forward a myriad of doctors
and psychiatrists willing to state that anyone who wished to end
his life, no matter in what state of pain, was not responsible for
his own behavior, "for the will to live is the paramount, the
undisputed instinct in the human being."

The defense called just as long a list of professionals who
were of the opposite opinion as to the right of ending one's life,
and why. It was an individual's *supreme right* to die in the face
of terminal torture, namely cancer.

Yes, the doctors for the defense would say, Dr. Wesgrove
had confessed to the act of finishing a life, but a man of his
stature had not committed a crime; by his lights he had be-
stowed a blessing. Only in the eyes of present-day laws was he
guilty. And, those laws could be changed by the acumen and
empathy of juries such as *this one*, sitting in this very courtroom.
One was not to minimize Riverhead, a doctor from California

said. History could be made in such a place, with the help of a Dr. Wesgrove, who had been his professor at Harvard. History was not confined to the metropolises of the world. History was made by superior people and their minds *anywhere*.

Euthanasia became a household word in that week of argument.

The prosecution called Dr. Roy Candleman to testify as a molecular biologist, that he had worked on the cells of Maxwell Treading months before his death and with an unusual degree of interest and directive from Dr. Wesgrove. The prosecution thought it might veer the jury away from the moral plea of helping a suicide, to the picture of a scientist using a human as a guinea pig and being responsible for his eventual death. It was shaky evidence, corroborating nothing but a mood, and the witness was even shakier than his testimony. What Candleman had *overheard* the day he cleaned out his office was of no importance anymore, since Wesgrove had admitted to *the final injection*. The teeth of Candleman's vengeance-act had been pulled. Candleman had fallen apart; his eyes were heavy-lidded, he could barely speak. The day before, the defense had called Dr. Wesgrove to testify as to why Dr. Roy Candleman had been fired. The disclosure of his falsified experiment, heard for the first time by anyone outside the small circle at the Research Center, damned poor Candleman for life, at least the life he had so earnestly sought for himself—the airy reaches of academic research.

Much to the prosecution's chagrin, Rosalind Treading changed her tune. Gone was the counted-upon vitriol, the accusation that her father had died not of sane mind. She did express dismay—that he had chosen such an unacceptable way, in her view, to die. Her testimony was cold, removed. She looked at no one, least of all Roy. He didn't exist. She looked ravishing. The newspapers described every detail of her dress.

Phoebe, on the other hand, was highly emotional. Her father had a right to die in any manner he wished and his doctor was a saint to have helped him. (The judge had allowed Max's letter to be introduced as admissible evidence the day before.)

She opened her purse, took out a copy of the letter, waved it in the air, saying . . . here was proof that her father was the bravest man who ever lived, brave for himself and for the future of science and the world. The prosecution had to ask the court to stop her because she wasn't testifying to a question, she was making a speech, and the judge agreed. But, the jury *heard* her.

The media made a great deal out of the difference between the two sisters. They were called "King Lear's daughters."

Hedda testified in almost a whisper. She was asked to recount the last two days of Max's life (again!). It became so unbearable, she was inaudible before she finished. But, what she said added up to a man not insane from disease, unusual as his plan to die had been, which she, herself, had not been aware of. *No, he had not shared it with her.* She testified that not once, in the whole year of pain and medical treatment, was he other than what he had been—a man of superior feelings and behavior, "a kind of prince . . ." She was not pushed to go further. She couldn't have. She burst into tears.

The prosecutor's summing up was lethal. Hiram Wesgrove, distinguished as he might be, was a mortal man, and let no one think there was any other kind. He had exploited a sick and dying person in a frightful charade. In order to obtain a huge grant for himself and the Cancer Research Center, he had coerced Maxwell Treading with promises of future life, which everyone in that courtroom knew to be the promises of a charlatan. Wesgrove had acted to gain financially and professionally in his egocentric and shortsighted pursuit of a cure for cancer. Thus spake the prosecution.

The judge, in his charge to the jury, spoke in an affecting manner that surprised Dinessen and gave him the tiniest ray of hope.

"I don't like this any more than you do," the judge said in very low key, so as not to be polemical. He cautioned the jury to think clearly, to the extreme of its ability, about the classic emotions behind an act of murder—greed, lust, jealousy, loss, anger, sexual aberration, and mental derangement; the lack of judgment as to right and wrong. He asked them to add another word to the list—*compassion.* They must also be mindful of the testimony as to the mental condition of the deceased and review it with considered care, as well as "the intent to murder" of the defendant.

The baggypants judge in the hinterland had turned out to be something other than what Dinessen and Markham had expected. He had been sitting for a week, Judge Lansing, hoping the jury would do something startling.

The jury found Hiram Wesgrove guilty of murder in the second degree.

When it was all over, the judge met with Dinessen in his chambers. "Juries usually do what the law requires," he said. "We know that, don't we? Juries favor incarceration, since the law requires guilt to be punished. Despite my inclination in this case, it seems to me I must go for twenty-five years to life." Despite his inclination, the judge had decided he had to be strict. It *was* premeditated murder, despite the extraordinary circumstances and nuances of this particular case, and to prevent others from thinking they could get away with it, under the guise of euthanasia, and until new law was made . . . he had no choice.

After the dreadful moment when the decision came down, the foreman of the jury asked if he might add a statement to the verdict. "It is the wish of the entire jury, Your Honor."

The judge allowed.

Now what? Sam said to himself, holding Phoebe's hand in his. Everything involving his dead father-in-law seemed to have a larger-than-life dimension.

The foreman said, "The jury was unanimous in thinking that Maxwell Treading was sane at the end of his life, Your Honor, and we didn't think that he was coerced by the defendant; but since the defendant did cause the death of the deceased, with a fatal injection, we had no choice but to look at the crime . . ." The man swallowed hard and was obviously feeling very emotional . . . "We had no choice but to think of the defendant as guilty of murder by compassion! We wanted that known, Your Honor."

Dinessen wanted to go for an appeal. "It will give you time, Dr. Wesgrove, keep you out of jail. Maybe we could parlay it for months, maybe years . . ."

Wesgrove wouldn't hear of it. "The end will be the same. We couldn't win, unless there's new law. It would sap my energies. I'd rather start paying now. I have too much to do in my life." He smiled the smile of a very tired man. "I'm almost looking forward to prison."

The media had been describing him for weeks as either a man of vision or an ogre with midnight fantasies. When he took the stand in his own defense, he gave a lecture to the world (it would be printed everywhere) about why he did what he did; what the field of cryogenics was all about; how, in years to come, long after a child born that very day was dead, there would be humans, frozen, flying in space, in capsules going to other places in the Universe. "If we do our work well, step by step . . ." (Wesgrove's tone was as rational sounding as Galileo's when he explained to the medieval church *his* concept of the heavens.)

The court in Riverhead, Long Island, also had the unusual privilege of hearing about the assurance of a cure for cancer, *if* all the disciplines of science and medicine were able to *afford* to work together toward that end. *If* . . . they were funded sufficiently toward that end, and, indeed, one man alone had made that confluence of disciplines possible—Maxwell Treading. A man of courage had foreseen that need, and it would be done, whether a Hiram Wesgrove was free or not.

The air in the courtroom, when Wesgrove spoke, was like the silence of good theater. People were listening, feeling, and you could hear them listening and feeling.

There was only one consolation to be drawn from it all. Max's will stood firm. The work of the Cancer Research Center would go on, whether Wesgrove was in prison or not.

Max's last wish and intention remained *alive*.

THREE

26

[*December 1993*]

"Time has a peculiar way of simultaneously galloping and standing still." Sam was trying to begin a New Year's editorial about the state of the world. He kept staring out the window at the tops of the nude trees in Central Park and the heavy snow falling. The snow had started the night before and was doing much better with its statements than he was.

He was sitting at the desk in the library that used to be his father-in-law's. It was Sam's favorite room, as it had been Max's —a comfortable sanctum with dark wood panels, muted red rug and drapes, a discreetly opulent stage for all the books.

Sam had gotten to know his father-in-law intimately through the books. What could be more revealing of character than what a person chooses to underline in a book or where he places a marker? Whether it was Puritan Jonathan Edwards or Norman Mailer, the modern fighter of devils, Max Treading had had something to say to every persona between covers in his massive collection of Americana. Sometimes, Sam would open a book, find a notation of Max's, read it, ponder over it, and almost say out loud, "Now, why did that statement interest you? Oh yes . . . I see . . . Aha . . . very good point."

Sam continued to stare out the window. What to say about the world? He disliked writing an end-of-the-year recap column, but it was obligatory for a newspaper columnist. He began to kick it around in his head.

"Dear Reader: Look what happened in your year, your decade! Sing 'Auld Lang Syne' and on to the next. Business on the planet as usual. Years later, it's called History, can you imagine that? Your lousy year, your good year, is History? Dear Reader, what did you do to help make History?"

No, he couldn't put his mind to *the larger issues,* not on Christmas afternoon. He kept thinking of himself—about to be forty on New Year's Eve. When he was small, he thought everyone was celebrating his birthday with a blowing of horns and a ringing of church bells . . . the whole world.

He was feeling slightly depressed, the way one does on holidays, sinking into a review of connections, belongings, loss, change; a sad, gentle poking about in the memory pile. He put a new piece of paper into the machine and stared at it, typed *New Year's,* and stopped. Hell, maybe he should just write a little thing about evergreens and deer huddled underneath waiting for spring, the April thaw, lighthearted peace in the warming sun, long idle months of plenty and no death, the dreams of deer as well as humans. Or, maybe he'd amuse himself and do a flip holiday column on fashion. If you wear a skintight bodysuit like everyone is wearing these days, does it give you the feeling you can get places faster? Like the new space shuttle . . . it's beginning to resemble a piece of metal spaghetti, or a needle looking for an eye.

Sam smiled to himself. He was imagining a conversation with Phoebe, who liked the bodysuits. "Don't you love me better in a bodysuit, honey?" she'd say.

"Better than what? I can see what you've *got* better, sweetheart, but it doesn't make me wonder much, and wonder is a rare occupation," he'd say. A thought struck him: There certainly was something mysterious about the mons veneris of an Athena, with thick folds of fabric blowing around it for centuries! Mystery. Wonder. Not to be so sure of what's underneath

—that was tantalizing. *How come I don't spend a lifetime carving you in marble anymore?*

Sam had done very well in the past decade. Twelve years ago he had arrived for an interview with an editor, only to find that he wasn't an unknown; he had been greeted with (he thought) undeserved enthusiasm—all because he was the son-in-law of Maxwell Treading. But he had gone on to prove his own worth as a reporter in three wars: first, the Syrian-Jordanian explosion that lasted for six months in '86; then, the one on the border of China and India; and the last, which had threatened to be the last war for everyone, between Brazil and Argentina, with tactical nuclear weapons of the Soviets on one side of the La Plata River protecting Brazil and U.S. tactical nuclear weapons on the other being Big Brother for Argentina. It was a damn hot, uncomfortable place to be in peace, much less war. That was in 1990, when another devastating incident took place, responsible for putting War on hold. A defensive weapon being tested and on its way up in a Russian space vehicle, fell—because of human error in assembling—and wiped out an entire section of Siberia. The shock of the event sent the world leaders to the conference table, where they've been ever since, trying to figure out, once and for all, world disarmament until further notice, which could mean half a generation if the Devil takes a holiday.

Max Treading, who died in '82, would have said, "What? The stupid world didn't explode because of the crisis in the Middle East? The Arabs, the Jews, the oil, access to the Persian Gulf?" No, it didn't. A Soviet-backed Syria had withdrawn when a U.S.-led alliance of European countries stationed itself on the Jordanian borders and threatened an all-out invasion of Syria if the Arab genocide didn't stop, if a homeland for Palestinians wasn't immediately carved out of sections of Jordan, Syria, and Israel.

But, from the Middle East, Man's stupidity had moved to Latin America, threatening itself with the final conflict . . . until the nuclear missile fell in Siberia . . . which led to the disarmament conference and other startling events. The United States and the Soviet Union, seeing that neither capitalist nor communist pressure was able to win the obedience, respect, or loyalty of hungry peoples, decided jointly to invest in the future of beleaguered countries, hand in hand, cheek to cheek . . . and it was working. It was tremendous for world trade. A minor miracle. The Disarmament Conference in Peking has been in session for four years. Old-fashioned phrases like "Peace on Earth" have been buzzing around hundreds of Peking duck dinners, like flies.

Sam Russell had his own weekly column in the *Times,* if the world behaved itself and he didn't have to travel, to report its mayhem. He had developed over the years an arresting style of writing that some people called "old-fashioned," the tall, blond-bearded, liberal westerner from the north country. His columns had a "Continental Congress" zing to them. He knew American history, if he knew anything, and never hesitated to ram it down some throats every chance he had. Max would have gotten a kick out of his son-in-law. The resonance in Sam's writing voice could have come from his easy access to the seminal. Max's original papers of Franklin, Jefferson, Hamilton, Emerson, Thoreau, Paine . . . they were all there, like letters from relatives, in Max's library.

Sam kept pulling the paper out of his old IBM Selectric, the model he had bought when he started on the *Times.* It was always being repaired, and he was going to keep on repairing it until someone said it wasn't fixable anymore. He disliked the *printers* everyone used, computers that even found the idea for you, if you were at a loss. His own brain-computer was doing the same thing without being asked!

"Snow." No, wrong word. The word you want is "father." He was worried about his father, still working the farm, wrinkled, smaller, more fragile, too old for the snow of a Montana winter. His mother had died five years after he and Phoebe were married. *Parents:* You're bonded and rooted to them, you measure yourself against them. His father, going through the same rituals for a lifetime, had made a kind of peace for himself, but his father had not changed.

Sam put a new piece of paper in his typewriter. *"Change:*

The one miracle of time." He was still trying to begin his column. Could he think of some minor miracles to write about, since there was no such thing as a major one? Well, if not in human behavior, there had been a galloping in science, he was thinking. Not since the beginning of the twentieth century had original scientific thought moved so fast as in the last decade, particularly in America. Good old Yankee ingenuity had walked in front of a mirror and recognized itself again—the same ingenuity that had founded the country, still enduring the tremblings of democracy, despite all efforts to twist it out of shape. Possible hook for his first column of 1994: "Science is galloping while society is still doing its awkward little dance—three steps back, two steps forward, take your partner if you don't wanna shoot 'em, an' turn around, turn around . . ."

No, that wasn't quite true. There *had* been a minor miracle in everyday life. *Solar or Sink* had become the slogan of 1987 after an atomic plant leaked in India, radiating thousands of acres and people. The world had sighed cynically—thank God it was India, its expendable millions, and not us! Solar energy was definitely a way of life in 1993, much as early television had crept into the patterns of the 1950s; particularly in America, with its M.T. solar batteries. People have to be reminded of minor miracles or they won't stand still to observe the wonder—yourself included, Sam said to himself.

He was finding it impossible to concentrate. There was much activity in the apartment and the thick door of the library wasn't keeping it out. His sister's children, two gangling adolescent boys, had flown in from Montana for the holidays . . . and his own Marianne and little Max were overexcited by the company, running around like banshees, in and out with sleds and skis, trying to show the Montanans the small delights of the first snowstorm in Central Park.

Himself and Phoebe? *They* were a minor miracle. Their love still had its original coat but was changing all the time. In a funny way, *they* were galloping and standing still. He was about to be forty, still measuring himself by the granite yardstick, his parents, and it would never go away, not completely;

that still feeling *the child*, longing to be *child* slamming doors in and out of time. And, Phoebe too . . . She was still measuring herself against the ghostly obelisk of Maxwell Treading, Sam reflected.

Yesterday, she had made her yearly trip to the cryonic storage facility of the Cancer Research Center in Long Island and left a dozen roses. She had done it every Christmas for twelve years, ever since her father died. Was she any more bizarre than those who went to cemeteries? In Phoebe's case, though, it was more difficult to get relief from the metaphysical by being close to the *remains* of a beloved spirit. The body of her father lay in its deep-freeze coffin, and although she wasn't allowed to view him, the awareness that he must look exactly as he did the day he died was totally disorienting. He was dead but not disintegrated; dead, but still of this earth. She always returned from her pilgrimage with a pinched, disbelieving, white look.

What Sam didn't know . . . (she had not shared it with him, it was such an outrageous impulse) . . . was that each time she went to leave her roses, she had an irresistible urge to make a scene, demand to see her father's body, then rip open the capsule with a sharp tool she would have hidden on her, and slice through the coffin. There he would be! white, frozen, but on this earth; and she could look at him and cry! What a strange privilege that would be—to look upon a father who was twelve years dead, but still *himself in his body*, like a pharaoh buried deep in his tomb and good for a thousand years, barring inquisitive shovels, like her sharp tool. It was such a real fantasy, it scared her to death.

Sam went back to his earlier thoughts about *change*. They had received a call from Roz that morning. It was from England this year. They hardly ever saw her except in transit—without any *gloria*. It was always "I've just arrived . . ." Or, "I'm just leaving." Talk about change? Roz had definitely changed. She was a minor miracle in reverse. There had only been backward movement for Roz.

When was it, a year after Hiram Wesgrove went to prison,

that she suddenly divorced Willard? She had been on the move ever since, under the name of Treading. Oh yes, "Rosalind Treading," with all the notoriety wreathed about the name, and she didn't mind. It was an antidote, a breakaway from Greenbriar, Willard; jail and jailer. She was still running. From the quickly written notes they received occasionally from every corner of the world, where the rich gathered for their seasonal parties, they could only deduce that Roz had become one of those longitude and latitude hoppers, a member of the gang who had the money to support their addiction—restlessness.

Sometimes, they would get a late-night call when too much liquor had probably induced homesickness or a longing to hear Phoebe's voice, maybe even his. She always asked to have him on an extension phone, too. The three of them would have a silly, verbal fandango meant to stand for a family visit; I-love-yous from Roz, not insincere, but it was hard to catch her true feelings. Her voice was so elated, skittering on ice.

The call from her that morning had been sober. She must have a new romantic involvement in London or she wouldn't be there. There was a new love every year, or if not love, an affair that hit the gossip columns. Sam had a picture in his head of men around the world fleeing from his sister-in-law's tongue. Stunning and rich as she was, even a defunct prince out for a steady income would have to run away from her, because that was her master plan—to be fled from. It all added up to making Phoebe very sad, but that was also Roz's intention, Sam was sure. Phoebe couldn't fulfill her promise to their father . . . "Look after your sister, even though you're the younger." You can't keep track of a bird in constant migration unless you put a band around its leg, he kept reminding Phoebe.

The noise in the apartment suddenly stopped. He knew where they'd all be. Max had gotten his first sled under the Christmas tree. They'd be on a hill fit for a five-year-old, that little monster with dimples, shaggy blond hair falling over his eyes. That five-year-old head! It knew exactly what to say to everyone to make them feel good, and knew how to wheedle anything it wanted out of everyone.

And Marianne, ten years old, tall for her age, with her white-white skin, dark hair, long delicate face, and big green eyes. Marianne looked as if she'd been cloned from her aunt! How do such things happen? There wasn't a bit of *his* family in his daughter. Thank God she didn't have her aunt's insides.

And Phoebe, out there in her ski suit? He knew how she looked—like Marianne's older sister!

To hell with writing on Christmas Day! Sam pulled the paper out of his typewriter, with another first sentence crumpled up and lost forever—"Social systems, as usual, except for a few sports of nature, have taken their three steps back and two steps forward in the past decade . . ." Into the wastebasket.

He put on his snow gear and tore out of the apartment to join his family, for those moments when nothing changes, either backwards or forwards, those precious moments of suspension and love . . . when someone is five or ten and the thing called family is a beautiful half-bloom.

While you're running across Fifth Avenue into the park, you're filled with wonder, because not so long ago, *you* were the child and the parents were other people catching their moments of love . . . when they were forty and you were five or ten.

27

The voice was firm and sure. It was only Wesgrove's face
that had been crushed by his incarceration. He was seventy-seven, still jaunty, testy, unusually testy today in spite of
what he was hearing. Arthur Lewisohn, acting head of the Cancer Research Center, was on the videophone with *the boss.*

The final data was in, on the twenty-four cancer patients
who had agreed to submit to the new serum they were calling
"the hero." They'd done it! The proof was in without one failure. Twenty-four indisputable cures. Lewisohn was asking permission to release the news beyond the walls of the Center.

Wesgrove's answer was, "No. Do it on another twenty-four
and then we'll see."

Typical, Lewisohn said to himself. The one person who
should welcome the sound of trumpets was saying—don't play
them. Lewisohn couldn't believe what he was hearing next from
the old man: "Start to pick up on *Project Dragonfly.*"

"You don't think we should wait, Dr. Wesgrove?" (It was
still "Dr. Wesgrove" after all those years.)

Wesgrove's answer was "Yes." Lewisohn, in his shock, either didn't understand, or was so taken aback he misunderstood.
"You mean, yes, wait? Or yes, don't wait?"

With unusual annoyance, Wesgrove said, "What's the matter with you? I said yes, don't wait. We know we've got it! But
do it again before we publish. However, I don't see any reason
to wait—to test the findings on *Dragonfly.* "

Lewisohn had one more question, hoping his head wouldn't
be chopped off. "If it's yes on *Dragonfly,* shall we inform the
family?"

The answer was an emphatic "No!" Then Wesgrove added,
"Get your chiefs together tomorrow evening, inform them, but
you and I talk together tomorrow morning . . . I want to go over
everything as I see it, step by step." He switched off the connection without even a good-bye.

Wesgrove's reticence to allow the announcement of a major
miracle was hard for the younger man to take. After the call,
Lewisohn sat for a long time trying to understand not only the
reluctance to announce the serum success, but the order to go
ahead with *Dragonfly.* After some agitated thought, he figured
he *did* understand. Wesgrove was sure of the serum (as they all
were), but he wanted it linked to *Dragonfly.* It was his right to
want to link the two—to justify the twelve years in prison. The
linkage was precarious and frightening. One success might not
make another. Miracles don't come in twos, yet that's what the
boss was demanding. It was almost too much to ask, but they
would *try* to do it. Of course they would! The Center owed it
to him to *try.*

Lewisohn couldn't help thinking, particularly now: What
a long, unbelievable journey of injustice, with Wesgrove still
there despite continual efforts to maneuver a pardon for him by
some of the most famous people in the world. He was still being
held up as an example. What an example! It was almost comic,
if it hadn't been so tragic. Every law in the books concerning
prisoners had been broken when it came to Wesgrove. What
warden in his right mind wouldn't be proud that there was a
Wesgrove having dinner under his roof every night? The warden had had a videophone installed so his prize prisoner could
talk and work with his staff at the Center whenever he wished.
That warden was an intelligent man.

And Wesgrove? He had accepted prison life as craftily as a river that had been rerouted by a natural calamity. It was going to continue to find its way until Nature should decide otherwise. He was far from that end. To the contrary, the older Wesgrove became, the more miraculous and dangerous a river. Didn't the two go together—miracle and danger?

Look how far he's taken us without a capsize, Lewisohn forced himself to admit. So, don't be afraid of *Dragonfly*. If the boss says yes, it's yes . . .

How *did* Wesgrove fare? His life in prison had been the same, except for the loss of his own laboratory, his favorite chairs, faded Orientals. He discovered he could think very well without a fireplace. He had his writing, his reasoning, his equations, his speculations, his chess, and even his brandy. He was in communication with Lewisohn at the end of each day, and in his spare time he had become a one-man rehabilitation system in the prison, with the warden's hearty approval. The prison boasted the best medical care and facilities in the country. One scribbled note from Wesgrove to a university president, and contributions, spare parts came like magic, to augment the prison's hospital equipment and library. Over the last twelve years, the prison had acquired a science teaching lab! Under the instruction of a Wesgrove, who could impart knowledge like speeded-up film, college requirements were filled and enough medicine learned to astound the entrance committees of the best schools . . . along with letters of recommendation for released prisoners that were hardly set aside, considering who the recommender was. *And* there were lifers in the prison who had become talented paramedics as well as students of the atom, the molecule, and philosophy. Talk about miracles. It was just Wesgrove rerouted, flowing though different terrain, but still changing everything around him in the process, making different banks, different outlooks, *even different fish*.

It was on February 4, 1994 (just a little over a month after Sam had sat at his desk ruminating about *minor* miracles and the galloping or standing still of time and social tide) that Lewisohn was sitting at *his* desk, faced with a *major* miracle not yet ready to be trumpeted, according to "the boss."

Wesgrove, more than fifteen years before, had chosen his protégés well. They were leaders in their fields of chemistry, biology, physics, medicine, the electronic and molecular sciences—disciplines that had made tremendous leaps in the past decade. Due to his orchestration from prison, the inevitable outcome (which he never doubted) had arrived. The cure and prevention of cancer in the human animal was now a reality. Einstein had been young when he arrived at the secret that set him above and apart from others. Wesgrove was to arrive at the unlocking of the secret he had devoted his life's energy to, in his old age. Namely: The brain's function in relation to the cells in its command. How to correct the destiny of aberrant cells. How to induce the awesome brain to signal a delinquent chemistry in a body not to misbehave. The discovery was twofold: immunization, regulation.

Wesgrove didn't like the nomenclature that, of necessity, was going to be used to describe his breakthrough—a fascistic solution if there ever was one. He consoled himself: A surge of power, a control of signals, brute determination wearing a velvet glove, isolation, insistence, a summoning and prevailing of will *was at the root of every imposing, creative act.* If a serum had to be injected to redirect the brain, which would then fascistically reeducate the molecules of the diseased cell; if genetic engineers had to run roughshod, in black jackets and boots, over anarchic behavior (because of chemical insanity or viral invasion, not to mention the *structural* obscenity of the few that caused the death of many) . . . then, the iron hand was the only way.

It was not for nothing that the letters DNA had saucily ridden the waves on the stern of his little sailboat. Wesgrove had found a way of talking in the language of the tiniest fragments of life, the structures that bore genetic information, bore them well, or bore them ill. With the brain as ally, twenty-four people on their way to death had been turned around. Their cells, drunkenly crashing into nerve, muscle, and bone, had been stopped, reprogrammed, slid into reverse like cartoon characters, by the shock of new orders in a tongue they understood. And, for those human organisms with imperfect regulators to start with, a control mechanism had been found to convince the body to function despite its disability, a new series of orders to create a correct immunization field when the body could not create one by itself. You lack the information, poor dears? Hear this! Don't go mad. Intelligence will out, though you are minus a full genetic deck.

Normal protein information encapsulated in an electromagnetic field—to correct the mistaken signals of crippled molecules. That was what it was all about. Marauding cells were stopped. Illiterate cells were reading Shakespeare in a matter of weeks. (Wesgrove enjoyed his private metaphor.) *All was one and one was all.* Whether it was science or art or an intricate structure of molecules, the secret was intelligence. *Intelligence could cure all.*

Lewisohn felt he had aged ten years between the end of his first call with *the boss,* and his meeting with his chiefs of staff the next evening. He had talked with Wesgrove two more times in preparation for that meeting.

They walked into a conference room where a table was set with pâté, shrimp, champagne and flowers. They looked at one another. No cold sandwiches? Ah . . . it's a celebration . . . for the serum, a job well done. It's not a celebration? Then, what in hell is it?

Arthur Lewisohn raised his glass. "No publishing, no glory, not yet. That's what *the boss* said. But, he's given us the go-ahead for *Project Dragonfly!*"

There was a gasp from the veteran scientists in the room. The younger ones—who had been at the Center for four or five years—had no idea what he was talking about. Lewisohn went on: "Wesgrove wants the two projects to coincide, if it's at all possible. I can understand that. If I were he, I'd want the same. I'd gamble for it, and we owe him that . . .

"Those of you who know what I'm referring to," Lewisohn

continued, "when I say *Project Dragonfly,* drink up and tell the others. To all of you, we're about to begin a very long, short journey. Not a soul in this room is to utter a word about it . . . not to your wives, husbands, lovers, kids, dogs, cats . . . to no one!"

When those who didn't know *learned* that *Dragonfly* was the code name for a frozen specimen named Maxwell Treading, the entire room fell silent . . . waiting.

Lewisohn looked around. There were many virtuosos in the room, ready to test their disciplines. "All right . . . down to work. Some of you have never met him, the man who made all our work possible in the last twelve years. He gave us the freedom to experiment without strings, the independence, the salaries, the equipment. The sky was the limit. We've been the most pampered, spoiled lot of researchers on this earth . . . thanks to Hiram Wesgrove *and* Maxwell Treading. We have one more stretch to run. We'll run it the best we can. If it works? We'll have a double whammy. If it doesn't? There need be no blame anywhere. It just means we've got to wait for another bunch of years. That's the first message to you—from Dr. Wesgrove."

There was a bit of champagne left in his glass. He lifted it again. "You look white as sheets. That's all right. We all feel the same way, but a little stage fright isn't bad. It gets the adrenaline going, sharpens the perceptions. And let's remember . . . the work in cryogenics has been running neck-and-neck with the cancer research. We've just got to be bold and put the two together . . . if it's written on the wall. So, here's to success *or* failure . . ."

He heard a whisper: "Failure is a dead man . . ."

Lewisohn answered with alacrity. "Maxwell Treading willed his body to science. It must be looked upon as a guinea pig."

The man who had whispered stood up, a young, very brilliant magnetic engineer with an added degree in medicine. His face was white. "I'm sorry, I can't be a part of this, I don't approve."

"That's your right," Lewisohn said softly.

The young man then said, "OK, I resign, I'm sorry."

"No you don't!" Lewisohn snapped. "And, you're not fired either. You just stay in your own department. We'll keep you informed, don't worry."

The young man smiled weakly and not without a little amazement.

"Is there anyone else who can't stomach the fact of a human guinea pig? For whatever reason, it will be accepted . . ."

No one reacted.

"Then, we begin . . ."

Lewisohn laid some notes on the table. "Wesgrove has sent us his suggestions on procedure. They're going to need a lot of talking. Each of you knows intimately the new attacks, equipment, the new applications—in your own field. But, he's put it all together and suggests they be used in a new way, as they've never been used before. For instance, the telemetered feedback and the scanning educator. Both instruments have been applied in relation to theoretical science, never in relation to a whole living being. He suggests we cross over and that it's time we try." Lewisohn paused. "We all know you can work for years on something, and then—suddenly—intuition! The unconscious puts it all together. Sometimes, scientists function like artists. That's not me, it's Wesgrove talking . . .

"But, as usual, we have to start with *A*. By the time we get to the middle of this mountain, we will have finished with the *Z* we know, and from then on, we'll be making our own alphabet.

"First, we start with defreezing samples of the Treading cells removed and frozen before his death . . ."

Shock and reality permeated the conference room. *Project Dragonfly* was a human being! They broke up into clusters, comparing reactions, thoughts, and projections on the work ahead.

In the next weeks, the Treading cells were analyzed and computerized for days. Laboratory animals were used to test the new cryonic-reversal techniques, over and over again. A great many of the reversals were successful; some were not.

The nots were analyzed into exhaustion. Wesgrove was consulted daily. Why did this cat die in the process of re-animation? Why did that monkey survive it? The reasons were discovered and they began again—with this cat, that monkey. Lewisohn was getting scared. He didn't want to begin *Dragonfly* with any nots. *Dragonfly* could end up a *not*. Wesgrove kept insisting they were ready to aim for a human re-animation or they would be "treading water." That phrase made Lewisohn burst out laughing.

A month went by, in which there were other kinds of activities related to the needs of *Dragonfly* . . . They had to acquire a scanning educator. There were only two in the entire world—one at Rockefeller Institute, the other in Moscow. Dr. Jeff Gruening, biopsychiatrist, was chosen to borrow or sweet-talk the loan of the machine, and he wasn't about to fly to Moscow to do it.

They would also use the telemetered feedback, but that was easy—it had been invented right there at the Center. However, it had to be tried out and applied to the mammal, and so it was . . . and Wesgrove was correct in his hunch about it. The telemetered feedback, slowly moving over the body of an animal, could give back more organic information than lab technicians working for months on specimens of organs. There had to be corrections and inventions for the machine, but those were made and doped out so fast, it was as if the Center were in total war; life and death strategies had to be decided in split seconds. The Center could have taken off into space—with the adrenaline being manufactured in every department concerned with preparation for the *Dragonfly* experiment. After all, when it did decide to take off, it was going to have to be a perfect shot into the air.

It was April 1. April "the cruelest month," "April with its sweet showers," depending upon whose heart was speaking. According to Arthur Lewisohn, it could very well turn out to be the most frightening month of *his* life.

With all the data collected, the personnel in readiness, he gave the order to transfer the Treading capsule from the storage building on Long Island to the Cancer Research Center in Manhattan.

The body of Maxwell Treading, frozen solid in its metal cocoon, was making its way along the same highways and bridges into Manhattan that it had left by twelve years ago. It was not sitting up and drinking coffee and looking at a rising sun. It was surrounded by temporary refrigeration and accompanied only by a solemn Dr. Arthur Lewisohn.

The staggering plan in the works was written all over his face.

FROM THE JOURNAL OF DR. HIRAM WESGROVE, MARCH 1994

"Be humble, you will be whole.
Bend, you will be straight.
Be hollow, you will be filled . . ."

It comforts me to write the lines from the Tao Te Ching . . .

"He does not show himself.
Therefore he shines.
He does not proclaim himself;
Therefore he is clearly seen.
He does not praise himself;
Therefore he wins victories.
He is not proud of his handiwork;
Therefore it lasts forever."

I am not that GOOD! I am proud to the point of bursting with what we have accomplished thus far, so proud I could be struck dead for it at this point and I would not mind in the least.

Wise words though, the ancient ones—"Be humble; you will be whole—To reach wholeness one must return!"

The excitement of what lies ahead has brought back the chest pains. I know them well, but I will keep my mouth shut. As I did with the seizures last year. Someone's going to find the scar tissue someday, if they do an autopsy. But they're not going to put me in a bed now, not yet! On second thought, I would mind being struck dead at this point because of a surfeit of pride. I must hide it from the Furies, ho, ho!

28

The Treading capsule was delivered to a lab filled with a maze of equipment, computers, closed-circuit television, scientists, doctors, and nurses.

The liquid nitrogen had been removed from the capsule at the Long Island facility. Still in a frozen-solid state, the body was lifted from its icy womb; the lithium foil that enveloped it was carefully stripped away inch by inch.

Max Treading lay on an operating table—a hoary statue of blanched marble. One of the nurses almost fainted. It was one thing to work with a frozen organ, a mouse or monkey, but a frozen whole man? The nurse wasn't the only one with a stomach that rose up and banged against heart muscles.

But as though it were a monkey, they would proceed with the unfreezing, armed with new knowledge evolved in twelve years. Treading's body was going to be like an early invention tucked away in an attic. If the basic concepts and theories applied to it were valid in '82, then the new techniques of '94 were going to be used to activate it, encourage, force it to function— maybe. That there be a minimum of physical and biochemical changes in the body before them was at one end of the spectrum

of their guarded hopes. At the other end was complete failure.
In the middle was the possibility of badly damaged cells, partially ravaged organs, in which case the body would be dissected
for analysis bit by bit, part by part.

Lewisohn felt his knees weaken at the prospects before
them. He wished he could be wafted backward into being a
pupil (again) under Wesgrove's tutelage. Now, he was the chief
in charge. They waited for his instruction. But he was off to the
side reading something. Wesgrove had placed his diagnosis and
projections in the capsule twelve years ago. Embedded in the
information was the sentence: "I injected the patient with L.L.
to suspend the brain first and to achieve as instantaneous a death
as possible."

Lewisohn announced what he was reading. A peculiar quality invaded the modern lab, a quality of myth-and-ancient-cob-
webs-about-to-be-torn-away. No one knew to what the letters
L.L. referred.

Lewisohn figured this moment to be the most dangerous—
the moment of distrust. It had to be stopped. Of course they
knew how to defreeze a mammal, and of course the brain still
eluded them. Most of their unsuccessful reanimations had involved the failure of the brain functions. He was going to voice
the mutual concern out loud and get rid of it. "We're all thinking the same thing . . . Even if the freezing itself had been
successful and the body put into a perfect suspension, something could happen in the defreezing and we'll never know
where the blame lies, in the beginning or the end. We must keep
steady. This is a guinea pig, not a man. Dr. Wesgrove said it
twelve years ago, it still pertains. Please, let's begin as though
under normal circumstances, or we're in the soup."

"I'd say—scientific mud," Gruening said under his breath.
Lewisohn started to throw him an angry look, but stopped when
their eyes met. There wasn't the usual sarcasm in Gruening's
eyes, there was fear.

"Start the needles," Lewisohn said softly to the eight people
standing around the body from head to foot. He knew he and
Gruening were probably having the same *déjà vu* sensation,

remembering just the three of them working over the body twelve years ago, and now there was an army; now there were control mechanisms calibrated, to a zillionth of a microgram, in comparison to the past capabilities.

Microscopic needles were placed in every acupuncture point in the body—heat infusers. Those designated for the internal organs were begun first, to warm from the inside out so that the inner organs would start functioning before outer regions and skin needed blood and body liquids. At the very same microsecond as the cells began to warm, the cryoprotectant had to be removed. It must happen in measured sequence, corresponding to the liquid forming in the thaw. The cells must not be shocked as they expanded in the unfreezing. As the slow radiation began, other needles were made ready to inject blood in the same rhythms as the withdrawing cryoprotectant.

It was now entrances and exits—the reverse of the image Wesgrove had entertained as he observed the freezing. They were all too aware that the procedures to be done by instruments and people had to be executed with the coordination of tightrope walkers, or at any moment the balance of the cells, in the process of reanimation, could be irrevocably disturbed or shut down.

The body couldn't be seen for the activity around it. It looked like a strangely textured collage of sensors, needles, tubes, all leading to their computers, that hummed and blinked verification of information. At the same time, like a hovering bird in flight, the telemetered feedback swung slowly back and forth, checking the Treading cellular identity and genetic data, cell after cell, as they warmed from the inside out. Pictures of the activity of regeneration under the dead-white skin were unfolding like stop-motion photography. A microscopic dance of life. Hurrah! The cryoprotectant was being removed as fast as water replaced it in the cells!

All the while, the measured blood introduction continued, going from drop to multiplication of drops into the major arteries. The computers recorded the so-far positive progress of the tightrope walking. The cryoprotectant was out! The blood was taking over, the body temperature was flashing on its computer, up and up. The cell data were matching those of the cells Wesgrove had analyzed for the year Treading had been his patient. They were halfway and beginning to hope. The original cryonic suspension might have been a good one. The skin was no longer hoary marble but more like pale pink rubber, with the slightest suggestion of pulsing underneath. The heart and lung monitors were beginning to transmit fluttering lines of life! The heart was pumping! It was operational!

Lewisohn motioned to the heart and lung resuscitation team standing in the second line behind the body to be ready for artificial aid, in case chest incision was going to be necessary to sustain life while they probed into the phenomenon of human organs twelve years frozen. But no . . . The computers were registering stronger and stronger responses; everyone hovered over the body as though they were practicing levitation.

"Blood replacement completed," a voice said.

Suddenly, Lewisohn became aware of a nurse holding a mirror to the body's mouth. There was moisture on the mirror. He snarled at her in outrage, "What in hell are you doing, you idiot? With all the equipment in this room, you're using a mirror to determine life?" The nurse pulled back with an impish look and he broke into a grin. The incident was the relief they needed from the incredible pressure; a laugh, a second of relaxation.

"Temperature ninety-six and stationary," another voice reported.

"Oxygen helmet," Lewisohn responded. Then he whispered hoarsely, "I think we're going to have a re-entry." He paused. "Of a body . . . God willing with a brain." He motioned to Gruening. "Scanning educator ready?"

"Yes, but look what's happening." The cardiovascular signs were becoming weaker not stronger.

A voice repeated: "Temperature, ninety-six and not rising."

"Jeff?" Lewisohn whispered. "What's wrong? Not enough pressure? Could we need *more* blood than was originally removed? Blood replacement in re-animation? Could that be the reason for some of the failures with the larger monkeys?"

Gruening whispered back, "Improvise! There's nothing to lose!"

"Right, I agree." He ordered more blood to be introduced, slowly, slowly . . . as they watched the body temperature rise until it hit 98.2. "Enough!" Lewisohn stood back. "Wrap from the neck down in diathermy blanket." He rubbed his forehead and began to talk to himself. "Frozen cells, moisture rejection or retention . . . must be retention capability during heat-return trauma. Frozen cells need a bigger zoom . . . oh boy . . . discovery by accident, using the larger body, more intricate, more space, more time needed for conversion . . . the time that could kill.

"Start the chicken soup in the I.V.," he said with a grin.

They all stood back from the operating table—to observe what looked like a normal human body with all signs Go. For the first time (because of the excitement) they heard the sounds of even breathing coming from behind the oxygen helmet.

"It looks real," Gruening commented.

"We'd better stop calling it *It* and start saying *He*," Lewisohn said with an edge.

"Not yet, Art," said Gruening, the cautionary. "You're going to have to substitute an oxygen tube in the neck for the helmet before we begin with the scanning educator. I have to inject the brain stem before we attach the educator."

As the oxygen helmet was removed and the respiration team operated, Lewisohn looked at the head of the body for the first time. It was the handsome head of Max Treading. He shuddered.

Gruening started an injection of isotopic carriers with intense calcium and protein infusion capability, to encourage brain cell activity, through the brain stem. The scanning educator, unknown to most of them, was brought close to the table and attached to Treading's head by means of twenty wires thin as spider thread. The wires, glistening, waved at the slightest breath, causing the head to appear as if it were wearing a surreal halo. Surging through the wires was rapid-pulsed particle energy.

It was Wesgrove's idea to use the scanning educator. He had voluminous correspondence with scientists in Moscow who had been using it for isolated brain cell investigation. But it had never been used on a body. Once again, Max's gift to Wesgrove was paying off, allowing him to mix science with imagination. Wesgrove was now seventy-seven and still jumping the high fences like a young goat—the sign of genius unabated. Since he'd given the go-ahead for *Project Dragonfly*, he had also been on the phone often with Gruening, whose expertise was the brain. The brain stem infusion was Gruening's idea, and Wesgrove had thought it equally inventive. Why not try on a complete brain what they were doing with individual cells or clusters of brain cells in test tubes? Bravo, Gruening.

Gruening, waiting for the injection to spread through the brain, began to talk swiftly and quietly. "We've got a live body with insufficient wave. It's emitting reflex signals and that's all. From now on, it's the new alphabet *again*. You cryonics people have been here before, with animals. You brought them back, but couldn't get the computer going. You considered them failures. We're going a step further with this one, maybe more than a step, maybe way, way out . . .

"If it works, it . . . Wesgrove's expectation is: The scanner will agitate, activate the memory chips—if they've not been dysfunctioned or permanently shut down by the freezing or unfreezing. Memory chip means—humanity. If we only fill half the order, we'll have learned about a mindblower . . . and that is *not* meant to be one of my usual puns," he grimaced.

What *did* the scanning educator mean? If it did work, it would have to get the uncountable sensory systems of the brain started, systems that recorded and retained *everything*, from an individual's response to gravity, to the geophysical universe; from lunar sequences to sunspots, to seasons; from the first sensations of an emerging embryo to the supposedly forgotten last word of a discarded lover . . . all sensed, recorded, and retained for a lifetime by the memory chips.

Gruening pressed a key on the scanning educator. Lewisohn moved away to let him take over. There was a large screen over the machine. "Everyone get the hell out," Gruening said sharply. "There's a viewing screen next door, if there's anything to watch. The less thought interference, the better. Out!" He looked around at his colleagues. "I'm sorry, I'm nervous; that shouldn't surprise anyone after what we've been through." He paused. "The damn thing's going to make images . . ." He looked at the surprised faces. "Yes, images, if it works at all. And if it really works, it will reconstruct the stored experience that builds a personality. It can unjumble and put into sequential order the brain's retention, if the cells respond . . .

"And if they do, we're stringing up a trillion beads. It's Wesgrove's caution that we have to be careful how we do it, or it might upset the re-entry completely. There must be absolute quiet. We do not know what to expect, if there *is* response. Even if we register patterns, they could have been thrown out of sync and what's here will never survive as a human, even if he survives the table. All I can say is, I wish Wesgrove were here. I dread the responsibility. No blame, anyone. You've already done more than has ever been done in the history of medicine. The damn brain still eludes us.

"Please clear the room. The infusion is completed. Turn off all lights but one. Arthur, you stay with me." He took a deep breath as they left. "This brain is gonna get a kick . . . if there is one."

The laboratory was in semidarkness. Lewisohn stood in a corner, animated, despite a terrible fatigue, waiting for a cue to something.

There was nothing but the sound of *three* people breathing; the sound of computers humming low, like life on leaves in a dark forest.

All at once, bits of light with a nimbuslike appearance were being discharged off the surface of Treading's body. They floated in the air and disappeared. They reappeared. There was a new hum in the room, then a crack like a tiny stroke of lightning, and the bits of light began to flash on the screen of the scanning educator.

The light became patterns *and* colors! Kaleidoscopic forms

shifted about, reassembled themselves. Suddenly! Out of focus, but definitely recognizable—shapes! Then, in perfect focus: A desert landscape! A woman's face! A large white meadow? No, a white meadow with a nipple. A breast!

The flow of images continued, first forward, then backward, then forward again, reassembled. And, then . . . only forward, in focus and sequence, clear moving pictures!

"My God, my God!" emitted from Gruening. "Are you seeing what I'm seeing, Art? A desert? A woman? A man on horseback?"

"Don't you know a man, a woman, and a desert when you see them?" Lewisohn hissed back in total hysteria and ran from the lab into the viewing room next door. "The brain is alive!" he yelled at the entire staff sitting there and looking at the piling up of images.

"*Quiet!*" they all answered as one, without looking at him.

"It's an absolute, fucking miracle," Lewisohn muttered to himself and stood there watching the pictures roll out faster and faster. A man's earliest imprints, he added silently, and ran back to his office to call the prison.

Almost too excited to speak, Lewisohn's sentences came out in cryptic explosions. "*Dragonfly* is working! The baby looks like it was born healthy. Congratulations. My God, congratulations! We think we're working on a perfect suspension. How was it done? There was a problem with blood replacement, but we improvised. What did the L.L. in your original notes mean?"

He waited for no answers. "I have to get back. The scanning educator is going like mad." He forgot himself completely: "Old man, it looks like there is no corpus delicti! Shall I inform the family, or should we wait?"

For the first time, Wesgrove was able to get a word in. "Yes, call his daughter Phoebe. It sounds advanced enough. Let her share it; otherwise, the shock might be too much." Wesgrove was shaking visibly. "Call me about how he looks. Call me about everything."

Returning to his cell, Wesgrove literally danced down the prison block, a smile of jubilation on his face, explaining to the guard that he'd just been made a grandfather and wasn't life the most fantastic, wonderful thing in life.

Maxwell Treading lay alive, but unconscious—still the best-kept secret since the first atom bomb was deployed. A day and a half had gone by. They were afraid to release him from the oxygen tube in his neck, lest the balance of life falter. He was being fed intravenously and was voiding normally, the latter activity creating great joy for his attending physicians. All vital signs were normal as the scanning educator continued to record his stored images, hour after hour.

Lewisohn was in touch with the prison, to discuss the progress of "the baby." Wesgrove insisted they maintain the supports, and conjectured a curious thing. "Keep the educator going, no matter what. We've got a burn-in, not a burn-out. If it's stopped, the acutely individual memory bank could be aborted. That would be dangerous. You've got to keep it connected until it goes blank. It might take days, or weeks . . . who knows? But, you might try to release him from the tube for a few minutes, then longer, if nothing is disturbed. It's the old tightrope, Arthur. I trust your instincts. Have you informed Phoebe Treading?"

"No, I'm leaving the lab for the first time. I'm going to see her today, in person."

Wesgrove ended the call and met the warden on his way back to his cell.

"One of the guards tells me you're a grandfather," the warden said discreetly.

"Just research talk, Warden. I used to call an experiment a baby until it grew up and was proven, or left home permanently, telling me I failed as a parent. My staff picked it up. I guess they're still using it," he added wistfully.

The warden was looking at him closely. "You don't look well."

"Me? I'm fine, never better. Nothing a few days of fishing wouldn't cure, fresh pine in the nose, muddy boots. You'll have to come fishing with me one day, up in Maine, Warden. Incidentally, I want you to know how I have appreciated your courtesies and treatment."

"Dr. Wesgrove, you sound like you're saying good-bye."

"One never knows, does one? But, oh, how I would love to ... with all your courtesies in mind, my dear, dear warden." The little old man bent very low, in a bow that almost brought tears to the man he was facing.

The scientists, doctors, and nurses continued to sit glued to their chairs in the viewing room, living on sandwiches and vitamin shots as they monitored the story of a very interesting little boy who was growing up in a ranch house between a mesa and a butte. Their eyes were falling out of their heads, but no one would leave.

Except Lewisohn. He was on his way, down a normal street, in a normal taxi—to see Phoebe Treading Russell.

29

Lewisohn tried to impart the astounding news as carefully as he could. Phoebe fainted. When she was brought around and the information began to penetrate, she sobbed uncontrollably. He had come prepared to face some kind of hysterical response and gave her a shot of light sedation.

"Let's talk, because I have to get back," Lewisohn said. "I feel like fainting myself now, more from exhaustion than shock."

"Would you like a drink?" Sam offered.

"Yes, scotch, please, straight."

"I'll join you," Sam said. "I need a drink, too."

"How long has he been alive?" Phoebe said shakily.

"Two long, incredible days."

"On his own, or on machines?" came from Sam.

"Pretty much on his own, except for a breathing tube in his neck," Lewisohn replied.

"Can he make it on his own?" Sam asked in as ordinary a tone as he could muster.

"We're going to try gradually . . . but he is on another machine—a scanning educator. I suggest you come to the Center this evening, you'll see better for yourselves."

Phoebe's equilibrium was coming back. "Is it *my* father? Is *he* there?"

"We don't know . . . yet," Lewisohn said guardedly.

"Oh, my God," she gasped. Sam was holding her tightly in his arms. She was trembling so, she felt like a tuning fork.

"Dr. Lewisohn, my wife is shaking . . ."

"She'll be all right. She's going to be strong. We need her to be."

Suddenly Phoebe looked at Sam. "Roz! What about Roz? She has to be told, too!"

"You don't know where she is, do you? We haven't heard from her since Christmas . . ."

"We can find out." She got to her feet. "I'll call a few people and see . . ."

"I don't think you should," Sam said quietly. "I don't think you should do *anything* right now. Her reactions are always unpredictable. No one needs that, at the moment."

"He's her father, too!"

"I agree with your husband," Lewisohn said. "Let's take it one step at a time."

The thoughts of the three were catapulted back to the time before the trial of Hiram Wesgrove, and the erratic, angry behavior of Rosalind Treading Clyde . . .

Phoebe looked at Sam. "She's not the same person . . ."

"Even so, darling," he said, "I agree with Dr. Lewisohn. One step at a time. I don't think you and I could handle any more than that."

She left them and walked to the windows, flung them open, and a blast of cold air came in from the park. She breathed deeply. "I don't believe it," she kept repeating.

Lewisohn stood up. "I have to get back. Please, share this with no one . . . or the Center will turn into a three-ring circus. We have to behave as if it were just another careful experiment in the privacy of our lab. The last thing a failure like this needs, is fanfare and exposure."

"Failure?" Phoebe gasped, and banged the window shut. "Are you expecting failure?"

"We're expecting nothing. We're learning."

"On my father?"

"That was his intention," Lewisohn said guardedly. "Wasn't it?"

"Yes," she responded curtly. "Yes, it was . . ." She looked at him with steady eyes. "Don't worry, I'll be all right. We'll see you this evening." She grabbed an arm of a chair. "What did you give me? I'm floating . . ."

"Fine . . . maybe we'll keep you floating. At the Center, we're feeling maybe we're discovering the world *isn't* flat. That's enough to disturb anyone's equilibrium."

Lewisohn's fair skin was blushing with the next thought that flashed through his head: "What a beautiful woman." He was amused with himself. *That* thought despite his exhaustion? He hadn't seen his own wife for four days.

Privately, he didn't agree with Wesgrove that the family be informed . . . if ever, unless there was a perfect re-entry. What was the point? It just complicated the atmosphere. One whiff of a human tie to a guinea pig and you were lost. But, the old man had insisted. His years away had made him forget the distance you need when you work with an animal and its beating heart on an operating table in a lab . . . not a hospital. You have no obligation to heal under the Hippocratic oath; your only obligation is to learn and find answers. Once you make a connection between that animal and its world outside, you're lost. It had happened to him too often. You look into a monkey's eyes and there, in the center of them, is its right to be in a green forest with its tribe; a cat, its right to be curled up on the best chair in the house, the inscrutable aristocrat . . . not strapped down to a table, its heart in your hand, or its brain exposed.

He looked at Phoebe, who seemed to be getting stronger by the second. Something very practical and courageous was rising in her; something was making her stand very straight, with an open, vulnerable, curious, intelligent thing flashing in her eyes —a challenge: I am his daughter! It made Lewisohn remember the only time he had seen Max Treading alive, when they were in the van together with Gruening and the boss, on their way

to the CRC storage facility on Long Island . . . and Treading was
insisting on being human, finding the humor of it, wanting to
ask questions to the end, with only Gruening ready to try it with
him. He and the boss, reaching for distance, had been struck
dumb. Maybe Wesgrove had learned something new about the
human factor and science needing each other in a crisis. The
human factor. There it was challenging him from those big, blue
eyes. Maybe it could tilt the outcome—that which cannot be
described or measured.

To his horror, Lewisohn knew he was standing there
blushing. He had arrived determined to be a rock for the lay
person who couldn't be expected to understand the lack of
emotion needed on a scientific journey of such magnitude
. . . but his resolve was falling away completely. "See you
later," he muttered. "Ask for the fourth-floor lab. It has its
own entrance on the floor. I'll be rung up and will come out to
take you in."

Phoebe was no more "daisy" or "little one" in defiant jeans
and ethnic cottons. She had matured into a commanding, self-
assured woman. She was no one's little girl anymore. Her physical presence was reminiscent of her mother's, she was clever as
her father, but nothing like either. She was *her own.*

At thirty-six, she was like a full-bloom peony. (More complicated and lushly structured than a rose is the peony. Left to
its own devices on the bush, its beauty lasts and lasts. Even cut,
it outstrips the rose-in-vase. The peony is a natural survivor.
Hard winters rarely take their toll on its tenacious roots.)
Phoebe was beautiful and hardy. Max would have been delirious
with what had happened to his "little one." She was one of those
young, fiery women of the '80s, educated and fearless, who
seemed to have learned and used well the lessons of the women
of previous generations. Without malice or anger, she could
attempt anything and do it well. But, not without the secret
ingredient. The secret was to have a man like Sam.

After their marriage she finished her Ph.D., at his insistence. Then she accepted the challenge of Global Materials like a trouper and became a most thoughtful, careful administrator of her father's empire. She lacked his ruthlessness, his gambling instinct, and that was just fine. The responsibility of power did not scare her (Max hadn't thought it would), and she carried on the power he had left to her, lovingly (he knew she would) . . . because he, "Daddy," had made it.

Phoebe's axes to grind weren't the same as her father's, either. To make it easier for her, the world had become a little saner. The inevitable conclusion that too much *poor* would destroy too much *rich* had finally dawned on the '80s like a warning from the gods, and only an idiot could deny that prudence and liberalism were going to be the way to bind the wounds of a globe in distress. Max's "love and money" axiom wasn't such arcane nonsense as she had thought in her *old days* of pure Marxist fervor. She had become, in comparison, conservative in the steps she took. They were in the same imprints as her father's, but walked more patiently and carefully. Bloody revolutions and the guns to make them had become fruitless exercises. Phoebe was pouring the Treading money into the raising of the intelligence, the knowledge, the economic health of peoples, not into the guns of anger. To Max's credit, the year he died, that had been his shift too, for the future he wouldn't see.

Phoebe also seemed to have managed being a good mother. But, without a man like Sam, she could never have juggled her roles of executive, wife, mother, lover . . . She knew very well that you couldn't be a full woman without a full man. Full, in every sense: outside, as far as one dared to reach; inside, to the very lining of the womb. *That* took two hormonal systems in love, male and female. There was no question, their marriage had made her doubly beautiful. A paragon of virtue? Hardly. Phoebe had developed quite a temper. Sam teased her that it probably had gone into "causes" and "rabid arrogance" when she was "a baby." And anyway, there must have been room for only one temper at a time and that was her father's. After he died she found her own. Oh, did she! She and Sam screamed a lot at each other. They discussed and fought and usually ended up feeling they were two of the most interesting people they knew . . . which is some kind of definition of a good marriage.

Except for the death of her father, Phoebe knew she was one of the very lucky ones. Feeling lucky can also make one look beautiful. You face everything with open eyes. Those were the eyes Lewisohn felt when he was leaving.

When he left, she ran into Sam's arms. "I'm going to see Daddy! He's *there!*"

"No, darling, he's not there. Don't do that to yourself. It's not your father, it's a guinea pig. Keep it low, or you're going to get very, very wounded." He took her face in his hands. "You . . . I will not let you get hurt by this act of your father's."

She looked at him with dumb questioning.

He tried to translate his feelings. "It's a first, in the wildest way, but it's still the Oedipal circus."

"I don't believe what you're saying!"

"Do you know, no one's ever felt what you're feeling? What you're going to feel? Your first love—dead and buried. And, here he is, back again! Not in a dream or a wish either. . . ."

She closed her eyes to block out what he was trying to say. "You're jealous!"

"Don't be an ass! I'm not jealous! Of what? I'm just trying to protect you from getting torn apart by the oldest feelings in the world . . . Christ! It's happening in a laboratory. Don't humanize, damn it, or there'll be pieces to pick up."

"It's in my genes to hope, Sam!"

That stopped him cold. "OK, it's in *my* genes to protect you while you hope! Stop yelling!"

"I'm not yelling! I'm breathing, so I won't faint again!" She started to cry. Nothing for him to do but hold her. There was something reminiscent about the way she felt in his arms—like the sad, hurt foundling he'd first met on *The Clearwater*. He *knew* he was right. What she was going to have to experience would be Greek drama squared and Freud unimagined. And if Roz were brought into it? He didn't dare to imagine . . .

. . .

As planned, Lewisohn met them on the fourth floor of the Center, walked them through a corridor to a closed door that said: *Do not enter—Sterile conditions operating.* They were given white masks and coats to put on. They walked down another long corridor, came to an open door, and Lewisohn stopped. He gestured toward a table with protective bars on each side.

Phoebe and Sam just stood there, taking in the scene—a maze of machines, two nurses monitoring them, two men whispering in a corner, the feel of dusk because of only one light on, a low hum . . . and in the middle of it, the table, on which was the long body of Max Treading, naked from the waist up, the rest covered with a light-green sheet. His skin looked pink as a newborn's, his strong jaw and cheeks paler, and around his blond-graying head was a halo of glistening, trembling wires.

Phoebe opened her mouth under the mask, took a deep breath, and closed her lips tight, so as not to scream. She made a move to rush to her father. Lewisohn pulled her back. He took her hand, led her to the table, and placed her hand on her father's. She felt the warm skin, patted it a few times as Lewisohn whispered, "That's all, no more . . ." He drew her back to the door. "We're flying blind," he continued to whisper. "If anyone approaches him with more than clinical necessity, the scanning educator falters." He pointed to the screen over Max's head. "Go into the next room and watch it from there."

Phoebe suddenly became aware of what he was talking about—a screen with flickering images. She was so overwhelmed, so intent on looking at the body, the screen had escaped her. But, it hadn't escaped Sam standing at the door. Phoebe watched, thunderstruck. She was seeing what looked like photographs from the family album come to life—Daddy as a little boy, moving!

There was the ranch! Images moving so fast, they were hard to catch. Lewisohn led them to the adjacent room where staff members were sitting and taking notes. The room had the feeling of a church filled with exhausted, drunken parishioners.

They sat down and began to watch the phenomena, with Lewisohn behind them, talking softly.

"In the beginning, it was all scrambled. As of two days ago, the focus became perfect. The images are pouring out faster and faster each day. We *think* they are unrolling a consciousness. It's called a scanning educator and has never been used like this before. There are only two in the world. The other one is in Moscow . . . where it was invented."

"Everything in his mind is being revealed?" Sam asked.

"We have no way to judge."

"It could be an abominable instrument," Sam whispered back.

"We think it's re-activating not only memory, but the life of the brain in all its functions, sequentially. Even the learning processes. . . ."

"This is the living end," Sam said.

"Right now, it could be the living beginning," Lewisohn said and slipped out of the room.

As Phoebe sat there watching the images of her father's vanished time, she remembered, with the stun of recognition, how she had once playfully said to him . . . "What a cheat it is, only to know your parents when they're big, stupid grownups." And there she was, watching the early days of the ranch, *like a myth revealed.* There was Martha Treading, the gangling little boy, not so little now, about eight, looking like a slightly older version of her own little Max. She didn't know whether to feel horror or the elation of a dream when your unconscious strews diamonds all over the floor and you begin to pick them up greedily. You stuff your pockets until the weight of the riches becomes unbearable . . . She sat there watching the images pass by with fast-frame speed. She was the only person in the Universe, a freak, living an original experience that had happened to no child ever—to see the inside of a parent, the intimate secrets, buried voices.

She jumped up. Sam couldn't stop her. "I have to find Roz! She has to be here!" She left to telephone friends who might know where Roz was. It took three frantic calls. Roz was in the

States, at the Plaza! How to tell her and not tell her? How to get
her to the Center without shocking her out of her mind? God,
Phoebe thought, have her there, please have her there. She
looked at her watch. It was eight o'clock.

Drink time, dinnertime. Roz was about to leave the suite
she kept for herself when she touched down in the States like
a migratory bird. She hadn't called "the Russells" because the
London lover had dematerialized. She didn't want to sit opposite Phoebe at lunch, and face the usual question: "How are
you?" It was such a repetitive bore, Phoebe's earnest, family
face.

"Phoebe? How did you know I was in town? Wait a minute,
what are you saying? You sound drunk, darling . . ."

"Roz, you have to come to the Cancer Research Center
immediately."

"The Cancer what?"

"Where Daddy was treated. You know where it is. I'm
there. I can't tell you why, but it's serious, a matter of life and
death. Please don't ask questions, just come." The magic words
tumbled out:

"I need you!"

"What's wrong with you, Phoebe?"

"I don't know . . . I'm not sure . . . Please come quickly.
Thank God you're here. Sam will meet you outside and bring
you to where I am. You *will* come?"

"Of course . . . I'll come."

Sam had no intention of doing it alone. Lewisohn and he
waited for her at the front entrance of the Center. The steadi-
ness of Lewisohn was going to have to pull off those first minutes, at least. Sam knew he couldn't do it.

She stepped out of her limousine like a queen made of some
translucent stuff, brilliantly dressed (she had been on her way
to meet friends for dinner) . . . her skin glowing and tanned from

a month of skiing in Switzerland. "You look marvelous," Sam mumbled.

"What's wrong with my sister?"

Lewisohn stepped forward and took her by an elbow. She stiffened and looked at him coldly, but they ushered her into the building. "What's wrong with Phoebe? Who are *you*?"

"I'm Arthur Lewisohn, acting head of the Center. Now, you must be strong, ready to accept anything . . ." As he talked, they entered an elevator.

"I never accept anything . . . what in hell is going on? I asked a question! What is wrong with my sister? Sam?"

The two men stared at the numbers of the floor indicator. "4" wasn't coming fast enough. She was realizing something was very wrong. Lewisohn continued to hold her arm. She felt trapped but curiously supported at the same time and began to break out into a sweat. Her perfume filled the elevator.

The fourth floor came. Sam knew he hadn't done it right, but it was too late now. As they left the elevator, all he could say was, "We'll face everything together."

How could she know what he meant by "everything"? She couldn't even ask. A crawling numbness was taking over.

They walked to the door marked *Do Not Enter.* She allowed herself to have a mask placed over her face and a white coat put on her. She was very frightened. As they approached an open door at the end of another corridor, she heard Lewisohn say, "The patient is not your sister, it's your father. We're in the process of re-animating him, bringing him back." He had her by an arm and felt her body contract violently as though hit by a bullet. Sam turned away. Lewisohn led a wordless Roz into the lab.

She took one look and let out a scream. (The scream that Phoebe had held back under *her* mask.)

(It was cruel, very cruel for them to have done it that way, Roz was to think later. Phoebe had been prepared as delicately as one could be for such a shock. Phoebe had had Sam to hold her. Everything had always been made easier for Phoebe.)

In the excitement of the moment, Phoebe hadn't thought.

She had just wanted her sister. ("Don't ask questions, just come.")

Roz was to think it over and over . . . later . . . when it was all over.

Her scream stopped the scanning educator. Lewisohn grabbed her and pulled her out of the lab. (Another assault.)

She leaned against a wall, green with nausea, and mumbled for a bathroom. He led her down the hall. She grabbed at the door marked *Women*, opened it, and banged it shut in the faces of Lewisohn and Sam. They stood outside listening to her retch.

The staff in the viewing room rushed out into the hall. "What happened? The screen went dead!"

Sam banged on the bathroom door to be let in. Roz wouldn't respond. She stopped throwing up and clutched the sink to keep from passing out, not only from shock, but from the smallness of the room. (It was tiny as an airplane's, just a relieving station for nurses on the crisis floor.) She lifted her head and looked at herself in the mirror over the sink. Terror throbbed, head to bowel. The taste of bile was in her mouth, stomach acids in her nose. She would never be able to fight her way out of the white-tile coffin she was in. She could hear Sam's voice: "I'm out here, let me help you. All right, don't open, I'll stay here. Take your time, pull yourself together. Phoebe needs you . . . Forgive me, Roz, I didn't do it right . . . no one could have, but that's no excuse. Phoebe's waiting for you."

She could do nothing but look in the mirror, mesmerized by the gross distortions of her face—a huge vein pulsing on her forehead, the whites of her eyes engorged red; her mouth was open in a breathing, silent scream for air. With disgust, she commanded herself. She had no pity for such a face.

In the lab, Lewisohn and Gruening nervously checked the scanning educator. Others inspected the I.V.s, the oxygen tube, the blood pressure monitors, the instant blood chemistry computers. Nothing was wrong.

Slowly, the images on the scanning educator screen started to register again and unscramble themselves into clarity.

Roz opened the bathroom door and walked out. She was pale but quite herself, face repaired, smelling of a lovely perfume and wearing dark glasses. Sam embraced his sister-in-law for the first time and held her, trying to make up, with his body, for the bad messenger that he was. She allowed it for that brief moment. The rest was behind the glasses. He brought her to Phoebe, who hadn't moved from her chair in the viewing room. She had sat there, still as a stone . . . when the scanning educator stopped. Phoebe saw the terror behind her sister's glasses. She embraced her and started to explain what had happened. Roz returned the whispers in fierce anger, hardly comprehending what Phoebe mumbled, ". . . The cure for cancer . . . Daddy's wish . . ."

"Why wasn't I told? Because you knew I wouldn't allow it, that's why! They're all mad!" Roz got up to leave.

Phoebe dug her nails into her sister's arm. "Sit down! I didn't know about it, either. This is no time for shit, behave yourself. Let go your anger, once in your life. There's too much love and caring in this place. It's what Daddy wanted, whatever it is. Look up at the screen. It's Daddy's brain re-activating. We . . . have . . . to . . . be . . . brave!"

Roz sat down.

"Don't leave me with this," Phoebe said. "It belongs to both of us."

Roz looked up at the screen and was startled into silence. The images were flashing by in faster motion than before her scream had shut them down.

There were Max and his mother in a two-seater, low-flying plane, its shadow chasing rabbits in all directions. The plane landed . . . there was an old man with a long white beard . . .

Roz gasped. "Granny and Daddy! It *is* Granny, but she looks like me in old clothes!" She clutched Phoebe's arm. "And the old man, that must be the one Daddy told all those stories about! What is going on? Where is it coming from? I don't understand . . ." She had pulled off her dark glasses. Phoebe took her hand. Roz's eyes were wide with fear. "They're pulling out Daddy's memory bank, Roz," Phoebe said softly, "in the hope that there'll be a working brain when it's over . . . we mustn't be afraid, darling, even though it feels like jumping off from the highest place there is . . . we mustn't be afraid . . ."

The images tumbled forward, from diggings, outcroppings, faces of American Indian miners, Martha Treading in her leather dress, a young Max in his twenties (as he saw himself), a collage of images whirling forward to. . . .

Young Sophia, the Walleby dining room . . . their young mother in rose silk looking across the table at Max, her eyes amused, glistening. "God, look at her . . . she was beautiful," Roz gasped in a whisper.

The sisters' eyes gaped at the phantasmagoria of their young parents . . . in love. Their eyes had to catch them fast as the pieces of pictures imploded and exploded into others . . . into. . . .

A baby! Young parents with a baby. It was Roz. Max was holding her up high in the air, kissing her. He looked so happy. Roz put a hand over her mouth. Daddy was kissing her, hugging her. He was loving her . . . She wasn't a baby anymore, she was a little girl, a white-faced, sober, wide-eyed little girl looking up at her mother, who was screaming. Sophia's face was cold, ugly. Roz saw herself when she was three, her thumb in her mouth, hiding behind Max's legs, her mother trying to pull her away . . . they were tugging at her. The images became faces close up, angry, yelling faces . . . dissolved into Max holding Roz in his arms, walking slowly through Central Park, just the two of them, two little figures disappearing under trees . . . his head was bent over hers, his lips on her cheek, as though they were bonded. . . .

Roz began to cry.

The images became a Catherine Wheel of Sophia's face filled with unhappiness, cruelty, anger. Max making love to another woman, another, a fast train of women. . . . Another baby! Phoebe! Daddy kissing her, smiling. . . . So many pictures of little Phoebe, none of Roz now. (Phoebe closed her eyes.) The abominable machine was turning years into split seconds; Sophia's face, tight and set, was among a montage of women;

again a fast train of women and their father making love to strangers. In the midst of it was Roz, a tall willow of what? Ten years old? Sophia was slapping her face. Max slapped their mother's face in return. "I don't remember that! Why? Why?" Roz gasped.

The sisters lowered their eyes. Science was committing violent indiscretion. It had glued them to their seats too long. The revelations were too cruel. It was no one's right . . . "I've had enough, this is monstrous," Roz said, got up, and went into the antiseptic, white corridor. Phoebe followed. They walked down the corridor to a waiting room, their arms clasped, but once in the room, they sat at opposite ends, each deep in her own thoughts, shaken.

Sam, accompanied by Gruening, joined them. It was late in the evening and no one had had dinner. Phoebe asked Roz to come back to the apartment and Cook would make up something. Roz declined.

Gruening jumped in. "May I take you out for a supper somewhere? Food couldn't be more important now. . . . Anyway, it'll give me the opportunity to explain what's going on, if I may, to fill you in, so we can all face tomorrow fully briefed." It wasn't so much an invitation as a professional command, but with just a hint of courtliness.

Sam and Phoebe were surprised to hear Roz say "Yes." They sighed with relief as they watched them walk to the elevator, Gruening's voice trailing behind, a hand on her elbow. . . . "You'll have to be patient with me, I'm very tired. I'll fill you in from the beginning, with what we hope was Dr. Wesgrove's perfect suspension . . ."

They heard Roz's response: (Laughter) "Suspension?"

"That's worth one martini for itself," Gruening replied. "Don't you agree? You must be very shocked, I'm sorry . . . each day is . . ." The elevator door closed behind them.

"Well," said Phoebe, "who else should be taking her out to dinner, but a psychiatrist? If anyone can handle it, he should. Do you think that's why he asked her?"

"Yes. There isn't a thing here that's accidental, you can be sure of that. But, he doesn't look like the ordinary, run-of-the-mill lion tamer."

"I think he does . . . right out of the Italian Renaissance." (It felt good to talk nonsense.) "Did they tame lions in the Renaissance?"

"Have no idea, but they did try to tame their viragos, without much success."

"Viragos?"

Sam pulled her out of her seat gently and they, too, walked to the elevator, Phoebe reluctantly. She didn't want to leave the body in the lab, not even the constant flow of images on that incredible, horrible screen. It felt like abandoning a baby.

Sam answered her as they walked into the elevator. "A virago was a brilliant, scheming, beautiful, plotting woman. . . . God, I'm tired. We've got to get some sleep and be ready for tomorrow, whatever it brings."

All that night, the staff remained in the viewing room to monitor the scanning educator, as the images continued the collage of Maxwell Treading's history. Familiar faces to the staff, newspaper faces, not just family faces, faces everyone recognized, from the 1950s on . . . and the fascinating part, the body on the table, right in the thick of it:

Lumumba, the African leader who was murdered. Hammarskjöld, secretary general of the United Nations, who died in a plane crash. A party in Paris with General de Gaulle. Jack Kennedy, Bobby Kennedy. Martin Luther King. Adlai Stevenson. Castro in Havana, hosting the American industrialist.

An angry lunch with Nelson Rockefeller. A strange barbecue on LBJ's ranch with both men looking strained. Arabs, Chinese faces . . . The staff forgot themselves, calling out the names of those they recognized—like a game. "That man knew everyone in the world!" someone said.

"It looks like he devoted his whole life to trouble," someone else commented wryly.

Lewisohn, bleary-eyed, staggered into the viewing room

from his office, where he'd been trying to sleep for a few hours. He put a stop to the game. "Everyone try and get some rest somewhere. There are two people on duty in the lab. I'll stay in here for a few hours. Come back and relieve me then. This can't go on forever. The man died in 1982. Tomorrow's going to be an off-the-wall day. That's one thing I do know, if I know anything."

30

The phone buzzed. They were disturbed out of deep, dawn sleep. He groaned and refused to answer. Hedda had to lean across his body to press the "on" button.

"Hedda? This is Phoebe . . ."

"I know, darling. What's wrong? It's . . ." Hedda looked at the bed clock. "It's six o'clock California time!"

"I know . . . I waited as long as I could."

(Phoebe's voice was sounding very strange.)

"Hold it a second, darling, let me get up, I'm in a very peculiar position." She rolled over and rushed to the other side of the bed. "Now . . . what is it? What's the matter?"

"Hedda . . . they're doing it . . . at the Cancer Research Center. They did it! They're doing it . . . it's going on right now!"

"Doing what?"

"They've unfrozen Daddy . . . bringing him back . . . maybe . . . First, they found the serum . . . Oh God, I'm saying it in jumbles. It's working!"

"Phoebe, I'll call you back in a few minutes." Hedda broke the connection abruptly and looked at Lew Koestler. "That was

Phoebe, Max's daughter. She sounds like she's in trouble. I have to call her back but I'm going to take a shower first and wake up."

Fifteen minutes later, Phoebe sounded very calm. "I don't know if you even want to know, but I thought you should."

Hedda listened, her face registering shock, amazement, and finally, very veiled emotions as she became aware of Lew watching her. She finally put the phone down as though it had burned her hand to the bone.

"You look like you've just had a call from the Devil."

"Close."

She told him the news.

Lew had known only too well about Max in her life, ever since he and Hedda had begun to live together three years ago. Three years later they were finally talking about marriage. Now she was packing and calling for the first reservation possible, saying, "I'm going to New York, today."

He was aghast. It was as though she were wiping away their three years in a second. He had to say so, bitterly. "You mean I'm being upstaged by a corpse?"

"Darling, no! How can I make you understand?" She sat down.

"You can't."

"You have to! Phoebe said Max is 'clinically alive' but not conscious. They don't know what's going to happen next . . . I must be there, don't you see? If he does come around . . . I was there at the end . . . I have to be there if there's going to be a beginning. I owe it to him. It has nothing to do with us . . ."

"What does it have to do with?"

"Loyalty. Can't you see that? I loved him very much."

"You think your making an independent decision is right?" He saw her desperately trying to hide what was on her face— the possibility of a *live* Max Treading. The only thing she could say was, "I owe it to the incredible thing I was a part of, I insist you understand." He knew he had no power to dispel the magic of the air around her. It would be as foolish as trying to stop the moon from making waves. Dumbstruck, he drove her to the airport.

Whose work was it, if it wasn't the Devil's, he thought as he watched the plane zoom into the clouds. It was sheer madness. She had clung to him when he kissed her good-bye. She said, "I love you, remember that . . ." But her mind was somewhere else and she was trying to cover it up with . . . "He might be nothing but a vegetable when it's all over. That's what Phoebe said, poor thing, I'll call you the minute I know anything . . ."

The year Max died, Hedda left New York for California, to get as far away as possible. She ran away from everything— to heal. The last year of Max's life had ravaged her more than she had thought possible. It had been like living through the *endless* climax of a tragic play that refused to finish. She would never regret having shared the last part of his life, but she never wanted that kind of excitement *or* love again. Once was enough.

With all the money Max had left her, she needn't have lifted a finger for the rest of her life; but it wasn't her nature not to be creating something. Gradually, she began to design costumes for movies and never went back to dress design. She bought herself a lovely house on top of a Hollywood hill, lived quietly in the mindless sun, painted for pleasure, and went on with her life, by choice, as if she were a widow in her fifties, not a handsome woman in her thirties. There were nine years of being a reluctant oyster, shells clamped tight. There were affairs, but nothing that she allowed to be important, until Lew, an English Jew, product of Oxford, the London theater, a tall, intense man with flashing eyes, a writer-director, passionately civilized and verbal. It must have been her fate to be brought to life by men possessed. Max had been possessed with changing the world, riding it like a horse. Lew was possessed with changing people's feelings, and he was very successful at it. Carefully, she fell in love with Lew. She had madly fallen in love with Max from the first minute. With Lew, she had almost been able to forget the difference between *carefully* and *madly*.

For a long time after the plane rose, Hedda kept her eyes

closed, trying to collect her wits. She wasn't sure she could. The rashness and violence of feeling that shot her out of the house after Phoebe's call were not to be reasoned with easily. The only thing she could do, now that she had done it, was to respect the explosive, overwhelming reaction—*get there!* . . . *be there!* She had managed to catch one of the three-hour, transcontinental planes. Someone had canceled a reservation. Was that an omen?

She opened her eyes and looked down. The large, silver ribbon of the Colorado River was looming up. Straight down was desert, plateau, endless tan, brown, rust silence. Max's land. Big, dirty-blond America, oh God! She was flying over it and into it again! She closed her eyes and prayed. It was the only word she could find to describe what her mind was doing. She pleaded with whatever made the silence below and above her— that she not be going toward another crash.

Phoebe and Sam were back in the viewing room by mid- morning. But, no Roz. They watched for a while. The watching was becoming unbearable for Phoebe. It was easier, less painful, to look at old images than the more recent ones in her own memory. Roz's coming-out party . . . The incompatibility of her parents was so repetitive, anguishing. She thought she would die of a heart attack herself when she saw, as Max had seen, her mother wheel about on the tennis court and drop to the ground, her father's hand in midair, about to return the serve.

And then came the first images of Hedda . . .

Phoebe got up. "I've had enough." She did *not* want to be a witness to that—Daddy making love to Hedda. Never!

They went out for lunch and came back. Lewisohn and Gruening walked into the waiting room, looking very grim. Lewisohn spoke: "Well, it's finally stopped. No more images are being transmitted. We've disconnected the scanning educator. There's nothing to do but watch and wait for further signs. I have to say, very frankly, we have no idea what to expect. Your father is unconscious . . . there *are* brain waves."

"Have you talked with your sister today?" Gruening asked.

"No."

"How did your supper go last night?" Sam asked guardedly.

"Very well, I thought, calm, rather pleasant . . . up until coffee. She suddenly got up and said she had to leave. She wouldn't let me walk her out to her car, and I didn't insist. She'd had a lot of pressure in a short time. But I did get her up on everything. She's completely briefed. No secrets. She said that when we sat down: 'I don't like secrets, I want to know everything.' She accepted a lot of technical information very intelligently."

"I bet she did," Sam said.

They all looked at him.

"What do you mean by that?" Phoebe said, critical of Sam's tone.

"I mean—your sister is capable of anything."

The doctors became alarmed. "What *do* you mean?" Lewisohn demanded.

Gruening spoke slowly. "He might mean she's capable of getting a *cease and desist* to pull all the plugs." He looked at Sam. "Am I right?"

"Yes."

"I might agree with you." He paused. "We didn't have a calm, pleasant supper, as I said. We had an almost analytic hour, very tempestuous and upsetting for her. I was not going to make mention of it, for professional reasons. But maybe I'd better. The images she saw on the scanning educator went to the core of what I think is her deep problem. I remembered her behavior before Wesgrove's trial, then the sudden change, after all the dirty work had been done, of course. Yesterday, I watched her closely. She was thrown into trauma by the shock of seeing her father's body. She pulled herself out of it . . ."

"I thought she did rather well," Phoebe said, tremulous. "She held my hand, made me feel we were in this thing together, sisters."

"She was shocked out of her mind, she said, looking at images of her father when she was small; he seemed to love her very much. She can't reconcile that with what she felt her whole life—that he ignored her, rejected her in favor of Phoebe, that he, in fact, hated her as she hated him. It lessens the guilt of the death wish, if you assume the hatred is returned."

He paused. "Now, what is she to do with *her* hate, which she *saw* was not altogether justified? It's one of those childhood misconceptions that often ruin our lives, and no one ever disabuses us of them. It's rare for a parent to have that opportunity or wisdom or humility, even though the parent is partially to blame, if not completely. Let me try for a point." He addressed himself to Lewisohn. "I'm picking up on it, Art, because I'm not sure her confusion won't turn into a punitive action. She might have to defend the structure of her feelings, the only self she knows . . .

"And she got *another* blow yesterday. The parent, the mother she loved, not hated . . . that person wasn't what Roz thought she was. Roz blurted this all out to me. She kept repeating . . . 'my mother's angry, cruel face.' Then she calmed down, became very abstracted, abruptly got up and left.

"She might not be able to face *again* the terrifying love she had for her father, if he were to be successfully re-animated. Do you see? She might have to do anything she has to—to keep him buried. Anything that could change that is a threat to her own life. Oh, she understood it all, I know that, I watched her very closely. She's a very intelligent person, a beautiful woman . . . and she's gotten no satisfaction from being either." He stopped, hit by a thought.

"You know, the possible ramifications from that damn machine have almost knocked me out. It's a monstrous vehicle, a fucker!" He looked at Phoebe. "Sorry . . . but I mean it. Two years of conventional therapy, or even drug therapy, or a lifetime of therapy might not come up with the truth, the insights. Yet, a couple of hours of watching that screen came up with the core of the psychic confusion. That's a brutal blow. I'm sure that's why she hasn't come here today."

Lewisohn was surprised by Gruening, the cool one, being so emotional. "What do you think she might do?"

"I don't know. Maybe nothing. Maybe she'll just run away

from it. Or, maybe she'll accuse us of grave robbing," he added dully.

"All she needs is a conservative judge, let's face it," Sam offered.

"I don't like what you're doing, Sam!" Phoebe was getting angry with him. "You don't really know my sister. You only know the bad part."

"Let's not push this any further than we have," Lewisohn interjected. "The newest information, which changes the picture somewhat, certainly the legal picture, I think: We removed the oxygen tube at noon. He's been breathing on his own ever since. There was no problem. Every organ is functioning. He's on his own, except there are no signs of consciousness. He's in limbo and we can't figure it out, not yet, anyway. . . ."

"So, he's not being kept alive, he *is* alive," Sam said, taking Phoebe's hand.

"Yes, and we don't think we should investigate anything for another four to six hours, maybe longer. I've talked it through with Wesgrove. He says, 'Let the body rest.' So, that's where we are."

Hedda arrived at the Research Center at four o'clock. Phoebe took her to the lab. They stood at the door. There was nothing to faint or scream about. There were no wires around his head, no tube in his throat. It was just Max sleeping! Hedda put an arm about Phoebe and they just stood there. Hedda was lucky. There was no Grand Guignol for her to witness. Just a *terribly* silent room with the heart and lung monitors humming low, registering their information through unobtrusive sensors.

Lewisohn was looking at the latest blood analysis. He beckoned them to come in. It was the first time he had allowed that. Was it over and didn't matter now? Phoebe wondered.

Hedda went right to the head of the table and put her hand on Max's forehead. It was almost an automatic gesture, a reflex well-remembered. She brushed her fingers lightly against the warm skin, up through the blond, peppered-gray hair. It felt as magical as if she had been able to lean out of the plane that afternoon and touch the desert when they flew over it. There was nothing real about where she was. Nothing to do but give in, as though she were under a spell.

She was full of questions when they went back to the waiting room.

"He's in limbo, that's all they know," Sam said. "And they don't know why."

There was no point in talking, they didn't have the energy, but Phoebe was relieved Hedda was with them. She knew there was a Lew Koestler in Hedda's life, yet Hedda here . . . made it more real, as if there had been no break in time. It was an utterly childish feeling . . .

Should they go out to dinner? Lewisohn thought not. "The first twenty-four hours off the oxygen tube are crucial; even in a *normal* critical situation, respiratory function can fail and fool you after a number of hours of going on its own."

Sam had been painfully right about Roz. She had had a very busy night for herself after she left that Dr. Gruening, with his thin, nervous face and inquisitive eyes that had brought more out of her than she had ever said to herself in her most frightening nightmares. She had called her lawyer, who had called a judge at home, who had received them both at two in the morning . . . and the secret was out.

Gruening's worry was dead center . . . about the *cease and desist.*

"For perverted use of a corpse for unauthorized experimental purposes, and for exhumation without the consent of the Coroner's Office of The City of New York . . ."

The paper was served on a hysterical Lewisohn at ten o'clock that evening. (The secrecy they needed for the reanimation had made the request for sanction impossible. Did they actually need official sanction? Treading's will had laid out the scenario, had it not? And, the will had not been challenged.) The worst had happened. The secret would have to spread. Lewisohn was forced to call the Research Center's own lawyers for immediate interpretation.

The entire staff of scientists were gathered in his office, as well as Phoebe, Sam, and Hedda. *Shock* was the only word applicable from the very beginning. Each progression had been a shock. Lewisohn, showing the wear and tear, fired questions into the phone. The lawyer at the other end was saying he needed time, his staff would have to consult.

"Then, consult, *now!*" Lewisohn shouted. "Can we be stopped?"

The answer must have been in the affirmative.

"You mean they could pull the plug on us?" was his agitated response. He hung up, drained and silent.

A sardonic voice broke through. "What do you mean, pull the plug? There are no plugs. The damn critter's lying there on his own. We pulled the oxygen plug today! He's breathing on his own, he's alive! He's of this earth, for God's sake!"

"If there's no consciousness," Lewisohn said slowly, each word an attempt to break through his fatigue, "we could be charged with creating an . . . an obscenity, a monster. They'll charge us with anything, it's headlines. Gruening! This is your department. What in hell is going on with the brain? What did the scanning educator do, empty what was there? That's all? Can you project *anything*?"

"What do you want me to do? Define the black hole right here and now, on a Friday night" (he looked at his watch) "at eleven o'clock? There are brain waves, but not like any I've ever seen."

Lewisohn lost his temper completely. "Goddamn it! This is no time for your black comedy dialogue!"

Gruening kept his maddening cool. "God doesn't have a sense of humor, it's an invention of Man, sorry. I think we need time out."

Lewisohn stormed back to the lab. He stood at the foot of the table and watched the body breathing in and out. He was having some frightening thoughts. Could what they had done be called "forbidden fruit"? A decoy to entrap Man in his pretense at playing God? Or was it the right of Science to tread, not with the angels but with what looked like the Devil? Which was it? He longed for Wesgrove to be at his side. He was losing courage.

The others followed him into the lab. There was an absence of purpose or plan, an odd quiet. They had proved a human body could be re-animated from a frozen state, but not the brain. Life was the brain. This body was like a fish returned to water, but it couldn't swim, it would sink. Without a brain, what was lying on the table wouldn't be human.

Phoebe began to cry.

The night-entrance bell was being rung. Outside, a detective, Roz, and her lawyer were waiting to be let in. They walked through the lobby and into the elevator.

In the lab, all of a sudden, soft whooshes of sound started to come from deep in the body's chest. Lewisohn moved swiftly to the head of the table and switched on an overhead light, at the same time ordering the cardiac and vascular people to hitch up the oxygen tube apparatus and be ready. Yet, the heart and lung monitors were registering nothing unusual. The chest kept moving up and down in full, rhythmic movement—like stretching and yawning. It was not movement showing distress, it was slow and easy . . .

Max Treading opened his eyes! He closed them! He opened them! Lewisohn, beet-red with emotion, leaned over the body like an Indian with his ear to the ground. "My God! . . . "I think he just said . . . *'Too much light!'* "

There was a groan of disbelief, and it came from Gruening. He broke into wild guffaws. "I don't believe it! Goethe said 'More light' before he died, and this one is saying 'Too much light'?" He couldn't stop laughing. The others joined him and began to clap.

Lewisohn shushed them fiercely. "Quiet! He could be shocked to death!" They fell silent and stood there . . . watching what seemed like a miracle. They watched Max try to lift his head. His lips parted, his tongue slipped through trying to wet them. A nurse scurried off and came back with a piece of gauze and water. Max swallowed the coolness with what seemed to be a faint smile of thanks. The white, stark lab smiled faintly with him.

There were sounds in the corridor, approaching the lab. A group of people stood at the door. The detective was about to move into the room, but stopped dead. Roz and her lawyer came from behind. All heads in the lab turned to look, appearing like animals startled at their watering hole.

Max was gesticulating with his hands, looking at Lewisohn and trying to say, "Who are you?"

"I'm Arthur Lewisohn, an associate of Dr. Wesgrove. Do you remember me?"

Max seemed to be nodding an assent. He made more sounds. Lewisohn said, "He's saying, 'Roz . . . Phoebe . . .' if I'm not mistaken."

Max made another assent.

(Even though his mind felt like a top whirling and piercing through the funnel of a tornado, he was conscious of *coming back.* There was another word he wanted to say, but wouldn't. Some final thought way, way in the distant past, a moment before, or a hundred years before, gave him no right to say it.)

Roz moved to the table like a sleepwalker. Max raised a hand. She took it. Phoebe did the same on the other side of the table.

Hedda began to cry, as well as some of the nurses and doctors.

Suddenly, the voice of the detective . . . "What's going on here? There's no corpse. He looks like a dying man, not a dead one."

"Dying, you idiot? The man's reborn, you ass!" Gruening exploded. "Excuse me, Officer, but you just banged into a miracle, it's not your fault. We've just entered the outer-galactic space of the brain, that's all!" He caught his breath and went on, to no one in particular; he was beside himself. "We don't know how we got there, but we did it! I need a drink. I'm going out and get drunk."

"You leave this building and you're fired," Lewisohn hissed. "I need you!"

. . .

In all the excitement, Roz released her grasp on her father's hand and slipped out. Gruening noticed it, followed, and found her at the elevator. "Let me join you . . . I want some air too. That's why you're leaving, isn't it," he lied, taking a giant, firm step to put her on a track he knew she hadn't planned to take. "You weren't escaping, you just needed air." He guided her into the elevator. "I meant it. I want a drink. Join me, then we'll come back. They're not going to need me for a while. Your father will be moved to a private room on the intensive care floor. He's a very sick man with cancer, same as he was twelve years ago."

They were out on the street. "I want more than a drink. I'm hungry. But let's walk first." He breathed in. "The air is good." He looked at her and said very gently, "What would you say, if I tell you I think you're going to recover too?"

"*Will* he?"

"Don't know. But, whether he does or he doesn't, you will."

She put her arm through his. They walked slowly down the street. It felt comfortable. He knew her secret.

"No talking, just breathing," Gruening said, casting a glance at the pale, beautiful woman on his arm. "Every cell in me is yelling 'Ouch!' Let's go find a loaf of bread and a jug of martinis."

Roz went back to the Plaza, and it was just as well. Lewisohn had sent Phoebe and Sam home. Hedda went to her hotel. Max had not asked for her . . . but she would be there tomorrow, there was no question of that, she had to.

There was no sleep for Lewisohn and Gruening that night. Max developed a high fever that kept going up and down like a yo-yo. There was no explanation for it—burning to cool, burning to cool, like a chemistry that didn't know what to do with itself. They decided not to inject or aid in any way, they simply watched. And, sure enough, by dawn, the body had righted itself. Max's temperature was normal and he fell into a deep, normal sleep.

The men went to Lewisohn's office for coffee with a lot of

brandy in it. They were facing a fantastic day. How to plan a scientific disclosure that would set the world on its head! *Wesgrove would be the first call.* Could Treading tolerate the cancer serum immediately, or did a body after re-entry need time to recover from the trauma? "Well, one thing we do know," Gruening said, "The old man made a perfect suspension. From the first look, doesn't it seem like the brain has been frozen and unfrozen successfully?" Lewisohn agreed with a grunt. "Did you ever go into it with him—the L.L. injection he put into the jugular? Or was it the cranium?"

"Who had time, once we got started? I brought it up in one of those phone calls, but he didn't answer, probably didn't want to load us with anything more to think about. Whatever it was, it suspended the brain, didn't it, the old fox. I'll find out today, believe me."

"Are you worried, Art?" Gruening asked.

"Yes," Lewisohn said.

"Me too . . . We've got an unknown quantity . . . I'm going to my office and collapse on the couch for an hour. My own brain feels like it's turned to water and if I lean over, it'll come pouring out of my ears. You think I went out for a drink? I was working. I had a long analytic session with Rosalind Treading . . . I don't even know what day it is, do you?"

"It's April, the eighth. *One week . . .* that's what it took."

"Wanna kiss me good night?" Gruening said.

"I want to shake the hand of a very fine scientist, the best I know."

"Me, too."

They didn't shake hands, they embraced with unabashed feeling.

31

Lewisohn had no way of knowing that Wesgrove was shaking and very pale when he was told the news of the complete re-entry the next morning, because they were not using the videophone. The momentous leap had been accomplished between that morning of June 1982, and a night in April 1994.

They could only afford a moment for the incredible. It was back to work. The situation with Treading was precarious. They talked chemistry, medical ifs and whereases. Should the cancer serum be started? Could the re-animated body tolerate it? Treading's temperature had gone up and down all night. It was normal this morning, but what should they expect? "You can't expect," said Wesgrove. "You're still making a new alphabet."

Lewisohn wanted to wait with the serum. They were disagreeing.

"You'll lose him if you wait," Wesgrove said. "What's the reticence? You can lose him either way, but at least we will have tried, with the serum. I say—push on, sir." (It was an order.) "You've got a man with terminal cancer on your hands."

Lewisohn smarted. "Dr. Wesgrove, what about the final injection you administered?"

"Ah yes . . ." was all the question elicited.

Lewisohn hesitated. No, he was going to say what he wanted to say . . . "Why did you withhold the information from us?"

Wesgrove grunted and Lewisohn waited for a response. In the silence, Wesgrove was feeling the span of years falling like dead weight, and he, with it.

Wesgrove began: "Have you ever written a poem under the influence of liquor and thought it the most brilliant utterance ever made?"

Lewisohn, mystified and annoyed with the curve—the old man was fencing—answered, "Once or twice, in college."

"What did you do with it?"

"Hid it in a drawer."

"Exactly," said Wesgrove. "I was out of my field with the laser."

"The laser?"

"We had to halt the brain in midflight, didn't we? And fast . . . How? Not the cells of the brain, but the synapses, the nondefined, the function of the brain, or there would be no point in freezing the human body, would there?" Wesgrove laughed, in spite of a heavy weight on his chest. "I had been thinking about it and working on it in the 'cold' lab . . . for a long time. Art, I had a hunch and I came up with something, but I wasn't sure, I couldn't test it and wasn't ready to share my figures . . . you know who I am—don't tout till you're sure. Something to penetrate as swiftly as light. Why not light itself? Liquid light. L.L., in other words."

"How?!" Lewisohn was astounded.

"I reduced the laser energy to a stationary state with a refractive gradient force field; in other words, I rendered the photons motionless. I congealed them. Stationary light . . ." Wesgrove's voice had gotten so small, Lewisohn could hardly hear him. "It's classical and modern physics, with the exception of the extrapolation into force fields and their effects . . ."

"Are you all right, Dr. Wesgrove?"

"Yes, I'm all right, just a little tired from all of this. Let me

finish for the moment. We'll go into it later, when things settle
down, if they're going to. What I came up with seems to have
worked. You see, when Treading told me he was determined to
commit suicide, I thought—why not test it? We have nothing to
lose. It actually influenced me to convince him to go through
with the cryonic procedure. It was rash, the rashest thing I've
ever done in my life and I paid for it, didn't I? I could have
shared the information, we could have worked on it together, on
animals, but the plight of Treading so affected me, I think, the
kind of man he was, made me go for it right away—test it on a
human, suspend the brain with the speed of light . . ."

Wesgrove was going over in his mind that last minute with
Max, which he would never forget. "I gave him acupuncture
first . . . then I went in with the gradient force that liquefied the
laser energy at the point of injection . . . it evidently worked.
Art, my hands are shaking, this is all too much for me. From
now on, you take over. I have complete confidence. Try to save
him if you can. If you can't, so be it. At least, I've lived to see
the serum successful. Now let's see if Treading can tolerate it.
He's still our guinea pig, remember that. That was the bargain."

Lewisohn was alarmed by the way the old man sounded. He
called the warden and told him the news of Treading's re-animation. "It will break by evening. Look, I want Dr. Wesgrove
transferred to the prison hospital. I don't like the way he sounds.
Do it immediately."

The warden was no exception with his explosion of wonder
about the news. At the Center, everyone had been saying all
night, "My God!" . . . "Christ!" The warden's response was,
"Holy shit! You mean to say the good doctor's victim is alive?
The governor should be informed!"

"That's my next call, Warden," Lewisohn said.

The governor of New York saw immediately that an un-
precedented decision was before him, since there was no corpus
delicti, but he was going to have to think about it, "petition the
files, take into account the letter of the law . . ."

"There can't be any letter of the law in this case, Governor," Lewisohn said angrily.

The governor promised to make an immediate evaluation.

Lewisohn's next call was to the mayor, who said, of course the street in front of the Center would be cordoned off, the press restrained, to protect the dignity of a scientific institution, and what an honor it was for the city of New York. When the mayor was told of the governor's reaction, he said he wasn't surprised. "He's a letter-of-the-law guy. If I were in his shoes, I'd spring Dr. Wesgrove today, and you can quote me."

Sam Russell was asked to release the announcement of the dual breakthroughs—the cancer serum and the re-animation of Maxwell Treading.

Lewisohn was worn down with the excitement and everything that had to be done that day; he didn't know where to begin. But this he *had* to do first: find Gruening and tell him about his conversation with the old man and the explanation of L.L., *the fatal injection* that had led them into the perfect suspension and re-entry, as far as the brain was concerned. Lewisohn repeated what Wesgrove had said, adding, "He didn't go further, said we'd all go into it later. He sounded too tired, Jeff. I put him in the hospital."

"You mean to say, he created a quasi-material out of the laser and the electrical impulses of the brain cells were arrested *in place?* The son of a gun must have made a quantum leap! And he didn't say anything for twelve years?"

"He said he wasn't sure . . . you know how he always called his work—a hunch, an intuition . . ."

Gruening asked Lewisohn to repeat the beginning explanation of L.L. again.

"I can't, I've got too much to do. The old man insists we begin the cancer serum on Treading today. I couldn't argue him out of it. He stopped me cold. So we go for it. If we lose him, we lose him. Wesgrove wants it tested on a re-entered body, said Treading was still a guinea pig."

By the next day, the church, legal, and medical professions, recovering from the first shocks—there was a live Maxwell Treading at the Cancer Research Center—were poising themselves to rethink their positions in an atmosphere of Galileo squared. Evidently, God giveth and taketh away in manners inconceivable.

❧

Max was slowly realizing he was *coming back*. He also knew he had to be quiet inside or he would explode with the realization. He and Wesgrove had gambled and won! He also knew he was still *coming through* something that felt like the thick cloud banks of a tornado. Just thinking words made him shatter inside. Words felt like bullets. The best thing was to stay away from them, make himself a blank. Impossible. His brain felt like a tree with a thousand branches, and millions of words were sitting on them chattering away; the sound was going to break open his head. The tree was scratching the sky that was the top of his head. Suddenly the tree was turning green. He clung to the word *green*, pushed all the other words off the branches and hypnotized himself. He slept most of the day, swaying back and forth on a swing that was attached to ozone.

By evening, his bed was raised and he was sitting up, having his first meal—chicken soup. It felt like liquid sun. He wasn't coming back, he *was back*. A nurse was feeding him. He clutched at his throat, it felt like a dragon's, on fire.

"You've had an oxygen tube in you for a week, Mr. Treading," she said.

He said hoarsely, "The week of what year?"

And so he learned for the first time: It was 1994. Lewisohn and Gruening had wanted to be the ones to tell him, but they had kept him sedated and he was too groggy for contact until late that first day, so he heard it casually, matter-of-factly, and it was just as well.

"Where is my family?" Max whispered, because it hurt too much to talk. "Where's Dr. Wesgrove?"

Lewisohn had given orders to the staff not to answer the patient's questions unless he or Gruening were there. The nurse scooted out with, "They're in the waiting room, I'll find out . . ."

Phoebe came in and walked to the foot of his bed. "Daddy . . . Daddy . . . They said 'no kissing,' I can't get near you . . ."

Tears rolled down his cheeks. "Look at you! All grown up! You're fatter . . . Where's Roz?"

"Outside. We can only come in one at a time, Dr. Lewisohn's orders." (Their talking, so casual? Insane! She wanted to *yell* "Daddy!")

"Who's he?"

"He's the head . . ." she stopped herself. "The acting head of the . . ."

"Where's Wesgrove? Don't tell me he's dead."

"No, Daddy, he's very much alive."

Lewisohn walked in and introduced himself. "Do you remember? Dr. Gruening and I were with you and Dr. Wesgrove the night before you . . . in the van." (Would he remember?)

"Yes . . . yes." Max looked at him closely. "You're fatter."

Phoebe laughed. "Everyone's fatter and older, Daddy, except you."

"What's this one person at a time, Doctor? I want to see everyone . . ."

"I'm afraid not. We're going to take it slowly. How do you feel?"

"Very weak, but I'm myself. Is that what you want to know? And my throat hurts like hell," Max croaked.

"All right, don't talk, listen. Let me tell you a few things in front of your daughter. We have a cancer cure or we wouldn't have reversed the cryonic procedure on you. You're still a very ill man, with cancer, and with a body whose functions might be new to us. So far, so good. You've received a first cancer serum injection already. It's watch and wait to see how you respond. Your cooperation is crucial, meaning quiet, strict control. You're still a guinea pig, I have to say that, and will be until you're out of the woods." He watched Max for reactions. He was taking the information well. "We're involved with firsts, we must remember that. Don't rush things. You've got twelve years to catch up on. Each thing slowly; that's an order. Let me say, we're hopeful for your recovery. Phoebe, let's let him rest now.

You can see him tomorrow, or someone else . . ."

"Like my husband . . ."

Max felt faint. "When? Who? I want to see Roz . . ."

"And two grandchildren . . ."

Max sank back and looked at Lewisohn. "You're right, it's too much." He closed his eyes and went back to saying "green" to himself.

The next morning, it was Roz. She lay her head on the bed, near his hand. He stroked her hair. They didn't talk. Max couldn't help thinking—so it takes a resurrection. Roz began to cry. "We'll do nothing but talk when I get out of here," Max said, still quite hoarse. "You know I'm going to make it. Then, we'll have nothing but Time with a capital *T.*" It was the first time he said that; he was going to say it over and over.

"Now, tell me a little, not too much, just a little." He learned that Roz and Willard were divorced, she had a villa in Italy, an apartment in London, and lived at the Plaza in-between, which wasn't very often.

"Wandering around the world, eh?"

He also learned that Phoebe's husband was "wonderful."

"It's time to stop and come home, baby . . ." Max felt exhausted.

Gruening came in. "Enough for now, you two." He was pleased to see that Roz's first contact with her father must have gone well. Her face was tear-stained (that was fine), but no anxiety or fireworks. "You know, Mr. Treading, the first name you spoke after your re-entry was Roz's."

"Re-entry? You mean like in space capsule?"

"That's what we're calling it, like in body coming back."

Max frowned in thought. "She was one of the last things on my mind before I . . ." he tried to laugh. "Died. I did that, didn't I?"

"And before you said 'Roz' and 'Phoebe,' you said 'Too much light.' Do you remember that?"

"No, I don't . . ."

"We'll talk about that some other time," Gruening said. He led Roz out of the room.

Max was doing so well, Sam was allowed to meet his father-in-law just for a minute or two. They smiled warily at each other. Max scrutinized the very tall, blond-bearded man who had acquired a slight stoop by his fortieth year; he noted the long, Lincoln face with early lines around the mouth. (She got herself a head-man!) Sam shook Max's hand and backed out of the room in embarrassment. No one had looked at him like that —with such intensity—since his mother had when he was small, trying to decide whether he'd told the truth or not.

Each day, Max had been given an excuse about Wesgrove's absence. By the third day, he insisted upon being answered, by that fellow Gruening, who'd been checking him out and asking him questions as though he'd come back a mental defective or a premature senility case. "Wesgrove is dead, isn't he! You've been keeping it from me. He must be, or he'd be here . . . so no more lies. If you won't answer, then get that other fellow, Lewisohn, to come in here." Max's hoarse voice could be heard down the corridor.

"Someone start talking!" Max demanded. Phoebe and Lewisohn had come into the room. They saw they couldn't fairy-tale it anymore, and, by the look of him, he seemed strong enough.

The news that he and Wesgrove had *lost* twelve years ago, the web of Candleman, Roz, his own letter, which had finally led the district attorney to prosecute, and Wesgrove's confession . . . it astounded Max so (he said later), that he listened to it as if it were a tale of other people. But when the tale was over and everyone stood there watching him, he reacted like the old Max. "Get the governor on the phone! What kind of legal game does he think he's playing? Get Dinessen, I have to put him on it . . . Wes should be released today."

Very quietly, Phoebe said, "Daddy, Dinessen died three years ago."

"Oh . . ." Max expelled. (Tears welled up, he sucked in his breath. Not now . . .) "Get the asshole on the phone!"

It was the old Daddy, Phoebe thought. There was nothing to do but get the governor on the phone.

"And, don't you guys say I can't!" Max added.

Max was in control. There was no anger. You used the

velvet, hoarse voice: "Good afternoon, Governor, this is Max Treading . . ."

(They stood there imagining the shock on the other end of the phone.)

Max talked to the governor about *absolute power,* when it's given to a wise person and to be used in greatness of spirit, "or you wouldn't be where you are . . ." He winked at his audience.

The result of the call? They couldn't believe it. When his doctors felt he was well enough, and the governor had heard that Dr. Wesgrove wasn't well either . . . well, when both men felt up to it, his *absolute power* could bring about a hearing right there at the Center, in front of the same judge who'd heard the case in Riverhead, because he was still seated, about to retire; that had already been ascertained. Max was assured it was "full speed ahead, although under ordinary circumstances, it could take weeks, maybe months . . ." Max added to that, "Fast is the word, Governor. Time with a capital *T,* it's too precious to waste. You've got it from the horse's mouth." He induced a laugh of complicity from the other end. The governor then obviously wished him well, because Max ended the call with: "Thank you, I'm going to be just fine. I have to be. Another corpus delicti would be very embarrassing, wouldn't it? Ha-ha."

After that, there was no stopping him. The next call was to the prison. He couldn't get through. There were strict orders for isolation and rest for the old man. The warden apologized. "He's fine, but weak from all the excitement. Believe me, if it were up to me, I'd string a line to his bed . . ."

"Send him my love, Warden, and give him a message, if you would be so good. Tell him I said: We fucked Fate, didn't we! And also tell him I know his answer: 'Be humble, you ass.' "

In Phoebe's mind, there was no doubt that her father would recover.

Treading walks! Treading tolerates cancer serum! Reporters had been practically scaling the walls. It was decided they would draw numbers. The winners were in a conference room of the Center, issuing their daily reports. "Treading eats filet mignon!"

Max was feeling almost ready for the biggest question of them all, the one he had avoided asking. "Phoebe, baby, what about Hedda? I'm ready to take it now."

"She's at the end of the hall outside your door, in a waiting room. She was here when you opened your eyes. She's been here ever since . . . waiting for you to ask."

"I don't believe it." He turned waxen. "Why didn't she just walk in the door? What kind of canard is that?"

"The psychiatrist thought it best that we wait until you asked. You didn't ask till now, did you?"

"I couldn't handle the tailspin, if you want to know . . ."

"Daddy, Hedda came from California, she lives there . . . She almost left yesterday."

"Almost left? Why did she come?"

"You'll have to ask her." Phoebe ran down the hall to get Hedda.

At the sight of her, he closed his eyes.

(What to do? What to do? Hedda stood in the doorway. Gruening had talked with her that morning. "He's up as high as a kite, pushing around governors, wardens, and everyone else. We want him up. He knows he has to be, to win this fight. Something inside him is telling him that. That's why he hasn't asked for you. He had every right to expect his daughters, but not you. He's being smart, without knowing. Loss makes a depressed chemistry. You know what I suggest, if he does ask for you? Behave like no time has passed. Can you do that? He can be weaned away from disappointment later. We can't trust his strength yet, it's too soon.")

She was still in the doorway. How could she make believe that no time had passed? She could not, even if Max was the guinea pig of all time. Why *had* she come? There was a flock of birds caught inside her chest. She could *not* lie, she should turn around, go away . . . far, far away. Max opened his eyes.

It was as though a knife had slit her open and the birds flew out. She walked to him, pulled a chair up to the bed, and put her cheek next to his. No words, not one could come.

Max spoke first. "You crazy person. I didn't love you for nothing. *Folie à deux.* That's the truth, isn't it? No matter what happened? You came."

There was that Max-smile she had tried to forget. It was a nightmare or magic. Nothing had happened in twelve years, it was like an enchantment. She was doing willingly what Gruening had asked of her. It was unbelievable . . . There was no Lew Koestler, no California, no bed she had awakened in a week ago, it had all slipped into the Pacific, there'd been a huge earthquake. She and Max were together. It was 1982.

"Phoebe said you came to welcome me," Max said calmly. "You made another life, didn't you?"

She nodded. (Max wouldn't accept a lie, Gruening was wrong.)

"I told you to, darling, you had to. If you and I had married, look what a problem you'd be in now—another first. Dead husband returns."

"I didn't marry anyone, Max. I'm planning to, very soon." She started to cry. "I had no right to come, but I had to. I just couldn't not be with you, but it's wrong, it's not fair to anyone."

"But you did come and it wasn't just to say hello. I can see it on your face, I know my Hedda-face. You know I'm going to fight for it . . ." He reached for her hand. "Stay with me until I'm out of the woods? Like time stood still?" His face had blanched.

Gruening walked in and knew immediately what had happened. She couldn't do it. Treading looked like he was going into cardiac arrest. He ordered her out and called for an emergency crew.

Max was furious over all the fuss. He'd pull himself together, oh yes, they'd see how strong he was. But he wasn't . . .

Max had a bad night. It was the first setback since the beginning of the serum injections. His chemistry went berserk.

With all the resolve in the world, he couldn't fight off the sense of loss. He vomited and developed a fever. Lewisohn thought it was the serum, and with great trepidation. But Gruening thought otherwise. He stayed with Max all night and made him talk. The problem was his love for Hedda and how to kill it, *if he couldn't get her back.* No, not kill it, make peace with it . . .

Gruening said later that he had never seen the *soma* react so immediately to the *psycho,* and thus the chemicals that flood the body when triggered by loss. Loss helps create cancer. Treading's body was a battlefield of conflicting signals all night —between the cancer serum and the rush of hormonal activity countermanding the serum, attacking it. He would have to talk to Treading about it later on. What incident of tremendous loss or death had occurred in early life? In a normal body, *a repeat of loss or mourning* could create a fertile ground for cancer. They knew that. They could name the secretions that did it with their nefarious signals. Could it be that with a re-entered body they had one that responded immediately to its psychic environment? The body had re-entered a week ago. Would it right itself, or always be vulnerable? What a field day for experiment, if it didn't.

32

Hedda couldn't face seeing Max again. She flew back to California and cried all the way, her face pressed to the window, watching the mountains of cloud with striations of light piercing through them, thinking of Icarus flying into the heavens toward the sun . . . She knew why she was crying. She had rejected *enchantment,* and it felt like a piece of her had been cut out forever. It wasn't like Max's dying the first time. This time she was making her own fate. No one was pulling the strings . . .

She hadn't let Lew know she was coming. She just arrived. At the airport, she was so distraught she forgot to pick up her luggage.

"No bag? You flew across the country to say good-bye?" Lew was furious. She hadn't called him from the moment she'd left. "Oh, I forgot. Witches don't carry luggage on their broomsticks."

"Lew, don't do that. I wanted to get here so fast, I forgot to go to the baggage counter, can you believe that?"

"Not easily . . ." But he looked at her closely and thought maybe he'd better. "You've come back? To me? To us?"

She nodded.

"Oh, Hedda, Hedda . . ." He grasped her in his arms. "You know what I was going to do, if I didn't hear from you in one more day? I was going to burn all your things, make a bonfire on the front lawn . . . the trappings of a witch. I was not going to understand 'star-crossed'! Fuck Shakespeare, I was losing *my* lady . . ."

"Your lady almost lost herself." She looked around the house that she had built, the house that had given her peace for twelve years, after three years of Max that had felt like shock treatment. She looked at her gardens through the windows. She looked at Lew. This was hers. *She* had made it. Max was the only one who *made* anything around *him*.

"I ran, Lew. Max was too weak for me to explain anything. They wouldn't have let me, anyway, not now, he wasn't going to be able to take it. I ran like a rat, I feel terrible . . . I . . ." She felt slightly hysterical. "I almost sank into the magic again, Lew; I ran to save myself, can you understand that? I almost flew into the sun! I almost got burned again when I walked into his room, I almost forgot this house, you . . . I have to say it! I have to hear myself say it!"

"Darling," Lew said quietly. "Let's have a drink, then we'll take a drive and pick up your bags. I need a great big gin and I'll make one for you."

Hedda curled up in a chair and watched him, the man she had fallen *carefully* in love with, the rangy, masculine form, but with a delicacy, his eyes that had such humor, the English accent that made everything sound more grand, civilized, sardonic sometimes, pathetic, beautifully human . . .

Lew handed her a glass. "When you rushed out the door, darling, I couldn't think of anything except the mad antics of Zeus, the grand fuckeur. He comes down out of the heavens, picks out a woman, says, 'You're mine . . .' and she's good for no other mortal for the rest of her life. And I wasn't big enough for myth, no matter how much I loved you. I was in a terrible place. I tried to reason that your flying out the door had to do with some kind of chemistry that had to be understood, a magic

that paints your life in another color, not a color that's better,
just a color that makes other colors not right; that you were
trusting my humanity to forgive. The civilized man must forgive, even if he doesn't understand, or there would be chaos,
anarchy. Oh, I worked myself into a fit of trying to forgive you
. . . But it didn't help. I wanted to burn you at the stake." He
lifted his glass. "To the queen who came back to the king, alive,
the tale of Penelope in reverse, 1994!"

"Don't do that, Lew. I don't want to play king and queen.
I had to do that once. I never want to do it again in my life!"
She was flooded with the memory of Max and her in bed, playing king and queen, to make him feel strong, to keep him from
dying. She burst into tears. Lew curled up on the couch next to
her and held her. She sobbed, "I have to write to him. What can
I say?"

"You're going to have to tell him, I suppose," Lew said
slowly, "that the miracle happened to him, to no one else; that
it was stop-time for him, not for anyone else. If you want
to . . ."

"I want to," Hedda answered, but she couldn't stop crying. "Why am I crying, Lew? Why can't I stop crying? Help
me . . ."

"You're crying for the lost things, darling, for not being
able to *go back*, for changing . . . I cry sometimes because I'm
insufficient for the dream, and, my God, you got caught in a big
one, this Dr. Wesgrove. The papers have been full of it here,
everywhere . . . not only a cancer cure, that would have been
enough. But the re-animation of a human! You're crying? Un-
derstandably so, you're in shock! The realization of a dream.
You were part of it! It swept over you . . ."

(Hedda stopped crying.)

"Do you think he's going to make it?" Lew asked, cautiously. He wasn't so sure she could extricate herself from the
miracle.

"I'm sure he's going to make it." Hedda jumped up. "I have
to call one of his doctors. He has to know what I did, that I'm
here."

"Staying here?"

Hedda looked around . . . her paintings on the walls (she hadn't painted when she was with Max; it wasn't his fault, it was hers! Lew had given her the love and space to listen to herself.) She looked at Lew in his old sweater, his head cocked; she had watched him look that way when he was directing actors, listening for their music, his encouraging face, full of empathy, his gray eyes waiting for the truth . . .

"Staying here," Hedda said, and went to phone Gruening.

33

"New beginning." Max clung to the phrase that fellow, Gruening, insisted he hang on to. He was trying, like he'd clung to *green* and then *steel* when he knew he was going to make it, after coming through the tornado clouds. *Hedda was lost.* It had to be "new beginning." He was still a guinea pig. He *had* to keep his body in control; he had to make it easier for the experiment that was *he.* He had to be the perfect guinea pig for Wesgrove. It was the second week of the cancer serum and there was one more to go. After that, he was facing an operation to reinforce the partially eaten-away fibula. Max was fighting depression. He wanted to go home, couldn't they give him the serum at home? He had to get out of the white clinic. He didn't know who he was. He wasn't in much pain, the serum was working, he could walk pretty straight with a cane, pee straight, everything was straight except his head.

"I want to go home!"

"We can't do the tests on you at home," Lewisohn said.

"Do you realize I don't have a home? I have to start over. Why am I saying 'home'?"

"Phoebe would disagree with that, Mr. Treading."

"Oh, for God's sake, call me Max! You know me well enough inside and out."

"You know what you could do today? I think you're strong enough. You've been walking up and down the corridors. You can go down two floors and talk to the media. They've been waiting for two weeks, they're starting to smell, they're eating us out of food. Do you feel like giving them an interview?"

"Absolutely, let off some steam, good boy." Max's face lit up.

"Do it this afternoon and get the world out of our hair."

Max left the intensive care floor for the first time. Even the elevator ride delighted him. He almost strode into the conference room and was greeted with cheers. "Here I am, a living corpus delicti. The doctors gave me five minutes, so I'll talk fast." He grinned, in perfect control. Gruening was in a corner of the room watching. They weren't sure he was strong enough, but he *had* been a flamboyant character, he needed to find it again; he *was* getting well, they were almost certain of that, in spite of his depression.

"I'm recovering, that's for sure," Max went on. "Dr. Wesgrove should be here with me today. Each day that man is in prison diminishes the human race. Sound purple? Sometimes I love purple. The governor is 'a good man,' as it was said in *Julius Caesar,* if I remember. He's gotten the machinery going to declare a man innocent, but even a day is too long in this instance. We all know how the state and the courts lumber around like drunken dinosaurs." Max stopped and smiled. "On second thought, maybe I shouldn't knock the dinosaurs, they gave me a couple of damn good fortunes." (There was that Treading smile, and didn't they take note of it.)

A young reporter raised his hand. "Mr. Treading, didn't you make your money in uranium?"

"Where have you been?" Max snapped. "I've been in a liquid nitrogen capsule for twelve years! Hell, I made my money in oil. I left uranium! The *modern* dinosaurs were using uranium to make bombs!" Max stopped. "Forgive me, I need some water."

The young reporter leaned over to an older one. "Do you think he's behaving normally?"

"Absolutely! He looks tired, but it's Max Treading. He had studs on his tongue. I interviewed him a couple of times when he was alive . . ." the older man laughed, "I mean before . . . B.C. Before Cryonics. Don't you use that, it's mine! Years ago, you should have seen him with Juan Perón. Treading was thrown out of Argentina. I was there. Remember Perón, baby? Adolf Hitler's cousin by marriage . . ."

Max was on his feet again. "I want to say something about Time. We think we know the meaning of *now* but we don't. I hear they've been sitting around a conference table for four years, talking about disarmament. They were thinking of doing that before I . . . before I left. What kind of use of Time is that? Time with a capital *T.* You only know how holy it is when you've lost it and found it again . . ."

(Gruening was pleased with that. Max was digging under his depression and finding *spirit,* not anyone's, his own, from what Phoebe had told him of her father. Gruening felt it was the most important thing that had to be done, for Max to fight the trauma of the miracle that had happened to him.)

"Imagine, the heads of the world, of every nation in the world, representing the peoples of the world . . . and they're wasting Time, still talking about nuclear weapons, lines of demarcation, peace through strength. Bullshit! Do you still use that word, or is there a more graphic one? Have you ever seen a conference of birds? They get together, make a decision, and fly off in the direction where the winds are best. They don't want nature to smash them to the ground. They don't want to die. What's wrong with us birds?"

(Laughter.)

"Don't we know yet that *no more war* is the only weather we humans can fly in and not get incinerated in a fire storm?"

Max stopped. There were no questions.

"You're looking at a guy who's walked across the bridge of sighs. I can pull rank on the whole world. I had a coin put between my teeth to pay for the trip, but I . . . came . . . back.

It happened through the genius of a Hiram Wesgrove. God offers it once or twice a century to the rainbow walkers—a Homer, a da Vinci, a Mozart, an Einstein, a Picasso . . . choose your own, there aren't many. God would give us the gift more if He thought we deserved it. He would . . ." Max's voice faltered. He was overcome with numbness, he tipped over in a dead faint.

The reporters ran in all directions, but the television cameras had it all. The whole world heard what Treading had to say and watched him faint from the exertion.

That's all it was, too much emotion, too soon. Max loved it. He was fine after a long nap.

Max's last week at the Center was going to be spent mostly with Jeff Gruening, preparing him for leaving and analyzing all that had happened.

Gruening had been having a nagging time because of questions put to him and questions he asked himself. Why did the scanning educator stop when it did? How did Treading's brain restart itself? They had attached the scanning educator to him again, a day after it stopped. It registered nothing. They had to speculate that the recording of the machine had something to do with dead storage, that it had animated an already written book, as it were. What kind of conclusion was that? A cloud is a cloud and forget the *because*.

Gruening spent days poring over the Treading charts. He spent much time with Max, testing, talking. The two found each other good company (which surprised Max, he hadn't liked him at all in the beginning).

Gruening, feeling Max was strong enough to participate not only as a patient, confided his problems—the lack of scientific explanation about what had taken place. Specifically, that space of time when the brain was not activated, although the body had been reanimated.

"We had to decide that it was an . . . an ineffable space, a crucial measure of time . . . now, don't laugh," Gruening said protectively . . . "almost as though a spirit were deciding to re-enter or not re-enter its body." He challenged Max with a look.

"I'm not laughing," Max said.

"The things that elude us," Gruening went on, though rather curious about the look on Max's face, not being able to define it. "Is the energy of the brain ever lost, or can it be triggered back as we have done? Is that what we did? Is the energy generated by a brain always in the atmosphere, once released? Metaphysics? Parapsychology? The Unknown? Are we being kept from the ultimate answer? Are we still as innocent as Adam in the Garden and God wants it that way? Always a little left unknown, unlearned . . . our fate always to be tantalized, never to be allowed to grasp the whole story . . . always a few pieces missing?"

Gruening stopped. "You know what Wesgrove said to me? He wouldn't engage. He said, 'We obviously have many more miles to walk. If there's an explanation, it will be found one day, with painstaking research. Treading is the first. We're still babies in the sphere of the brain and spirit.' "

It was uncomfortable territory for Gruening, the scientist. Having no answers was hardly unfamiliar for a psychiatrist involved with biology and the soul, even if he sometimes behaved like he knew all the answers, Max noted. Why had Gruening opened this up with him and not his staff of experts? Wasn't this Wesgrove territory? If the experts had no answer, why him? Why, indeed, him! He was flattered by Gruening's having rendered himself dumb before him. He liked the chap more and more . . .

Gruening went on to confess: "Dealing with human behavior, no matter how much you think you know, is like flying blind. The givens of the psychiatric trade make two kinds of doctors. We're either poor slobs torn apart by empathy, or we turn ourselves into comedians, to hide from ourselves, to deny our futile knowledge about the magic healing of the word *love*, 'cause no one listens."

"It's always been a few, Jeff," Max said. "A few make

change, cause it, and the insane world follows . . . always late."

They talked, Gruening watching as a working doctor—to see if Treading had returned as the self he remembered.

"You know," Max said, in one of their sessions, "it could disturb the whole balance of the economy in the future, if people choose to want to come back to the vale of tears, and you guys choose to perfect the way. Although, it looks like only the rich could afford a cryonic comeback, for a long time to come. It's too expensive. But if that time did come, would just anyone be allowed to come back, or would there be a pick-and-choose by a self-serving power? I feel like a freak; that's what I have to work on, and I know you've been trying to help."

Whenever the word *soul* was used, Max would get a funny look and go silent, which, as Gruening came to learn, was not the Treading style. The subject Gruening kept digging away at was: "What about the re-entry? You now say you remember saying 'Too much light.' "

"Yes. It comes back like a dream. It didn't in the beginning." Max's face had a queer look as though he were going to offer a thought but decided not to.

Gruening affirmed, only for himself, that *the space* between the time the scanning educator stopped and Treading's full entry with normal brain waves—it was another black hole, nameable in no other way. Someday it might be answered, but in the 1990s that hiatus of the brain was as mysterious as the moon rising and the sun setting for prehistoric Man. The thought amused Gruening. Maybe there always had to be some Knowledge withheld, or Man would forget who he was—naked and dumb enough to think he could eat the fruit of the whole Tree and not get a cosmic bellyache.

As Gruening's work tapered off with Max, he brought up the subject of Roz more and more, her childhood, her marriage, as Max saw it, her classic distress. Max said to himself, How does he know so much about it? He began to feel himself the butt of the prosecution, so he imparted his own feelings gingerly, thinking, Why should I admit my guilt to anyone but her? He was also seeing that Gruening's questions weren't so clinical. They seemed to indicate something else that the brilliant oaf thought he was hiding.

"What do you think of her?" Max asked.

"She's a beautiful woman," was Gruening's very small answer on that subject.

Gruening had one more thing on his mind; he had kept it to the end because he knew by the last week that Max was ready to take it. "The miracle happened to you, to no one else. They discovered the world was round? A week later, it was commonplace. A walk on the moon? A week later, it was ordinary. We're an insatiable species when it comes to wonders. But when they happen, we don't wonder long, we scramble back to the ordinary for safe harbor . . . The extraordinary is unhealthy," he added wryly. "I've been told that you were a manipulative man, an outspoken man, a maverick, and you fought for your own way. You were used to being effective. You're going back to people who've made a new structure for themselves, who've changed. I'm not saying *you* have to make a new structure for yourself, but you can't behave in the same way with them. Your first blow was Hedda. Phoebe isn't the little girl you left. Roz isn't the same, either. It's all going to be different. *And* you have to be prepared for it. In some myths, people slept for years, or wandered for years; they came back to everything as it was when they left. You've come back and it's not myth, it's real. You're going to have to let go what was." He began to laugh. "Max, laugh with me. You're the victim of the biggest magic there ever was—science."

The Wesgrove hearing was scheduled for the day Max was to leave the Cancer Research Center. No media, just the family, the Center's heads of staff, lawyers, and the governor, who chose to be present at the legal *happening* he had arranged. The judge from Riverhead arrived, tickled by what the governor had pulled off despite Max's press statement about the state lumbering around like a drunken dinosaur. The governor *was* a good man to have cut through due process and the letter of the law so quickly.

Hiram Wesgrove arrived. He looked tinier than Max had remembered. There was the pixie, less white hair, but what was left was still standing up in confusion.

The first words out of Wesgrove were: "I got your message about Fate. You were right about what you thought my answer would be—'Be humble, you ass!' "

The two men embraced, kissed each other, embraced again.

"Far cry from the last time I saw you," Max said. I was mumbling 'Now I lay me down to sleep . . .' "

Both men broke down and wept.

Lewisohn wasn't sure which one would collapse first. Neither did. You can swoon with joy, but it will never kill you.

The judge asked everyone to be seated, then: "This is going to be short, but I am honored to be here to play my part. There is no precedent for what is about to take place; therefore, I, as judge, have only to invoke the writ of *coram nobis,* meaning the decision handed down today in this case—the State versus Hiram Wesgrove—will come from *the breast of the court.*" He looked up. "In other words, we have a unique situation demanding justice, and something must be done about it in the name of justice.

"It is the court's pleasure to vacate the judgment under which Hiram Wesgrove has been imprisoned for twelve years. By virtue of the judicial powers granted me under the laws of the State of New York, I hereby declare Hiram Wesgrove released from the custody of the state, exonerated from the previously charged crime of homicide against Maxwell Treading, *not deceased.* The previous conviction is herewith overturned and the record expunged." He paused.

"I have a personal addendum to this proceeding. I've spent my life in the law . . ." (Max liked him—the man had laugh lines around his eyes) "but I have never been party to the making of new law. I bet my bottom dollar, though, that before too long, and because of this case, there will be new law! It will go something like this: A person has an absolute right to command his own death if he is sane *and* dying; therefore, he also has the right to demand help for that act.

"We are now entering upon a new Time, capital *T,* and God willing."

Max whispered to Phoebe, "How does he know about Time with a capital *T?*"

"He read your statement to the press, Daddy. Everyone knows about Time with a capital *T.* "

34

At home again! The view of Central Park! His library! At
first, the only thing Max was suffering from was euphoria.
The apartment was overflowing. Roz was there, they were all
living together again; there were the children; Phoebe, Sam.
They were sharing an extraordinary time. Max was checked
medically every few days, sitting for it like an impatient child
having his shoelaces tied. He was fifty-five, not sixty-seven! Seize
the moment. He was on fast-forward. He was insufferable. He
made everyone feel they were walking in deep water, slow-
motion.

Who was he?

That damn Gruening was right. *He was in a different play.*
He couldn't get over the change in Phoebe as she filled him in
on the workings of Global Materials. There was no Global for
him anymore, it was hers! So much hers, he didn't want it.
Maybe he didn't want it anyway.

Max's head was reeling. When he picked up little Max,
it felt like picking up himself, looking at himself starting over
and wanting nothing less than perfection. He fell instantly in
love with Marianne, who looked so much like a little Roz. He

broke every discipline with her. He exclaimed, "Phoebe, Sam, honor the looks in their eyes, they're not to be taught just for ceremony's sake. They're new, like unscaled peaks. And, they're recording. Beware what you say and do. It's all being imprinted . . ." (He was saying things in such oracular, pompous ways, hearing himself and not being able to stop.)

Phoebe was provoked. "Don't you think we're doing a good job? They wouldn't be the way they are, if we weren't." She tried to understand her father's rush *to seize,* put to rights, his saying, "Do it this way, it's the only way . . ." but it was unnerving.

Sam watched it all, their being the first family of the world for a moment, all together. He and Phoebe had moved out of their bedroom to give it back to Max. Roz was running in and out, very different, but somewhat the same. She and Phoebe were having little cat fights . . . "It's what you always used to do, damn it!" But they would be followed with "I'm sorry . . ." Sam knew it wasn't going to last long.

Curiously, it was with Roz that Max felt most easy. Both he and she were changing at the same time.

Max and Roz were in the library less than a month after his return, the middle of May. He looked out the windows of the room he had felt most comfortable in for a great part of his life. It was Sam's now, and it would stay that way.

"Daddy, I don't like the way you look. First of all, you're pushing everyone around like chess pieces. It's as though nothing pleases you and you have to make it better."

"Everything pleases me, I just want it perfect."

"You should get back to work. You're going to take over Global, aren't you?"

"No!"

His sharp negative startled her. She decided not to pursue it.

Roz laughed. "Perfection? I've been in a perfect rage most of my life. So much for perfection."

Max turned about. "Sounds like you've been talking to that fellow Gruening. You know, he had me in instant therapy for a couple of weeks, sneaky fellow."

"He has that way . . ."

"Roz, I'm going for broke with you. There might be more of me in you than in Phoebe—the looking-for-justice business. It made you freeze up. We gave you an awful time, I ask your forgiveness. Now, what about Gruening?"

She was silent in disbelief. "I can't believe the distance you think you're covering."

"You deserve each other. There *is* something going on, isn't there?"

"Yes."

"That's going to be your punishment, living with a psychiatrist for the rest of your life."

"Daddy, mind your own business. It's very far away from that. And if you don't calm down and stop acting like some immortal soul, I'll tell Jeff and he'll tell Lewisohn and they'll put you back in the lab for more testing."

"And another thing," Max said, "Gruening explained to me about that damn machine they used on me to activate my memory chips; I don't ever want it mentioned, you tell Phoebe that. No one's going to think they know what's inside my head! I might change just to make sure of it."

(Roz decided she wouldn't say, "But it changed my life . . .")

"You know, Roz, the way I'm behaving, it's just covering up terror. I'm frightened, I feel like a baby. I'm rushing around like a bull in a china shop, trying to discover myself, remember who I was. Phoebe and Sam have made this a happy place, but it's not mine. You're all currying me and treating me like a senile. I have to get out of here!" He choked up. "I miss Hedda."

"You could take over the Treading Foundation, Daddy. You'd be proud of what it's done since . . . since you've been away."

"No."

"Have you seen Dr. Wesgrove?"

"No. He's in Maine recuperating. He had two heart attacks in prison, you know, and didn't tell anyone. He'll be back at the end of the month."

"Why don't you come to Italy with me, Daddy? I have a lovely house there . . ."

"No."

"How about Southampton? The beach in June is wonderful."

"Absolutely no, I never want to see that house again!" Max said. "I want to go away, but I want to see Wesgrove first. Then I'll start over." Max began to laugh, but he was also crying. Roz was taken aback, it was all so new, talking with him, loving him, mixed up with memories of her old self. She ran to him and took his hand. "Don't cry, Daddy, please . . ."

"Why not? I want to cry. I have to come back to humanity, damn it. I'm the victim of a blast, the blast of a miracle. Everyone can protect themselves from it, except me. I'm alone! I have to make a new place for myself, in myself." He began to laugh uproariously. Roz became alarmed.

"Daddy? Are you all right? Do you want a sedative?"

"Sedative? Are you kidding? I take one every day and two before they check me out at the Center, so they won't find out how hard my heart is beating. And, don't you tell Lewisohn and Gruening.

"Do you know, my darling Roz, why I'm laughing? I just remembered something. I have a million dollars in the bank and twelve years of interest. I had George Dinessen put it away. You should have seen his face when I said, 'Do it!' I called it my Re-animation Fund. It was one of my little playing-with-Fate jokes . . . ha . . ."

"You're worried about money, Daddy? Phoebe will transfer any amount of Global stock to you. I can return as much as you want . . . for heaven's sake."

"Not on your life, baby, that will stands! Even though the lawyers are having a fit trying to figure out how to view an estate that isn't one anymore. That's their problem . . .

"I'm going to start over with my Re-animation Fund." He sat down and was silent for a moment. "Hedda would have liked that idea—beginning fresh. Can you see the difference between *continuing* and *beginning?* To me, right now, it feels like the difference between old age and youth. After all, my darling, I've got a resurrection on my hands, don't I? *And other things* . . ."

Max decided, *that moment* that he was going back to Utah. He was going to sit in the kitchen, get the fire going, listen to the gophers scurry, ride out to the mesas and buttes . . . when the doctors said he was strong enough to cut the strings. He was going to sit there for a long time . . . and *then* start over.

35

Max and Wesgrove, back in his office at the Center, were playing chess together and drinking innumerable brandies. Wesgrove, as of old, was winning. Max was trying, but he had never been a match for his old friend. Wesgrove had mastered the board. He was on the verge of saying, "Check." Max was abstracted.

"Make your move, man, I'm waiting," Wesgrove said impatiently. Max didn't respond. Wesgrove looked up. He saw that Max was a million miles away. "What's the matter?"

"I want to talk to you about something . . ."

"Can't it wait until I've beaten you?"

Max leaned over and grasped the doctor's arm. "Wes, what was it that you injected me with, that killed me?"

Wesgrove winced. "Don't say it like that. I've been exonerated, my friend." He leaned back in his chair. "Something that would perform as swiftly as light, the laser liquefied, so I called it Liquid Light. It was to protect your brain. It obviously did, but it didn't make your chess game any better."

"Too much light," Max mumbled to himself. "So that's why Gruening kept at it, looking for something."

Max leaned over the chess pieces. "Wes? I can't keep it from you any longer. I have to tell you what happened to me . . ."

Wesgrove looked at him anxiously. "What are you talking about? What do you mean—what happened to you? What's the matter? You don't look right." Wesgrove gave Max one of his piercing, diagnostic looks.

"I don't mean what happened to me yesterday! I mean the twelve years!"

"Oh, my God . . ." Wesgrove put a hand over his heart.

"That's right," Max said. "You hit it right on the nail."

"You don't mean . . . you're not telling me . . . there's a . . ."

Max shook his head *yes,* then broke out in his glorious grin. "Yes there *is!*"

"Oh, no . . ."

"Oh yes, my friend, there is!"

The old man was alarmed, anguished. Post-entry delusions? Delayed manifestations of brain impairment? He would have to alert Lewisohn and Gruening in the morning.

Wesgrove kept shaking his head.

"I know what you're thinking," Max said solemnly. "I'm not mad. I had to share it *with you,* before I went away. I owed it to you."

Strange, Wesgrove said to himself. The man's never looked better!

FROM THE JOURNAL OF DR. HIRAM WESGROVE, MAY 1994

"How long shall I stay in the world?
Why do they not leave my heart in peace?
Why do I torment myself so vainly?
Shall I stay, shall I go?
I have no love for honors,
I have no love for riches.
Paradise is beyond my hopes.
And therefore in the clear daylight
I shall walk among my fields and
*   among my flowers,*
Singing a little and sighing,
And climbing the mountains of the east
To the accompaniment of a liquid stream,
Chanting a few songs,
Till the time comes
*   when I shall be summoned away,*
Having accomplished my destiny,
*   with no cares in the world."*

The above was the last entry. Hiram Wesgrove died of a
massive heart attack, sitting at his desk, pen still in hand, as he
copied out the words of an ancient Chinese poet, which had
been his custom for a number of years—in search of tranquillity.

AUTHOR'S NOTE

This book is in remembrance of Elizabeth, my sister; Isaac, a fine composer; Charlotte, an innovative painter; Jean, who insisted upon living artfully; Doren, an exquisite young poet. They all died of cancer.

Elizabeth was a dancer. She danced her way through life, moved through the air in great beauty. She died in 1979, three years before Maxwell Treading's death. Oh, that his fate could have been hers and theirs.

May we keep learning that the human spirit is capable of an almost unmeasurable reach.

D.S.

About the Author

Doris Schwerin's acclaimed memoir, *Diary of a Pigeon Watcher*, was published in 1976, followed by the novel *Leanna* in 1978. Born in Peabody, Massachusetts, a graduate of Juilliard, she is an accomplished composer of theater music as well as the author of five plays and several children's books. She lives in New York City.